Try

THE TEMPTATION SERIES I

ELLA FRANK

Also by Ella Frank

The Exquisite Series
Exquisite
Entice
Edible

Masters Among Monsters Series
Alasdair
Isadora
Thanos

The Temptation Series
Try
Take
Trust

Sunset Cove Series
Finley
Devil's Kiss

Standalones
Blind Obsession
Veiled Innocence

The Arcanian Chronicles
Temperance

Sex Addict
Co-authored with Brooke Blaine

PresLocke Series
Co-Authored with Ella Frank
Aced
Locked
Wedlocked

Dedication

It's simple, this is for Logan and Tate.

Prologue

PLANES—LOGAN WAS not a fan.

Although, the warm pussy that his cock was currently balls deep inside of was a definite improvement to the cold blue leather of seat 1D in business class, where he had been sitting by himself earlier. Luckily for him, just before the plane taxied out onto the tarmac, the vacant seat, which he'd thought would remain empty, had filled.

And even though it's changed my plan from sleeping to—

"Shh, hon. If you're going to moan, I'll have to shut you up." Logan brought his right hand up to cup over her parted pink lips.

At first, he'd been under the assumption that this would be the same old boring flight from L.A. back to Chicago. He'd settled back with his usual gin and tonic, unbuttoned his suit jacket, and crossed his feet as he waited impatiently for the trip to get under way. He'd figured if he were lucky, he could have several more drinks and sleep through half the trip.

And what a lucky bastard I am.

While he was draining his small plastic cup, he'd heard a woman's voice moving closer and closer to the cabin door, calling out, "Wait! Wait! One more!"

And that was when he'd seen—*Oh fuck yeah, more*—Jessica.

She was a leggy blonde in a pink miniskirt, who had made her way through the door and essentially let him right into hers.

The flight attendant had given her a quick smile. "You're lucky. We were just about to close the cabin door."

Jessica had laughed.

And *that* was what had made his cock take notice.

"Well, I'm glad I ran then."

"Let's get you seated. What's your seat number?"

"Looks like 1C."

And that, as they say, is that.

Currently, Jessica's bare ass was seated on the miniscule sink in the back lavatory of Virgin America, Flight 201, and—well, there was absolutely nothing virginal about the way her skirt was shoved up around her waist. In fact, Logan would guess that she couldn't even remember what the word *virgin* meant, especially considering how her creamy thighs were spread wide apart with his cock sliding in and out of her soaking wet pussy. And that was just fine by him.

When she'd first stopped near his seat, he'd let his gaze wander from her black heels up to her smooth, long legs. He had made no apologies and offered no excuses for eye-fucking her while sizing her up as a potential—*or as of right now*—fuck buddy.

She hadn't seemed to mind though—*obviously*—
because when he'd finally met flirtatious green gaze, the
woman had grinned as she indicated the seat beside him.

"Looks like you're stuck with me."

"Yes, it looks that way," he acknowledged.

After she'd stowed her bag in the overhead bin, she
slid slowly into the seat beside him and turned, holding out
her hand.

*That same small hand is currently gripping my suit lapel
right now,* Logan mused as he punched his hips forward,
sinking inside her, as much as the cramped and
uncomfortable position would allow.

"I'm Jessica," she had told him with a bold and
assessing gaze, much like his own.

He had looked at the petite fingers tipped with
manicured pink nails, and suddenly, the flight had become a
whole lot more interesting.

Taking her hand in his, he'd winked. "I'm Logan."

"Harder Logan!" she moaned, now putting his name
to good use.

Well, I'm not going to say no to that, was Logan's only
thought as he braced his feet, which was difficult to do when
the toes of his shoes were bent against the plastic vanity
taking up the majority of the fucking area he was standing
in. But, like a trooper, Logan steadied himself, clasping
Jessica's ass cheek with his left palm and holding the counter
with his right, as he started to pound into the woman just as
she had requested. He was pushing them closer to that

elusive moment, directing them to that heavenly place.

He'd never really thought about getting off on a plane until it had rumbled down the tarmac and moved out of the holding pattern to line up for takeoff. But that had been all he could think about after Jessica had made a show of crossing her legs, and flashing a *whole* lot more than her upper thighs.

"Well, Logan, I have a feeling this trip just got interesting. Thank you for that."

He'd given her a smug look that was as depraved as the thoughts now running through his head.

As the plane had shot down the runway with the full force of two jet-propelled engines, Logan had buckled in, preparing himself for the ride. While the front of the plane angled up, much like his throbbing cock, he had finally replied, "I try. So, are you going back home to the husband and kids?"

When Jessica had licked her glossy lips, Logan had immediately imagined that tongue performing the same slick move down between his legs.

"No kids and no husband."

With that, Logan had known he would be joining the exclusive club, which had nothing to do with virgins.

"*Yes*," he hissed out as his balls tightened and his ass cheeks clenched.

Wrapped firmly around his waist, Jessica's leg strained against him, pulling him in closer, as her eyes widened above his palm covering her mouth. Then, her sweet, juicy muscles clutched his cock like a goddamn vise, and they both found it.

For the admission price of $543.90, they were inducted into the exclusive Mile High Club, and it was worth every last penny.

Part One

Recognition: Realization of an existing truth.

Chapter One

MONDAY EVENING, NINE fifteen, and predictably, I'm still at work.

Sitting in his chair, Logan pushed up his glasses and rubbed the bridge of his nose. The office was quiet right now, and he knew he was the only one left on the floor.

This was the best part of the day. This was *his* part of the day. It was the time when he could unwind, drop all titles, proprieties, and appearances, and just *be*.

Standing, he cracked his neck from side to side as he loosened the blue tie from its perfect knot at the base of his throat. It was time to hit his usual spot for a quick drink before heading home. Picking up his briefcase, he walked to his office door, switched off the light, and made his way to the elevator. Waiting for it to arrive on his floor at Mitchell & Madison, he glanced around at his place of business.

Huh, who would have thought?

He and Cole had really made something of themselves. It was a bit of a shock, considering his wild college days, but as far as he was concerned, that was what college was for—to try a little of everything and everyone—and after…well, *him*, Logan had made sure to try everything.

Cole was always on him to think about settling down with someone. That would probably be a fucking stellar idea, but he wasn't like Cole, who was well into his third year of wedlock.

Logan had no desire to bind himself to anyone, woman or man, especially when it was so much more exciting to take exactly what was offered. A city this large provided too many choices, and until the moment his cock only got hard for one person, he planned to use it to its full potential.

When the elevator doors opened, Logan got on with a single goal in mind—to have a drink.

A gin and tonic, and then life will pretty much be fine and dandy.

He had a successful job, a downtown condo, and an office located next door to his favorite bar. If he were an arrogant man—

Well, hell, who am I kidding? I'm one lucky son of a bitch.

* * *

PUSHING THROUGH THE double doors of After Hours, Logan left the cool night air and stepped into the cozy surroundings of his favorite hangout. As the familiar dimly lit interior invited him inside, he was reminded of why he loved coming here. It was the perfect place to sit, observe, and if he wanted to, *hunt,* and he could accomplish all of that without the constant harassment typically found at a pick-up joint.

Save those particular spots for the weekends.

He craved quiet after work, and maybe—

Oh yeah, he thought as a voluptuous brunette brushed by him, her breasts grazing his arm. *Maybe a piece of that, too.*

The dark secluded booths lining the sidewall were calling to him, but at the last minute, he changed his mind and bypassed several suits as he made his way up to the bar where he found a vacant stool at the end. He put his buzzing cell phone on the bar top and ignored the text from—

Ah, yes, L.A.-to-Chicago Jessica.

After placing his briefcase on the floor, he sat down and moved it between his feet, securing it there, while he waited for the bartender. Looking around at a few of the people mingling, Logan spotted an attractive woman standing farther down the bar. He was guessing she was in her early thirties. She was a petite redhead, dressed in a snug black jacket and a skirt that hugged her round ass as well as his hands would.

As she inclined her head in his direction, Logan spied the drink in her hand and decided he would send her a second one as soon as the damn bartender showed up. Afterward, maybe he'd take her up to his office and introduce her face to the top of his desk and her perky ass to his—

"What can I get you to drink tonight?"

Finally.

Logan turned his head toward the deep baritone who had just addressed him, and with the way his body reacted, he was thankful he was seated. The guy staring back at him, waiting for an answer, was fucking hot.

Clearing his throat, Logan reminded himself to keep this friendly. "A gin and tonic. Start a tab for me? Thanks."

"Sure thing. Coming right up," he told Logan before turning away to make his drink.

Logan quickly assessed the loose brown curls, broad shoulders, trim waist, and—

Speaking of asses...

Turning back to him, the hot bartender slid the glass across the wooden bar top and gave him a wide friendly grin. He then placed his large hands on the surface and angled in closer, like he was about to divulge a secret. Logan felt his cock react to the mischief sparking in the guy's eyes, and he found himself inching a little closer, deciding that *this* option was far more interesting than the first.

That was, until the bartender turned his head, looking down the length of the bar. "So what about her?"

Logan glanced in the direction of the redhead, who was still facing his way. It was a pity really because, until around two minutes ago, getting laid tonight had been a sure thing.

Looking back across the bar to a face full of humor, Logan was now thinking about how to get this guy alone and on his knees. That pompous vest and tie, which was part of the After Hours uniform, would look even better if he was staring at it from above, while the legs in those dress slacks were kneeling on the floor.

"What about her?" Logan finally responded, taking the drink and lifting the glass to his lips.

When the bartender chuckled, Logan focused on his Adam's apple bobbing in his tanned throat.

"Playing it cool, I see," he joked, as he lifted a white towel and placed it over his shoulder.

"I'm sure you don't." *If you did, you'd more than likely be moving farther away.*

"What was that?"

"Nothing. I guess I just changed my mind."

"Jesus, man, why would you do that? She's sexy as hell."

Logan took another quick drink, draining the contents of the glass, when his body tensed, reacting to the word *sexy* coming from that smooth voice. It was as if the bartender had just run his hand over Logan's groin.

Usually, the employees at After Hours weren't exactly chatty, and if they were, the conversations were always polite. This place was high-end, not like the local pub, and the fact that this guy was standing here, blatantly checking out the clientele, made Logan do a double take of the woman.

"Agreed. She is hot."

"Want another?" He gestured toward the empty highball glass.

"Sure. So…you're new here."

The bartender nodded, his dark hair shifting with the motion of his head, as he looked across at Logan. "You're obviously not since you know that. I started yesterday."

"Well, I guess you could say I'm a regular. I work next door."

The new drink was pushed in his direction, and Logan picked it up without taking his eyes off the man. He was getting some kind of vibe from him, but he was pretty sure it wasn't the one he was hoping for.

Probably just a new employee appreciating a decent customer.

But every thought running through Logan's head right now, especially one in particular, was definitely *not* decent.

That was when the bartender gave another pearly-white grin as he motioned his head down the bar. "Well, have to get back to my fans. Let me know if you want to buy the sexy redhead that drink. You look like you need to unwind, if you know what I mean."

Before Logan could even get a word out—much less, *No, I fucking don't. What do you mean?*—the guy had moved away, and he was now flirting with a blonde woman. She was giving him an exclusive view down her ample tits, and Logan couldn't stop himself from watching the newest After Hours employee while he drained his second drink.

Fuck, things just got a little more complicated.

Just when he figured life was going to be easy and hand him a woman to bend over his desk, it threw him a nice fucking curve.

Batter up! I want to play with some balls.

* * *

STANDING OPPOSITE A curvaceous blonde, Tate concentrated on mixing her cocktail. This was only his second night working at After Hours, but he'd been bartending for years.

Only one of the many things Diana hated.

No matter what he'd done during their marriage, nothing had ever made her happy.

They'd been inseparable when they first started dating. If she'd been in a room with him, he'd likely ended up inside her. They hadn't been able to keep their hands off each other, and although that made for one hot bed at night, it sure as hell hadn't stopped the ice-cold jealousy from trickling through the cracks of their faulty foundation.

Their life or love or whatever the hell it was, had been built on lust, and when lust had morphed into the green-eyed monster, their marriage had fallen into the toxic bin.

Now, the mere sight of her made Tate want to punch something.

After he finished shaking the fruity concoction, he poured the bright red drink into a tall glass and added a slice of pineapple, a straw, and miniscule paper umbrella. He then slid it across the bar to the blonde.

"That'll be twelve." He winked and gave her a sexy smirk, knowing it would get him a tip.

It was the same expression he'd offered only minutes ago to the guy at the end of the bar—the same guy that Tate could feel was still watching him.

The lady slid a twenty across the smooth surface, and she made no apologies as she eyed his body. When her gaze came back up and met his own, she flicked her tongue out and played with the straw as though she were licking the tip of his cock.

"Keep the change," she offered in a provocative tone.

Tate took the bill and picked up a small black napkin. As she leaned closer, he made sure to admire her impressive breasts, and then he placed the small square in front of her for her glass.

"Thank you," he accepted.

Without a second thought, the woman placed her cool hand over his. "It's my pleasure."

Tate knew this was all part of his job. *Be flirtatious with the ladies and friendly with the men, and obviously, never cross too far over the line.* He also knew that most of the businessmen and women in the area usually frequented the bar after work on their way home...or maybe they came in to avoid going home. *Who knows, and who cares?* Either way, his job was to be the friendly ear, get them what they wanted, and make them want to come back, so that was what he did. If he threw a little flirtation into the mix, it was only because he'd perfected it to a fine art. Plus, he always got better tips that way.

"Mine too, but I need to get back to my other customers." He gently removed his hand and straightened up from where he'd been leaning on the bar.

"What time do you finish tonight?"

Tate smoothed a hand down over his black vest. "Late. What time do you start work tomorrow?"

"Early," Blondie drawled. She sucked the end of the straw between her shiny, red lips.

"Ah, now, that's a shame, isn't it?" Tate commiserated and found that he actually meant it as his cock showed signs of interest for the first time in a long while. "Guess we're just two ships in the night."

Boldly, she ran her gaze down his body once again. "You here tomorrow night?"

Tate nodded as he pulled the bar towel from his shoulder. "I'm here Tuesday through Saturday nights. Haven't you heard? I'm the new entertainment," he stated, making his way down toward the guy at the other end.

Leaning against the bar, Tate stared at Mr. Gin and Tonic and noticed that his glass was empty once again. "Want another?"

"No."

Tate's eyes moved from the highball glass to the blue ones peering back at him from behind narrow, black hipster glasses. This guy screamed sophistication, from his styled black hair, slickly parted to the left, to the perfect amount of stubble. He clearly took his image seriously.

Tate had once heard Diana refer to a man as *geek chic*. This guy had that look about him, except for the eyes. Tate couldn't quite pinpoint what the difference was, but with the silence between them, and the intense stare, he became slightly uncomfortable. He also noted that the interest the blonde had stirred in his cock was not subsiding, but he quickly shoved that thought aside.

"Anything else I can get for you?" Tate asked.

"Why didn't you get her number?"

Taken off guard by the complete change of subject, all Tate managed was, "Huh?"

"Her number?" Mr. Gin and Tonic repeated, glancing across the bar in the direction of the blonde. "Why didn't you get it? She was obviously interested."

Still holding the small towel in his left hand, Tate started to wipe down the surface of the bar. It was already pretty clean, but he needed the distraction.

"No fraternizing with customers." Raising his gaze, Tate gave a shrug accompanied by what he hoped was an easygoing smile, as he continued wiping the bar.

The man staring back at him didn't return it. "That's a shame."

Tate stopped moving the towel and held it between his hands. *What the hell does that mean?* Looking around, he noticed that Amelia and Stacy, his coworkers, were nowhere in sight, so he was confused by exactly who the man was referring to. When Tate turned back, the steady gaze behind the glasses were now creased at the sides with what he swore was amusement—at him.

"It's a shame because she's…how did you describe the redhead earlier? Sexy as hell?"

In shock, Tate stood there, silent. He couldn't think of one thing to say. For a brief moment, he'd jumped to the wrong conclusion, and thought the man meant it was a shame that he couldn't fraternize with *him*. Instead of responding, Tate remained mute with the towel in his hands, contemplating the man across the bar.

Mr. Gin and Tonic stood and picked up his briefcase from the floor. He reached for his vibrating phone on the bar top and glanced down at it. Obviously deciding it wasn't important, he looked back at Tate as he pulled his wallet from his pants pocket. He took out some cash and slid it across the bar.

For some unknown reason, Tate felt that it was important to stand his ground, so he didn't glance down at the money. Instead, he offered his fail-safe—the easygoing grin that *usually* let him get away with everything.

"You should get that number from her. You look a little stiff, like *you* need to unwind, if *you* know what *I* mean."

With his own words flung back at him, Tate watched the man make a call on his phone before he turned and left the bar.

It wasn't until Stacy came up and said his name that

he realized he was still standing where he had been for the last several minutes, and his erection hadn't fully relaxed.

Staring down at the bar, he saw a fifty on the surface, and he shook his head.

Damn, that's one hell of a tip. I don't care how strange that interaction was. If he's a regular, I'm making him mine.

Chapter Two

YEP, SECOND NIGHT in a row, and I'm back at the bar.

This time though, Logan came earlier. He glanced down at his watch, seeing that it was only five fifteen. He never left the office that early unless he had somewhere to be or someone to do. This was definitely *not* one of those times. Nevertheless, whatever he'd felt after that initial encounter compelled him to return to the bar tonight. It was lingering in his perverted head.

So, best not to let it linger. Better to go and take a second look.

Making his way through the busy after-work crowd, Logan made sure to keep his head down. He didn't want distractions, and he didn't want attention. He wanted to sit at the end of the bar and observe.

Tonight, Logan had only come armed with his cell and wallet. He had made sure to leave his briefcase at the office. He didn't want to worry about what was between his legs. *Well, between my ankles anyway.*

He scanned behind the bar, but he didn't see the man from the night before. *Hmm, maybe he isn't working tonight.* He was sure though that he had heard the guy say Tuesday through Saturday. *Yeah…hello stalker.*

Taking a spot at the far end of the bar, Logan unfastened his black jacket and loosened his tie.

Stacy, one of the bartenders, came over with a smile. "Usual tonight? Or do you plan to shake things up?"

Logan was about to answer, but before a word could come out of his mouth, he heard that deep baritone from behind him.

"I'm guessing he wants a gin and tonic. Why stray from the usual?"

Turning his head, Logan saw the bartender from the previous night. He was walking over to the bar pass, dressed in the same black uniform. It shouldn't have surprised Logan when he felt his pants tighten in response, especially when he lowered his gaze and noticed the guy was carrying a black leather jacket in one hand, and holding on to a red motorcycle helmet in the other. Logan's cock twitched with interest.

The man's hair looked as though he had just removed the headgear. His brown curls were all over the place. He moved through the pass and turned back to face Logan. When the guy flashed that same relaxed grin from yesterday, Logan's erection went from interested to rock-fucking-hard.

Christ, it's official. I have a hard-on for a straight guy. That's just terrific.

"That's your poison, right?"

"Right," Logan agreed.

Stacy quickly gave Logan a wink.

I really need to get his name.

"I'll leave you to it then," she told her coworker, walking farther down the bar toward a newly seated customer.

As the guy opposite him turned, picked up a bar towel, and poked it into the waist of his pants, Logan took the opportunity to have a good, long look at the way the guy's black fabric molded to his ass. Wishing he already had a drink to soothe the urges riding him, Logan made sure that his face was neutral when the bartender came back to him.

"Give me one minute. I have to put my gear in the back and punch in."

As he sauntered down the bar, Logan noticed several customers' eye him, and he had to wonder why the guy had gone out of his way to interrupt Stacy before he was even settled in.

Interested? No, you moron. It's because of the tip from last night. He's back for more.

Logan told his body to calm the hell down. This was nice scenery, but that was all it would ever be. The guy was obviously just doing his job, and here Logan was, fixating on him, like some fucking weirdo. Logan hadn't been able to stop thinking about the man all damn night, not to mention while at work today.

Finally getting his body to cooperate, Logan felt his phone vibrate, and he turned it over to see a text from Jessica.

Jessica: So, are you free next month?

Sure. Why not? That woman's pussy had been tight and warm, and he wouldn't mind revisiting it. But right now, right this second, his interests lay with a body that was completely different in physicality.

He picked up the phone, opened the message, and replied.

Next month sounds fantastic. Can't wait to see you—all of you.

When he placed the phone down, he was surprised to find the bartender now standing across from him.

Oh, so the guy is stealthy, too.

"Here's your drink." He pushed the glass across the counter.

Logan saw those brown eyes almost smiling at him as the bartender waited, and Logan wondered what *exactly* he was waiting for. "I would thank you, but I don't know your name."

The guy reached behind his back to the towel tucked into his pants, and he pulled it in front of him and started moving it over the bar top. Logan was curious if it was a habit of his, or maybe it was just something he did when he felt nervous or unsure.

"You can't thank a stranger? I just served one."

"That's true." Logan lifted the glass to his lips.

He didn't look away as he took a sip, and he became curious when the other man didn't turn away either. Lowering his drink back to the bar, Logan kept his fingers wrapped around it as he swirled the glass around.

"I'm Logan."

A confident smirk crossed the bartender's lips, and he moved his hands to tuck the towel back into his pants, immediately drawing Logan's gaze to his waist.

"Well, it's nice to meet you, Logan. I'll be back when you need a refill."

Well played. Logan watched the back of the still-nameless guy move away from him. *Well fucking played.*

* * *

TATE COULDN'T HELP but feel somewhat cocky as he walked away from Mr. Gin and—*Logan.*

Last night, when he was finally at home relaxing, he'd found himself replaying the entire conversation with Logan, trying to pinpoint why it had seemed so unusual. Finally, he had worked it out.

It was because the guy had been checking him out.

This guy, *Logan,* had been flirting with him.

It had been subtle, but when Tate thought about the words exchanged, they'd definitely had a flirtatious undertone, and that was when he came to his final conclusion. Logan was gay. He had to be.

Tate couldn't believe that he hadn't realized it sooner. In his profession, it wasn't like he was a stranger to both women and men hitting on him, but for some reason, he hadn't seen it right away with this guy.

Maybe he'd missed it because he had witnessed the look between Logan and the redhead. Or maybe he was delusional and totally off base, and the guy was just a little odd.

Why else would he say no to the redhead? Unless he's married? But the way he looked me over...it was like he thought I was—hot?

Well, no matter what it was, now that Tate had his theory, he figured there was no harm in flirting right back. Usually, he kept the charm for the women, but if it made this Logan guy a regular paying customer, Tate saw no harm in it. He was comfortable enough with his sexuality.

"Hey, Tate, looks like you caught the attention of one of our regulars."

Tate turned his head toward Stacy, who was standing beside him, pouring some ingredients into a blender filled with ice.

Choosing to act ignorant, he asked, "Oh yeah? Who would that be?"

"Logan, the guy at the end of the bar. Suit, glasses, gorgeous blue eyes. Flirts every time his mouth is open." She let out a dramatic sigh.

When Tate looked over his shoulder, he saw that Logan was actually staring at both of them. He wasn't smiling, and Tate made sure to have a neutral expression on his face as he stared back at the man.

Turning back around, he grabbed a bottle of water, opened it, and lifted it to his lips, then returned his attention to Stacy. "Do you know anything about him?"

"Other than he oozes sex and has dated half the women who work here? Although, I'm not sure you can call it dating."

Tate choked on the water in his mouth. He recovered as quickly as he could as Stacy laughed and placed the lid on the blender.

"You're shocked? I'm pretty sure he could date the manager if he asked Pete nicely. That one comes with one hell of a reputation."

Okay, so nix the gay theory. The guy must play for both teams. Well, I can still work with that.

* * *

STACY AND THE MAN who has all of my attention are definitely talking about me.

Logan brought the glass back up to his lips. After taking a sip, he placed it down on the bar. He'd had been tempted to wink at the hot bartender when he'd glanced his way. It was more Logan's nature, but he wasn't sure how that would have been received, so he'd refrained.

He was almost positive that the man had flirted with him only minutes earlier. *Maybe that was some wishful thinking,* because, right now, the guy was giving no emotion away. He'd turned back to his coworker, making Logan believe he was more than likely, imagining things.

Before Logan could think anything else about it, his

phone started ringing. He picked it up and accepted the incoming call.

"Jessica. You are impatient, aren't you?"

As a relaxed laugh filtered through the phone, Logan pictured her smooth, long legs parting for him as they had only a couple of weeks earlier.

"Well, after your last text, I wanted to hear your voice."

"So, should I just start reciting the alphabet?" Logan asked, dropping his voice to an intimate tone.

"You could, or you could tell me how much you miss being inside me and how you're dying to get back there."

Logan chuckled, and his lips curled as he let her words sink in. Although he would have to wait another month, he was looking forward to sliding his dick back inside her.

"Well, that wouldn't be a lie," he agreed just as he felt someone stop in front of him. He raised his gaze to meet the current object of his lust, and he felt the devil on his shoulder as he licked his bottom lip. "I wouldn't mind getting you out of your clothes. When can we arrange that?"

Who he was really addressing was anyone's guess. Logan noticed the bartender's eyebrow arch, as he listened to Jessica's husky laugh. He imagined the man in front of him saying, *Right now*, and removing all his clothes, starting with that black vest.

That didn't last long though because the guy angled his head like he was about to leave, but Logan didn't want him to go anywhere.

He held up a finger, and contemplated the man in front of him as he said into the phone, "I'm out right now, Jess. You think we could have this conversation a little later?"

Hot bartender reached for the ever-present towel with his left hand, and he started to once again wipe down the bar. His repeated actions came close to confirming Logan's earlier suspicions.

That's a nervous habit. It's got to be.

"Yes, tonight is good. I'll talk to you then. Bye, hon."

As he ended the call and placed the phone on the bar, he waited for the man opposite him to talk. When nothing came, Logan leaned in and decided to stop being polite. *What the fuck, right?*

"I think the bar is clean. You can stop wiping it down now."

Immediately, the towel stopped moving, and the guy stood back up, tucking it into his pants.

"I'm sorry if I made you uncomfortable—" Logan started but was cut off quickly.

"No, you're not."

Logan scoffed at that and started to finger the rim of his glass. "Okay, you're right. I'm not. I figured you deserved it after talking about me with your coworker. Isn't that frowned upon or something? Gossiping about your customers?"

His bartender—*Yeah, that's how I'm going to think of*

him—leaned his hands on the counter.

"I suppose it would be. Dating the customers is also frowned upon, but you don't seem to mind that rule," he replied steadily.

"Ah," Logan said. *It was the usual work gossip.* "The new guy has finally been informed."

"Informed of?"

Logan didn't know what had provoked him, but the cap he normally kept on his personality had finally been unscrewed.

He pushed up a little from the rungs on the bar stool and rested his palms on the bar top as he leaned across the surface. "That I like to fuck, and that I've slept with almost all of the women and a couple of the guys you work with. And just so you don't worry about them, they all thanked me afterward."

Sitting back on his stool, he was proud to see that his little admission had shocked the bartender. The man's mouth was parted as he remained focused on Logan.

"Isn't that what you were discussing with Stacy? Oh, come on, we aren't strangers anymore. You know my name, remember? But I still don't know yours. Should I just keep thinking of you as the hot bartender? Or maybe that's offensive. You should give me your name, so I stop labeling you in the same way you are trying so desperately to label me."

* * *

WHO IS THIS guy? Tate stood there, completely stunned by the words that had just come out of that perfectly shaped mouth—*Wait. Why do I care about his mouth? Fucking Stacy, talking about how good-looking he is.*

"Would you like another drink?" He needed to quickly get this conversation back on track. This guy could have him fired on day three of his employment.

"Oh, I've shocked and scared the man behind the bar. That's amazing really, considering only..." He stopped and looked at the clock on the wall. "Fifteen minutes ago, you jumped to take my order."

Tate was trying to keep up with what the hell was going on while looking at the man peering at him from behind the dark-framed glasses, but he was coming up with absolutely nothing.

"It's okay," Logan assured, dropping the heavy sarcasm. He gave a relaxed smile. "I'm only inappropriate when I'm sober."

That finally made Tate laugh. Somehow, he doubted it.

"So, I just have to get you drunk to shut your mouth?" As soon as he'd said the words, he knew they were the wrong ones, considering the current conversation.

"Well, that's definitely one way, but I can think of a more preferable one, not to mention more pleasurable," Logan responded.

Tate recognized the same voice he had heard Logan

use on the phone with Jess when he'd said he wanted to get her naked. *Or maybe Jess was a he?*

"Do you hit on everyone you meet?" Tate heard himself ask as he stood, frozen to the spot by some perverse curiosity.

Yes, he'd been the object of affection over the years, but there was something different behind Logan's comments. Logan's scrutiny was a lot more intense than a casual once-over. Logan was looking at him like he wanted to see him *without* his clothes on, as soon as possible.

"Do you?" Logan countered, looking directly at him.

Well, he has a point. Tate had been flirting with him earlier when he thought the guy was gay and interested enough to give him a good tip. *Yeah, joke's on me.* Now that Tate knew Logan thought he was hot, Tate was thinking that flirting hadn't been such a great idea. He was actually thinking it would be a very dangerous one, if he continued.

"It's part of my job, I guess," Tate tried explaining.

As soon as an I-don't-believe-you expression crossed Logan's face, Tate knew that whatever was about to come next would be highly inappropriate.

So, Tate interrupted. "Do you want another drink?"

Logan inclined his head forward, "Yes, please."

Tate was relieved that Logan had let the conversation go, and turned away quickly. He went about making his drink, all the while telling himself to pull his shit together. The guy was just confident and went after what he wanted.

Right now, he's playing with me because he thinks I was

talking shit about him. I will not let him get to me. At least he
doesn't know my name.

Tate moved back to the bar and slid the drink across
the counter. He watched as Logan's large hand stopped the
glass.

He lifted it in a mock salute. "Thanks for the drink,
Tate."

Tate narrowed his eyes on the laughing ones looking
back at him, and he couldn't help the annoyance bubbling
up inside of him. *Logan knew my name all along.*

"By the way, Stacy was right about you grabbing my
attention, but the next time you gossip, you should do it
quietly."

Tate had nothing to say to that. Instead of trying to
come up with anything, he turned on his heel and made his
way down the bar to the other waiting customers, getting as
far away from Logan as he could get.

* * *

LOGAN TOOK ANOTHER sip of his drink, enjoying
himself immensely.

Tate. He now had a name to go with the currently
bewildered face. *Poor guy.* Logan knew he was sending out
more mixed signals than a broken down traffic light, but
fuck, he was having fun. With every cryptic comment he
had thrown, Logan could see the questions running through
the man's mind.

Well, let him wonder, and while he's wondering, I'm going to concentrate on watching.

Tate hadn't punched him yet, so that was a plus. No, Tate had almost flirted. It wasn't until he'd realized *how* interested Logan was, that things had changed. That was when Tate had backed off.

Logan always went after what he wanted though. That was half of his problem. He had no boundaries. *Thanks, Mom.* Throughout his life, his mom had been so busy apologizing to him for his worthless sperm donor of a father that Logan had pretty much done whatever he'd wanted to.

But wanting this guy? That was a stupid choice in every way.

First, Logan had no clue if the guy was single. Second, every indication thus far had proven Tate was one hundred percent straight.

So, what the fuck am I doing?

He stood, getting ready to leave, when Tate turned and started walking toward him.

Logan stopped what he was doing and took a moment to admire the way he moved. Long legs encased in black slacks confidently stepped across the space with a purely masculine stride, but the look on his face was not half as certain. He looked worried.

He stopped in front of Logan. "I hope I haven't offended you in any way tonight, sir."

Aw, he thinks he pissed off a customer.

It was a pity he couldn't just say, *Relax, Tate. I want to see you naked, not fired.*

Instead, Logan took his wallet from his back pocket and pulled out some money. Placing it on the bar, he said, "The only offensive thing you did tonight was forget my name. It's Logan, not sir. Well, at least it is in this setting." He pushed his wallet back into his pocket.

Tate shook his head. "There you go again."

"Excuse me?"

"Being inappropriate," he pointed out.

Logan hadn't even realized. "Ah yes, it's a curse."

"So I've noticed."

That response intrigued Logan more than he should allow. "What else have you noticed?"

Tate picked up the empty glass. "I don't know what you mean."

"Okay..." Logan lifted his cell and quickly dialed a number. "You keep telling yourself that."

Raising the phone to his ear, Logan winked at the silent man standing opposite him.

I don't care if I have to be here every fucking night. I'm going to have him.

Chapter Three

DAY THREE AT 11:01 p.m., and Logan still hasn't shown.

I definitely pissed him off last night. Tate toweled down the top of the bar where one of the customers had gotten sloppy. If only he'd kept his mouth shut and done his damn job, he would have a regular customer who tipped big. *But I couldn't do that, could I? What do I care about the personal lives of my customers?* Usually, he didn't care at all. He wasn't the type to gossip, but damn, this Logan guy had deliberately provoked him.

Screw it. Just move on.

At least Logan hadn't reported him. That was a bonus. Tate had been worried about coming into work this afternoon, only to find out he no longer had a job, but that hadn't been the case. So, he pushed aside his annoyance and got busy with the Friday night crowd. The fact that *the suit* hadn't shown up was bothering him, and *that* was really starting to piss him off.

It wasn't as if someone who had slept with nearly the entire staff of women *and* a few of the men would be sitting around here on a Friday night.

And why am I still thinking about it? Jesus, move on already man.

It didn't help that before he'd shown up at work, he'd received a call from Diana, who proceeded to tell him that she'd just gotten engaged. That, of course, meant that everything between them needed to be resolved now, and the divorce she'd been putting off would be finalized. Diana had claimed she was doing him a favor by calling, and she'd wanted him to hear it from her first instead of finding out from someone else, or worse, his parents since they all still talked.

How fucking nice for them to all remain friendly. Granted, Tate's sister had been best friends with Diana before they got married. *But where is the damn loyalty? And how on earth did she find some other schmuck to take her on? It's only been a little over a year.* Well, as far as he was concerned, she could go and suck the schmuck as much as she wanted. *I'm free now.*

Tonight just needed to be written off. It was going down the shitter for sure.

While grabbing a bottle of water for himself, he observed the door being pulled open, and Logan stepping inside.

Tate couldn't decide if he was relieved the guy had shown or if he was worried about what would come out of Logan's mouth once he was seated. He wasn't exactly in the mood to be dicked around, and this guy seemed to push his buttons—and he delighted in the pushing.

Watching objectively as Logan made his way through the crowd, Tate noticed he looked different this evening. The glasses were gone, and he was in jeans and a black V-neck shirt. Although the outfit looked casual, Tate was pretty sure each item of clothing was designer-made. Logan must've shrugged his coat off outside because he was holding it down by his leg as he shouldered through everyone, including several women who turned to look him over.

As he got closer, Tate was astounded by the sexual confidence and pull that Logan exuded. It was so obvious and potent that Tate knew Logan could have any pick of the women he wanted. Finally, he made it to the bar and sat down in his usual spot, immediately seeking out Tate and inclining his head in his direction.

Making sure not to give any reaction at all, Tate casually tipped his head back and took a gulp of water, securing his fingers around the bottle. He had always thought of himself as self-assured, someone who knew his way around, especially when it came to playing the game of cat and mouse. He made a living off of it. He was always the cat that never caught the mouse, but he sure played with it for a while to make good money. But in this scenario, with *this* guy, Tate found himself feeling a lot like the mouse—and that pissed him off.

Pulling the bottle from his mouth, he noticed that Logan's focus was still on him. He twisted the cap back on and placed the bottle on the bench behind the bar, wondering if he could get the upper hand back. He made his way toward the end of the bar, but just before he got there,

Amelia, one of the girls he was scheduled to work with regularly, grabbed his arm.

Tate looked down at her and found wide brown eyes sparkling back at him.

She gave him her best *please* smile. "Do you mind if I take him?"

Trying to think of a good reason to say no, considering the last two nights Logan had tipped him extremely well, Tate, instead, came up with nothing. "Sure, go ahead."

Amelia leaned up on her tiptoes and pressed a kiss to his cheek. "You're the best."

Then, she walked down the bar with an extra sway in her step right before she stopped and leaned across the counter to greet Logan.

* * *

FUCK. LOGAN WATCHED as Amelia intercepted Tate and made her way over to him.

"I was wondering if you'd be back in this week. I haven't had a chance to see you."

Logan tried to be polite as he turned his vision to the blonde, who had been in his bed a couple of times, but all he wanted—and all he had wanted for the last three days—was currently at the other end of the bar, laughing and smiling at someone else. It was wise to note, Logan supposed, that the other someone had long brown hair and was wearing a rather revealing dress. *She* was also currently touching what Logan wanted to touch.

Focusing back on Amelia, Logan gave her a friendly wink. "You know me. I'm always in at least three nights a week."

"I know." She giggled as though she was embarrassed she'd given away how much she wanted to see him. "It's just, each time you've come in this week, Tate has snagged you before I had the chance."

"Hmm, yes, the new guy," Logan mused.

Tate had definitely *snagged* him, and as he looked beyond Amelia's shoulder, he noticed that Tate had turned to the back of the bar to grab a liquor bottle from one of the top shelves. As he reached above his head, the snug vest pulled his shirt from his pants, revealing a smooth strip of tanned skin.

Logan licked his lips, wondering just how good Tate would taste. His olive skin was such a delicious complexion. It was definitely natural because, in Chicago, no one looked like that coming out of winter unless it was natural. *And I'm volunteering to inspect every fucking inch of him as soon as possible.*

As Tate placed the bottle on the bench, he turned his head as if he felt Logan scrutinizing him, and Logan couldn't help but give in to the urge to openly check him out. He trailed his gaze down Tate's long frame, at least six feet, and as he came back up in his overtly sexual once-over, he made sure to connect with the disconcerted eyes staring back at

him.

Logan offered nothing in the way of his thoughts, which were all centered on getting Tate out of his clothes and his cock into Logan's mouth, as he turned back to Amelia, who was still chatting about—

Shit, what is she talking about?

"So, what do you want to drink tonight?"

Wow, I've been coming here for years, and I order the same thing every time, yet she still asks. Funny, Tate just assumed after the first night, and his assumptions so far have been correct.

That made Logan wonder, *What exactly is he assuming right now?*

* * *

WHAT WAS THAT all about?

Tate was shocked to find his hand was shaking as he placed the bottle on the bench, taking a moment to look in the mirror behind the bar. He just stared at himself.

Breathe, you idiot, and let it go. He's just trying to rattle you.

Going back to making his customer's drink, Tate poured what he needed, added a wedge of lemon and then turned back to whom he was currently serving. He decided that the minute he was free, he was going to go talk to Logan. He wouldn't let Logan mess with his job or his head, and Tate was determined to find out if he had anything to worry about after last night.

Around fifteen minutes later, there was a break in the service, and Tate started to make his way down to where Logan was sitting. Taking a breath, he reminded himself that this was just some random guy he hadn't even known four days ago. But as he got closer, he could have sworn he felt his palms grow clammy at the expression aimed his way.

When he finally reached the end of the bar, he noticed the glass in front of Logan was empty. "Another?"

"Is it polite to poach another bartender's customer?"

Tate really wasn't in the mood to play games tonight, so instead of answering him, he rested against the counter and crossed his arms. "Fine. No drink."

"And no small talk, I see," Logan pointed out as he tilted his head to the side. "Something wrong?"

It annoyed Tate that he noticed how blue Logan's eyes were, and he thought that maybe Logan was wearing tinted contacts. Tate knew they sold that shit because Diana had liked to wear the green ones.

"Not really in the mood tonight," Tate answered with a shrug.

"Really? You seemed to be doing okay with the brunette over there."

Tate could have sworn that within that comment, he detected a hint of—

What? Jealousy?

"Well, the brunette was easy, and I know she wouldn't report me for anything I might say."

Tate watched Logan lean back and mirror his pose

by crossing his arms, which in turn made Tate notice how broad Logan's shoulders and chest were under the short-sleeved shirt.

Funny how misleading a suit can be.

"You think I'm going to report you?"

Tate looked around and then shook his head slightly. "I have no idea what *you* are going to do."

"I think I might take that other drink," Logan decided, his eyes narrowing slightly.

Without a word, Tate turned to get him his usual and then pushed it across the bar. Before he could remove his hand from the glass, Logan closed his fingers over his, and Tate jerked his head up. Tate couldn't mistake the sexual invitation in that stare. Logan had worn the same expression when he'd looked Tate over only moments earlier.

"For the record, I would never report you, and I'm probably the easiest person sitting at this bar tonight—for you, anyway."

Tate tried to remind himself that women and men had every right to hit on whomever they were attracted to, and he had no problem with that. His current problem was how to react to being so blatantly pursued.

"I don't understand you. You pick a woman one week and a guy the next? So…" Tate trailed off, wondering *what* exactly he was asking.

When Tate felt Logan's hand finally move away from his own, he quickly released the glass as if it were on fire. He watched Logan intently as he lifted the drink to his lips, seemingly contemplating the question.

After taking a sip of the liquor, Logan lowered the glass slowly. "So...I like to try a little bit of everything and everyone."

The words sank into Tate's head, settling in, and then they started to make a whole lot more sense—until Logan, as usual, threw another can of gasoline on the fire.

"I'd like to try you."

* * *

LOGAN MONITORED TATE'S face closely as he seemed to digest exactly what he'd just said. First came the shock, his face flushed, and Logan *almost* laughed. The embarrassment though was accompanied by such a look of bewilderment as if he didn't know what the fuck to say.

Logan decided to let him off the hook. "It's okay, Tate. I don't expect an answer, but I thought it best to be up front, considering..."

Out came the white towel, and Logan stared at it as Tate ran it between his hands.

"Considering? Considering what?"

"Considering you seemed so confused when, really, there is nothing to be confused about."

"Except for the fact that I'm straight," Tate finally announced.

Logan toyed with his glass for a moment before he conceded. "Yes, well, I don't let little things like that stand in my way."

Tate started laughing and seemed to regain his footing as Logan let the robust sounds reverberate through him.

"You're full of confidence, I'll give you that. But I have to tell you, you're barking up the wrong tree."

"Am I?" Logan responded quickly.

"Yes. I just got out of a horrible marriage. Even if I *were* interested, why would I try something with you? Last night, you told me yourself that you've fucked everyone I work with. Now, I'm just wondering which women *and* which men."

Logan, not the least bit deterred, lifted his glass. "Wouldn't you like to know?"

"Well, I can just ask them all and cause mass anarchy in the After Hours ranks."

"You could. Or you could get to know me better and ask me again at a more appropriate time."

Tate's dark brow rose in suspicion. "And when would that be?"

Logan knew that Tate was expecting something sexual to come out of his mouth, so he leaned in close, and he was delighted when Tate followed suit. He wondered for a moment if Tate even realized he did it.

"When Amelia isn't making her way over here to kick your ass."

Logan gave him a shit-eating grin and sat back as Tate turned to see exactly what he had been referring to.

* * *

TATE FOCUSED ON his coworker, who was glaring up at him as if he had stolen her personal property, while he tried to make sense of everything that had just happened. Amelia was a good distraction really, as she stepped around and ignored him completely, only to smile at the man who was currently baffling the shit out of him.

"I'm sorry. I didn't realize your glass was empty, Logan."

Tate didn't know why, but the fact that she used his first name irritated him. It also made it abundantly clear that she had definitely been one of the coworkers who had been fucked—and thankful.

"It's fine, hon. Tate and I were just talking guy stuff."

We were? News to me. Tate glared at Logan, from where he stood beside Amelia.

"Yeah, he was telling me about his bike. You make sure to come see me before I leave."

Tate had to hand it to the guy. He was smooth under pressure.

I wonder what he does for a living.

"Okay, I just wanted to make sure you were taken care of."

As Amelia's words floated through the air, Tate locked eyes with those vibrant blue ones.

Logan replied, "I am most definitely being taken care

of."

Shit. The guy needs to cool it and stop being so fucking obvious. People are going to start talking when there is nothing to even say.

"Amelia?" Logan turned back to her and gave a quick wink. "Don't go too far, okay?"

Tate groaned quietly in disgust and shook his head as she giggled and aimed a triumphant grin in his direction.

He offered a smile that he hoped was happy. "Sorry, I didn't mean to get in the middle."

Placing a hand on his upper arm, Amelia squeezed as she licked her lips. No longer annoyed, she flirted in the same way—he was positive—she had just done with Logan. "Oh, you didn't, but that's a great idea," she said in a seductive purr.

Tate's eyes widened slightly as he turned back to Logan. He felt like Logan had somehow set the whole thing up, but even Logan looked somewhat shocked. However, instead of remaining mute like Tate, Logan raised his glass.

"That's a fantastic idea."

Tate patted Amelia's hand and removed it from his arm, as she grinned at him and then walked away.

Tate aimed a glare in Logan's direction. "You think this is funny, don't you?"

"No, I actually think it's a fantastic idea."

Tate shook his head. "You're unbalanced. It's never going to happen."

"Scared?" Logan inquired, showing his teeth in a

warped version of a grin.

Tate knew Logan expected him to run, so he stood his ground instead. "I like to think of it as smart."

"Yet, you're still here, talking to me," Logan reminded him.

"Well, it's quieter now, and you're rather entertaining once I look past the inappropriate comments."

"What? It's inappropriate to tell you I want to fuck you? Would it have been better if I were drunk?"

Tate completely lost the ability to form words at that blunt declaration. As he looked around quickly, he heard Logan laugh.

Tate turned back to the cocky asshole. "Jesus, would you keep your voice down? I don't give a shit what you want to do. I have a brain and a mouth, and *no* has worked so far on people like you."

Logan placed his palm on the counter and stroked the wood with his fingers. "People like me?"

"Yes, as in pushy, arrogant, and full of themselves. What do you do anyway?"

Tate waited patiently as Logan picked up a small black straw from the container on the bar.

"Guess."

Flinging the towel over his shoulder, Tate looked Logan over quickly, but since Logan was in his casual clothes, Tate knew he'd get nothing from that.

"Investment banker," he threw out.

Logan let out a loud rumbling laugh, and as

customers turned to face them, Tate gave a polite smile before looking back to the oblivious man sitting opposite him.

"Seriously? Do I look like a numbers guy?"

"No, not really," Tate answered truthfully. *You look more like a model.*

"Thank God for that. What *do* I look like?" Logan inquired, lowering his voice.

Tate placed his palms on the bar. "Stop it," he told him pointedly.

"Stop what?"

"Stop flirting with me," he demanded.

Logan brought the straw to his lips and bit down on the end of it, and then slowly pulled it out. "I think you like it."

"And I think you're deranged. Used car salesman."

Logan frowned. "Now, you're just trying to be insulting."

"You're right, I was. I would bet the last two tips *you* gave me that you're a lawyer."

Logan twirled the black plastic between his fingers. "And if you're wrong?"

"I'm not."

"You're awfully certain all of a sudden. Did you ask someone?"

Tate answered almost immediately, "No."

"Then, why so sure?"

"You're smooth, too smooth, and you always have

an answer for everything."

"Maybe I like debating."

"Maybe you're full of shit. Just admit it. It's okay that I'm right," Tate announced, full of confidence, as he leaned even closer to add on a whisper, "I won't tell anyone."

And that, right there, was his biggest mistake.

He saw the precise moment when Logan dropped his focus to Tate's mouth, and his expression changed from interest to lust, and Tate found himself preparing to fight off an unwanted kiss.

"Careful, Tate."

"Huh?"

"I am a lawyer, and I'm always looking for a loophole. And I think you do like this, but don't worry," Logan told him before promising, "I won't tell anyone."

Tate quickly straightened away from the bar and grabbed the towel off his shoulder, kicking himself in the ass for getting caught up in conversing with this man—again.

"You're left-handed," were the odd choice of words that broke through his thoughts.

"And you're observant," Tate mumbled, still trying to work out if he did like the attention he was getting from Logan. *And if I do, what does that say about me?*

"You know," Logan drawled, "there are lots of interesting facts about left-handed people. Over history, left-handedness has been seen as all kinds of things from a nasty habit to a sign from the devil, a rebellious nature, even…homosexuality. Hmm, I've never had a left-hander before."

Tate stared back at the man who was talking so casually he might as well have been asking about the weather. Nevertheless, every single sentence coming from Logan's mouth was pushing Tate further out of his comfort zone and straight into the I-must-be-going-fucking-crazy zone.

"And yes, I am observant, sometimes." Logan lifted the glass to his mouth where he finished the drink and then placed it back on the bar top.

Going into self-preservation mode, Tate asked the usual job-related questions. "Will that be all?"

"Drink-wise, yes."

"That's all that's offered at this hour. Food shut down at ten," he stated plainly.

"That's fine. I'm not hungry for food." Logan clasped his hands on top of the bar.

Tate didn't know what to say to that unless he was going to slip into the same behavior he had a moment earlier. It was obvious that engaging in conversational-sparring matches with Logan, no matter how innocent, led to dangerous territory and wreaked havoc on Tate's mental health.

"In that case, I'll go and let Amelia know."

"Oh, could you? Because she is exactly who I've been picturing naked and bent over for me since I sat down here tonight. And yes, I know that was inappropriate. But, Tate?"

Tate focused on the shameless lawyer, who was

definitely checking him out this time, and tried to remain professional. "Yes, Logan?"

"That's when I'm at my best."

Tate turned away silently and heard laughter follow after him as he moved farther down the bar, and at that moment, he wondered if Logan was laughing at his own comment or the moron walking away from him.

* * *

LOGAN KNEW HE had been pushing it tonight. Hell, if there was one speed he didn't have, it was slow. But he figured if he didn't make his case with Tate, the opportunity—*wait, when did that become a word in this scenario?*—would disappear.

After that last drink, the time hit twelve thirty, and he decided he was probably now bordering on the pathetic line—especially considering he was sitting at a bar and drinking alone just so he could watch a certain bartender move around in front of him.

Logan felt the familiar stirring in his cock as he tore his attention from the other man. He got down from the bar stool and made his way into the restroom, trying to decide what he'd seen in Tate's expression when they had been going back and forth.

Confusion was the first expression that came to mind. It hadn't once been accompanied by disgust though, and *that* he could work with.

Finishing up, Logan washed his hands and stepped out into the dim corridor, leading back to the bar, where he practically ran into Amelia.

She stepped in close to him. "Leaving so soon?"

Logan glanced around, and when he saw they were alone, he peered down her black shirt and vest to where she had the top three buttons popped open. Running his tongue along his top lip in contemplation, Logan raised his eyes back to hers.

"I was about to—unless there's a reason I should stay?"

When Amelia placed her hands on his lower abdomen, stroking his rigid muscles, Logan knew exactly where this was going.

"Well, I was thinking..."

Stepping back into the corner of the hall, Logan wasn't surprised when she followed.

"What were you thinking?" He was now thinking about her lips around his dick.

Warm hands burrowed under his black shirt before fingers dipped into the top of his jeans. She turned her face up to him, and he watched expectantly as—*ah, yes*—her tongue came out to moisten her lips.

"I was thinking that I want this," she whispered daringly as she moved her right hand down to cup him through his jeans, "in my mouth."

Putting his hand on hers, Logan rubbed it up and down his throbbing cock.

"Then don't let me stop you," he invited, and then added, "Did you at least clock out? I'd hate to think you might be fired for inappropriately servicing a patron."

Removing her hand, Amelia laughed softly as she unbuttoned his jeans and lowered the zipper. Dropping to her knees in front of him, she tugged his pants down and freed his insistent hard-on.

"Well, if worse comes to worst, we can just tell them I was giving exactly what the customer wanted." Fisting the root of his shaft, she lowered her lips over his sensitive, swollen head.

Logan shut his eyes and imagined a different person altogether kneeling down in front of him—a person with hands as large as his own whose face revealed uncertainty and shock during their conversation tonight. He envisioned brown curls and dark eyes looking up at him as firm lips opened and took him into that mouth he wanted to taste.

As Logan moved his hands to the wall behind him, he didn't dare open his eyes. He was too busy enjoying the fuck fantasy he was imagining in his head, and when dainty lips slid down his shaft, taking him as deep as they could toward the back of her throat, he tried not to think about the fact that he wanted it harder.

Yeah, I'm an asshole.

He bucked his hips forward into her mouth, but all he was picturing was how much quicker he'd lose his shit if he could reach out and touch cheeks that were rough with stubble—*dark stubble like Tate's.*

When a small hand clutched his thigh, Logan was pulled back into reality, and his eyes slid open. That was also the moment they locked on to the man standing at the entrance of the dimly lit hall, who was staring at what was going on with an intense focus that Logan had never seen.

* * *

TATE COULDN'T BELIEVE what he was looking at, and even more disturbing, he couldn't look away.

At first, as he stood in the hall leading to the restrooms, he was hit with the visual of Logan backed up against the far corner wall, his legs parted, with Amelia kneeling at his feet. From the silent shadows, Tate could see that Logan's head was arched back as though the pleasure was so fucking good.

That was all bad enough for Tate until he felt his cock react as though he were the one on the receiving end of Amelia's mouth. Then, Logan's eyes opened, and that was when Tate's reality became one huge blur.

As his stare collided with the other man's, Tate realized that it was Logan's focus, not Amelia's, that made him finally reach full-on, rock-hard, aching status—and there was nothing he could do to try to fool himself into believing otherwise.

Tate absorbed all that he was seeing as Logan moved his hands from beside the wall to direct the head moving rapidly over his cock. Tate felt his breathing accelerate as his fists clenched by his sides. Silently, he watched Logan pump his hips forward, pushing his shaft farther down his coworker's throat, all the while looking at him and licking his lips.

Unable to make himself move, Tate found that he was entranced by the scene unfolding in front of him. He couldn't take his eyes off the man who was eye-fucking him, while face-fucking the woman on her knees.

When Tate dropped his vision to the back of Amelia, he saw the large hands on her head, and he couldn't help but wonder how strong they were as they flexed and fisted her blonde hair.

Jesus, I'm thinking about him touching me now? Walk the fuck away. Just turn around and walk away.

However, his feet weren't listening to his brain, and instead of walking away, he continued to play voyeur to a man who was becoming a menace to his normally sane life.

* * *

LOGAN HADN'T EXPECTED this twist of events, but as he slid free from Amelia's lips, and his gaze trailed over Tate, he felt his climax building in the base of his spine, causing his balls to tighten. There was something so depraved and deviant about being watched while performing a sexual act, but being observed by the one person he wanted and didn't think he could have was even fucking better.

As he continued to use Amelia's mouth, Logan

remained fixated on who he really craved, Tate. Having him standing there with an expression that crossed from shock to straight-up heated lust, Logan wondered if Tate even realized how much he was giving away.

First off, Tate was not looking at Amelia. *No, his attention is all on me.* Second, Tate's hands were balled up into fists as if he was trying to stop himself from touching. It was a wonder he hadn't broken his fingers. And last, as Logan eyed Tate's pants, he could see a bulge that made him want to push Amelia out of the way and get down on his own knees to finish his bartender off.

That was it. That was the visual Logan needed.

Parting his lips on a groan, he imagined sucking Tate's cock into his mouth and it was all over. His balls tingled as his hands seized the blonde hair they were entangled in. Focusing on Tate, Logan watched the man's tongue as it slipped out and slid along his bottom lip. When it disappeared back into his mouth, Logan wanted to be the one to fucking chase it, and taste inside, *after he swallows, of course.* He knew it was a fantasy but with that final thought, he stared at the man he truly wanted, and immediately came down Amelia's throat instead.

Chapter Four

TATE COULD FEEL his chest rise and fall with each labored breath he took as he remained fixated on Logan, who had just very obviously come in a jaw-dropping way.

As soon as the dimly lit space went from combustible to a silent dark hallway, Tate thought, *turn the hell around and go.*

Do not wait to see what happens next. Move! Move! Move!

But no, he didn't move. Instead, Tate stayed where he was and watched Logan run his hand over the back of Amelia's head as she moved away and he licked his full bottom lip.

Tate unconsciously moved his hand over his stiff cock, adding pressure to the ache behind his work pants. Of course, Logan didn't miss the gesture at all. He glanced down to where Tate was rubbing himself, and his lips tipped up into a full-on arrogant-as-hell smirk.

That was what finally had Tate turning on his heel and getting the fuck out of Dodge.

What is the matter with me? Standing here and getting off on Logan? Sick fucker is screwing with my head.

Quickly, Tate made his way back out to the bar

and to the break room to grab his gear. It was time to go, and he wanted to leave immediately. Punching out on the time clock, he made his way back out, hoping to God that Logan had left and wasn't waiting out there to further torment him.

When he got to the bar, he noticed it was practically empty. He sighed with relief, until he remembered exactly why he had gone to the back restrooms in the first place.

Better if I go now than need to on the back of my damn bike.

Making his way back over to the hall, he almost made it when Logan stepped out, and they both stopped in the empty space.

Oh, this is just great.

Tate stared at the man standing opposite him. There was no expression on Logan's face, and Tate wasn't exactly sure he had one damn thing to say. So, he stood and waited and hoped like hell Logan would do the one thing Tate figured he would not—leave silently.

* * *

LOGAN COUNTED IN his head, waiting for Tate to flee, and then thought, *fuck it,* and went into action, not wasting any time. Taking a step forward, he felt the thrill of the chase skate up his spine as Tate automatically backed up and hit the wall behind him.

"Logan," Tate acknowledged in a way that screamed he was trying to keep things distant, professional even.

Well, tough shit. You just watched me get head. It's too late for distant and professional.

"Tate."

"You just leaving?"

Logan felt his lip curl, as he saw Tate quickly look to the only means of escape. Or maybe he was checking to make sure no one was witnessing what was going on.

"I was about to since I got everything I came for. But now, I'm not in such a rush." Logan dropped his gaze to Tate's mouth and watched as he nervously ran his tongue over his lips, nodding.

"Well, I'm sure Amelia hasn't left yet. She'll be waiting for you."

A low rumble left Logan's chest as he raised his right hand and placed it beside Tate's shoulder, effectively blocking his escape.

"I think we both know I'm not in the least bit interested in Amelia."

"And I think I made it clear that I'm straight. Take a *hint*, sir," Tate pointed out and glanced at the hand against the wall before turning back to him. "You need to move your arm."

Logan straightened slowly and stroked his fingertips down the dark hardwood beside Tate's arm.

"Straight, huh? You know, funny thing is, often the straightest of trees have crooked roots."

As he removed his hand, he angled his body closer, getting within a few inches of Tate's.

"You forget my name?"

"No."

"Then, don't call me sir. It turns me on," Logan admitted, finding that the word *sir* from Tate's full lips really did turn him on.

"Doesn't everything turn you on, Logan? You seem willing to do anything at every opportunity."

Logan tilted his head to the side and pursed his lips. "Why not, if it feels good and someone offers? However, fucking wise? As of a few days ago, I just want one thing, and since he hasn't punched me in the face yet, I'm thinking I may have a shot at it."

"Like I said earlier, you're delusional, and right now, you need to get the fuck out of my face."

"Or?"

"Or it might just meet with my fist."

Logan felt the blood and adrenaline pumping through his veins at the pissed-off expression crossing Tate's face. Stepping back, he shoved his hands into his jeans pockets to try and shift the erection that was once again trying to rear its head as it painfully pushed against his zipper.

"Threatening a customer? Doesn't seem very professional. Are you upset because of what I did tonight?

Or because you stood there, watching and wishing it was *you* on your knees instead?"

Choosing to ignore him, Tate clenched his jaw and his fists, and Logan thought it was probably smart that he had taken a step back. Tate looked explosive.

"We're all told during training that sexual harassment will not be tolerated—by employees *or* customers."

Logan tipped his head back and laughed derisively. "Oh, trust me, Tate, I haven't started to do anything sexual *to* you, and for the record, I had a third drink tonight. It may have tipped me over the edge of sober."

"A man your size? I doubt it."

"You noticed my size? I'm flattered."

"Don't be," Tate spat at him. He finally pushed off the wall and took a step toward Logan, lifting his head and squaring off with him. "I thought you were only inappropriate when you were sober. So, what would you call this?"

Licking his lips, Logan boldly ran his gaze down Tate's black shirt and vest to the pants he was becoming obsessed with undoing. "I call this going after what I want."

A waft of air brushed against Logan's face as Tate scoffed and pushed his face in even closer to his own.

"Then, in case I'm the first, let me introduce you to what me walking away is called…"

Logan watched Tate turn and make his way into

the bathroom.

Over his shoulder, Tate called out, "Rejection."

For the life of him, Logan couldn't decide why that made the guy even more appealing.

* * *

TATE FINALLY MADE it into one of the stalls and shut it. He locked it quickly just in case Logan decided to follow him inside and do—

Hell, who knew what.

The man had no fucking boundaries. Not to mention, he seemed to have a death wish.

What if I was a homophobic asshole and decided to beat the shit out of him?

Tate turned in the stall and leaned his back against the door. Then again, the likelihood of that happening was slim. Tate could hold his own, but Logan was a big guy.

Lifting a hand, Tate ran it over his face and up through his shaggy hair. Squeezing the back of his head. He tried to ignore the fact that his hands were shaking as he brushed both of his palms down the front of his thighs, and realized for the first time that he was still sporting a major erection.

Jesus, he thought as he jammed his hand against the traitorous cock in his pants, *what the fuck is Logan doing to me?*

Tate had no answers. All he could hope for was that the guy would be gone when he came back out and that he would *not* turn up tomorrow night.

* * *

"YOU'RE LEAVING?" LOGAN heard from behind him as he made his way to the front door of the bar.

He turned to see Amelia jogging over, slinging her purse on her shoulder. Her blonde hair was now tied back for the evening, and her cheeks were a nice rosy pink from their earlier activities.

Logan shrugged into his black jacket and looked down at her with a wink. "I was about to. You just get off?"

"Not yet," she replied with a saucy grin, tucking her hands into her black pants, pushing her breasts up into his face. "Want to help with that?"

Logan was positive the answer here was yes. He was single, she was single, and they could so go back to his place and finish what they started. But he also knew that she was not the person he wanted.

As he looked just beyond her shoulder, he saw Tate come back out from the hall, and he glanced around the emptying space. Their eyes met, and then Tate moved his to Amelia. Logan wasn't surprised at the contempt he saw crossing the other man's features.

Why the hell not?

Logan touched Amelia's chin and looked down, so

they were eye-to-eye. "I'd love some company if you'd like to join me."

The smile that slowly spread across her lips made Logan's cock take notice, and he was relieved to know that it still functioned without him looking at Tate.

She let her top teeth bite into that ripe bottom lip as she nodded. "I'd like."

"Good." He took her hand. "Just so happens, so would I."

* * *

TATE PUSHED THROUGH the front door of the crappy apartment he'd moved into after the divorce, and threw his black backpack along with his jacket on the floor. Moving down the narrow foyer, he placed his helmet on the kitchen countertop and made his way to the fridge where he opened it and took out a beer. He was about to shut the door, but at the last minute, he grabbed a second.

Well, if ever there is a night for two beers, tonight is it.

Slumping down onto his couch, he picked up the remote and turned on the TV as he kicked off his boots. As the sports channel replayed a baseball game from earlier, Tate uncapped the first beer and took a large gulp.

After undoing the buttons on his vest, he lifted his hips and pulled his shirt from his waistband, sighing at finally being able to relax and unwind. As he started to zone out, he lifted the drink back to his lips and took another gulp, reflecting on everything that had happened and his own reaction to it. He knew that Logan was no doubt screwing Amelia's brains out, and he was happy to find that the thought of *that* was welcome.

Why? Because, otherwise, he might have gone home to jerk off while thinking of me?

Finishing the first beer, Tate reached out and grabbed the second.

Taking it with his left hand, he tilted it up to his mouth, and all of a sudden, he had a flash of Logan looking at him while Amelia was sucking his cock. Tate recalled the way Logan's eyes had seemed to spark and heat. If it was physically possible to feel heat from a look, then Tate could have sworn he had felt it lick along his skin at that precise moment.

Tate just needed to be more alert when Logan was around. Logan had admitted he flirted with anything that talked, but that didn't mean Tate needed to worry. Surely, Logan wouldn't push anything that wasn't welcome.

And it is not *welcome*, Tate told himself as he glared down at his currently under control lap.

Whatever had happened earlier was just some kind of involuntary chemical or physical reaction. *Something that couldn't be helped, right?*

Yeah, right.

He was pretty sure it wasn't normal for a straight man to get a raging erection from a guy coming, but then again, he had nothing to compare it to.

I just need to get laid.

Starting to feel more relaxed, Tate shuffled further down into his couch and assured himself that was all it was as he cradled his beer.

I'm frustrated. I just need to find a woman. Of course, I'm going to get hard while watching a guy like Logan getting head, especially with all the sex talk he threw around.

The guy was basically a walking hormone.

It was only natural, right?

Chapter Five

SATURDAY, SUNDAY, AND Monday passed by without incident.

Thank God for minor miracles, Tate thought as he rode to work on Tuesday evening.

Sunday and Monday were his days off, and Logan had stayed away from the bar Saturday night. The only reason Tate knew *that* was because his dumb ass had watched the door all night.

Logan had managed to somehow stay on his mind all the way through lunch at his mother's on Sunday where she and his sister, Jill, had spent half of the conversation grilling him about his love life. It irritated Tate to no end that all he could think about was the fact that the most intimate contact he'd recently had was with a guy who wouldn't leave him alone, but he didn't think his mother would appreciate that little tidbit. Actually, his entire family would flip out.

Today though, he was determined to move past it all. Fixating on a stranger in the bar was not smart in any way, especially when that stranger was male. He needed to find a woman to focus on.

A hot, curvy, available woman.

Pushing through the bar's front door, Tate carried his helmet under his arm and made his way over to the bar pass where he saw Amelia wiping down the counter. She must have arrived early, which was fine by him because it gave him a little extra time to clock in.

Once in the break room, he quickly hung his jacket and placed the helmet on top of a crate. The door swung open, and Tate turned to see Amelia come through, pushing a towel into the waist of her pants.

Tate looked over his shoulder at her and gave a friendly smile. "Hey."

"Hey, yourself." She leaned her hip up against a table opposite him.

"You have a nice weekend?" Tate asked conversationally.

Amelia nodded, giving him a sassy wink. "Yep, sure did. Went out with some friends Sunday night. What about you? Anything exciting?"

Tate laughed, shaking his head. "Ah, that'd be a negative unless you count going to my parents' for lunch after church exciting?"

Amelia's eyebrows rose as she scrunched her face. "Um, no. I don't call that exciting at all. Torture maybe?"

"Torture is exactly right," Tate mumbled as he punched in.

There was a slight pause in the conversation and then, "So, Tate, you dating anyone right now?"

Jesus, not her, too.

Looking over his shoulder, he noticed she was focused on his ass. "Nope. Not right now."

If he were smart, he'd ask her if she was dating anyone either. Tate didn't think hooking up with Logan for one night counted. Maybe he could finally put an end to his sexual frustration. She did have a nice set of breasts, and her ass was perky and round, just how he liked it. But like an idiot, he didn't. That didn't stop her though.

"Me neither."

Tate faced her, pushing his hands into his pockets, and before he even knew it, he opened his mouth. "What about Logan?"

Immediately knowing it was the wrong thing to say, he watched her face light up as she moved in close, placing her hand on his arm.

"Logan is...Logan," she replied with a small shrug.

She went to move past him, and Tate let her, but not before asking, "What does that mean?"

She chuckled as they made their way into the main bar area.

"Logan's got high standards, but he's also the kind to try anything that captures his attention. That's what makes it so much fun to make him yours." She paused and stared into the mirror at the back of the bar. She pulled out a tube of lip gloss from her pocket, painted her mouth, and stuffed it back into her pants. "For the night at least."

Tate frowned at her casual assessment of using someone for sex, and he wondered why it made him feel bad for Logan. It wasn't like Logan gave a shit where he stuck his cock. He would be the first to admit that.

"Well, I'll take your word for it." Tate moved around her and was about to head out to the bar.

"You don't have to, you know."

Stopping, Tate rounded back to see a sneaky grin come across her innocent-looking face. "Excuse me?"

She sidled up close and touched his hand, which was resting on the bench for support—or from the shock of the comment, he wasn't sure.

Have I really been out of the dating game for so long that this shit is now normal to discuss?

"He'd let you join in with us."

Tate swallowed once and shifted his feet, looking down at the small hand covering his. When he felt his cock harden, he wondered exactly which part of the scenario it was reacting to—the thought of Amelia naked, the invitation to a threesome, or the man who would watch him as he slid inside the woman now peering up at him.

Removing his hand slowly, Tate made sure not to say anything offensive as he shook his head. "Nah, not really my thing. After a bad relationship, lunch at my mother's is about as much excitement as I can handle for a while."

Amelia tilted her head to the side and batted her eyelashes as she giggled. "Maybe it's time to let us corrupt you."

Somehow, Tate figured she wasn't the one who would do the corrupting. *That* particular person was missing for this conversation, yet somehow, his fingerprints were all over it.

"I don't think so, but thanks for the, uh…invite."

Just as Amelia was about to reply, a noise from the door had them turning to see four businessmen, mid-twenties, pile into the almost empty bar. With that, she turned to Tate and indicated with a tilt of her head that she would take them.

She gave him a quick wink. "No hard feelings. The offer is open."

I'm sure it is, Tate thought, moving to the opposite end of the bar, *but it's a little too open for me.*

* * *

LOGAN SAT BEHIND his desk, staring at the clock on the wall. It was just turning seven, and he could still hear a few people moving around in the outer office.

His weekend had passed by without too much incident. He'd heard briefly from his mother about her visiting in a few months, but as usual, she'd been all over the place, and she hadn't officially given him a date. She was still deciding if she wanted to stay with the new boyfriend or come and see him for Memorial Day weekend. It was sad that Logan couldn't even find the desire to try and convince her to pick him. He'd given up that fight a long time ago.

After the night with Amelia, he'd decided to skip the bar on Saturday to give Tate some downtime. *Time to simmer.*

Time was up though. It had been three days, and
Logan was definitely heading there tonight.

Tate was a walking contradiction. Although relaxed
and easygoing with others, he always became unsettled
around him. And when Logan went out of his way to push a
boundary, Tate either stood mute or pushed back. Not once,
however, had he gotten overly angry or violent.

It excited Logan—just thinking about getting into an
argument with him and ending it with Tate bent over
something. Yes, the idea of grappling with Tate was a very
appealing one.

As Logan was adjusting the hard-on in his pants,
there was a knock on the door. Calling out for the person to
come in, he was surprised when Cole stuck his head inside.

"Well, hello. What are you doing here so late? Don't
you have a hot wife to bed?"

Cole stepped inside and pushed the right side of his
jacket out of his way, as he stuffed his hand into his pocket.
"The hot wife is out with *the girls,* and I wasn't invited. And
Mason and Josh are watching football, which I hate."

After making sure he was decent, Logan stood and
made his way around to his business partner and half-
brother. "Aw, and you're lonely? Well, as flattering as it is
that I am your *last* choice, I have something to do tonight."

Cole raised a blond brow at him. "Something to do?
Or someone?"

Logan didn't take offense as he moved to the couch

by the window. He picked up his gray jacket and shrugged into it. "Wouldn't you like to know? Come on, you know you miss it."

"Miss what? Hit-or-miss sex? No. Call me logical, but I much prefer having guaranteed hot sex with my wife whenever the hell I want it."

Logan barely resisted rolling his own eyes, but he'd known Rachel for a long time now, and the woman *was* sexy, no doubt about it.

"Yes, well, there's no need to be a show-off. It makes you ugly."

Cole stood exactly where he was, silent as usual when he wanted something.

Logan grabbed his briefcase and sighed. "Okay, fine. Want to come with me?"

"Yep."

"Wow, you are desperate."

"No, I'm not, and it's been too long since we hung out."

"Well, that's true. Okay, I was heading down to After Hours. Does that work for you?" Logan moved past Cole and shut off the light.

Apparently it did, because that was where they turned up ten minutes later.

* * *

TATE HAD JUST finished with a rush of customers when a

tall blond man took a seat at the end of the bar. Making his way in that direction, Tate was ready to take his order when the seat beside the guy was filled by—*fuck*—Logan.

The two men were chatting, and the blond must have said something particularly funny because Logan let out a loud laugh and slapped his palm on the bar top. Deciding to just suck it up and deal with the cards he was dealt, Tate stopped in front of the two just as Logan turned to him.

Tate made it a point to look at the blond. The guy could've been an actor or a model. He was so well put together. Like Logan, he was wearing a suit and palming a cell phone, but unlike Logan, his expression was the usual distant friendly one of a stranger sitting down for a drink. Tate didn't think Logan had ever looked at him like that once since they had met.

"Hi. What can I get for you tonight?"

Tate waited as the blond brought his free hand to his chin. He rubbed it once and then looked to Logan.

"You getting your usual?"

Tate watched the exchange curiously.

"You know me, creature of habit."

The blond laughed at that and turned back to Tate.

"I'll have a scotch, thanks. Macallan, if you have it, and this guy will have a gin and tonic."

Tate flicked his eyes to Logan's, framed once again by black glasses.

"Anything to eat?" Tate hoped the spark he saw there didn't mean he was about to be handed his ass.

"Nothing to eat," Logan told him, and as Tate was about to move away, he added, "Right now."

Choosing to ignore that, Tate turned away to grab the scotch off the back shelf, but he kept his focus on the two men in the mirror he was facing. Logan was angled toward the blond and was chuckling at whatever the much more serious guy had said.

He wondered how they knew each other. *Maybe they work together? That's the most logical explanation,* Tate thought, until he saw Logan push the big guy's arm and leave his palm on his bicep in a familiar fashion. *Or maybe they are something altogether different. Lovers, maybe?*

Turning back to them, Tate pushed the drinks across the bar top, and with a quick, *"Thanks,"* from them, that was it. *Over, painless, easy—right?*

Walking away from the men, Tate found that he was relieved, yet at the same time, he was also experiencing a different emotion, an emotion he didn't understand—anger.

He was pissed-off. All of last week, this guy, this *stranger,* had decided to wreak havoc on his brain. Not to mention, all weekend it had bothered him and made him worry about coming to work today.

And now, this! Fucking nothing? After all that worry? But then again, did I want something to happen?

Logan was lucky that Tate wasn't a violent man because, at that precise moment, he wasn't sure he would have been able to keep his fists to himself.

* * *

"SO, THAT'S HIM?" Cole deduced as the bartender turned and walked away.

"Yep, that's him. What do you think?"

Cole lifted the tumbler to his mouth and took a sip of scotch. "I think he hates your guts."

Logan shrugged. "Yeah, I think you might be right."

"I also think he's straight."

Logan looked down the bar to where Tate was now laughing with a group of women. He then glanced back at Cole. "So? When has that stopped me?"

"Never," Cole admitted. He took another sip as he turned in Tate's direction. "Just be careful."

Logan laughed. "Don't worry, dad, I'm always careful. I use condoms too."

"Not because of that, you idiot. The guy looked pissed off. Be careful you don't get into something you can't get out of—like a back alley with a group of guys about to beat the shit out of you."

Logan glanced back at Tate and lifted his own glass. "I don't think that will be a problem. Plus, he doesn't seem the type."

Cole's eyebrow rose, as Logan took a quick sip of his drink, "I think he's pissed about something else entirely."

As Cole placed his empty glass on the counter, he narrowed his eyes at Logan. "Do I even want to know?"

"Probably not."

"Okay, then just be careful."

"Okay," Logan added as he signaled for another round.

This time though, Amelia stepped forward, and she proceeded to flirt outrageously with them as they chatted and drank their second drink—Tate free.

* * *

FINALLY, CLOSING TIME.

Amelia had gone out the back around ten minutes earlier to do God knows what, and Tate was doing a final round of the bar tables and booths. As he made his way down the side row, he saw that someone was waiting in the last booth, and he knew instinctively that it was Logan.

The two of them hadn't had any more interactions throughout the evening, and when he had seen Logan leave with the blond guy, Tate had figured that would be the end of that. But as he moved to keep walking past the booth, ignoring Logan completely, Tate was out of luck.

"Not even a hello tonight? You *are* mad at me."

Tate stopped and looked down to where Logan was sitting, relaxed into the side of the booth. He had an arm up on the back of the seat, and his suit jacket was undone, showing off his white shirt and blue tie. Tate also noticed a glass between Logan's fingertips. Amelia must have served him before heading out the back.

"I said it earlier when you were at the bar."

"Well, you didn't say it to me. You said it to Cole."

Tate glared at the man staring up at him, and with the mood he was in, he decided it was better to walk away, so he did just that. Tate made his way around the wall separating the two main rooms of the bar before he felt a hand grab his shoulder.

Spinning around quickly, as though he had anticipated the touch, Tate almost ran into Logan as he came face-to-face with him.

Tate gritted his teeth, and as calmly as he could, he stated, "You need to take your hand off me—around four seconds ago. You have a nasty habit of taking liberties."

"I have a lot of nasty habits. Want me to tell you about them?" Logan countered, removing his hand.

Tate felt his blood starting to boil. "You don't fucking quit do you?"

"What can I say? I don't like to lose."

Tate had finally had enough of the cocky attitude and decided it was about time to put Logan in his place. Moving forward, he snarled, "Well, you aren't going to win anything here. I'm not interested in this little game you're playing. I work here. You drink here. *That* is where it ends."

Tate felt his ears ringing as Logan licked his lips and argued right back. "Are you so sure about that?"

Disconcerted, Tate fumed, "Am I sure I don't want to have sex with you? Yes." Pausing, he took a tense breath, and before he thought better of it, he continued, "Surprisingly, I don't want to fuck you, and I don't want to be the third invite to your party of three. So, stop licking your lips like you want to suck my dick."

It wasn't until Logan raised his hands, palms up, that Tate realized he'd backed Logan up against the wall.

"You're pretty pissed off, Tate. What's wrong? Afraid you might like it? How do you know unless you try?"

Tate took a step back from the man who was radiating as much heat from his body as he was. But where his was from anger, Tate was positive Logan's was from something else entirely, and for some fucking reason, that thought was making *him* hotter by the second.

Instead of acknowledging his body's meltdown, Tate grabbed a hold of the emotion he understood and let the anger thrum through him. "That's your motto, right? To try everything once? Well, newsflash, some people just know they won't like something."

With the adrenaline coursing through his veins, Tate didn't even think to move as Logan pushed off the wall and came closer.

"Again, you didn't answer the question. How do you know—unless you try?"

Tate tried to think of something, *anything*, to say in response, but he had nothing, so he stayed stubbornly silent.

"Because Tate, for someone who isn't interested, your body certainly has different ideas. I'm all about doing what *feels* good. You see, I've never had a left-handed hand job, but I'm almost positive I would love it."

Without even thinking, Tate raised his hands and shoved hard against Logan's shoulders. The man didn't budge. Instead, his eyes turned from the usual cocky blue to a steely don't-fuck-with-me gray.

"You get to do that once. Unless the next time you shove me violently, it's to fuck me against a wall, you got it?"

Tate jammed his hands into his pockets, disgusted with himself for reacting as he had. Glaring at Logan, he tried to rein in his bitter contempt—for the man before him, himself, or the situation he was now in, he wasn't sure. "Stay away from me."

"I don't want to."

"Why? I don't even like you."

"Your cock says otherwise. Stop fighting so hard, Tate."

Logan brushed by him, and their shoulders met.

Tate couldn't bring himself to look at Logan as he heard, "And just try."

Before Tate could say anything else, Logan moved past him and disappeared from the bar, leaving him with about fifty-thousand questions and not one good goddamn answer.

Chapter Six

TWO DAYS LATER, Logan was sitting in the conference room, listening to Cole trying to placate one of their clients. She was a tall, dark-haired woman around five-eight, if he had to guess, and she was dressed like a sexy librarian or perhaps a schoolteacher. She was wearing a white pencil skirt, ending just above her knee, with a little black blouse and a red cardigan over it. The overall look was sexy and demure, and it made Logan want to yank her skirt up and lay her back on the conference table.

Maybe then she would leave satisfied, and the morning would be over quickly.

He wasn't a fan of dealing with ugly divorces, but Cole was about to leave town with Rachel for a couple of days, and he'd assured Logan that this particular case was pretty much over, it just needed to be wrapped up. Today was about tying up loose ends and finally signing on the dotted line.

Logan was already bored.

He much preferred working with businesses than petty husbands and wives with trivial issues. That was part of the job though, and right now, as he looked down at his watch, the defendant still hadn't shown.

"I'm sure he will be here soon," Cole assured their client.

Seated in the corner of the room on a couch pushed up against the window, Logan watched her patience wear thin as she paced back and forth.

"Yes, I'm sure. He's always *so* punctual. He can't even be on time for something important."

"The guy is probably avoiding this," Logan thought.

And then, he realized he'd said it out loud.

The woman spun around to pin him with an icy look, and Logan shut his mouth real quick, but that was more due to the glare Cole was throwing his way than pissing her off.

"I'm sorry," he mumbled, anything but.

As the woman turned away from him, Logan let his focus shift to her ass, and he took a good, long look at it. Maybe he just needed to let go of his pursuit of Tate. The guy was obviously conflicted, not to mention furious at him. *And this woman?* Logan knew if he worked it right, he could have her within the hour, and in turn, satiate the ache that had been building in him for the last several days.

He had come to a final decision to do just that when a knock sounded, and the conference door opened. In walked a harried-looking, short, bald man. His suit was slightly crumpled, and he was shaking his head as he held the door open for, presumably, his client, the defendant.

"So sorry we're late. Mr. Morrison got held up on his way here."

"Big surprise there," Logan heard their client mutter.

The fifth person finally walked through the door, and Logan found himself staring at none other than—

Tate. Tate Morrison apparently.

* * *

TATE RAISED A hand and pushed his fingers back through his hair as he stepped into the conference room. Situated in the center was a large oval table was surrounded by at least, Tate would guess, fifteen to twenty chairs, and the back wall was made up of large windows covered by thin blinds letting in the muted morning sunlight.

Holding his helmet by his leg, he scanned to room, and he was shocked when they landed on the blond man from a couple of nights ago.

What the—

Before he could say anything though, Mr. Branson, his lawyer, indicated a seat opposite from—*ugh*—his pissed-off and soon-to-be ex-wife.

"What did you do? Walk here?" Diana accused from across the table.

Tate resisted the urge to flip her off as he placed his helmet on the floor beside his leg. "There was an accident, okay?"

"You couldn't call?"

Tate shook his head and glared at the woman he'd stupidly wasted three years of his life on. "Sure, Diana, when would I have done that on my bike?" Turning to face his lawyer, Tate sighed. "Can we just begin and get this over with?"

Mr. Branson nodded and opened his briefcase with two clicks of the locks. "Of course, of course." He fished his glasses out of the case and pushed them on. "Well, first, this is Mr. Madison, the plaintiff's lawyer. He'll ask you a few questions today, and then we'll go over some paperwork. Do you have any questions about that?"

Tate glanced at the blond man sitting opposite him. *Um, no, but I do have a question about him. How does he know Logan?*

He was considering asking the question when something in the corner caught his eye. From where he was sitting, his view was obstructed, but it was obvious that someone else was also in the room with them.

Great, she needs two lawyers? Nice to know that Daddy's money bought her good representation, and she still took twelve months to sign.

Right now, as a final hurrah, she was after his Kawasaki Ninja 650, and he would be damned if she took it. He loved that thing—probably more than he'd ever loved her.

"Do you really need two lawyers, Diana? How many times do I have to tell you? I am not selling my bike. Bringing me to a fancy lawyer's office for a little over seven grand is ridiculous, even for you, but I suppose you actually need me here this time to sign the papers I filed over a year ago."

"And you being a pigheaded ass about a bike is nothing new either. It's a toy, one you don't need, and we bought it together."

"Bullshit, we've already split everything, and I—"

"Mr. Morrison," the blond guy finally spoke up.

Tate pinned him with a fuck-you look. He was surprised when the big guy glanced over his shoulder, obviously looking toward the second lawyer, who was still silent.

"Yes, Mr. Madison?" Tate snapped, bringing the man's attention back to him.

"If we could keep this civil, it would probably work out much better for all involved."

"Is that right?"

Mr. Madison nodded once as the look in his eyes changed from serious to one of—

Is that sympathy? Fuck that.

"Fine," Tate conceded, slumping back into his chair and crossing his arms over his chest.

"Okay then, if you could have your lawyer read over these terms and either agree or disagree—"

Tate glared stubbornly at the blond, "I don't need to read it. I disagree. She's just being spiteful."

"*She* is sitting right here."

"Yes, I'm well aware of that," Tate replied caustically. *I am so sick of this shit. It's not my job to listen to her petty crap anymore.*

At his comment, Tate heard a sound from the far corner that he could have sworn was a laugh, but in the end, it was disguised as a cough.

"You're such an ass, Tate."

Tate shrugged. "Well, good thing you found a replacement for me then, huh?"

That seemed to be her breaking point.

Placing her perfectly manicured hands on the table, she pushed up from her chair and looked at her lawyer, who stood slowly beside her, dwarfing her by several inches. "I don't have to sit here and listen to this anymore, do I?"

Tate watched Mr. Madison button his suit jacket as he shook his head.

"No, we can contact you if we need anything else. Have a good day, Mrs. Morrison."

Diana swung her gaze to Tate's and sneered at him. "I'm going back to Ms. Cline now."

Tate uncrossed his arms and showed his palms. "Oh stop, you're hurting my feelings."

She aimed daggers his way before turning on her heel, marching around the table, and heading straight out the door, slamming it behind her. The noise didn't even bother Tate. He'd become used to slamming doors a long time ago.

"Well, that went well," Mr. Madison announced.

Tate looked to *his* silent lawyer, wondering what exactly he was paying him for. He was about to stand and leave the suffocating room, when a person clearing their throat had him turning his head. Tate felt his mouth fall open as the second lawyer finally stood, and he was face-to-face with Logan.

* * *

LOGAN HAD BEEN trying to decide at what point it would have been smart to announce his presence, but really, there hadn't been one. *Had there?* Except now, as he stood, staring across the silent and volatile space shared by all four men, he knew that he probably should have said something sooner.

Tate's lawyer was oblivious to everything that was going on as he removed his glasses and threw them into his briefcase. Logan wondered where the hell Tate had found the guy, as Cole turned in Logan's direction and his eyebrows rose as if to say, *what now?*

Yeah, well, I'd love to answer you brother, but I have no clue.

That was quickly cleared up though.

"What the *hell* is he doing here?" Tate stood and slammed his hands onto the conference table, much like his ex just had.

Cole had the good sense to look uncomfortable as he glanced back at Logan, searching for an answer.

Tate's lawyer looked up and connected gazes with Logan. Then, he told his livid client as calmly as he could, "Oh, this is Mr. Mitchell. He's Mr. Madison's partner. They own the practice. He sat in because Mr. Madison is going to be out of town. It's just a small technicality. Nothing to be upset over."

Somehow, Logan didn't think that was going to cut it, and from the death stare Tate was aiming his way, he knew this was far from over.

Tate muttered, "Unfuckingbelievable."

That was when Cole jumped in. "Um, Mr. Branson? Can you please come with me? I have a few things I need you to sign, and it might give your client a moment to calm down."

Wrong thing to say, Cole.

Tate turned his furious look onto his brother. Cole wasn't worried though. In fact, he looked as though he was trying to control a laugh as he made his way around the table toward the door.

"Of course, of course." Mr. Branson picked up his briefcase and followed Cole out of the room.

For the first time, the conference room felt tiny.

As the door firmly shut behind the two men, Logan took his time as he moved cautiously toward the opposite side of the table.

"Did you know all this time? Did you know who I was?" was the first accusation thrown at him.

Logan pushed his jacket aside and stuffed his hands into his pockets as he took a moment to really look at the enraged man across from him. Tate was dressed in faded jeans and a blue T-shirt under his leather jacket. *The guy looked totally fuckable.*

"No. I had no clue until you walked in the room today."

Logan observed closely as Tate raised a hand to run it through his hair—a gesture Logan was now realizing came from nerves or agitation. He felt the need to once again reassure.

Making his way carefully around the table until he was standing with only several chairs between them, Logan reiterated, "I didn't know who you were, I swear. By the time you were in the room, it was too late for me to get up and leave without making you lose your focus."

Tate's head snapped toward him, and Logan met his glare head-on.

"Oh, how nice of you, Logan."

Logan didn't know why, but he loved the way his name rolled off that pissed-off tongue.

"I can be nice."

Tate scoffed, "Yeah, I'm sure you can be—when you want to get laid."

"Well, that, I won't deny, but even then, I'm not always nice."

"I can imagine."

Oh, that comment is too good to leave as is, so of course, Logan pushed, "Can you?"

"I didn't mean *that*." Tate was quick to clarify. "Don't fucking start with me."

Logan stepped closer and felt his need to reassure

disappear as it turned into an altogether different kind of need. "Don't start, what?"

Tate shifted his entire body to face him. "Your usual shit."

Logan felt his lips twitch as Tate—for the first time and without even realizing it—voluntarily looked him over. He stood as still as he could, enjoying the feel of Tate's focus on him, and when they finally came back and met his, Logan raised a brow.

"And?"

"And what?" Tate snapped. "Nothing."

Logan took one more step until only one chair was between them. "You really are pigheaded, aren't you Tate?"

"Excuse me?"

Moving the final step forward, to where Tate was standing, so he either had to hold ground or back up, Logan was happy when Tate chose to stay where he was.

"Why are you so irate right now?" Logan asked bluntly.

"Why do you think? I just found out that you're working for my ex."

Narrowing his eyes on the dark ones searching his, Logan countered, "And why would that piss you off?"

"Because—"

"Because isn't a good reason and *never* an acceptable one to a lawyer."

Logan watched Tate's tongue come out and lick his bottom lip, and he knew—

This is it.

He just needed to do it or walk away. Tate was either going to hit him or—

Without another thought, Logan reached out and clasped the back of Tate's neck and tugged him forward.

* * *

SOMEWHERE IN THE back of his mind, Tate had known it was coming, but as he watched Logan reach for him, he did absolutely nothing to stop it.

As Logan's large hand cupped the back of his neck and firmly pulled him forward, Tate placed his palms on the solid chest now intimately pressed up against his own. Almost as though it were in slow motion, Tate watched Logan's focus drop to his mouth before he tilted his head and finally crushed his lips against his own.

At first, Tate remained frozen, his hands against the smooth fabric of the jacket until he realized exactly *what*, was happening. That was when he curled his fingers into the lapels and shoved Logan from him, but kept a hold of the jacket. Breathing hard, he felt Logan tense, as he seemed to brace himself.

Tate ran his eyes over Logan's neutral expression, and he finally focused on the heated blue that was cautiously staring back at him, waiting.

This is the moment, Tate thought. *This is the moment you punch him and tell him to fuck off.*

As he clenched his fists around the material, he
slowly released his left hand, determined to do just that. But
as Tate raised his arm, he saw Logan's attention shift to his
fist, and Tate was shocked to find himself reaching forward
to take the back of Logan's neck instead. Before he knew
what he was doing, Tate yanked Logan in and pressed his
lips back against the hard ones that had apparently tempted
him beyond his sanity.

All of a sudden, Logan's large body moved into
action as he walked them backward in the room until a wall
was against Tate's back with a hard, solid man against his
front.

Holy shit. Is this hot as fuck kiss, really happening? was
screaming through Tate's head.

Logan's palms came up to brush over the stubble
lining his cheeks. Then, before he could fully register
everything, those same hands slid into his hair and
tightened.

Tate was telling himself, *pull the hell away*, from the
insistent press of firm lips and the muscled body grinding
against his own when he felt the sharp sting of teeth bite
down into his bottom lip, hard. Jerking his head back, he
grunted as he hit it against the wall.

"Jesus, you bit me," he accused as if *that* was the only
thing he should mention at this point in time.

It was best not to focus on how disconcerting it was
to have his ass and back pressed against a wall by someone
taller, and slightly bigger than himself. Not to mention, *the*

someone in question was looking him directly in the eye and not giving him an inch to, perhaps, escape. But that was exactly where Tate was as Logan licked his own lips and grinned shamelessly back at him.

"I did. I couldn't help myself."

Tate ran his tongue along his bruised lower lip, trying to soothe the still stinging spot, and his breathing became more labored as he realized he could feel more than his own erection throbbing against him.

"Um—"

Logan, arrogant as ever, cut him off. "Yes, Tate?"

Tate cleared his throat. "I think you should back up a bit."

In usual Logan fashion, he didn't follow any kind of direction but his own. He stepped in closer, if that were possible, and then pushed his hips hard against Tate's.

"I think you like me exactly where I am. It's just taken you until now to realize it."

Tate's heart thundered uncontrollably in his chest as he noticed he was still gripping the lapels of Logan's jacket. He quickly let go as if his hands were on fire.

"Back up, Logan," he repeated.

Something in his tone must have broken through because Logan slowly took a step back. He pushed his hands into his pockets as though he didn't trust himself. Tate silently thanked him for that because he didn't trust himself at this moment either. He wasn't sure if his feelings stemmed from violence or—

Or what?

"You must feel really great right about now." Tate ran a seriously shaky hand over his face.

"I do actually, but not because of the reason you think."

"And what do I think?" Tate dropped his hand to his side.

"You think it's because I finally got you to admit that you want me."

"I didn't admit that."

Logan looked to the zipper of Tate's jeans, and it took everything Tate had not to cover the erection pounding behind the denim.

"Yes, you did."

"Fine, whatever. If that isn't the reason, then what is?"

Tate knew he should move past Logan, grab his helmet, and leave without engaging in a post wrap-up convo, but instead, he stood where he was, waiting for an answer he wasn't ready to hear.

"I feel great because *you* are even better than I first fucking thought. And I love being right."

Shaking his head in adamant denial, Tate straightened and went to move away from the wall. Before he even got one foot in front of the other, Logan took a step of his own toward him and put a hand up on the side of his chest, stopping him in his tracks.

THERE WAS NO way that Logan was letting Tate leave the room without getting at least one more taste of his mouth, and this time, he intended to make it a nice, long one.

"Boundaries, Logan. I think you've crossed enough with me today," Tate warned.

"We've also established that I have none."

"This changes nothing. It was a lapse in judgment."

Logan couldn't help the low laugh he let free as he tested the firm muscle under his palm. "On the contrary, it changes everything. You didn't push me away, *you* kissed me back, and you haven't taken my hand off you yet."

As soon as the last word left Logan's mouth, Tate's hand came up and gripped his wrist tightly as he pulled him forward.

"I don't know why you have fixated on me, but this game you're playing is a dangerous one."

Logan was sure the smart thing to do would be to agree and back off, but he didn't.

"I agree, but I never said I'd play fair, and you sure as fuck didn't fight me off."

Tate's scowled, and Logan wondered what he was thinking as the pressure around his wrist intensified.

"You know what you want to do," Logan encouraged in a seductive tone, thinking he must be losing his mind to be making such a bold move, even for him. "There's no one here, and no one is going to come in. Just do it," he whispered, eyes locked on to conflicted brown orbs, "*Try.*"

As the word left his lips, Tate spun him around until *his* back was up against the wall, and Tate was crushed against his front, with Logan's wrist clasped firmly between them.

"Do you ever shut the fuck up?" Tate questioned.

Logan touched his tongue to his top lip as though he'd already had the second taste of the mouth that was sneering at him.

"Only when I have a good incentive. Give me one." He hauled his arm back closer to himself, drawing Tate in that final inch. "*Make* me shut up."

He didn't really expect the taunt to work, but something in Tate seemed to snap as he lowered his head, attacking his lips for the second time.

Logan, never one to waste an opportunity, parted his mouth, determined to get a full taste of Tate this time around. He raised his free hand and sank it into the curls he'd gripped earlier, but this time, he took a moment to enjoy the feel of them under his palm as he pulled the stubborn man to him.

He felt a tentative tongue touch his lips, and he groaned as he slid his own directly into Tate's mouth. The hand on his wrist tightened at the intimate intrusion, and then the grip was released. Two large palms reached up and cupped his cheeks, and Tate finally let go.

Angling his head to the side, Logan heard a low

rumble leave his own throat as Tate sank his tongue inside, rubbing it up against his own. The sharp taste of cinnamon flooded Logan's mouth along with the faint hint of coffee and something he couldn't quite pinpoint. Whatever it was, the combination and the fact that it was Tate made it fucking addictive.

The ache that was thrumming in his balls and the constant throb in his swollen shaft was nothing compared to what he felt the moment Tate shocked the hell out of him and bit *his* bottom lip.

Logan tugged his head back and stared into eyes that were almost black but not showing signs of anger or annoyance. This time, they were dark with lust.

"So?" Logan managed.

"So?" Tate taunted him right back.

Logan, whose back was still up against the wall, looked around the conference room, trying to get his shit back under control. When his eyes finally came back to Tate's, he raised a questioning brow at the man who had taken a step back. Then Logan watched him move over to the table as calm as he pleased. Tate bent down and picked up his helmet, and Logan couldn't help but stare at the firm ass covered by those jeans.

Standing silently was definitely new to Logan, and just as he was about to say something witty, he was sure, Tate walked to the door and reached out a palm to grip the handle. Before he turned it though, he looked to Logan and trailed his gaze down over him, and then Tate did something completely out of character.

He winked at him. "So? Now, I've tried."

With that, the sexy fucker walked out the door.

Chapter Seven

TATE HAULED ASS out of the office quicker than he'd even realized he could walk. He was holding his helmet in a death grip as he flew past his lawyer and mumbled, "Call me," on his way directly into the open elevator.

As the doors slid shut, Tate was relieved to find he was alone for the descent. Slumping back against the wall, he brought his hand up and touched his mouth.

Fuck, fuck, fuck!

Removing it, he closed his eyes and tried to push aside the feeling of Logan's lips moving so surely against his own. He needed to think about this objectively, and then maybe he would be able to make sense of it all.

To start with, Logan had provoked him. At every opportunity, Logan had pushed and pushed until, like a normal person, Tate had finally snapped—

Right?

Yeah, right.

Tate stared at his reflection in the shiny silver doors. He didn't look any different than he had before. No, he didn't look any different, but he sure as hell felt it. He felt it in his whole body, including his confused-as-hell cock.

What was I thinking when I kissed him back?

By the end of the whole exchange, he'd convinced himself that it had been a matter of finally putting Logan in his place. Tate was sick of always being the one left questioning everything after each encounter. So, this time around, his main goal had been to leave the smug bastard wondering. He just hadn't expected to be left wondering as well.

The elevator hit the ground floor much smoother than his descent to reality, and after the doors pulled open, Tate moved into the lobby of the building. He was halfway to where his bike was parked when his cell phone started buzzing in his jeans.

Stuffing his hand into his pocket, he pulled it out and accepted the call, thinking it was probably his lawyer wondering why he hadn't waited for his paperwork.

"Hello?" he snapped.

"Running away so soon?"

He would know that voice anywhere.

Damn it.

"So, now, you're poking around in my file?"

Logan's familiar chuckle came though the phone. "I could come up with an obvious joke there about poking, but I'll refrain."

Tate felt his mouth itch to smile at the other man's nerve. He had to give it to Logan, for always saying what he thought, unlike himself.

"Is there something you want, Logan?"

"There are several things I *want*, Tate."

Tate moved over to the edge of the sidewalk, out of the way of others, and waited.

"Stubborn to the end, I see."

"I'm not being stubborn. I'm trying to work out exactly *why* you're calling me."

Logan sighed as though he was feeling particularly put out. "Well, you left so abruptly that I hardly had a chance to speak."

"No, that's not how I remember it. You were standing shocked shitless, if I recall."

A loud laugh hit his ear then as if Logan couldn't help himself. "Proud of yourself?"

"No." Tate wouldn't dare say that he kind of was. "Why would I be?"

"Because I can't remember the last time a straight guy *bit* me into silence."

Tate curled his fingers around the helmet, and as though others could hear, he whispered, "You have no filter, do you?"

"And this is news?"

"No," Tate muttered. "Just confirmation, I suppose. So, what do you want, Logan?" He regretted the question, but he knew he wouldn't stop wondering until he received a reply.

"I want to see you tonight."

Tate was positive on that answer. "No."

"You can't stop me from having a drink after work."

"Are you an alcoholic?" Tate just wanted to annoy him now.

"No, but I would become one, if need be."

"Why are you pushing so hard? Is it because you've finally met someone who's told you no?"

Tate found himself picturing the way Logan's mouth might move as he thought over—

Shit.

"Maybe," Logan surmised. "But I think it's more because you just slammed me up against a wall and kissed my fucking brains out. And whether or not *you* will admit it, you loved it."

Tate swallowed and felt his cock taking notice of the words coming through the phone.

"Don't act like you didn't, Tate. I felt your whole body vibrating against mine. I want to feel it again."

Wow, Tate thought, *the guy's persistent*. Somewhere in the back of Tate's mind, if he were willing to admit it, Logan's confidence and interest were both hot as hell, and scary as shit.

"Tell me," Logan urged.

Tate turned his feet on the sidewalk and stared once again at his reflection mirrored from the building in front of him. He couldn't even escape his own damn self, let alone Logan.

"Tell you, *what*, exactly?"

"Tell me you didn't like it, and make me believe it."

Tate studied himself, from the too long hair on his

head, to the dark stubble on his jaw. He ran his eyes over the leather jacket, T-shirt, and jeans, wondering why he'd thought he would look different due to what he'd done only minutes earlier.

You don't look different, dipshit, he thought with disgust. *You're thinking differently.*

"Tell me," Logan demanded through the phone.

Before Tate even thought about what it meant that he *couldn't* say the words, he ended the call.

* * *

NOTHING AND NOBODY will keep me away from that bar tonight.

Logan got on the elevator and made his way down. Unsuccessfully, he'd tried to push aside the incident in the conference room, but no matter what he did, all he could think about was the fact that Tate had kissed him back, and even better, the guy had played rough. Just thinking about it had Logan tracing his tongue over his bottom lip where those strong teeth had sunk in.

Hmm, I can't wait to feel those lips again.

Gripping his briefcase in his hand, Logan took a quick look at his watch and decided to skip going home first. It would be too much of a pain in the ass, and he wasn't in the mood. He wanted to know how things were going to go—if it had just been a fleeting moment. And now that Tate had time to think about it, Logan wondered if the moment was over.

I sure as hell hope not.

For the first time ever, as Logan stood waiting for the elevator to come to a halt, he felt an emotion he hadn't before, and he was pretty sure he hated it.

He felt nervous.

When the doors opened, he reminded himself that he did this kind of shit every day. Chasing shiny, sexy things was a familiar hobby of his, one he usually enjoyed and excelled at. He went in with only one motto—try, take, top.

Try a sample, take the goods, and then come out on top. Never let things get messy.

And this wouldn't be any different.

But as Logan opened the door to the bar and stepped inside, he immediately searched through and found the shiny object he was currently chasing. Right there, in that moment, Logan knew that somehow, this time, everything was going to be different.

* * *

TATE WASN'T SURE if he saw him first or felt him, but the minute Logan was through the front door of the bar, Tate knew it.

Obviously, Logan had come straight from the office. He was dressed in the same gray suit as this morning, and as he stared through the crowd to where Tate was standing, Tate knew he was giving Logan the same inspection he was receiving before glancing around the bar.

What am I looking for? was all Tate could think as Logan started through the crowd toward him. *Am I trying to see if anyone knows that he kissed me today? Or that I kissed him back?*

Tate wasn't sure, but the look in Logan's eyes sure as shit wasn't helping.

As several people moved aside and Logan drew closer, Tate could feel his palms getting clammy, and he wiped them on the sides of his pants. The expression on Logan's face was predatory as if he were hunting, and Tate knew that he was the prey.

Tate always prided himself on being a man of principle, a man of conviction. He was someone who owned his actions and held himself responsible for the outcomes that came from them. But as Logan stopped directly opposite him with only the wood surface of the bar as a barrier, Tate wanted to abandon all of those morals instilled long ago and get the fuck out of there.

Instead, he stood where he was and reminded himself that just because he'd done something once did not mean he needed to repeat it—even as his eyes dropped to Logan's lips.

"Evening," was the first word out of the lawyer's mouth.

Tate reached out with both hands to brace against the bar's edge.

"Evening. The usual?" Tate figured if he had

something to do, he would stop thinking about other things he had already done *earlier.*

"Do you really need to ask?" Logan quipped, moving to place his briefcase by his feet.

"Well, it is my job."

"It's also your job to know your customers. How serious are you about that?"

Tate ignored the obvious comment and poured the gin and tonic before sliding it across to Logan. Looking around himself, Tate was satisfied when he saw that no other workers were near him, and all the customers seemed to be taken care of for the moment.

"I told you not to come here tonight," Tate pointed out in a lowered voice.

He watched Logan's fingers as they reached out to grip the glass, and in a split second, Tate was reminded of how they had felt in his hair. Pulling his eyes away from the highball, Tate met Logan's daring look and wondered what he was thinking.

This is the longest he's sat silently, if I don't count this morning with his back against the wall after I had —

Yeah, hell.

Then, Logan finally spoke, "I decided to ignore you."

Tate shook his head at the smart-ass remark as Logan calmly held his gaze and raised the glass to his lips. After taking a sip, he placed it back down.

"And you're avoiding my question. How well do you get to know your customers?"

Just as Tate was about to reply, he noticed Amelia out of the corner of his eye. Glancing her way, he felt his heart start to do a damn tap dance inside his chest as she looked at Logan, and a sensual wide smile stretched across her lips.

Does she know? No, of course she doesn't know. She's smiling at the man she spent Friday night with.

As she got closer to them, Tate tried to act natural.

Nothing is different, nothing is obvious, and nothing is out of the ordinary, except for the fact that I had my tongue in Logan's mouth —

Just like Amelia has.

And *that,* Tate discovered, bugged the shit out of him.

"I didn't see you come in. You're becoming sneaky, Mr. Mitchell," Amelia accused good-naturedly as she rested her hip up against the bar.

"That's okay, hon. Tate, got me fixed up."

Tate was still looking down at Amelia, who now turned to stare up at him.

"I'm sure he did."

What does she mean by that?

"Yep, he knows exactly what I like," Logan added.

Tate faced him across the bar, all the while resisting the urge to tell him to shut the hell up.

Jesus. Now I'm turning into a paranoid fucking lunatic.

Luckily, Amelia started to laugh and also turned to a grinning Logan before leaning over the bar to show off her ample cleavage. "Yes, he does, but he turned us down."

Tate's stare didn't waver as Logan winked at Amelia and then raised his blue ones to him.

Is it the dark-framed glasses that make his eyes so damn blue?

"Well, that's a shame. I'm sure we could've had a *very* good time."

Feeling like he was in some kind of parallel universe, one where he'd gone crazy and was busy checking out the guy inviting him to a threesome, instead of the girl that would be in the middle, Tate frowned and shook his head.

"Sorry, not really my scene."

"Ah…look, Amelia, he speaks."

Logan's eyes were full of dare and sex as he raised the drink to his lips again, making Tate's temperature jump up a little higher.

Not only was Tate irked at being their inside joke, he was finding himself really wanting to shut Logan up—the same way he had earlier. And *that* impulse was scaring the shit out of him.

"Excuse me." Tate glowered at Logan, who raised a questioning brow at him. "We have other customers. I'll leave you in Amelia's capable hands."

Tate didn't tack on the end that he was sure Logan was already familiar with those hands, but he sure thought it as he turned and made his way down the bar.

* * *

LOGAN FOLLOWED TATE'S retreating back as he moved further away, and he wondered what exactly had ticked Tate off first. The fact that he'd turned up at the bar, the reminder of their earlier meeting, or Amelia's interruption. It was too much to hope that it was the last reason, but as Logan sat there, mulling over the idea, it seemed more and more accurate.

Up until Amelia had turned up, Logan had been positive that Tate was checking him out. Oh, he'd been subtle about it, with his slow once-over, but Logan had felt him linger on his mouth, and he knew that Tate had been recalling exactly what they'd done earlier.

"So, no Tate. Sad, huh? He's super hot."

Logan returned his attention to Amelia, who was also staring over at Tate.

"It is sad. But hey, we tried."

Amelia looked back to him, grinning, as she gave him a quick sexy wink. "We sure did. He's just out of a bad relationship, so that's probably got something to do with it too. I think I shocked him." She giggled.

"Oh?" Logan queried, not really paying attention.

"Yeah. He seemed scandalized but didn't want to offend me. Man, his eyes almost fell out of his head when I suggested it. Bet it would have been different if you were a chick."

Logan could imagine Tate's reaction to the suggestion of a threesome, and yes, he had to admit it had probably been more to do with the fact that the invite had been to a threesome with him, but he would have paid money to see it. Actually, he wanted to try his own hand at convincing the man.

"Maybe I can change his mind," Logan mused out loud.

"You could try, but I don't think you'll have much luck. Want another drink?"

"Sure."

She moved to make him one, and when she placed it in front of him, she whispered, "If he does come around, count me in."

Logan flicked his eyes to her as his mouth pulled into a wicked grin. "Well, I actually think you'll count *us* in, but that's all in the details."

With that, he raised his glass in a mock salute.

* * *

AN HOUR AND a half later, Tate was feeling pretty proud of himself. He'd managed to avoid dealing with Logan and was finally taking his break. Moving into the back room, he cracked his neck and grabbed his time card from the holder on the wall. Inserting it into the punch machine, he enjoyed the sound of twenty minutes of freedom as he clocked out.

Tate made his way over to the couch in the far corner and settled down onto it, resting his head back against the wall and shutting his eyes. He was content for the time being to just zone out and forget all about today.

"And here I was, thinking you couldn't look any hotter than when you're scowling at me."

Tate's eyes snapped open to focus on the door where Logan was leaning up against the frame with his legs crossed and his hands in his pockets.

"Well, that can be arranged." Tate stated, feeling surly as hell. "You're not allowed back here."

Logan blatantly checked him out where he was seated, and Tate immediately wanted to sit up straight and shut his widened legs.

"I have connections."

"Who? Amelia? She's hardly the boss." Tate told himself to stay where he was and not give any indication of his nerves.

"Not Amelia." Logan lazily pushed off the wall and took a step forward.

When he was in the room, he turned to shut and lock the door, and that was when Tate decided he needed to get the fuck up.

Logan behind a shut door meant a Logan who had no boundaries, and Tate had already met and given in to that guy once today.

No need for a repeat, Tate *again* reminded himself for good measure.

"Going somewhere?" he asked Tate impertinently.

"Open the door."

Tate hated the familiarity of Logan's lip as it curled

at him. He hated it, and at the same time, he was fascinated by it.

Then, the arrogant ass told him, "*You* open the door."

To do that, Tate would need to get close to him, and Logan knew it, so instead, Tate crossed his arms stubbornly.

"Okay, now that we have that sorted out, how long is your break?"

"I'm not spending my break talking to you," Tate replied peevishly.

Logan walked farther into the room while giving him such a thorough once-over that Tate could swear he felt it as effectively as the man's hands.

"Why? Would you rather spend it doing something else?"

* * *

LOGAN COULD SEE the conflict and curiosity swirling in the man staring back at him. He could tell Tate was confused by the feelings he was experiencing, and he *knew* Tate was feeling them because Logan had deliberately looked to find out. Just as he was, Tate was hard as a fucking rock.

It was actually *unlike* him not to push that knowledge in his favor, but Logan figured that wouldn't be an issue in around ten seconds. The room was practically vibrating with sexual tension, and a whole fuckload of testosterone.

"What do you expect my answer to be, Logan? Please suck my dick?"

Now, there's an idea. Best not to get ahead of myself though.

"I want you to tell me the truth." For once, Logan meant it.

"The truth?" Tate asked.

Logan moved then, across the room until he was in front of the other man, where he repeated, "The truth. Did you enjoy what happened this morning? It's as simple and as easy as that."

"Really? It's *that* simple, *that* easy?" Tate questioned in a tone indicating that he thought Logan was certifiable.

Refusing to give an inch now that Tate was talking, Logan gave a slight nod of his head. "No one in this room is going to judge whatever comes out of your mouth. So. Tell. Me. The. Truth."

Tate clenched his jaw, and almost as if he had given himself permission, he explained, "Did I like it? *Yes.* Do I understand it? No, I fucking don't."

That was all he'd been waiting for. Logan took the final step to bring him close enough to smell Tate's cologne, and the guy smelled amazing.

"Do you need to understand it to know that it felt good?" Logan raised his hand to touch Tate's arm, testing the hard, lean muscle. "Do you want to do it again?"

Logan kept watchful eyes on the man coming to terms with all of his decisions today, and when Tate's hand came up to grip his own, Logan waited.

"It's like you expect me to flip a switch and just

accept that everything I ever believed about myself has changed, and that I should be okay with that. Do you know how insane that is?"

"I do. But do you know what else is insane?"

"What?"

"That you still haven't told me no."

* * *

HE'S RIGHT. TATE stared at Logan, who was still holding his arm.

"What do I need to get you into my bed?" Logan asked boldly.

Tate couldn't help the laugh escaping his mouth at Logan's directness. "A vagina?" He raised a brow at the man.

Releasing his arm, Logan took a step back and removed his cell phone from his pocket. He dialed a number and placed the phone to his ear.

"Hi, hon." He then met Tate's eyes and smirked as he mouthed, *A vagina, I can get.*

"Hang up," Tate demanded through clenched teeth.

Logan shook his head, trying not to laugh.

"Logan, *hang* up."

Pulling the phone away from his ear, he pressed it to his chest. "Why? I thought you wanted a vagina."

Tate took a step that put him as close to Logan as he could get without touching. "Hang. Up."

Very slowly, Logan did as asked. He slid the phone down his chest and placed it in his pocket. "But you said—"

"I know what I said," Tate told him in a clipped tone.

"Then what's the problem?"

Tate was trying to think of one, but all he managed was, "I don't fucking share," as he reached out to Logan. This time, there was no mistaking what he wanted, as Tate gave in to his curiosity and took Logan's mouth with his own.

* * *

DAMN. WHEN DID I lose the firm grip I had on this game? Logan thought in the back of his mind.

He was always the one in charge—*always* the one who made the moves, came on strong, and got off stronger. That was not the case this time. As Tate's mouth dominated his, it was all Logan could do not to beg the guy for more.

Just as that thought left his mind, Tate's body swayed from his. Not wanting the man to go anywhere, Logan smoothed his hands under the brown curls and held on. There was no need to worry though. Tate merely angled his head for a better connection and then slid his tongue across Logan's lower lip. Not even thinking twice, Logan opened for him and groaned when he felt teeth scrape his bottom lip in a rough caress, just like this morning.

"You like that," Tate stated against his mouth, experimenting.

Logan thought it was a fucking miracle he didn't come right then.

"I do," he managed. "I like it harder, too."

Tate's lips curved against his own, and Logan clutched the back of his neck, trying to get him to move again.

"Does every word that comes out of your mouth have to do with sex?"

Logan smirked against Tate's mouth. "Usually, eighty / twenty, but with you, it seems more ninety-eight / two."

As the words rolled off Logan's tongue, Tate's palm moved across his cheek and into his hair as if he was testing all the new textures and how far he wanted to go.

"And the other two?"

Tate's warm breath brushed over Logan's lips.

I'm supposed to fucking think? "The other two I have spent trying to convince you."

When Tate—*yes, sexy-as-hell Tate*—slowly slid his tongue out and traced it along Logan's top lip, sampling him as if for the first time, Logan gave a throaty moan.

"And do you think I'm convinced?"

Logan wasn't sure if Tate was convinced, but his cock sure hoped so.

"I think you're getting there."

"And when I do? What happens to the two percent? More sex?"

Logan couldn't believe he was being so compliant. It

was completely unlike him, but he knew if they were going to move forward, it ultimately had to be Tate's move. That didn't, however, mean he had to be idle.

So, he decided, *What the hell?*

Taking his free hand, Logan slid it around Tate's waist and pulled him hard, bringing him in as close as he could get him. This time, Tate grunted, losing a little of the control he'd managed to hold on to.

"I think when you get there, you'll never want to leave. One thing about guys—we like sex. How long has it been, Tate? I'll give you the best sex you've ever had."

With what sounded like a frustrated growl, Tate twisted the hand in Logan's hair and brought an end to the talking. Tate pushed his tongue between his lips, and Logan's whole body shuddered in response. Their tongues tangled, and while in the wet heat of Tate's mouth, Logan thought of how he'd love to shove his cock between those perfect lips. He didn't know when Tate had decided to let down his barriers, but Logan wasn't about to stop and ask.

Moving the hand he had on Tate's waist, Logan slid it down over the snug black pants to grip his ass, pushing their hips together. Nothing could conceal the stiff shaft throbbing up against him now, and he couldn't help but grind against Tate, letting him know he felt it, and showing him that he was just as aroused.

When Logan heard a low rumble from the chest pressed firmly against his own, a thrill skated down his spine, and as Tate removed his hand from Logan's hair and gripped his jacket, Logan thought it was all over.

This moment of sexual perfection is about to end. I knew it was too fucking good to be true.

But instead of stopping, Tate's fingers tightened around the material. Testing the truth in Logan's words, he bit Logan's lip hard enough to almost bring him to his knees before tugging on his bottom lip and pulling away.

"What the hell have you done to me?"

Logan pressed himself harder against the man driving him crazy. "I have no clue, but I'll be the first to say, I'm glad for whatever it is."

Tate shook his head. "I don't know if I can go any further than this. It's all so…so…"

Grabbing Tate's ass in both hands this time, Logan thrust his hips against him. "This doesn't feel good to you?"

Tate closed his eyes and tipped his head back, exposing the Adam's apple that Logan really wanted to lick.

"I think it's obvious how good it feels, Logan."

Sensing the moment was over, Logan removed his hands and took a step back, trying to resist the urge to manhandle Tate down onto the couch and say *to hell with it all*.

"What's the biggest problem for you?"

Tate crossed his arms as though he didn't trust himself. "You're a guy, Logan. Pretty big problem."

"Why?"

"Because I like women!"

Logan shook his head calmly. "Do you know how

ridiculous that sounds? Especially when you have plenty of evidence to the contrary."

"Thank you for pointing out the obvious, counselor."

Logan shrugged, deciding now was the time to leave—before things turned to shit, before they got into an argument. *Give him time to digest.*

"Okay, okay. I'm going to go." Logan walked back to the locked door, but before he left, he had one more thing that *needed* to be out in the air between them. "Tate?"

Tate's stare met his own.

"This? *This* changes things. If you think I'm going to walk out of here and you'll conveniently forget about what happened, you should think again. This wasn't a fluke, no matter how much you try to pretend. You wanted it as much as I did, and you should remember that tonight when you jerk off, thinking about my tongue in your mouth," Logan said, using a tone more serious than even he knew he was capable of.

Satisfied that he'd said everything he wanted to, Logan turned, unlocked the door, and left, wondering where this thing, whatever it was, would inevitably go.

Chapter Eight

THE RED GLARE of Tate's digital readout shined brightly on him as he lay in bed, staring at the ceiling. *It might as well be a fucking spotlight.* He placed an arm across his eyes. With a lone sheet across his waist, he tried to relax, but it was no use. He was agitated and restless.

Tonight had not gone according to plan, which was to ignore Logan at all costs.

No, instead, I kissed the bastard until I gave myself a major hard-on.

Gnashing his teeth together, he tried to ignore the fact that the stiff cock in question had reappeared at the memory of it, just like Logan had said it would. There was nothing more infuriating than knowing the cause of his sexual frustration was also the cause of a whole lot of self-doubt.

This was a time in his life when he was single. If he wanted to go and sleep with two-dozen women, he could. But no, his erection was fixated on a guy—an extremely hot guy but a man just the same. With his black hair, and eyes which were insanely blue, Logan was undeniably sexy.

Tate wasn't sure why, but he also found it...*exciting*

that Logan was taller than him. When they'd argued and he had Logan's back up against the wall, Tate had felt alive for the first time in months. Not to mention, he'd been extremely aroused. It was as if arguing with Logan and gaining the upper hand had somehow put Tate in control to do whatever he wanted.

Which is what exactly? What do I want?

Tate knew it would be different if he had no reaction to Logan at all and could just brush him off, but ultimately, he kept coming back to his all-around curiosity with Logan Mitchell. He couldn't deny it. It was there, and even more disquieting was his fascination with the man's smart-tongued mouth.

Logan's lips were—*go on, admit it*—bitable, and he had licked them at every opportunity he got, making Tate hyperaware of them. The bottom was much fuller than the top, and although Tate would have thought a man's mouth should be hard, Logan's was soft.

Soft, malleable, and yes, very fucking bitable. Damn!

Tate rolled over to look at the time—three fifteen in the morning. *Great, just great.* He noticed, sitting by his clock, his cell phone, and he reached out to pick it up.

Switching it on, he scrolled through to the call from Mitchell & Madison and wondered if the number was from the office. Placing the phone on his bare chest, he thought about it for a few minutes, and then—*fuck it*—he dialed the number.

He was all ready to leave a message on Logan's office

voice mail, preparing to tell him *not* to come by the bar anymore, when the phone connected.

* * *

LOGAN'S VIBRATED LOUDLY on the wooden side table by his bed. It wasn't like it had awoken him. He'd just been lying there, staring at the ceiling and thinking about Tate—

Jesus, this early in the morning?

He really hoped it wasn't a client that needed him for some urgent matter.

Rolling over to his side, he scooted up from beneath the covers and snagged the cell. Swiping the screen to accept the call, he lifted it to his ear and managed a sleepy, "Logan, here."

Silence.

Pulling the phone away, he leaned to his side and glanced at the number on his screen seeing a name displayed across the top that he'd programmed in earlier yesterday. It was a name that immediately had him waking *all* the way up.

"Tate?" Logan's heart started to pound almost as hard as his *now* rapidly swelling erection. "I know it's you. You might as well talk to me," he pushed, not wanting Tate to hang up without saying what he'd called for.

"I thought you'd be asleep, and I could leave a message."

Logan shifted back against the mattress and down in

between his sheets, enjoying the sound of Tate's voice when it finally came through the phone.

"Well, this is my office number. Calls get routed for clients." He was trying to keep things neutral and easy, wanting to do anything to keep Tate talking.

"Oh," was all he got in response.

Running a hand across his chest, Logan massaged his shoulder and waited, wondering what the hell he should say next. After all, the likelihood of *why* Tate was calling this early probably wasn't good, but shit, someone had to say something.

"So, you were going to leave me a message?"

More silence.

"At three in the morning?"

Still, complete silence.

Well, almost—Logan was sure he could hear Tate breathing softly.

"You going to say something? Or do you want me to do all the talking? Because we both know the direction I'll take this, especially since I'm lying here in—"

"I was calling to tell you not to come back to the bar anymore."

Logan didn't know why, but that comment actually—

Hurt?

"I see."

The silence at the other end was starting to irritate him now, so Logan decided to stop playing neutral, decided to stop playing easy.

"And why's that, Tate? Because I've made you think about things you don't want to?"

Finally, that seemed to penetrate Tate's silent self-intervention.

"No. Christ, you're arrogant," he announced in an annoyed rush of air. "Because you're making my fucking head hurt. You never take no for an answer, and you *don't* take a fucking hint."

Logan laughed with disdain as he imagined a frustrated Tate running a hand through his hair. "I might have taken no for an answer—if you *ever* said it."

"I did say it!" Tate's voice boomed through the phone. "And I also told you very clearly that I am straight."

Anger was definitely riding the man, but it seemed mixed with something more, something that hadn't made him hang up the phone yet.

"Yeah, I remember that, too. It must've been before you kissed me and changed *your* fucking mind!"

From the other end of the line, he heard a loud growl.

Then, Tate spat out, "You're impossible, you know that? Do I need to quit my job? You'd really make me do that?"

"I'm not making you *do* anything. I'm not even making you talk to me right now," he pointed out before adding, "but you're still here."

The muted seconds following that particular

observation were almost tangible. Logan knew whatever happened next, whatever was to be said had to be from Tate.

"I don't know what you expect from me."

Logan didn't even realize he'd been holding his breath until that confession hit his ear, and he let it out in a rush.

"I don't expect anything." He thought that was a pretty basic response. He *didn't* have any expectations. He never did since a certain person had crushed all of his.

Tate didn't give him time to dwell on that though as he interrupted his thoughts.

"And that's just another part of this whole mess, isn't it?"

"What is?" Logan asked, even though he was positive he didn't want to hear the answer.

"You can't even decide what gender you want to screw this month, yet *I'm* supposed to pick you. What kind of joke is that, Logan? Let's see. First, there was Jess, whoever the hell that is. Then, apparently, everyone I work with, not to mention Amelia's invite. Is there anyone you don't want?"

Okay, so the guy has a point, but—

"Then, why are we still talking?" Logan expected to hear a click and then nothing, but instead, he got—

"Because I can't seem to get you out of my fucking head."

And that *is all I needed to hear.*

* * *

TATE WAS BREATHING hard at this point, feeling
extremely disconcerted about everything that had been said
and the fact that he was also turned-on from listening to
Logan's voice.

"Tate?"

Tate clamped his eyes shut. "What?"

"Talk to me. Stop thinking for a minute about what
you believe is right and wrong. Just talk to me, like you
would anyone else."

Laughing derisively, Tate shook his head at no one.
"But that's the problem, isn't it, Logan? You're *not* just
anyone, and I have to consider everything that comes out of
my mouth."

"Why?"

"Why?" Tate repeated back, in disbelief.

"Yes. Why? Just say what you want to say, and if you
want to be inappropriate at any time, I'm okay with that,
too."

Tate relaxed a little. "See?"

"What? Don't act like you don't want to flirt with me.
You do it with all your customers. I've watched you."

"You do too." Tate realized too late what he'd just
given away.

Logan, of course, didn't miss it. "And you know *that*
because you watch me, too. Don't you?"

In the darkness of his room, Tate decided to do

exactly what Logan had suggested, and say what he was thinking. It wasn't like the guy was here in the bedroom with him. He couldn't reach out and...touch him.

"Yes, I do," he finally admitted to Logan and himself. After no response, he added, "Watch you."

"What if I told you, you could ask me anything right now, and I would answer you. I'm open to all questions. Would you ask me what's on your mind?"

The tone in Logan's voice matched the serious tone Tate had heard earlier in the break room, and Tate discovered that he wanted to ask a million questions. He just had no clue where to start.

"Jesus, I don't know. This whole conversation is so far from normal that I don't even know where I'd begin." Tate heard rustling at the other end and blurted out, "You're in bed?"

Logan's chuckle came through the phone and immediately Tate felt foolish.

"Um, yeah. At almost three thirty in the morning, I'm generally in bed. Aren't you?"

"Of course," Tate mumbled and then had a horrible thought. "Alone?"

"Yes." Logan laughed louder this time. "In a cold bed all alone after someone got me all hot and horny this afternoon. It was a sad night, crawling between my sheets."

Tate moved down his own bed until he was flat on his back and staring at the ceiling again.

"I really got you hot and—"

"Horny?" Logan filled in the word.

"Yes."

"Tate? You got me so hard this afternoon, I could have pounded a nail through a two-by-four."

"And that's not normal—for you?" Tate couldn't believe what he'd asked.

I sound ridiculous.

"Well, I'm a guy. It's not like an erection is difficult to get. I just need to think about your hair, and I get hard as a rock."

"My hair?" That was last thing Tate had expected.

"Yes, your sexy fucking hair. Are you kidding me? The curls..." Logan groaned out loud. "Tate, they're—just trust me."

"Okay."

"Smart move."

Tate's breathing became more labored as his heart continued to beat rapidly in his chest. He thought about everything he wanted to ask and then decided to just dive in.

It's not like anyone is here to hear me.

Hesitantly, he pushed forward. "What else do you...*like* about me?"

"Like? That's not the right word."

"Then, what word would you use?"

"What else *turns me on* about you?" Logan suggested.

Nodding absently, Tate held his breath for whatever was about to be said.

Then, Logan answered with, "Everything."

Huh? That wasn't what he'd expected to hear, and Tate was—

Disappointed? "That's it?"

"What do you mean? That's…everything," Logan told him in a tone dripping with devilry. "Oh! You want details?"

Tate remained silent as Logan made fun of him, and clear as a picture, he had an image of the man in his head with his sly smirking mouth.

"You already knew that, didn't you?"

"Yes," Logan confessed unapologetically. "But I wanted you to ask."

"To torment me?"

"No, to torment myself. Don't underestimate the power of a good tease. Aren't you lying there right now, dying to know what it is about you that turns me on?"

"I don't know about dying, but I'm curious."

"Your throat." Logan surprised him again.

"My throat?"

"Yes. It's thick, tanned, and strong. Your Adam's apple protrudes, and it moves when you swallow, especially when you're nervous. I want to lick it."

Tate's cock responded immediately to the way Logan's tongue delivered the word *lick,* and he swore he could feel it against his throat as if the man had done what he'd suggested.

"Your hair, which I already told you. I like that it's a

little long and that I could really tug on it when you were wrestling me up against the wall." Lowering his voice until it sounded like he was whispering directly into Tate's ear, Logan finished with, "And let's not forget, all your lean muscles *pushing* me against that wall. I would kill to see them naked. Fuck, Tate, everything about you turns me on. Just thinking about it right now—I might actually pass out from the lack of blood flow to my head."

A smug-ass grin stretched across Tate's mouth at the frustration in Logan's voice, and before he knew it, Tate was asking, "So, are you turned-on now?"

* * *

FUCK YES, I am, Logan wanted to say, but just to be sure, he clarified, "Are you asking me if I'm hard right now?" Logan wasn't sure he'd get a response, but he did.

"Yes."

"Then yes, I am very turned-on right now." He paused. "Are you?"

"Turned-on?"

Logan smiled into the darkness. "That was the question." He wondered if he would get anger or truth.

"Yes, I'm turned-on. I've been hard since you picked up the phone."

Logan closed his eyes, and this time, he let an unmistakable full groan escape his mouth as he pressed his head back into the pillow. He barely managed to keep his free hand above the covers as he imagined Tate lying in bed, talking to him, with an erection.

"I was thinking about your mouth before I called you," Tate continued just to further torment him.

"And you think I fight dirty."

Tate immediately backtracked. "I shouldn't have said that?"

"You can say whatever the fuck you want to, but be prepared for what comes after comments like that. Pun intended."

"Such as?"

"Such as me wanting to know more. And by more, I mean details, Tate. Tell me what you were thinking about my mouth."

Deciding there was no harm in it, Logan pressed his palm to the sheet currently draped across his arousal, and waited to hear what words would come from the inquisitive man at the other end of the phone.

"I was thinking about how soft it is even though I expected it to be—"

"Hard?" Logan added. *Like that's a word I can forget right now.*

"Yes. I expected your lips to be hard, but they're soft and big. Your bottom lip is bigger than your top."

Logan licked the lip under discussion, remembering the way Tate had bit it yesterday, as he palmed the steel rod under his sheet. "Do you like it?"

"Yes."

"Does it turn you on?"

Logan waited for and got Tate's ragged confession.
"Yes."

"Are you touching yourself, Tate?"

Silence—and then, truth.

"Yes."

* * *

TATE CUPPED HIS throbbing shaft and arched up into his hand as he gave the admission over to Logan.

"Above the sheet?" he barely heard Logan ask.

Tate looked down to where he'd kicked the sheet from his body. "No sheet."

"Christ. At least tell me you're wearing something."

It was almost comical—the more agitated Logan was, the more comfortable Tate became. It was as if the other man's loss of control gave Tate some kind of power, and the sexual high he got from it was intoxicating.

It was so intoxicating that Tate found himself sliding further into the feeling. "I'm wearing something."

"Oh, look who's being a tease now? So, you're killing me here, you know that right? *What* are you wearing?"

Tate looked down at his gray boxers and the hand he was using to stroke himself. "Boxers."

Immediately, Logan fired back, "Cotton?"

Tate ran his palm back up against the fabric under his hand. "Yes."

"Tight or loose?"

"Tightish but tighter than usual right now."

"Oh, fuck you," Logan complained like he was in agony.

Tate couldn't help the throaty chuckle that came from him, surprised to find he was enjoying the hell out of himself. "You?" he asked, picturing Logan lying in the same position he was in.

"I have a sheet over me," Logan informed him sensually.

See, this isn't so bad. I can do phone sex.

Hang on—phone sex?

Stop thinking. It feels good, right? Go with it.

"And what are you wearing?" Tate pressed, interested in the picture he could conjure up in his head.

"A sheet *is* all that I'm wearing."

Tate didn't mean to, but as soon as the image was relayed and imprinted in his mind, his fingers curled around his cock and pulled roughly as he released a guttural sound and arched up hard into his palm.

"Hmm, that sounded fucking good."

Logan's rumble met his ear, somehow breaking through the red haze of lust currently swirling all around Tate.

"So, you like the idea of me lying here, naked and turned-on, touching myself while you're talking to me?"

"Oh God." Tate thrust his hips up again.

"Spit on your palm, Tate. Get it wet, do whatever

you have to. Then, slide it back inside your boxers and touch yourself, just like I am."

Tate lifted his palm, spit into his hand, and then without a second thought, he pulled the boxers away and watched his erection spring free, pointing guiltily toward him.

"Wrap your fingers around yourself, and when you do, I want to hear you."

Feeling as though his heart was about to fly right out of his chest, Tate gripped his shaft. He couldn't have held back the raw noise ripping from his throat even if Logan hadn't told him he wanted to hear it.

"*Yes*," Logan hissed.

Tate knew that he, too, was fisting his cock at the other end of the phone.

"Tell me how it feels," Logan demanded bluntly.

The first word out of Tate's mouth was, "Hard."

"I fucking hope so." Logan gave a strained laugh.

"Hot. It's so hot in my palm—and throbbing. I don't think I've ever been this fucking hard in my life."

"Jesus, Tate," Logan cursed. "What else? What do you look like?"

"You mean, my cock?"

"Yes. You cut, uncut? Veiny, long? Describe it to me."

Well, that was something Tate had never done, but eager to keep Logan talking, and for him to continue feeling this way, Tate did as asked.

"Cut, and I'd say average size, lo—"

"Don't be a pussy, Tate. Give me an approximate length."

Tate laughed, barely, at Logan's put-out tone.

"Okay. I'd guess approximately seven inches, maybe a little more."

"Fuck, fuck—*fuck*."

Liking the strain he'd heard behind each cursed word, Tate really started to work his length. Logan's breathing became heavier in his ear, and suddenly, Tate couldn't shut his damn mouth.

"It feels like I could fuck for hours, I'm so turned-on. I swear, every time you groan or curse in my ear, it makes me even harder, if that's physically possible."

Logan's breath rushed out and into the phone, sliding through Tate's ear, and he could have sworn it was like the man was lying in the bed beside him.

"It's insane how slick my cock is," Tate muttered absently as he spread pre-cum over the swollen head. "I'm so close to coming. I don't think I can stop myself."

Finally, Logan seemed to find his tongue. "Then, stop fucking teasing me and come. I'm about to, and I want to hear you when I do."

As though Tate had been waiting for permission, he clamped his fist around his agitated shaft and listened to the huffed groan at the other end of the phone as though Logan had finally given himself permission, too.

Like two marathon runners sprinting toward the

finish line, there was nothing but gasping breaths, grunts of mutual pleasure, and right when Tate thought he couldn't feel any fucking better, he heard Logan shout out his name, and that was it. With a snap of his hips, Tate pushed up and moaned loudly as he came all over his taut stomach in a rush unlike any he'd felt for years.

Breathing harshly, Tate looked down at the sticky mess he'd made as everything came crashing in on him. He'd just had phone sex…with Logan…and he fucking loved it. His right hand was still holding the cell to his ear, and Tate could hear similar breathing to his own through the line.

"You alive?" Tate didn't know what else to say. He had no idea what guys said to one another after this sort of shit.

"I think so. Holy shit, Tate."

Tate didn't know why, but the awe in those three words made him proud. "Yeah?"

"*Hell* yeah." After some movement on his end, Logan asked, "You?"

"Yeah." That was as much as Tate could admit, and then he laughed. "Definitely, yes."

"And? Feel better?"

Tate could hear the smug tone, but he decided to finally give the guy a break. "I feel fucking fantastic."

The satisfied sound coming through the phone made Tate happy that he'd told the truth.

"Tate?" Logan asked of him.

"Yes?"

"It's going to be even better in person."

As Tate swallowed, he was aware, for the first time, of his Adam's apple bobbing in his throat.

"It can't be at the bar."

Logan laughed loudly, and Tate actually looked around his empty room as though he'd been caught jerking off.

"Well, I wasn't thinking of doing *this* at the bar. Kind of unhygienic."

Tate wasn't so sure. He knew Logan liked taking opportunities whenever he could get them, and Tate needed to be crystal clear that this, whatever *this* was going to be, needed to remain separate from work.

"Okay. Well, you need to leave me alone at work if you want me to—"

"To?" Logan urged.

"To *try* this—in person."

This time, instead of the silence coming from Tate's end, Logan seemed to be waiting for him.

"That is what you want, right?" Tate started to slightly panic, thinking that maybe he'd misread everything.

"Are you messing with me, Tate?" Logan demanded, voice serious, tone flat.

"No," he answered and quickly added, "I don't think so. I need to know what this is, whatever it is, and the only way I am going to do that is to do what you said, and try it out."

"Wow."

Tate felt his chest shake as a laugh came free. "I've shocked you?"

"You've almost killed me—twice tonight."

Tate licked his lips. "I want to talk to you about this first though, somewhere private. I have questions and things I need to know before—"

"Yeah, okay, whatever. You just say when."

Tate thought about it for a moment and decided he wanted some time to think this all through before he went ahead with it.

"How about Sunday night? I can be there by nine?"

There was a pause before Logan's voice came through from the other end. "Okay. And until then?"

"Until then, let me think about this some more."

"What if you change your mind?"

This time, Tate felt a genuine smile hit his lips as he told Logan sincerely, "I won't change my mind about meeting up with you."

"But maybe about the other?"

Tate couldn't make any promises, so he decided to be candid. "I guess we'll just have to wait and see. But Sunday works best for me."

Logan let out a long sigh. "Okay. Sunday, it is."

Just before Tate was about to say good night, he requested one last thing. "Oh, and Logan?"

"Yes?"

"Keep your zipper closed until then, huh?"

Logan groaned. "Okay, but I won't be held responsible for what happens to it on Sunday."

Tate decided to end with a tease—*why the hell not at this stage?* "No. I will be."

Chapter Nine

SUNDAY MORNING, TATE was at church from nine until approximately ten thirty. By noon, he was seated at his mother's kitchen table right alongside his sister, Jill, and her husband, Sam, for lunch until two thirty. It wasn't as though he was consciously watching the clock, but he couldn't seem to drag his eyes away from it.

It was around that time he excused himself and rode home to sit in his crappy apartment and further contemplate everything he'd been thinking about since he woke up this morning.

Now, here it was, Sunday night, and he was standing in front of Logan's condo door after traveling up the elevator, at exactly nine fifteen.

Tate had *never* been so aware of a timeline in his life, but as he stood twenty-two stories high, he tightened his fingers around his motorcycle helmet and counted back from thirty.

For the last couple of days, Tate had thought about nothing except what would happen right here, this minute— and now that the time had come, he still had no idea what that was going to be.

Tate was about to lift his hand to knock on the door when he felt his phone buzz in his pocket. Shuffling the helmet to his other hand, he pushed his left into his jeans and pulled out the cell. A smirk crossed his mouth at the name currently flashing on his screen. *Logan*—whose personal number he now had, as of a day ago.

Bringing it to his ear, Tate answered, "Impatient much?"

"I buzzed you up over ten minutes ago. I'm just making sure the elevator didn't get stuck."

"It didn't."

There was a pause that didn't help Tate with his indecision.

Then, Logan asked, "Where are you, Tate?"

Tate bumped the helmet against his thigh. "Standing at your door."

He could hear shuffling through the phone and presumed Logan was moving closer to open it.

"And how does it look from out there? I always thought it was pretty boring—cream paint, doorknob, standard black peephole to look at strange men lurking in front of my place."

Tate felt the corner of his mouth tilt up. "I'm not lurking."

"But you've been standing there for the last—"

"Five minutes," Tate supplied.

"Ah. And?"

Closing his eyes, Tate tried to think of a response.

"You sure you're ready for me to open the door, Tate?"

Biting his lip, Tate nodded silently, hearing the underlying message in Logan's words, and he was surprised when Logan murmured, "Good thing for the peephole."

As the phone disconnected, Tate heard a chain rattle and a deadbolt turn. When the door finally opened, he knew he was standing face-to-face with a man who was about to change his entire life.

* * *

LOGAN DIDN'T KNOW what was different about Tate, but as he stood a few feet away, he recognized a change. Maybe it was the direct way Tate was looking him in the eye instead of making an excuse to turn from him, or maybe it was the fact that he wasn't scowling.

Moving back, so the door was wide-open, Logan gestured for Tate to come inside. As Tate went to move by him, Logan reached out and touched the arm of his leather jacket. Tate stopped and looked down at the hand on his arm before raising his gaze to meet Logan's. And that, right there, was the difference—the heat.

Tate's focused on his lips, and Logan swore his mouth became dry in an instant from the scorching once-over Tate gave him.

Clearing his throat, Logan let go of his arm. "So, you found the place okay?" he asked as casually as he could.

Tate continued moving down the hall and into the living area where Logan had a large flat-screen mounted on the wall above a marble fireplace. He stopped, looked around the space, and then glanced back over his shoulder to where Logan had moved to lean up against the wall.

"Yeah, it wasn't hard at all."

Don't make a joke, Logan told himself. He really wanted this to go the right way. He wasn't sure what to expect, and he had no clue what Tate had finally decided. So, until it was obvious one way or the other, Logan was going to play it cool and try *not* to be the pushy asshole he'd been accused of.

Well, that was the plan until Tate bent down to place his helmet on the floor, and his jeans stretched across his ass. Logan let his gaze wander down below the black leather of Tate's jacket, and he imagined sliding his hands into the snug pockets and cupping his—

"You looking at my ass?" Tate stood and turned around.

Logan raised a brow and freely admitted, "Yep."

"And?"

Pushing off the wall, Logan crossed his arms over his chest, figuring now was the time to get everything out in the open. "From the first time we met, I thought it was fucking impressive. Nothing has changed."

* * *

TATE WASN'T SURE if the comment should upset or disturb him, but as he looked at the man staring him down, he decided that it was neither. In fact, it'd had the opposite effect. It made his temperature spike.

Logan looked good as he stood across the room from him with his arms crossed.

He definitely has a different build than me. Tate took a moment to really study the man without the fear of anyone catching him.

He was dressed as casually as Tate had ever seen him. Barefoot, Logan had on some loose, gray track pants and a black T-shirt that seemed molded to all his muscles, and the guy had some serious muscles under those suits.

He definitely works out to get those.

Tate acknowledged Logan's shoulders and incredibly built biceps, and he had to admit, they were fucking awe-inspiring, not to mention sexy.

Wow, who knew that would flip my switch?

"Done looking?" Logan's voice questioned in a way that told Tate he was enjoying being the object under scrutiny.

Tate didn't respond immediately. Instead, he took his time finishing his one-stop visual feast before finally shrugging and pushing his hands into his jacket pockets.

"Yep."

"That's it? No details?"

Yeah, see how that feels. Tate tilted his head to the couch. "Mind if I sit?"

He watched Logan's eyes narrow as he shook his head. Moving around to the recliner, to the right of the loveseat, Tate sat and crossed his legs at the ankles as Logan walked toward the opposite end of the double.

"Would you like a drink?"

"Ah, the irony. You sure I shouldn't be in the kitchen, mixing you one?"

Logan pointed to where he was seated. "No, you stay right there. I'll serve you tonight."

The remark was meant innocently—probably for the first time in Logan's life. Tate, however, twisted it in his own mind as he began thinking of all the ways Logan might want to serve him. He felt the blood rushing down between his thighs, and his cock started to ache from the ideas now flashing through his head. Tate also discovered that the more he observed the muscles shifting across Logan's back, the more turned-on he became.

Logan looked back and caught him looking, and the cautious but interested expression on his face told Tate that Logan knew he was being watched.

"You never said. Drink?"

Tate shook his head. "Just water, thanks."

"Seriously?" Logan turned to fully face him from behind the kitchen counter.

Tate ran a hand up and through his hair, and Logan's eyes shifted to the gesture.

"I want a clear head." Tate appreciated the fact that Logan didn't push the issue.

When Logan was back in the living room, he made his way between the couch and the wooden coffee table until he was directly in front of Tate, looking down with two drinks in his hands.

Slowly, Logan leaned down toward him, and Tate thought for a full overwhelming moment that he was going to hyperventilate, but at the last second, Logan's mouth tipped up into a grin.

Tate focused in on that full bottom lip, fixating on it, as Logan placed his water on the table next to the couch. Thinking the man was about to move away, Tate reached out and snagged Logan's free arm.

"Your eyes…"

"Yes?"

Tate tilted his head to the side. "They're so fucking blue."

* * *

LOGAN CONVINCED HIMSELF that the way Tate was looking at him was due to nerves and curiosity. It wasn't because Tate was about to attack him.

The guy wants to talk, so move away from him and talk, Mitchell.

"You should let go of my arm." He was pretty damn proud of his self-restraint, but apparently, Tate had his own agenda.

"Why?"

Logan almost groaned. That seemed to be Tate's favorite question. *Why?* The big problem with that was everything Logan wanted to say back was one hundred percent inappropriate and not where they were supposed to be going—yet.

Reminding himself that he could be an adult—*sometimes*—Logan lifted his drink and took a sip. "Because you want to talk."

"You can't talk with me touching you?" Tate released his arm.

Taking a couple of steps back, Logan sat down in the far corner of the loveseat and stared Tate down. "Not about anything that requires me to actually think."

He watched Tate's mouth open slightly as he wiped his palms on his jeans.

"That was the plan, right? To talk about what happened the other night? Or have you changed your mind?"

"I haven't changed my mind."

Those five words pretty much guaranteed Logan's erection for the rest of the evening. "You haven't?"

Logan tried for casual as he lifted his glass and sucked the alcohol back. Tate must have noticed because he heard the guy laugh.

"Nope, I haven't," he responded as if this was a normal conversation for him.

Logan leaned forward on the couch and slid the empty glass onto his coffee table. Remaining bent over, he rested his forearms on his knees and turned to face the calm—*apparently, up until now*—straight man sitting in his favorite seat.

"Why are you so relaxed all of a sudden?" Logan demanded before the obvious answer hit him. *Of course, Tate is relaxed. He knows where this night is going to go. He has the advantage.*

Tate knew what Logan wanted—*well, maybe not exactly*—but Tate knew his intentions. It was him who had no clue what was going on, and that was starting to make him act like a nervous shit, which he hated.

I'm never nervous, except with this guy.

"Trust me, I'm not relaxed. But why are you so tense?" Tate uncrossed his legs and sat forward on the couch, mirroring Logan's position.

Okay, so maybe the guy isn't as relaxed as I thought.

"Do you really want that answer?"

Tate lifted his face and locked purposeful eyes on him. "Yeah, I really do."

With a pent-up sigh, Logan told him bluntly, "I'm tense because I don't know what *you* want to happen." He gave a self-deprecating laugh. "And I'm tense because of what *I* want to happen."

He caught Tate adjusting his pose, to sit up straight.

"Do you mind if I take off my jacket?"

Logan let out a long-suffering grumble and sprawled back on his couch in frustration. "No, I don't mind. Take off all your fucking clothes if it makes you more comfortable."

Shutting his eyes, Logan told himself to be patient, and waited for Tate to talk. What he didn't expect was to feel the couch beside him sink down.

He saw that Tate was now seated at the opposite end of the two-seater, facing him with his jean-clad leg bent up on the cushion, and his arm resting along the back in a short-sleeved red shirt. His fingers were only inches from Logan's shoulder, and Logan wondered if he'd done that on purpose.

"I'm not sure I'm ready to strip just yet, but this is much more comfortable."

Oh, fuck this. Logan turned on the couch, so he could stare Tate directly in the eye. *If the guy wants to drive me crazy, fine. I can play that game, too.*

"Tate? Start fucking talking before I decide to really shut you up."

* * *

TATE REGARDED THE man opposite him, and he knew that he wanted his mouth on Logan's. Problem was he didn't know how to go about it.

Do I just lean forward and grab him?

All of their personal encounters in the past had been brought on by anger and adrenaline. This time though, it was premeditated. Tate *wanted* to kiss him. He wanted to feel those lips under his, and as the thought settled, he leaned forward and slid his palm along the back of the couch.

When his fingers were in line with Logan's shoulder, he asked in a voice he barely recognized as his own, "How would you shut me up?"

Logan didn't move a muscle as he watched him intently. "You want me to tell you—or show you?"

Tate knew that answer. He'd thought about nothing else for days. "Show me."

* * *

LOGAN DIDN'T WAIT around for Tate to change his mind. He raised his hands to Tate's face, letting the scratch of his stubble abrade his palms. Sliding his hand to the back of Tate's head, he asked at the last moment, "Are you sure?"

That seemed to trigger something in Tate because the hand he had on the back of the couch moved onto Logan's shoulder and squeezed right before Tate tugged him in that final inch.

This time, when their mouths met, there was no fury, no annoyance, but there sure as hell was one wicked, hot burn. Logan could feel the heat radiating from Tate's skin as he touched his jaw with his fingertips.

When Tate's lips parted beneath his own, Logan slid his tongue over them, tracing and testing their shape and size as the hand on his shoulder flexed, and there it was again—cinnamon and something else that blended and made it all...*Tate*.

With no more hesitation or subtlety, Logan pushed both hands into Tate's hair and thrust his tongue between the other man's lips. As if he couldn't help himself, Tate groaned against the invasion and let go of Logan's shoulder to clutch his waist, trying to pull him even closer.

Pushing up and onto his knee, Logan angled his body above Tate, whose neck tilted back. From the position Logan had put himself in, he gained such a deep slide into Tate's mouth that he thought it would be a miracle if he ever decided to leave. As he continued to devour the lips moving under his, Logan wished like hell he were naked because this kiss was about to blow his fucking mind.

Rubbing their tongues together and imagining their cocks doing the same, Logan took from Tate every breath and sigh he could get, and he was finally relieved not to hold back. It was the most sexually driven mating of the mouths Logan had ever been a part of, and his brain needed to get a handle on itself and stop listening solely to his dick.

Tearing his mouth away, Logan wrapped the curls around his fingers and looked down at eyes that were heavy with lust and staring up at him.

"You taste like cinnamon. Why?"

Tate's breathing was coming hard, and his fingers were flexing into Logan's side as he answered, "Gum."

"Gum?"

"Yep, Big Red."

"You just like the taste?"

Tate licked his top lip, making Logan want to

followed that tongue back in to his mouth.

"Something like that."

"Hmm, we'll come back to that. Any questions so far?" He hovered above Tate, ready for round two.

Tate blinked once. "Why'd you stop?"

Logan felt like he was close to attacking, so he closed his eyes for a second, blocking out the man below him as he tried to remind himself to breathe.

"You okay?" he heard Tate ask around what sounded like a swallow of air.

The laugh that came from him was strained. "Yes, I keep telling myself that you've never done this, and I need to slow down."

As the final word left his mouth, Tate's hand moved across his lower back.

"It's funny you know, I expected you to be different."

Logan's brain was trying to stay with the program at hand—initiate the new guy. *But come the hell on. What am I supposed to do when the new guy keeps changing all the fucking rules?*

"What do you mean, you expected me to be different?" He released Tate's hair, and reluctantly sat back on the couch.

Tate removed his hands from Logan's waist and ran a palm up over his face. "Nothing bad. I just expected you to be more…"

"More?" Logan pushed.

Tate looked away then. It seemed his nerves had finally caught up with him.

He shrugged. "More forceful. Less willing to stop."

Logan raised a brow and took Tate's chin between his fingers, pulling his face back, so he was looking right at him. "I was *trying* to let you talk. You told me you wanted to. You had questions, remember?"

Tate's mouth opened and closed, but nothing came out as his eyes clouded over, and he once again let them focus on Logan's lips.

"But I don't think you want to talk anymore, do you? You want to do exactly what I want to do," Logan taunted as he leaned over, and an inch from Tate's lips, he suggested, "You want to fuck."

As their eyes connected, Logan slipped his tongue out and touched Tate's upper lip. "Don't you?"

Chapter Ten

TATE COULD FEEL every single pulse in his engorged cock as Logan's tongue teased and tormented his mouth. As he listened to the suggestive words coming from Logan's lips, all Tate wanted was to ease the ache between his own legs. If that meant fucking Logan, then maybe that was what needed to happen.

But damn, am I ready for all of that?

Before Tate could respond to the question hanging between them, Logan palmed his chest and pushed him back into the corner of the couch. When his back met with the soft leather, a strong thigh slid between his legs, and Tate groaned from the relief of finally having something hard to press against.

"*Yeah*, that's it," Logan encouraged, placing a hand on the back of the couch and the other on the armrest behind Tate's head. Using them as an anchor, Logan rolled his hips downward and proved just how forceful he could be.

Tate's head was resting against the couch as Logan looked down between them while he thrust his hips, over and over, creating a heated friction that had Tate's mind spinning out of his head. The sexual hunger on Logan's face as he watched their clothed bodies connecting made Tate wonder just how combustible things would be when their clothes finally came off.

Feeling the need to touch, now more than ever, Tate grabbed a hold of Logan's hips and pulled the man down against him with much more force than he'd intended. The delicious pressure of having Logan's shaft grind against his own was too much to forgo, so Tate arched up, anxiously meeting the steady rub Logan was giving with every single punch of his hips.

"Fuck," Logan muttered.

Tate's fingers dug harder into his hips, and his left hand slid down to Logan's ass, squeezing it, as he propelled himself up again, trying to reach for something more.

* * *

LOGAN LOOKED AT the man under him. *Jesus, Tate is gorgeous.*

They weren't even naked, and Logan was pretty sure he could die happy from merely dry-humping him all night, but that was *not* how he wanted this to end.

Slowing his hips down, Logan moved away and quickly pulled his shirt over his head. Naked from the waist up with one leg supporting him on the floor and his other kneeling between Tate's thighs, he heard, "Wow," as Tate looked him over.

Logan went to laugh, but it came out more as a

cough when he looked down to where Tate, once again, shocked him by pressing his hand between his thighs to palm his own erection.

"Feeling good there?" Logan questioned.

Tate's response of a mumbled, "Mhmm," made Logan's desire to touch him even stronger.

Lowering his gaze to the uncomfortably tight-looking jeans, Logan fingered the button. "Yes?"

With an arch of his pelvis, Tate replied on a rush of air, "Yes."

Quick fingers went into action as Logan undid the button and unzipped Tate's jeans. Spreading them apart, he raised his eyes to where Tate was watching him intently. "Lift."

No hesitation was shown as Tate lifted his hips, and Logan pulled the denim down to his upper thighs, revealing black cotton boxers—the exact kind he'd imagined the other night when they'd been talking on the phone.

Visible beneath the shorts was the obvious proof of Tate's excitement. His thick shaft was distinctly outlined by the fabric, and the sight made Logan's confined cock jealous. Slipping his fingers into the waistband, he tugged the material down Tate's lean hips, and he almost thanked the guy for automatically lifting his lower half.

"Christ, look at you. You're going to kill me," Logan swore when he was finally staring at the cropped curls surrounding Tate's flushed and straining erection. Not having any lube handy, Logan spit into his palm a couple of times.

Welcome to my world, Tate. Now, you just lie there and let me devour you.

Logan fisted Tate's steely length, mesmerized by what he was finally seeing and... *mmm, squeezing*. Satisfied by the loud, gasping response, he started to stroke and pull at the cock that was finally in his hand. Glancing back up to where Tate was sprawled on the couch, Logan noticed that he'd tipped his head back and shut his eyes.

Not wanting him to forget where he was and whom he was with, Logan leaned over and did something he'd been dying to do. He licked Tate's throat, right across his Adam's apple. Tate grunted and lifted his head to look at him, as he jammed his hips up into the palm giving him a solid hand job. Then, just as Logan was about to say something, Tate grabbed the back of his neck and he pulled him down until their lips crushed together, forcefully pushing his tongue into his mouth.

* * *

I AM BURNING up, was all Tate could think.

The strong hand jerking him continued to work his flesh like a fucking pro. Logan's mouth was eating at his, like a starved man, and Tate was finding it difficult to slow his body down. He didn't want to come yet. He wanted something else. He wanted—*more*. So, he did what he knew would get Logan's attention—he bit down on the man's lip.

Instantly, Logan stopped and lifted his head. With his fingers still wrapped firmly around Tate's cock, he smiled down at him like a fucking deviant.

"Want something, Tate?" Logan stopped moving his hand altogether.

Tate nudged his hips up into the hold Logan had on him, but the man was not budging.

"I asked you a question. Do you want something?"

"I don't know."

"Yes, you do. What do you want? Tell me, and I'll give it to you."

Tate's mind went into overdrive at the sexual promise.

"Just open your mouth and say, Logan, I want you to…"

Tate bit down on his own lip and squirmed slightly at the first thought that popped into his head. That was when Logan's expression went from patiently waiting to blazing inferno as he looked at the hard-on in his hand.

"Damn Tate, something just got you extra excited. I swear to God your cock just grew an inch. What's going on in that head of yours?"

That mouth of Logan's was going to get him every fucking time. Not only was it dirty, it was sexy, and it drove Tate right over the edge of his sanity and into the most dangerous of waters.

Ever since he'd met Logan, he'd wanted him to shut his mouth, punch him in it, or dive inside for a taste—and right this second was no different. All Tate could think about was pushing what was in Logan's fist between those smart-ass, arrogant lips and making the guy shut up by sucking his dick. But thinking it and asking for it were two totally different things. So, he remained stubbornly silent as Logan continued to hold him captive with his warm palm and his taunting stare.

"Do you want me to stop?" Logan asked.

Tate shook his head as Logan crowded down over him and braced his free hand on the armrest. He could feel Logan's breath in a hot sigh by his ear as he stroked his fist up Tate's length in a slow, torturous pull.

And then, Logan asked exactly the right question, "Do you want me to suck your cock, Tate?"

Letting out a groan of pure frustration, Tate turned his head on the armrest, so he was nose-to-nose with Logan. As he stared into devilish blue eyes, his whole body vibrated against the couch.

And finally, Tate gave in. "Yes."

* * *

LOGAN PRESSED A hard kiss to Tate's mouth before he backed away and released his fist. Pushing off of Tate, Logan stood in front of him. "Sit up with your back against the couch."

Tate shifted to a seated position, and spread his legs out in a straddle as far as his jeans would allow.

Oh hell, was all Logan could think as Tate's cock pointed proudly toward its owner. There was no need for it to worry. Logan knew exactly who it belonged to, and he wanted to make it his.

Dropping to his knees in front of Tate, Logan didn't wait around as he pushed them apart and moved closer between. Tate was silent as he watched from above as though he were witnessing the act, not actually experiencing it.

But that is all about to change, Logan decided with a smug grin.

He lowered his head to drag his tongue from the base of Tate's erection right up to the very tip, and that was when Tate decided to join in on the action. A firm hand came up to grip Logan's hair, and he winced at the force that was used. But as soon as the shock from having Logan's mouth on him was over, Tate's hold loosened, and Logan brought his hand up to smooth his palm across the muscular thigh beside him.

As he flicked his tongue around the broad plum-shaped head, he could taste the salty evidence of Tate's arousal. Feeling his own erection pounding out a staccato rhythm, Logan decided now was not the time to play around and tease. That could happen later. Right now, there needed to be release, and it needed to be fast.

Spreading his palms out on Tate's thighs, Logan smoothed his hands up until his thumbs were framing Tate's pelvic bone, and he could cup the root of his agitated flesh.

Logan lifted his head and made direct eye contact with the bewildered man above. With a wink at him, Logan then lowered his mouth to slide his lips down over Tate's beautifully cut cock.

The harsh curse that pulled from Tate's throat as he pushed into his mouth with more force was almost enough to make Logan come. The hands in his hair tightened as Logan started to drag his lips up the rigid length pumping in and out from his mouth.

Logan could hear Tate's breathing pick up as his pace increased, and Logan found that he didn't even need to employ skill this time around. Tate wanted something to fuck, and Logan's mouth was the lucky winner. So, Logan held on to his thighs, opened his mouth, and let Tate shove in between his lips like they'd been doing this for years.

When Logan felt one of the hands at the side of his head come around to his cheek, he closed his eyes, enjoying the moment where rough fingers stroked the day-old growth. They then moved down to his chin where Tate tugged it between his thumb and index finger, signaling he wanted more of Logan's mouth around him.

Opening his eyes and getting up high on his knees, Logan lifted his mouth off of Tate with a soft popping sound and curled his fingers around the glistening shaft, angling it straight up at him. Bending back down, Logan circled the tip of Tate with his tongue.

Concentrating on the sensitive glans, he heard Tate mutter a soft, "Fuck," before Logan took him all the way to the back of his throat. With a slight grunt and cough, Logan slid his lips back up and waited for Tate to move. It didn't take long.

Confident hands took Logan's head and started to direct his mouth at the speed and pace Tate wanted. Methodically, he thrust between Logan's lips, cursing and groaning with every gratifying entry and exit his cock made from Logan's mouth, and when Logan moved a hand to cup Tate's balls, he seemed to lose all finesse.

"Logan," he warned grimly.

Logan's fingers cradled and massaged the sensitive sac tucked up between Tate's legs. Logan knew what was coming, and he wanted it. He craved every last drop of cum to hit his tongue and slide down his throat. Only then, would he know exactly what Tate Morrison tasted like.

Holding Tate's leg with one hand, he gently squeezed the balls he was palming in the other, and he fastened his mouth around the intrusion shoving relentlessly down his throat. Logan closed his eyes as Tate pushed into his mouth for the final time, and then Tate let out the most satisfying shout Logan had ever heard as he came in a hot, sticky torrent down his throat.

* * *

JESUS H. CHRIST.

Tate was slumped back against the couch, trying to catch his breath, and staring at Logan, who was still kneeling between his legs. He couldn't even think right now as Logan's mouth left his sensitive flesh, and he sat back on his heels.

Logan's sexy—not to mention, talented—mouth was now swollen from having been wrapped around him for the past several minutes.

Or was it more? It'd seemed like a fucking eternity to him.

As Logan licked his lips like he'd just eaten the best meal in the world, it occurred to Tate that he couldn't remember the last time anyone had ever swallowed. Diana had hated it, but Logan had refused to move away. In actuality, he'd sucked harder and faster until the end where he'd seemingly taken immense pleasure from swallowing everything Tate had given him.

"Um…" Tate reached a hand up to scrub it over his face.

That was when a low laugh hit his ears. Dropping his hand down, he quirked a brow at Logan, who was still on his knees, laughing.

"What?" Tate demanded.

"Nothing."

That got him curious. As he looked down, he noticed that he needed to cover himself, and he found it interesting that it hadn't even occurred to him. He just wanted to know what was so damn funny.

"What?"

"Nothing. You just look like I sucked your brains out

through your cock."

Tate couldn't disagree with that assessment one little bit. "You might have."

The look Logan gave him was satisfied and smug, and at that moment, Tate realized that he hadn't done anything for the guy in the last portion of the *initiate Tate program*. He hadn't kissed him, touched him, or sucked him. He'd just sat on the couch and selfishly gotten a brain-destroying blow job.

Well, the guy did offer.

"Ah...sorry, I...you know, came before you—"

You lame ass. Tate groaned, lifting his hips to pull his boxers and jeans up. Just as he had them back in place and covering his groin, he felt a hand on his and saw that Logan was touching him and giving him a look full of irony.

"You didn't," he said.

Tate didn't understand at first until Logan looked down at himself and shrugged.

"I came in my pants, like a fucking high schooler."

Tate couldn't help the laugh that escaped him at the self-disgust he'd heard in Logan's tone.

"Oh. Well, at least those were just your track pants."

Logan's brow rose. "I'll have you know that these are Armani track pants."

More at ease now, Tate sat forward until he was only an inch from Logan, and reached out to cup his face. Bringing Logan the rest of the way forward with a slight pull of his hands, Tate pressed their lips together and marveled at the rough texture of Logan's cheeks.

"Huh," Tate mused out loud, still running his palms over the coarse hair on Logan's face.

When he pulled away, Logan frowned, and Tate wondered for a moment if he shouldn't have done that. Then, Logan's mouth morphed into a smile. "So, what do you want to try next?"

Chapter Eleven

"I THINK WE should have that talk now, don't you?"

Letting his head fall back, Logan groaned. "If you insist. I, personally, think we should do something different altogether."

"I'm sure you do," Tate told him.

Logan looked at the man who'd completely surprised him in the last half hour and raised a questioning brow. "Well, I don't know about you, but I need a shower."

"Yeah, uh...that's probably not a bad idea. Is there somewhere I could go to have a smoke first?"

Moving to his feet, Logan winced at the sticky condition in his pants. *High schooler was right.* He couldn't remember the last time he'd come while still wearing his pants, but damn, Tate finally giving in and letting him suck on him had done it.

"You smoke?" Logan asked. "Ah, that's what it is." He thought about the faint taste of tobacco under the overpowering cinnamon as he made his way to the dark drapes behind the single recliner. "That's a nasty habit, you know?"

"Yeah, I know." Tate stood and pushed his hand into

his back pocket, presumably to get out his pack of cigarettes. "I only smoke when I drink."

As Logan pulled the curtain back, revealing the door to his balcony, he looked over to where Tate had moved around the couch. "But you're not drinking."

When Tate got to him, he brought the white pack up and tapped it against his palm before opening the flap. Bringing it to his mouth, he pulled out one of the white cylinders between his lips.

"No, I'm not," he mumbled around the tip in his mouth. "But I just came from a guy giving me a blow job, so my nerves are shot to shit." Fishing a blue lighter out of his jeans pocket, Tate gave him a wiry smirk. "Don't judge me."

Logan chuckled, holding up his palms. "I'm not. And for the record, this guy enjoyed giving you head. So, if you want to get used to it, just ask."

Tate's eyes moved to his mouth, and Logan knew he was remembering exactly how it had felt to have his cock sucked by him.

Unlocking the door, Logan pushed it open and felt the cool night air hit him as Tate made his way outside.

"I'm going to go and have that shower," he said as he watched Tate lean against the railing, lighting his cigarette. "Unless, of course, you want me to wait, so you can join me?"

Logan paused as Tate looked back at him. The wind ruffled the loose hair around his face as he took a drag of the cigarette and then blew out the smoke.

What a turn-on, Logan thought.

Watching Tate smoke might have just become a new fascination of his. The man looked striking, standing there with the city lights as his backdrop, and the smoke sensually curling away from him.

"I'm not sure I'm ready for…all of that just yet."

As Logan raised one of his arms up and stretched it above his head against the doorjamb, he felt immense satisfaction from the way Tate's eyes skidded down over his naked chest and abdomen.

"You sure about that?" Logan reached his free hand across his body to rub his shoulder.

Still looking back at him, Tate watched him like a dog eyeing a bone. It was obvious he liked what he was looking at, but at the same time, he still seemed to be holding back.

When it was clear that Tate wasn't going to answer, Logan tried his name. "Tate?"

"Huh?" He brought the cigarette back to his lips.

"You sure you don't want me to wait?"

As Tate took another long drag, he turned around completely, leaning back against the rail, as he unapologetically checked him out.

"You're really good-looking. It pisses me off."

Logan brought his arm down and leaned against the door. "Funny, I was just thinking the same thing about you, minus the pissed-off part. Why does it annoy you?"

Shaking his head, almost as though he didn't believe

his own thoughts, Tate admitted, "Because you make me want to do things that I shouldn't."

Logan wanted to know *every little thing* Tate was thinking, but he also knew he desperately needed a shower. So, he walked forward to Tate, reached out, and took the cigarette from him. Bringing it to his own lips, he took a drag, and as he gave it back, he blew the smoke out just past Tate's face.

"Sorry, I just really wanted to suck on what you were sucking. I'm going to go and take a shower. If you want one, the second bedroom has an en suite. Then, Tate?"

Tate was staring at him with unflinching focus, holding the cigarette down by his leg, forgotten.

"I want to know all the things you want to do but shouldn't."

Tate's tongue came out to moisten his lips.

Logan couldn't help himself as he added, "So, we can start crossing them off the list."

With that parting comment and Tate's long exhale, Logan turned and made his way back into his condo.

* * *

AS LOGAN DISAPPEARED inside, Tate turned back to face the lights of downtown Chicago, and he had to wonder for the millionth time, *What am I doing here with him?* But the answer was pretty obvious now—

Isn't it? Just say it. Just admit it out loud, and then maybe it will get easier.

"I'm sexually attracted to Logan Mitchell—a man," he muttered into the quiet night.

Nope, that didn't help.

He couldn't seem to turn off his brain, and all Tate kept thinking about was what everyone in his life would think if they knew what had just happened here. Even more perplexing was the fact that he knew the shitstorm it would stir, but it wasn't going to stop him from doing it all again.

Finishing his cigarette, Tate crouched down, pressed the butt to the concrete, and made his way inside to look for the garbage. As he stepped back into the living room, he looked at the couch where he and Logan had been earlier. Automatically, Tate was hit with a vision of everything that had taken place, and he realized that he wanted to go and find Logan.

Moving to the kitchen, he placed the butt in the sink, not wanting to snoop, and then he walked through the living room and down the hall to where he could hear the shower running.

Stopping outside the door, Tate thought about exactly what he wanted to happen here. He knew that going down this rabbit hole would turn his life completely upside down. Yet, even as he thought it, his feet were carrying him closer to the partially shut door.

Pushing it open, he stepped into the bedroom and took a moment to look around. It was full of dark mahogany wood and cream walls. Tate didn't allow himself long to linger, knowing that if he did, he'd more than likely leave. So, instead, he made his way toward the open door where Logan's track pants were on the floor.

Closing his eyes for a second, Tate told himself, *I can do this. Hell, I want to do this*, and moved farther into the humid bathroom. The shower was on the left side of the tiled room, and up against the right was a double vanity. He could hear the steady stream of water as he rested his ass up against the edge of the first sink, and he waited.

The glass door was shut and covered with steam, only allowing him a partial view of the man inside. As Tate leaned on the sink, he imagined what would happen when the door was pulled open, and his cock stiffened to full mast.

And that's what it really comes down to, he thought. *My cock wants Logan. I want Logan. Hell, standing here in the same bathroom, thinking about him naked, turns me on more than anything or anyone else.*

Just as that thought slammed home with the force of a Mack truck, the water shut off, and the glass door slid open.

* * *

LOGAN HAD RESISTED the urge to spend too long under the warm spray, instead wanting to get out and find Tate— or more importantly, make sure that Tate hadn't left. Lathering up all the important areas, he then rinsed off and pulled the door back, ready to go and hunt down the other man.

That wasn't necessary though. Tate was standing in the bathroom, up against the vanity, with his arms and legs crossed, staring directly at him.

"Hello," Logan stated calmly, not wanting to spook Tate, as he ran a hand through his hair.

Tate shifted his hips against the counter, lowering his eyes to zoom in on—

Yep, my now swelling cock.

"Hi."

Not possessing one shy bone in his body, including the one standing tall and erect, Logan stepped out of the shower and walked steadily toward the man who was frozen against his sink. When he was close enough that he was dripping water onto Tate's jeans, Logan stopped and waited for Tate to look at him.

Slowly, Tate raised his head, and the heated connection they shared, was what had Tate shifting off the vanity. Logan was sure it happened much sooner than it seemed but as Tate's fully clothed body brushed up against his naked thighs, and—*fuck yes*—his cock, Logan bit back a curse.

Deciding he needed to speak or he'd end up humping Tate's leg, Logan stated, "I thought you wanted to take a shower."

"I decided I wanted something else."

Hell, how does this guy always shake my steady footing?

"And what would that be?" Logan asked.

He watched Tate reach out a seriously shaky hand to trace a line down the center of his chest. The rough finger moved between Logan's pecs and down to his navel where it stopped and flirted with the damp hair just beneath.

"I want to touch you."

Logan had been all ready to talk around five minutes ago when he'd been in the shower calming himself down. *But now?* Now, he was ready to go again, and Tate was driving him out of his mind.

Clenching his jaw, Logan stepped forward, muscling Tate back to the sink, and then kept advancing. Tate's ass hit the edge, and Logan moved slightly, so he had one foot between Tate's spread ones, and one on the outside of his right thigh. Pressing his naked cock against the rough denim, Logan groaned as he clasped Tate's arm for support.

Tate shocked the hell out of him by wrapping his arms around his waist and clutching Logan's bare ass as he hauled him in closer.

Tipping his head back, Logan ground his hips down on Tate's strong thigh as he growled out, "Jes-us."

"Fuck," Tate sighed.

Logan brought his head back up to look Tate in the eye. Parting his mouth, Logan licked his lip and continued to rub himself off on Tate's leg.

"You still wanna talk?" Logan somehow asked through his lust.

He could feel Tate's hot breath against his cheek while moving his mouth to Tate's ear where he bit down gently. "If you want to talk, talk, or I am going to unzip your jeans and rub my cock against that fucking hard-on. And trust me, there will be no talking after that."

Tate reluctantly released his hold, and Logan slowly took a step back.

"Talk or get undressed, but pick something in the next two seconds, so I don't lose my goddamn mind."

* * *

TATE DEFINITELY WANTED to talk, but as soon as Logan was in front of him, completely naked, wet and erect, his brain had shut down, and his body had taken over.

The man was ripped. From his solid arms to his muscular chest, which had a fine dusting of dark hair, and then his abs and that treasure trail leading down to…

Jesus, how am I supposed to talk? Tate barely had blood left in his brain to remind himself to breathe.

"Can you maybe put some clothes on?"

"No. Next question?"

Tate frowned. "It would help if you put something on."

"Why? You seemed comfortable enough a moment ago, and if you weren't, you should have waited for me to get dressed." Logan reached out, snagged a towel, and dried himself. When he got to his hair, he rubbed it a couple of times before throwing the towel on the floor.

"That's hardly the problem," Tate muttered.

Logan moved toward the door leading to the bedroom, and Tate found himself looking at the firm, round ass he had been kneading just minutes ago.

"I didn't think so. Well, come on then. Let's get the talking over and done with, so we can move on to the fun part. You know, the part where my cock gets to meet yours?"

As Logan exited the room, Tate shook his head incredulously. The guy really did walk to the beat of his own drum. Stepping away from the sink where his ass had taken up residence, Tate made his way into the bedroom to see Logan lying casually on the mattress with his arms behind his head. He had a sheet draped across his waist, and somehow, Tate was positive that Logan had not put on any clothes.

"How does this work?" Tate finally voiced the number-one question that had been bugging him.

"Well…" Logan removed one of his hands to lay it down beside him on the bed.

Tate's eyes were drawn to where Logan's hand had landed, right beside the discernable tent that had formed under the sheet.

"That depends on *what* exactly you're referring to. The first thing that needs to happen is for you to take off your clothes."

Tate walked over toward the foot of the bed. "Yeah, that much I know, thanks. I'm unsure of the details, smart-ass. You know, like who…" *Yeah, saying this is much harder than thinking it.*

"Like, who fucks who?"

Apparently, it wasn't an issue for Logan.

"Jesus, do you have to be so—"

"So, what? To the point? Come on, Tate, that's the thing you're most worried about, right?" Logan raised a brow. "I'll make it really simple. I can't wait for you to fuck me. Does that clear things up for you?"

It sure as hell does. But somehow, Tate didn't think that was all there was to it, and he was right.

Logan moved his hand to where the sheet was covering him and started to stroke himself. "For now."

Tate couldn't think of anything to say to that, so he just stood there with his lips pulled tight.

"Take off your clothes, Tate."

Tate grabbed the hem of his shirt, removed it swiftly, and threw it off to the side, not even caring where it landed. Tate's mouth finally parted as Logan started to move his feet, pulling the sheet down, and—

Yeah, the guy didn't bother with clothes.

As Logan's nude body came back into view, Tate wondered how it would feel to press his own nakedness against him.

"And the rest," Logan told him in a voice that seemed to have the same effect as hypnosis.

Tate kicked off his shoes and undid his jeans, removing the rest of his clothes. When he was finally undressed, Logan had both hands down between his thighs.

One was jerking his thick shaft, and the other was dipping down to play with his balls. All the while, Logan's intent gaze focused on Tate's body.

"Fuck, just stand there. I can do this all day. You don't have to do anything for me to get off on you."

Tate felt some of his nerves and apprehension leave as Logan continued pleasuring himself.

"I don't know when I'll be ready to…you know, do everything you want," Tate finally spoke, answering sincerely.

Logan stopped what he was doing and leveled steady eyes on him. "We'll go as slow as you like."

"Which for you is full speed ahead?"

"Usually."

Huh, Tate thought, and then asked the other question that had been on his mind, "Why are you being so patient with me?"

Logan let go of the hold he had on himself. "Why are you even *here* with me?"

Good comeback, damn lawyer.

"Tate, you're sexy as fuck. The minute I saw you, I got hard. When you opened your mouth, I became one hundred percent interested. And when you kissed me? I lost my damn mind. I'll be as patient as I need to, to get you inside me. Anything else?"

Tate's cock seemed to understand because it proudly proclaimed its interest in the action it wanted.

"Get into bed," Logan coaxed.

"I think I better stay here while we talk."

"We're still talking?" Logan asked in a tone that suggested he was over the conversation section of the evening.

"This is a big deal for me. You might be used to putting your dick wherever and whenever, but mine has only visited pussy, and I'm freaking out a little. So, would you hang on, and cut me some slack?"

* * *

WHILE TATE STOOD, seemingly trying to get his brain to catch up with his eager body, Logan took in all of his lean muscles and smooth, tanned torso. *Mmm.* Tate hardly had any body hair over his burnished brown skin, and Logan couldn't wait to run his tongue all over it.

Deciding to play nice, Logan relented, "Okay, I'll cut you some slack. Why don't you tell me what else is bothering you?"

Logan hadn't known what to expect, but it wasn't what he got.

"You, sleeping with everything that moves." Tate moved cautiously around to the empty side of the bed.

Logan tried to concentrate, but all he kept coming back to was, *Tate is standing here, naked in my bedroom.*

"Logan?" Tate waited for a response.

Turning on his side, Logan watched as Tate slowly placed a knee on the bed. "What?"

"Are you even listening to me?"

"Honestly? No." Logan sat up, grabbed Tate's hand, and tackled him down onto the bed until he was hovering over him.

"Mmm," Logan half-groaned as he finally pressed his naked erection against Tate's. "You're worried about me with other people while I'm fucking you. Aw, I think you care, Mr. Morrison."

"I think you mean while *I'm* fucking *you*. Don't you?"

Logan became amused as Tate glared up at him, obviously aggravated he'd been overpowered, and even more so at Logan's words.

It may have been crazy, but seeing Tate irritated was fast becoming one of Logan's biggest turn-ons.

Placing his hands by Tate's head, he lowered himself until he was by his ear. "Minor details."

Tate turned his head on the pillow until their lips were only inches apart, and he released a low grunt as Logan rolled his hips over him.

"Important ones, wouldn't you say?" Tate asked.

Logan flicked his tongue out, tracing it across Tate's upper lip, and when they parted, he promised, "I know what we agreed to, and what you think you want. But I *will* end up inside you." He emphasized exactly which part of him he was referring to, by flexing his hips against Tate. "And you'll beg me to be there. I guarantee it."

A hand slid up into Logan's wet hair and palmed the

back of his head as the other held his pumping hips, halting his moves.

"And everyone else?" Tate asked on a labored breath.

Logan noted with great interest that Tate hadn't objected to what he'd just told him, and for the first time in his life, he answered, "Right now, there is nobody else."

That seemed to be what Tate was waiting for because he pushed up and rolled Logan to his back where he waited for Tate's next move.

Chapter Twelve

TATE STARED DOWN at the man whose naked body was perfectly aligned with his, wanting to look at all the muscles he was feeling. He also wanted to touch, and he was positive, while glancing at Logan's full mouth, that he wanted to take a good, long taste as well.

Logan's legs bent, and parted at the knees, so Tate took a moment to settle against the groin cradling him.

God, that feels really good.

It was so good that Tate nestled his hips against Logan's shaft—only this time, harder.

Tate continued to test out the new sensation as Logan's eyes slid closed, and his jaw clenched. Everything about this moment, with his new choice of bed partner, was so different, yet it was all essentially the same.

"Jesus, this…this feels fucking amazing." Tate applied more pressure to the downward grind of his hips.

Blazing blue eyes opened to focus on him as Logan's hands smoothed down his sides, causing Tate's body to shudder.

Logan rose up from the mattress to press his lips to Tate's ear. "We haven't even gotten to the best parts yet," he promised as he bit Tate's lobe, pushed his hips up, and really started to move.

The guy's hips were like a well-oiled machine. Not only did he press them firmly up against Tate's, but Logan then also arched his body at an angle, gliding his steel-like length, firmly along the sensitive underside of his own. It was all done in the exact right way to make Tate's eyes want to roll to the back of his fucking head.

With a strangled groan, Tate pulled back and shuffled down the bed a little, moving away from Logan. When he was kneeling between Logan's legs, he took a long look at all that was spread out in front of him.

Logan's feet remained planted on either side of him, and his erection pointed directly to the face that had first captured Tate's attention. Tate trailed his eyes over the rigid abdomen until he reached that face where he found an expression of heated lust looking back at him, and immediately, Tate began fisting his own cock.

That was when he also discovered that being watched by Logan ramped up his urge to come by around one hundred notches.

"Come back down here," Logan invited as his hands moved between his legs.

Tate's fist tensed around himself when Logan dipped his hand down to cup his own sac while he pressed his other palm against his shaft.

"Not just yet. I'm getting used to this view," Tate replied.

A grated curse left Logan's mouth as he elevated his hips off the bed, allowing Tate a better view. "You'd enjoy it even more from down here."

"I don't know," Tate pondered, watching Logan's hand fondle the flesh he was cradling. "This is working pretty good for me."

"Well, do you at least want some lube? It'd make things...easier." Logan teased his bottom lip with his tongue.

Nodding, Tate was almost disappointed when Logan had to stop what he had been doing as he rolled to his side, opened a drawer in the nightstand, and grabbed a small black bottle. Instead of handing it over, Logan kneeled in front of him and looked him in the eye. As the bottle was undone, Tate stopped moving.

And Logan told him, "Let me."

* * *

LOGAN POURED SOME of the cool liquid into his palm and shuffled in closer. "Here, let me."

Tate slowly let go of his straining erection.

Logan clasped the back of Tate's neck, drawing him in to take his lips. This time, there was absolutely no hesitation in the way Tate opened his mouth, or grasped his shoulders to steady himself while he granted the access Logan was demanding of him. Dipping his tongue inside the heat of Tate's mouth, Logan moved his hand forward and wrapped a firm fist around the base of him.

"Logan," Tate groaned, wrenching his head back as his eyes shut and his teeth came down to sink into his lower lip.

Logan stroked his slippery palm up Tate's engorged length, watching his face go from sexual torment to one of pure, unadulterated lust while his hips moved, driving his cock through Logan's fist.

"Open your eyes," Logan demanded as he continued to pump his hand up and down.

When Tate obeyed, and met Logan's stare, he could tell that Tate had finally let go of all thoughts and was just *feeling* in this moment.

"Good?"

"Fuck yes," Tate rasped, right before he cupped Logan's face and tackled him backward onto the bed.

When Logan's back hit the mattress, he managed to get his legs out from under him and parted enough before Tate landed back between them. Raising his knees on either side, he tightened them at Tate's waist while he continued to stroke the pulsating hardness in his hand.

Logan could feel his own cock restricted between their bodies as Tate took his mouth in a rough kiss, and his hips rocked forward on top of him. As a greedy tongue shoved between his lips to tangle with his own, Logan released his hold and shifted positions, so his own shaft came into direct contact with Tate's.

Just as he was about to encircle them together in his

hand, Tate lifted his mouth and pinned him with a stare.

"Why'd you stop?"

Logan wrapped his palm around them both, groaning as he gave a solid squeeze of his fist, and he was satisfied only when he heard a similar noise leave Tate.

"I wanted to give you your first cock rub, or as it's sometimes referred to, and my personal favorite, an *Ivy League* rub. You don't mind, do you?" Logan asked the inquisitive man above him.

Arching his pelvis, Logan pushed through his palm, creating a hot friction against Tate's sensitive erection.

"Oh, *holy shit*," Tate cursed out on a sharp breath.

"My sentiments exactly," Logan agreed and craned up to press his lips to Tate's. "Now, stick your tongue in my mouth and *feel* me."

* * *

TATE HAD NO problem with that. Pressing his mouth to Logan's, he plunged his tongue between the lips that had been driving him crazy since they'd first met as the raw pleasure of his first—*What did Logan call it? Ivy League rub? Of course, it sounds pretentious*—flooded through him.

Tate really wanted to see what was going on between his legs. "I want to…"

"You want to what?"

"I want to watch what you're doing to me." Tate emphasized by propelling his hips forward.

The fist around him disappeared, and he was rolled onto his back, a position he wasn't quite comfortable with yet in the presence of—*well, this man.*

"Um…"

"Relax, Tate." Logan lay on his side, angled toward him, smoothing his hand over and around Tate's eager cock. "Now, roll this way, would you? And turn your fucking brain off."

Tate did as he was told and turned to face Logan with a scowl.

"I should tell you, that expression on your face? It doesn't upset me. It just turns me on even more."

"Fuck you," Tate groused, feeling the hand around him tug hard enough to make him grit his teeth and hiss.

"Are you sure you're ready for *that* just yet?"

Tate, determined not to be provoked, slid his fingers into Logan's black hair and took a firm hold until he saw Logan wince. Pulling him the short distance between them, Tate told him, "Probably not, but maybe a good fucking would finally shut your goddamn mouth."

The palm around him stroked over his aroused flesh, and Tate angled his hips toward it, watching as a depraved smile spread across the lips only inches from him.

"You're welcome to try, but unless something's shoved in my mouth, I have to tell you, it's next to impossible to *ever* shut me up."

Tate decided to ignore that comment, and instead, he dropped his gaze down between them, prompting Logan to follow suit. The sight that greeted Tate took his breath away as much from the unfamiliarity of what he was seeing as the wonderfully salacious feelings he was experiencing.

Both of their engorged cocks were lined up against one another, dripping with excitement, and as Logan's hand clasped them both, Tate couldn't resist wrapping his own palm over the top.

Fascinated at what he was witnessing, Tate watched avidly as Logan's slightly longer shaft glided up against his and poked out from where their hands ended, rubbing against his own aching erection. As a rasping breath was torn from Tate's throat, Logan's free hand wrapped around his neck and pulled him forward.

"Seen enough?"

Tate glanced back to Logan, "Why?"

"Because I really want to come all over you."

Tate's breathing faltered at the thought, and he stilled Logan's hand. "What should I do?"

Logan leaned in, kissing him quickly. "Whatever feels good."

Tumbling to his back, Tate forgot his aversion to the position as he brought Logan up over him, stretching out, so their bodies were touching from chest to toe. When Logan's hand left him, Tate moaned from the loss until it came up to rest by his head, and Logan started to thrust against him in earnest.

Tate didn't know how he felt in that wholly defining moment.

As he lay beneath Logan, he concentrated on the hot ache between his legs and the amazing pressure Logan was grinding down onto his shaft, with every perfect stroke. At the same time, Tate was clinging to two strong arms supporting a man who was currently undulating his entire body against him.

That was when he realized that Logan was dominating him. Logan was clearly the one in control in this position. It was a position that Tate usually used with women, and as he focused on Logan licking that sexy lip of his, Tate admitted to himself, *I fucking love it.*

Tate pressed his head back into the pillow and bent his legs as Logan had earlier, so he could lift himself up to receive more of the full-bodied massage Logan was giving to him.

Over and over, Logan's brawny frame stroked his as Tate registered all the differences about him—the hair on his body, the power in his thighs, and the cut muscles of the abdomen— moving against his own. The moment was almost surreal. Reaching for a way to anchor himself to reality, Tate stretched his hand up to touch the coarse hair lining Logan's chiseled jaw.

He was in bed with a man and not just any man. Logan Mitchell, who was about as manly as Tate could find—

Does that bother me? No, Tate discovered, *it really fucking doesn't.*

* * *

WHILE LOGAN LOOKED down at Tate, and continued his sensual assault, he noticed something in his eyes change. The hand on his jaw moved toward his hair, and Tate took his mouth in a savage kiss, finally enjoying the full strength and power humming between them.

Logan returned the kiss equally as hungry, nipping at the lips under his before sliding his tongue inside to twist with the eager one that met him. With a stifled groan, Logan inched his way down Tate's body and kissed the guy's chest. Giving one of his nipples a quick lick, Logan continued his trail down to suck and taste the heated skin of Tate's ribs, navel, and finally his abs, just as he'd been fantasizing about.

Looking up at Tate from where he was now situated down between his thighs, Logan could feel the other man's erection pressing against his collarbone while his own was trapped firmly against the mattress, and all he could think was, *What a lucky bastard I am to have him in my bed.*

* * *

RAISING HIS HEAD off the pillow, Tate peered down his body at Logan. The guy was running his tongue all over the muscles of his stomach, and occasionally dipping it inside his navel. Staring at his erection pressed up against Logan's chest, he thought, *What a turn-on to see him using that mouth on me.*

A rumbled moan escaped from within, as Tate let his head fall back to the pillow, and a case of nerves kicked in. Logan's arms moved under his bent legs, and as his body was lifted off the mattress, Tate felt the tongue that had just been flirting with his navel lick up the underside of his shaft.

"Yes," he hissed out on a shaky breath.

With one hand, Tate reached down to grip the base of his cock, and pushed it up for Logan's insatiable mouth. Tate watched eagerly, as Logan glanced up at him and seductively swiped his tongue across the head and slit of his cock.

"Oh, fucking hell. Your mouth is a goddamn menace."

As the words left Tate's lips, Logan removed his mouth and hands and crawled up his body until he was back between Tate's thighs, and then Logan's mouth was kissing the hell out of him.

Tate felt a hand in his hair as their shafts became reacquainted in a deliciously hard and sticky slide. He held Logan's head with one hand and moved his other to his ass, and all Tate could think was, *I want him closer.* Digging his fingers into the firm ass cheek under his palm, he pulled Logan as near as he could get him.

Oh, would you look at that?

Tate's fingers clenched into the solid muscle again, and Logan's hips slammed into his.

He likes that.

And just as Tate thought it, Logan tore his mouth

away.

* * *

"DO THAT AGAIN," Logan requested on a harsh rush of air.

When Tate's fingers curled over his ass cheek, he'd thought that would be it. Just the fact that Tate was anywhere near his ass was getting him beyond excited—

And that he did it himself without me having to ask? Even better.

It had first happened in the bathroom, but he'd chalked that up to Tate being in shock from all the nudity—

Apparently not.

"You mean this?" Tate inquired, as he squeezed Logan's ass again.

Yes, you tease.

Logan let out a shaky laugh. "You're a cocktease, Tate Morrison. Who would have known?"

Logan was stunned that Tate was comfortable enough to laugh, and—*ah, fuck yeah*—grab his ass with both hands.

"Now, that's something I've never been accused of before."

"What? Being a tease?"

Tate brought his head up and kissed him quickly before whispering against his mouth, "No. Being a *cock*tease." He emphasized with a quick jab of his hips against Logan's.

Bracing his palms on either side of Tate, Logan watched him slowly lower his head back to the pillow as he continued to knead his ass.

"But you *have* been called a tease?"

Tate gave him an arrogant look he'd never seen before.

"I prefer to call it foreplay."

Logan shook his head and nudged his body against the groin cradling his not-so-patient erection. "I call it torture."

"Ah, don't lie," Tate admonished with the same shit-eating expression. "You like me playing with your ass. Every time I do, you buck your hips against me like you wish you were inside me."

Logan cursed loudly as Tate traced a curious finger across the top curve of his ass cheek, stopping at the base of his tailbone, hovering directly over the start of his crack.

"You're playing with fire," Logan warned the daring man under him.

"Am I?"

"Yes. Don't think I haven't noticed you like to tease and talk dirty."

Tate's sneaky finger drew flirty tiny circles over his tailbone. He was totally caught in the moment, aroused, and ready to try anything.

"Tate?" Logan asked in a voice that sounded as though he'd swallowed gravel.

"Yeah?" Tate's curious gaze focused on him.

"Give me your left hand."

Logan wasn't sure that he would, but apparently, the time for hesitation was over. Tate wanted this as much as he did. He raised his left hand, and Logan took it, bringing it to his lips where he sucked the two middle fingers into his mouth.

As he stared down at the man beneath him, with the messy curls and the fiery eyes, Logan swirled his tongue along the long digits until they were wet, and Tate's body was now writhing under his own.

When he released them, Tate's arm fell down to his side.

Logan lowered himself over him and whispered, "Now, stop being a fucking tease, and slide your fingers in my ass where I really want them."

Logan immediately felt the chest beneath him rise and fall rapidly against his own.

Tate turned his head on the pillow. "I don't know...what if I hurt you?"

Logan licked the corner of Tate's mouth. "You won't, but if you do, I just might like it."

* * *

TATE WASN'T SO sure about this. In the back of his mind, he'd known this would eventually come around, but he also had no clue what he was doing. He'd played with Diana a couple of times, but she'd never really liked it.

Moving his hand to the curve of Logan's ass, he took a moment to knead the firm flesh. The thrill he got from the satisfied sound escaping Logan's throat prompted him to act and push past any doubts he was having.

With both hands, Tate started to really put his whole effort into giving Logan what he wanted. Legs bent and raised, Tate curved up against the man above him, making sure they were fused at every conceivable point. As Tate did that, his mouth was busy being destroyed by a ravenous Logan, who was driving his groin across Tate's with a momentum that was quickly making him lose focus.

Slipping his wet fingers to the warm crease of Logan's ass, he separated one firm cheek from the other and heard a moan leave the chest that was now resting against his.

"Jesus, I knew getting you here would make me crazy. But you haven't even really touched me, and I'm hornier than I've ever been."

Tate took that moment to start teasing the soft, narrow channel between Logan's cheeks.

"I'm touching you now." He slowly pushed the tip of his fingers against the taut skin.

"You're fucking with me," Logan accused, his body tensing.

"No, I'm not. Well, maybe a little, but I'm learning." Tate moved his hand farther down until he was rubbing the pad of his fingers against the tightly puckered hole.

Logan began pushing his hips back toward them.

"So, am I doing this right?"

"Yes," Logan grunted.

Tate eased the tip of his finger past the sensitive ring of nerves, breaching it to his first knuckle.

"*Ah*, Tate. *Fuck*," Logan cursed.

Tate clenched his right hand against the ass cheek he was holding, and was about to ask if he was okay.

Until Logan grounded out, "More."

* * *

AS THE WORD left Logan's mouth, Tate's finger slid deeper inside him and—*ah, holy...yes*—the guy did it slowly. He could feel the sticky trail their pre-cum had left as Logan slid himself up and down Tate's abdomen.

His ass clenched around the intruding finger as it started to pull out, and just when he thought Tate would remove it altogether, the guy reversed his momentum, and this time, he pushed his finger back in with much more force than at first. With a loud hiss, Logan looked down at the face staring up at him intently. With his mouth opened and eyes wide with lustful curiosity, Tate was undeniably sexy, and Logan felt his balls start to tingle.

He finally had Tate in his bed. *He* had Tate, in his bed, underneath him, and Tate had his finger inside him. It was a miracle they'd even gotten this far, and by the hungry look Tate was aiming up at him, Logan didn't think he was going anywhere anytime soon.

Lowering his mouth, he took Tate's with his own as Logan reached down between them and curled his fingers around Tate's erection and began to work him.

Hell yeah, my life's sweet. My hand is wrapped around Tate, and Tate's finger is gloriously fucking me.

Logan couldn't think of anything better right at that moment until the single finger inside him was removed, and he felt two timidly probing against his hole. When he locked his eyes on Tate's, Logan thrust backward toward them.

Greedily, Logan's body chased after what it wanted, and as Tate's thick fingers slid roughly into his narrow channel, Logan watched the other man's shock and pleasure at the new power he now held.

"God, your ass is so tight inside. How will I even fit in there?"

"*Jesus,*" Logan swore and felt his climax threatening at the base of his spine.

"Do you like it when I do this?"

Tate widened his fingers inside him, and Logan almost lost it.

He wished he had time to let Tate really experiment and wriggle those long fingers around, but—

Fuck me. I don't have the goddamn patience.

The thought of Tate stretching him, so Tate could slide his iron-hard cock into his ass was all too much for Logan to take.

Unable to answer, Logan concentrated on the slight

burn inside him as Tate continued to palm his ass with one hand, and move the fingers of his other. Logan looked right back at the man and bared his teeth in a snarl before closing his eyes and arching forward. Shouting out Tate's name, his fist clasped the man's erection, and Logan felt his internal muscles clench around the two invading fingers as he finally came on a loud roar.

Shooting jets of sticky, warm come all over Tate's abdomen, Logan let out a long satisfied sigh as Tate punched his own hips forward through Logan's hand and called out his name. That was when he got to watch Tate's powerful climax as he came on a curse and a prayer all over him, and the sexy treasure trail Logan was once again fantasizing about licking.

Especially now while it's covered with both of our come.

Panting as if they had both just run for their lives, they stared unblinkingly at one another. Hands, fingers, and eyes were all still connected. Reluctantly, Logan removed his hand from around Tate, and drew his fingers over the line of hair that was now sticky with their pent-up frustration, and Tate started to laugh.

Logan glanced at him as he felt the thick fingers inside his body slowly withdraw.

"Jesus, Tate," Logan mumbled as they came free. "Something amusing?"

Tate placed his hands behind his head. "No. I was just thinking about how my whole life just changed because I enjoy having your tongue in my mouth, and my fingers in your ass."

Logan tried to control his own amusement, but really, the serious tone in which that had been delivered followed by the ironic brow Tate raised as he turned his head on the pillow was too fucking much.

"Well, I hate to be the one to say I told you so."

"Then, don't," Tate suggested, rolling his head back to stare at the ceiling.

Logan moved up on his elbow beside him and looked down with a wiry smile. "Okay, I won't."

"Good. Because I hate know-it-alls who brag."

"Well, shit, you're going to hate me then."

Logan didn't really mean it, he hoped, but when Tate's eyes met his, he wondered for a minute how he would feel if he ever did end up making Tate hate him.

"We'll see, won't we?"

At that ambiguous comment, Logan pushed, "What's that mean?"

"It means just that—we will see."

"As in, you're going to see me again?"

Rolling in toward him, Tate took Logan's lips with his own and kissed him. It was chaste but lingering, and as it ended, Tate smiled.

"You make me hard as soon as I think about you. I need to know if there's more to it. I want to know why I respond the way I do with you. If it's just the way you look…"

"You like how I look?"

"Shut up. You know everyone wants you. I guess I'm no different."

Logan ran a finger across Tate's smooth chest to his nipple, where he circled it. "Well, that's where you're wrong."

Tate's hand pressed Logan's flat over his chest. "And why's that?"

Logan wanted to tell him that he'd never wanted or pursued anyone as hard as him. He'd also never agreed to wait and go at any other speed than full throttle.

But as he looked at Tate, who was now staring at him, waiting with an I'm-not-going-to-believe-you look on his face, Logan ended with, "You just are," and then he told himself to be satisfied with the nod Tate gave him as he shifted and got out of the bed.

"Mind if I have that shower now?"

"Not at all," Logan told him.

Tate moved away from the bed. When he was almost at the bathroom door, Logan called out his name. Tate stopped and turned around, once again displaying that sexy, lean body, now covered with their come, and Logan felt the stirrings of desire in the root of his shaft.

"Yes?"

"How much did you like it?" he asked, even though he knew it was completely egotistical.

But when Tate's body responded, he was glad he'd asked.

"Enough that I'm thinking about it right now and

wanting to do it again. Will that do?"

Logan widened his legs provocatively, and Tate's eyes dropped to watch.

"That's perfect. Now, go take your shower before I forget you are new to all of this."

"I'm hardly a virgin."

Putting one arm behind his head and continuing to casually touch himself, Logan replied with a wink, "You are where I want to go. Now, go take a shower, Tate. You're too tempting right now, and I'm too horny."

Raising his palms, Tate backed into the shower, as he replied, "Okay. I'm going, I'm going," and then he firmly shut the door.

Chapter Thirteen

TATE CALCULATED THAT he'd been staring at the ceiling for a little over six hours, and it still was not producing any answers to his questions. First and foremost being, *What am I supposed to do now?*

Last night seemed so long ago, but every time he shut his eyes, he could see and feel all the things that had happened as if Logan were still lying beside him. He wasn't, of course, because Tate had left him back in his condo as soon as he'd been done in the shower.

He figured he'd held it altogether pretty well, casually strolling out of Logan's place as though he made out with men daily. But really, somewhere halfway through his shower, Tate had started to question everything he'd done since walking through Logan's front door only hours earlier.

Rolling over onto his side, Tate spotted the jacket thrown over the chair in the corner of his room and was immediately pulled back to the night before.

* * *

"YOU SURE YOU won't just stay?" Logan asked as they made their way to his front door.

Tate shrugged into his leather jacket and took the helmet from Logan as they stopped in the entryway.

"Nah, I think I should go." Tate turned toward the door and reached for the handle.

"Tate?"

Looking back over his shoulder, Tate saw something he'd not yet seen in Logan — concern.

"You okay?"

Am I? Probably not.

Making his way over to stand in front of Logan, Tate searched his face, trying to decide if anything about it would turn him off.

He came up with nothing.

"I'm fine."

"Just fine?" Logan questioned mindfully.

It was as if Logan could sense a change in Tate since before and after the shower.

"I just need some time to —"

"Worry? Convince yourself that this was all wrong?"

Stepping forward, Tate braced his left hand on the wall beside Logan's head. "I need to think, to process all of this."

"To freak out."

"Shut up."

Logan's gaze held firm as he assured, "It's okay to question things."

"I'm not."

"Not even a little?" Logan joked. Taking the sides of Tate's jacket and tugging him close, Logan flicked the side of Tate's mouth with the tip of his tongue. "I am."

"Liar." Tate slid his own tongue along that bottom lip he was fascinated with.

"I thought you were leaving?" Logan reminded.

"I am." Tate nibbled the top of Logan's mouth as he pushed his hips into him.

"Doesn't feel like it."

Lifting his lips, Tate pointed out, "That's because you're hanging on to me."

"Well, your mouth was kind of molesting mine."

Tate took his hand from the wall, bringing it down to cover Logan's right fist. "I just need some time to think, okay?"

"Okay." Logan released his hold on the leather. "But not too long. Tomorrow, lunch. It's your day off, right?"

"You memorized my schedule? How sweet."

"Fuck you."

"You already told me I wasn't ready for that, so keep your offers to yourself."

"So, it's an offer now? Not a threat? Look at you, warming to the idea. That makes me fucking hard."

Tate shook his head and stepped away to walk back to the door. Over his shoulder, he called out, "Give you an inch…"

"And I'll want six or seven more," Logan called back.

"Jesus." Tate laughed as he opened the door and left, knowing that he would be at lunch the next day. He just wasn't sure what would happen after that.

* * *

GRABBING HIS CELL phone from the nightstand, Tate
opened his contacts, found Logan's number, and decided a
text would be better than dealing with Logan's smart mouth
this early. Punching in—**Morning**—he hit Send and
wondered how quick of a response he would get. It was
almost immediate.

> **Logan: You're up early for a day off.**
> **Couldn't sleep.**
> **Logan: Should I apologize?**
> **Are you sorry?**
> **Logan: Good point. No.**
> **Then, don't apologize.**
> **Logan: Why couldn't you sleep?**
> **Busy head.**
> **Logan: Are YOU sorry?**

Tate must have stared at that text longer than he'd
thought because his phone vibrated again.

> **Logan: I keep telling you, turn your brain off, Tate.**
> **It's not that easy.**
> **Logan: Why?**
> **Because.**
> **Logan: I've told you already that because doesn't**
> **work for me. Why?**
> **Cause I can't stop wanting you & you're a GUY. I**
> **don't like guys. Ugh, I don't understand why**

I'm…shit…no one I know will understand.

> Logan: Like who?

Friends, family…

> Logan: Hang on, we're meeting family now?

Tate rolled his eyes at the question. The mere suggestion of something other than casual, and Logan changed from flirtatious and demanding, to sarcastic and blunt.

> Forget it.

> Logan: No, don't do that.

Do what?

> Logan: Get pissed-off. You're so stubborn.

And you're impossible.

> Logan: Are you scowling?

Tate pressed his fingers to the frown between his brows before lowering them back to the phone.

Yes.

> Logan: Hmm, we both know how I feel about that.

The same way you feel about everything?

> Logan: And how's that?

Horny.

> Logan: Around you, Tate? 24/7. Now, what time are you coming to get me for lunch?

I'm not coming to get you.

> Logan: So, you want ME to come to YOU? Give me your address. I'll be there ASAP.

Tate glanced around his bedroom and imagined Logan in his room a little too easily, and that had him

reaching for his thickening erection. But at the last second,
he stopped.

> I'll come to you.

> Logan: Thought you might.

> What will we tell people?

> Logan: People? Like who?

> I don't know. Anyone?

> Logan: Nothing. It's none of their business.

> But what if they ask?

> Logan: Then, I'll tell them to fuck off.

> What. If. They. Ask. Logan?

> Logan: They won't. But IF they do, I'll tell them
we're going to lunch to discuss your case.

> You're on the other side.

> Logan: Well, everyone knows I like to play both
sides.

> Not helping.

> Logan: Are you laughing or scowling?

> Both.

> Logan: Well fuck, now I want to kiss you.

Tate looked at that line and read it over and over
before another text came through.

> Logan: Would you let me?

> Yes.

> Logan: That was quick.

> That was honest.

> Logan: And THAT is sexy. Jesus, I can't be hard at
work. Okay, so tell me, what time will you be here?

Tate glanced at the clock on his bedside table to see it was now nine thirty.

How about 12:30?

Logan: How about 11:30?

You'll be hungry then?

Logan: Yes, but not for food. Tate?

Choosing to ignore the first part of the text, he replied with, **Yes?**

Logan: I can't stop thinking about your mouth.

And just that easy, Logan had him lying in bed with a grin.

Well, you better try.

Logan: Oh, I've tried, and I can't wait to again. See you at 11:30.

Yep. See ya.

Then, as quickly as it started, the connection ended.

A precursor of things to come? Tate wondered. *Only time will tell.*

* * *

LOGAN SAT BEHIND his desk with the phone to his ear and an eye on the clock.

Eleven fifteen, Tate should be here soon…if he shows.

He'll show. He said he would, and if Tate is anything, he's undeniably honest.

As he hung up from the call, Logan's door opened, and Cole stuck his head through the space, motioning in a way as if to ask, *Can I come in?*

Lifting his hand, Logan gestured for him to enter, and as the door was pushed farther open, Cole's face changed from serious to a shit-eating grin. Behind him stood Tate, looking anything but comfortable, and he was currently glaring at him around Cole's large frame.

I'm going to kill him, Logan thought as his eyes met his brother's.

As Cole strolled into the room, he unbuttoned his perfectly pressed black jacket and pushed his hands into his pockets.

Motherfucker is having a great time.

Tate, on the other hand, looked strained as if he were visiting the dentist. He moved two steps into the office and stayed as close to the far wall as possible.

What did Cole say to him?

Logan's attention moved to Cole, who was standing by the corner of his desk, *pretending* to look at the mail in the tray sitting there. It was so unlike his stuffed-shirt brother to be taking the time to nose around the way he was, so Logan knew something was up, and not in a good way. It was more like an I'm-about-to-fuck-with-you kind of way.

Logan carefully looked to Tate, who was staring at the red helmet in his hand and had his other one stuffed into his jeans. He was wearing a white shirt with that sexy leather jacket, and when Logan finally tore his focus away from him and turned back to Cole, his brother raised a brow and then opened his fucking mouth.

"Mr. Morrison said you called him about a business meeting today."

Logan narrowed his eyes on Cole as he pushed his chair back from the desk and stood. Buttoning his own jacket, he made his way around to where Cole was.

"Yes, that's right. We need to go over a few things."

Cole turned toward him, and pulled his mouth into a thin line while dropping several envelopes back into the tray on Logan's desk. Silently, he inclined his head and made his way back to the door and past Tate, who still hadn't said a word but was looking at Cole with no expression on his face at all.

Cole acknowledged him, opened the door, and at the last moment, looked back.

He then addressed Logan in a voice that made him want to throw something at him.

"Funny that I wasn't informed about this meeting since *I* handle Mrs. Morrison's—oh, I'm sorry, his ex's case."

Logan continued his *die-now* stare.

Cole turned to Tate and told him in his controlled-as-fuck voice—*asshole had that down to a T*—"If he doesn't give you all the answers you came in for, make sure you let me know, and I will try my hardest to clear things up."

"Get out, asshole," Logan advised, looking on his desk for something to throw.

"Going," Cole replied over his shoulder, leaving the office and closing the door behind him.

Logan stared across the wide space to where Tate

was pinning him with a fuck-you look if ever he'd seen one. Crossing his arms over his chest, Logan rested back against the desk behind him and perched his ass on the surface. He crossed his legs out in front of him and remained silent as Tate continued to fume. Just when Logan figured he would have to be the one to say something, Tate took a step forward.

"What did you tell him about us?" he spit out at Logan.

That right there, Logan knew, was Tate's biggest fear, presented to him like a giant fucking billboard. The thought of people knowing exactly what he'd done and enjoyed the night before—

Screw that, Logan thought. *Time for a reality check, Mr. Morrison.*

* * *

TATE WAS MORTIFIED, and he was pissed. He knew coming here was a terrible idea, but he'd stupidly let Logan and his silver tongue talk him into doing it anyway. As soon as he had stepped off the elevator and told the receptionist he was there to see Logan, Tate had been instructed to go straight through. Halfway inside the actual offices, he'd run into the tall blond guy, whose name he couldn't remember, that he'd first seen at the bar, and second, at his fucking ex-wife's meeting.

At first, Logan's partner had sized him up as if he

were trying to remember if he had forgotten something, and then Tate had watched his shrewd—*yes, they are definitely shrewd*— eyes almost smile, if it were possible for eyes to do so.

"How can I help you today, Mr. Morrison? I didn't realize we had a meeting?"

The minute that had come out of his mouth, Tate had known he was screwed. He'd stammered around his words and pretty much tripped all over the damn place until he'd finally told the lie that he was called by Logan.

Something on the guy's face had given away the fact that he knew Tate was lying, and Tate had felt the heat in his cheeks as he followed, like an obedient child, to Logan's office. As if that wasn't enough, the interaction that had then taken place inside the office had confirmed everything.

The guy knows about us for sure, and *that* angered Tate more than anything.

He was still fuming at Logan, who was casually propped up against his desk, with his arms crossed.

"What did you tell him about us?"

Still gripping his helmet in his hand, Tate was determined not to put it down because once he got an answer from the man opposite him, he was getting the hell out of there.

What he hadn't expected was for Logan to quietly push away from the desk and move forward.

Jesus, the man is enough to drive me out of my mind.

When Tate finally wanted him to say something, of

course, he kept his mouth shut.

"Would it have killed you for one minute of your life *not* to say something to everyone about who you're fucking?"

That was when Logan stopped directly in front of him and finally spoke, "I'm not fucking you…yet."

Tate scoffed and decided this would all be over after this conversation. *Might as well throw my own jab in.* "And now, you never will be."

Before Tate could anticipate the move, Logan reached out and grabbed the helmet from his hand. Dropping it on the floor beside them with a loud thump, he then moved in close, shoving Tate until his back hit the wall.

"You have a bad temper, Mr. Morrison."

"Get the hell off me," Tate snarled through his teeth.

"I'm not on you."

"Yes, you fucking are."

"I'm against you. There's a mighty big difference. Take last night, for example, when you were lying on my bed, naked, with your legs spread and me in between them—that was me *on* you."

Tate's breathing quickened as Logan raised a hand and placed it against the wall by his ear.

"Do you understand the difference?"

"I don't give a shit about specifics. Get. Off. Me."

Instead of listening to him, Logan placed his other hand by his head in the same position as his opposite one. "Shut up, Tate."

"Fuck—"

"*Don't* offer unless you're going to follow through," Logan warned.

Tate swore if he had agreed, Logan would have undone his pants right there.

"Now, if I remember correctly, you told me that I could kiss you the next time I saw you."

Clenching his fists by his sides, Tate felt his jaw tick. "I didn't say that, and that was before."

"Before?"

"Before I found out that you can't keep your fucking mouth shut!" he thundered.

Logan blinked at him from behind his glasses, his face a mask of annoyance. "And what exactly do you think I said?"

"Get off me," Tate reiterated.

"No. Talk," Logan said with a calmness that further infuriated Tate. "What do you think I said?"

"You obviously told your partner about us. I bet you had a real good laugh about the straight guy who's sleeping with you."

Logan brought his face to within an inch of Tate's, and Tate could feel his heart hammering inside his chest. Logan was so close that his black hair ghosted over Tate's nose as he shook his head from side to side before raising his face again and licking his tongue along his bottom lip.

Yeah, fuck me, I looked.

"Well, let's clear one thing up right now," Logan

stated in a lowered voice.

That should have probably indicated to Tate that Logan's temper was steadily climbing to the boiling point, where his was now teetering.

"That work partner of mine? His name is Cole, which I already told you, and he also happens to be my brother. He was merely speculating because I told him I wanted you when we were at the bar the other night. He's giving *me* shit, not you, and I didn't say a damn thing."

Tate was beyond listening at this point, and he just wanted to leave. He tried to take a step forward, only to have Logan muscle him back to the wall by connecting their hips.

Logan asked quietly, like the calm before a storm, "Is that all cleared up for you now?"

Refusing to budge, Tate lifted his chin, scowling back at the unyielding man in front of him.

"Jesus, you're pig-headed. Fine. If you aren't going to talk, you just stand there and try not to enjoy exactly what you're too fucking scared to admit to wanting."

As Logan moved his head toward him, Tate lifted his hand and placed his palm against the strong chest that had been naked against him last night, preventing that mouth from touching his own.

"You're so brave, aren't you, Logan? Walking around life, pretending to have all your shit straight. Oh, I'm sorry, that's the wrong word, right? Who are *you* trying to hide from? You're even more messed-up than I am. You want me to accept everything that's going on, but you can't even pick a side."

When the final word fell from his mouth, Logan's hand left the wall and circled his wrist in a viselike grip. "Stop talking, Tate."

"No."

"Stop. Fucking. Talking. You're really starting to piss me off."

"Too fucking bad." As Tate spit those three words out, he thought Logan looked like he wanted to punch *him* for a change. But instead of getting hit in the jaw, Logan pulled him off the wall, and in one quick move, turned him around.

Before Tate could even ask what the hell he was doing, Logan shoved him up against the wall front on, so Tate had to move his head to the side or break his nose, and favoring his nose, his left cheek met with the cool surface now in front of him. His left arm was twisted up behind his back, and Logan pressed his hips so tight against him that Tate could feel the outline of his cock, long and rigid.

"Now. Do I have your attention, Tate?" Logan rumbled against his right ear.

"Let me go," Tate demanded through a lump that had formed in his throat.

Logan punched his length against the crack of his ass, covered by the denim of his jeans.

"But you were the one who wanted me to pick a side," he reminded. "I pick this side for now. Fuck-me hair, broad shoulders, your hand trapped in mine with your ass cradling my cock."

Tate's body vibrated, and he hated the fact that he was really turned-on while being held prisoner against a fucking wall. "Yeah, for *now*, and only because you haven't had me. It's all about the thrill of the chase for you. Don't act like this is more than that."

Tate paused as Logan's free hand slid around his waist and moved down to his front zipper. Tate bucked his hips back, trying to get away, but only succeeded in getting his ass massaged by Logan's unyielding body.

"You'll get exactly what you want from me, then you'll be done, and I'll be stuck on my own, trying to decide what on earth I just let happen."

* * *

LOGAN COULD FEEL Tate's entire body shaking against his, and he wasn't sure if it was from lust or from the words the man had just spoken and was finally letting sink in. Tate was obviously conflicted by what he was feeling, yet he was still here, he'd still come to see him.

"Tate. I swear, I didn't say anything to Cole," Logan promised against the shell of his ear.

"But he knows, doesn't he? He knows something is going on?"

Logan allowed his hand to fondle the bulge he could feel behind Tate's jeans, and when Tate sighed and moved his hips against his palm, Logan felt his temperature spike.

"He's a smart guy, and he knows me." Logan admitted.

"So, in other words, he knows you get whoever you want between the sheets before you just throw them away."

"God, you're fucking mean when you want to be."

"I'm telling the truth. Are you?" Tate finally turned his head back to look Logan right in the eye.

Instead of answering, because he didn't know what to say, Logan took Tate's talkative mouth with his own and pushed his tongue inside. Pushing forward, he wedged his stiff cock against the jeans covering Tate's firm ass and trapped his own hand against the wall.

"Oh *fuck*," Tate cursed as he tore his mouth free. "Touch me. No...no...don't. Christ, I don't know, Logan. I don't fucking know what I want!"

Logan massaged his hand up the zipper to the button of Tate's jeans. "Yes, you do," he challenged gently, trying to calm the man pressed back against him, as he undid the button and slowly pulled the zipper down. "You still don't get it, do you, Tate? I'm not looking anywhere but at you."

Dipping his hand between the denim he'd parted, Logan thought he would feel cotton, but as his fingers brushed over wiry hair, he groaned out loud. "Commando? You came to see me fucking commando?"

Tate's hard stare locked with his as Logan's hand dug into the jeans. He watched Tate's mouth part and a shaky breath leave him, as Logan's fingers grazed the plump, wet head of the cock trapped inside the material. Unable to help himself, Logan ground against Tate and slid his hand farther inside, so he could wrap his fingers around Tate's iron-hard erection.

Tate powered back against him. "No, stop. Not in here, not at your office."

Logan's hand and hips stilled as he looked at the eyes now staring at him. They were full of desire, frustration, and once again, that annoying fucking emotion—confusion.

"Stop thinking so much. Tell me, what do you *want*?" Logan held his breath as he waited for Tate's frank response.

"You. Everything else aside, I still want you."

Removing his hand from Tate's jeans, Logan also released the arm he had been holding at Tate's back, and as Tate turned to face him, Logan cradled his face with his hands and pressed his mouth to his, kissing him fervently.

When he felt Tate's hands on his waist, Logan moaned and angled his head to stroke his tongue against the other man's in a kiss that bordered sweet as much as it did hot. As Logan felt his control and desire to stop climbing, he pulled back.

Still holding Tate's face, he told him, "Then, go with that. Forget everything else and see where that leads you."

With Tate's anger seemingly kissed out of him, his lips curved slowly into a half-smile. "It led me here, to your office, and right into a hell of a lot of trouble."

"And that's *exactly* why you should follow where it

leads."

Logan dropped his hands from Tate's face and took a step back. As he did, his vision trailed down to the parted denim, and he shook his head.

"Zip up, Commando, or I'm about to find out real quick how bad this hardwood would be on my knees."

"So, lunch?" Tate queried, zipping his jeans.

"If we go to lunch, I won't be coming back to the office."

"Okay…"

"Dinner?" Logan suggested.

Tate seemed stumped. "Actual dinner? As in, food? Because I was under the impression I'd eat when I got here."

Logan walked around his desk and took a seat. Sitting back in his chair, he pressed a hand against the erection that was still apparent but was finally starting to behave. He then reached up to take off his glasses before he rubbed the bridge of his nose.

"Actual dinner. Tell me where to meet."

Tate thought about where they could go, and walked over to stand in front of the desk. "O'Malley's?"

"The pub?"

"Yeah, the pub. Sound okay to you?"

Logan nodded and put his glasses back on. "What time?"

Tate shrugged as he offered, "Eight?"

"Make it nine, so I can get home and shower."

As the word left his mouth, he saw Tate's eyes

darken and knew he was recollecting the last time they had been together in his bathroom.

"Okay," Tate agreed as he walked backward, still focused on where Logan was sitting in his chair.

Tate bent down, picked up his helmet, and then tilted his head to the side before shaking it.

The expression made Logan curious, so he had to ask, "What?"

"You look sexy, sitting there all professional, in your suit and glasses behind that desk."

Well, I fucking asked for it. Tate's lack of subterfuge will eventually get me into a shit-ton of trouble, Logan thought as Commando turned and left his office.

Chapter Fourteen

LOGAN GOT THERE first, which he hadn't expected, although he probably should have based off his previous meetings with Tate. The guy was always running around five minutes late. Making his way into the pub, Logan was happy to see that not too many people were about. Monday night wasn't exactly the busiest night of the week.

Logan had opted to go casual, wearing some comfortable jeans and a white button-down shirt. He'd brought a jacket with him, but really, it wasn't even cool tonight. Taking a booth against the wall, he made sure to slide into the side facing the door, and he sat, waiting.

He was waiting on a date. *Hell, when did that happen? When I met Tate,* he thought with an ironic shake of his head.

Usually, by now, Logan would have chased, caught, and released. But with Tate, he was still chasing, and who knew if he'd ever catch him. The guy was constantly dodging him, like a startled animal. One minute, Tate was paralyzed, and the next, he was running for his life. But there were those couple of occasions when Logan had caught him, and—*damn, if the man wasn't worth the time*—he was delicious.

Just as the thought entered his mind, the pub door opened, and Tate stepped through the entryway. Logan's body went on high alert as he watched the object of his attention scan the dim space. He supposed he could stand and wave him over, but—well, he didn't. Logan was too busy enjoying his unfettered view.

Tate was wearing jeans, just like himself, but with a short-sleeved black shirt that came into view as he shrugged out of the leather he wore everywhere.

I need to see him on that bike.

Tate scanned the pub and when he found him, started to make his way toward their booth. As his long legs ate up the space between them, Logan felt his cock twitch in anticipation of what was going to happen later—*well, hopefully.*

Tate stopped by the empty seat and threw his jacket into the corner. Sliding in, opposite him, Logan felt their knees bump as Tate seemed to relax into the wide straddle he favored.

"Sorry, I'm late. Got held up."

"What do I care if you're a little late? This way, I get to watch you walk in."

Tate chuckled as he snagged the small menu on the table. "Well, that's a first. Usually, I get my ass handed to me for being late."

Logan knew exactly who he was referring to after the exchange he'd witnessed between Tate and his ex, and not being one to beat around the bush, he decided to just lay it out on the table. "I'm not your ex, Tate. I'm not going to wonder where you are or bitch you out if you're five minutes late. Now, if you're an hour late, you better have a damn good excuse or at least offer to make it up to me on your knees."

Tate placed a hand on top of the table and tapped his fingers in a quiet tattoo against the wood.

"As in…" Tate joked but stopped on the follow-through.

"As in? Go on, ask."

Tate's mouth kicked up at the edges. "You mean, as in, me giving you a blow job?"

Logan raised his brows. "Shocking, isn't it? That I'm so easily appeased."

Tate regarded him in a way that made Logan's cock extremely excited.

"What are you thinking?"

Raising a hand, Tate ran it through his hair and shrugged. "I was wondering if I'd be any good at it or if I'd even like it."

Logan couldn't help the rumble of laughter before he told Tate quite adamantly, "You could be the worst in the world at giving head, but the fact that *you* would be the one with your lips around me…" he savored the thought for a second, and then winked at Tate, "*Mmm*, I'd go out of my fucking mind."

Now knowing Tate, for the tease that he was, Logan wasn't shocked when Tate licked his lips, the idea obviously growing on him.

"Really?"

"Really," Logan assured as he lowered his hand under the table to adjust his agreeable cock.

He was so busy ogling Tate that Logan didn't even notice the pretty brunette who stopped beside him and greeted them both.

"Hey, guys. How are you doing tonight?"

Tate's focus moved from him and shifted to the waitress, and then the wide smile, the one Logan hadn't seen since that first night they'd met, spread across his mouth. It was flirtatious, open, and so fucking sexy.

"Good, thanks. You?" Tate asked conversationally.

The waitress turned her body toward him, and Logan could tell she was giving him her best I'm-interested look, and for one quick moment, Logan could have sworn he felt—

Shit...jealous.

"I'm *very* good."

Logan rolled his eyes and smiled when he felt Tate's knee brush against his own, remaining and connecting them beneath the table.

"What can I get you to drink?" she continued, talking only to Tate.

Logan sat patiently, and watched the man opposite him.

Tate focused on the woman and told her, relaxed as he pleased, "I'll have a Corona, and he'll have a blow job, thanks."

The knee under the table pressed firmly against his own as Tate's eyes met his, and the woman beside Logan turned to finally look down at him, giving a small laugh.

"We don't get too many guys asking for that. You got a sweet tooth?"

Not one to easily embarrass, Logan felt a wicked grin curve his lips. "Nah, not particularly, but this guy owes me one."

Quickly, she looked to Tate, whose attention was now solely on him. Logan was hard-pressed not to laugh when he felt a heel jab down onto his foot.

"I made him try one the other night, you know, as a joke?" Logan informed the woman, as he heard Tate cough from across the table. "You okay?"

"Yes," Tate managed.

Logan was pleased to note that Tate now looked flushed and a lot less cocky about his little joke that had been turned back on him.

"Oh, I see. So, this is payback for buying a girlie drink, huh? Well, don't worry, I'll make sure it's a good one."

Logan touched the tip of his tongue to his top lip and lowered his voice as he agreed suggestively, "Oh, I'm sure you will."

With a light, airy giggle, she turned and walked away from the booth, leaving Logan staring across at the man currently shaking his head.

"What?" he asked.

Tate leaned back in the booth, and his knee pressed back against Logan's again. "You can't help yourself, can you?"

Placing his arm along the back of the seat, Logan angled himself, so he was comfortable. "Can't help, what?"

"The sex. It just comes out of your mouth—with everyone."

"You started it. A blow job? You need to try better than that to embarrass me."

"I wasn't trying to embarrass you."

"Yes, you were, but it didn't work. All it did was make me think about putting my cock into your mouth."

Tate shook his head again with a chuckle. "I've never met anyone like you."

"Oh?" Logan wanted to know more but shelved his curiosity as he saw the waitress coming back toward them with a tall bottle stuffed with lime and a short shot glass with—

Jesus, whipped cream. Ugh.

She placed them down, the bottle first, and as Tate reached out to take it, she made sure their fingers connected. Logan knew because—

Hell, I'm watching her with him like a jealous boyfriend.

"Thanks." Tate smiled as he took the beer.

She then turned to Logan and placed his shot glass down. "And here's yours. You do know the traditional way to...drink this, don't you?"

Logan could think of around one-hundred different, inappropriate responses to that, but instead of saying them, he played it dumb. "No. How am I supposed to drink it?"

The waitress started to explain, but Logan got caught up in Tate pushing his lime into the beer with his long index finger. All of a sudden, he had a very clear recollection of that finger elsewhere, and Logan found it difficult to even comprehend what the woman beside him was rattling on about until she said, "So, no hands, just a wide open mouth. Most put their hands behind their back."

Logan nodded his head as if pondering her suggestion, then asked. "But what's a good blow job without hands?"

He watched her face go from a lovely pale white to a bright shade of red as she lowered her eyes.

She floundered around a little and before replying, "Ah, yes…well, of course, hands are good too, for other things."

Quickly, she looked back to Tate just as Logan did, and they both found him sitting back in the booth, cradling his beer. As their eyes connected, Tate lifted the bottle, put it to his sexy mouth, and took a swig of the beer without saying a damn thing. But Logan knew Tate was thinking about his own recent experience, concerning mouths, hands, and —

Yes sir, blow jobs.

"Well, if that's all," she muttered, about to walk away.

"Actually, can I get the cheeseburger medium well, with fries?" Logan asked and then also added, "And a Heineken."

She nodded before turning to Tate for his order.

"I'll have the wings, thanks."

"Mild or hot?"

He flicked his glance to Logan and looked at—*my mouth, fucking tease*—before saying, "Hot, please."

* * *

TATE STARED OVER at Logan, who seemed determined to shake the very foundation he was used to standing on. Everything about him called to Tate—from the relaxed way he was lounging back in the booth to the I'm-cool-and-collected arm he had resting along the back of the seat. Not to mention, those blue eyes, minus the glasses, that were constantly watching him. The man was completely charismatic, and Tate had a hard-on for him that just would not quit.

"What are you thinking about?" Logan questioned as their waitress walked away.

Deciding he needed to just have this conversation and get it out on the table, Tate replied with, "You."

"What about me?"

"I want to know where you see this"—Tate indicated between them—"going. Is this just a quick hook-up to you? Because...I don't know. I can't just change my whole fucking life for a night in your bed."

"How about for two?" Logan remarked flippantly.

"How about you get serious for a moment?"

Logan brought his arm down and moved to lean across the table. "I want you. Tell me how I can have you."

Tate brought the beer to his mouth and took another swig of the contents. Slowly placing it back down, he brushed his knee against the leg pressed on the inside of his own. "For a night?"

Logan eyed him hungrily, and offered, "For as long as you want."

With that, Logan bent his torso down over the table with his hands behind his back and opened his lips wide over the shot glass in front of him.

Tate watched with rapt attention, as Logan lifted his head and swallowed the sweet contents of the drink in one gulp. Reaching up with one hand, Logan took the glass from between his lips, but before he lowered it, he made sure to stick his tongue as far into it as he could, licking clean all of the creamy liquid from the inside. When done, he placed it down on the table, brushed his thumb along his bottom lip, and smirked.

Tate was equally frustrated and turned-on by what Logan had just done, but at the same time, he was still unsure of everything he was feeling. So, he remained silent as Logan casually sat back and once again, placed his hand along the seat.

"Hmm, always gotta make sure you lick up every

last drop. Don't want to waste the end of a good blow job."

Tate cleared his throat, pulling himself out of the sexual haze he was in and blinked across at him. "Is that right?"

"Well, that's my rule anyway."

"To lick up every last drop?"

"Of you?" Logan asked with a cocky wink. "Count on it."

Stretching out both hands, Tate shuffled the bottle back and forth between them as he chewed on his lip.

"Okay, let's come back to that later. How about you tell me a little about yourself?" Logan prompted.

Tate couldn't help the burst of laughter that left him.

Logan raised a brow. "What's so funny?"

"I was just thinking about how long it's been since I've gone on a date."

"So, this is a date?"

Tate shifted in his seat and looked around to make sure no one was listening. "Well, isn't it?"

"I don't know. Do I get to kiss you at the end?"

"Logan, come on, be serious."

"I am being serious."

Tate lifted the bottle again, and this time, he finished the beer as he waited for a better answer than what he'd just been given.

Then, Logan gave it to him. "Yeah, it's a date. I'm out with someone I find extremely attractive. I'm going to buy him dinner, and hopefully, walk him outside and kiss him good night."

"Walk me outside, huh? In case I get mugged in the big, dark, scary alley?"

Logan's eyelids lowered until the look he was aiming Tate's way lit a fire in his stomach and made his cock weep.

"No. So, I can kiss your fucking brains out and then watch you get on your bike and drive away. I've been fantasizing about seeing you straddled over that vibrating piece of metal since you walked into the bar with your helmet."

"Really?"

"Yes, really. You have the whole sexy-rebel thing down."

Tate shook his head. "Rebel? Not me. I'm straight as they come."

Logan barked out a teasing laugh. "That's way too easy. You can't just hand me lines like that and expect me to sit here silently."

"I would never expect you to be silent—anywhere. Tell me something about yourself. You said Cole's your brother? Do you have any other brothers or sisters?"

Logan shook his head as the waitress appeared with their food. She slid the wings down in front of Tate and placed the cheeseburger down for Logan.

"Would you like another beer?"

He was about to answer when Logan spoke up, "Yeah, grab him one, would you, hon?"

She smiled down at Logan before spinning to walk

away.

"I *can* order a beer, you know," Tate pointed out.

"Yeah, but then I have to watch her drool all over you."

"Jealous?" Tate joked, grabbing a piece of celery and dunking it into the bleu cheese dressing.

"Yes. I want you drooling all over me."

Baring his teeth in a grin, Tate bit down on the vegetable and chewed slowly.

"Cole is my only sibling, to answer your question. And he's my half brother. We met when he turned eighteen."

Bringing the celery back to his mouth, Tate finished it. "Why eighteen? Or is that too personal?"

Logan grabbed the ketchup bottle, shook it a few times, and then put some near his fries before dipping one into the sauce, and stuffing it into his mouth.

"Hungry?" Tate questioned around a mouthful.

"I'm fucking starving. I missed lunch, remember?"

Tate picked up a wing, pushed it into the blue cheese, and then brought it to his mouth. After taking several bites, he dropped the bone back onto the plate, and then he began to lick his fingers one by one. Once they were all clean, he looked back across the table to find Logan had zeroed in on the finger closest to his mouth. Feeling relaxed and playful, Tate took a moment to suck that one back into his mouth and make a big show of it.

Logan coughed and shifted on his seat before

focusing once again.

"I lived with my mother. She had a relationship…well, affair, I guess you would call it, with our dad when Cole's mom was pregnant. He remained married to Cole's mother, and they lived as one big, happy family."

"Oh…wow."

"Yeah. Great guy, huh? Such a shame he's dead."

Tate could tell by the clipped way Logan had finished that particular story that the subject was now closed. Trying to think of something to say, he decided that eating seemed like a good fallback plan when Logan picked up his burger and took a bite.

Silence. Sometimes it was much more effective at solidifying a bond than all the talk in the world.

* * *

LOGAN SAT QUIETLY as he took a third bite of his burger, and internally he cursed at himself for being a giant asshole. It wasn't Tate's fault that he'd just happened to ask him the one thing that pushed all his buttons.

He could tell Tate was trying to think of something to say, but he seemed to have given up for the moment. When the waitress appeared with two more beers, neither of them acknowledged her. This time, they were just sitting in brooding silence.

Come on, man, snap the fuck out of it. You finally have him sitting across from you, and you're screwing this up!

Lifting his beer to his lips, Logan opened his mouth and continued on the fucking stupid route of doing everything wrong this evening. "So, how long were you married?"

Tate had been halfway to bringing a wing to his lips but paused and glanced at Logan, lowering it back down to the plate. Wiping his hands on a napkin, Tate slowly picked up his Corona and took a long gulp.

"Sorry," Logan told him. "That's none of my business."

Rubbing a hand over his face, Logan thought, *Why am I screwing this up so badly? I'm never like this, especially with people I want in my bed. Get with the program, Mitchell.*

"Four years."

The words came out like a curse, and as Logan met Tate's eyes across the table, Tate continued, "I spent three and a half of them trying to work out how to leave."

"And in the end?" Logan asked curiously.

"I woke up one morning, opened the front door, and walked out."

"Just like that, huh?"

Nodding, Tate answered, "Just like that."

"She's an idiot."

Tate picked up the wing that he'd put down. "Why do you say that?"

Logan watched him move his left hand over to the blue cheese sauce where he dipped the chicken in and then brought it up to his mouth.

"Because I'd never let you just walk out."

Tate swallowed once before he challenged, "What would you do instead?"

Logan shrugged. "Probably fight with you, and then drag you to the bedroom."

"Is that how you've solved all of your past relationships? I hate to point this out, but you're single."

"I've never been in a relationship," Logan admitted, picking up a french fry.

"Ever?"

"Ever," he confirmed and stuffed the potato in his mouth.

Tate grabbed his beer again and took a long gulp before managing, "Wow."

Not wanting to make a huge deal out of it, Logan explained, "I just wasn't interested."

Tate, of course, was not letting him get away with that. "And now?"

"Now?" Logan repeated back, like he hadn't understood the question.

"Yeah, now?"

Logan felt a genuine smile cross his lips as he very openly inspected every inch of Tate that was visible. "Now, I'm really fucking interested."

"I don't know about all of this, Logan."

Logan felt his heart pounding in his chest as he pushed his plate aside and leaned across the table toward the man currently holding—

What exactly…my happiness? In his hands.

"Look, I know you probably think I'm the worst choice you could ever make."

Tate said nothing to disagree with that, but ran a hand up through his hair.

"But you already know all the bad shit about me. Come on, what else is worrying you?"

"Really? You're asking me that?" Tate questioned incredulously almost as though he thought Logan was crazy. "Let me list it for you. Let's say I do this, *all* of this, and for a week, you're happy, content, and you get what you want. We continue, and my coworkers start asking questions, my soon-to-be-ex-wife somehow finds out, and God forbid, my family does, too. Then, you get bored a week later and say, 'I'm sorry, Tate, but it was fun.' *That's* all that's worrying me—the entire upheaval of my life. And all because you want to sleep with me."

Logan sat back, and this time, he straddled his legs out and around Tate's before he pulled them in, trapping the other man's between his own.

"First off, I would never do that to you."

"How do I know that?" Tate demanded.

"You don't. You'd have to trust me."

"Do you know how ridiculous that sounds? I'm sorry, but do you know what I see when I look at you?"

Logan was pretty sure that this was not going to be flattering, but he went ahead and asked anyway, "No. What do you see?"

"I see reckless. I see untrustworthy. I see someone that I'm terrified to take a risk on because I don't know if he'll be there to grab my hand if I jump off that cliff." Pausing, Tate leaned in. "You said earlier that I'm a rebel. Well, I'm not. I'm boring, I'm everyday normal, and I haven't dated since I left my wife. But you came along, and now, I don't know what to think."

"So, that's it then? Tate, every decision, whether it's between a man and a woman or two men, always comes with risks. To think otherwise is naive, and you're not that. But I can't give you guarantees. I can only give you my word, and if that's not enough…"

Tate shut his eyes for a second, and Logan had to physically stop himself from reaching across the table to try to soothe the man.

"If that's not enough," he started again, "then why are we even here?" Logan wanted to know as his temper rose.

Tate peered back at him. "Because you're the first person who has made me *feel* since I walked away from that disaster. And you're the *only* person that I think about when I can't fucking sleep at night."

Logan pushed his hand up through his hair, frustrated. "Okay then, so now what?"

"I don't know." Tate shrugged and threw his napkin on the table.

"Tate?" Logan waited patiently for Tate to look at him. "Tell me what you want from me, from this?"

Tate seemed to mull over the question before answering, "I want you to either stop coming by the bar, or..."

Logan grasped at the word now hanging between them. "Or?"

"Or prove me wrong."

Breathing out in relief, Logan sat forward, placing his arms on the table. "And how do I do that?"

"I'm not sure. But maybe *you* should try something new," Tate suggested.

Logan raised his hand for the check while asking, "Such as?"

Then, with determination, Tate told him, "How about trying to see where this goes with me—and only me?"

Chapter Fifteen

TATE SAT IN SILENCE as Logan paid the bill, and then
stood, looking down to where he was still sitting.

"You ready?"

Ready for what? Tate grabbed his jacket and slid out of
the booth.

Logan still hadn't said a word about what they'd just
discussed. Sure, Tate had thrown out the scary idea of seeing
how things between them would progress, and as predicted,
Logan hadn't said more than a few words. He might have
said he was interested, but as Tate had suspected, the
actuality of it had made Logan uneasy.

Tate hadn't meant to issue that particular request,
especially tonight, but before he had known it, the words
had tumbled out of his mouth. After all, the thought of
going any further down such an unfamiliar road, with
someone who could just up and leave, was really stressing
him out.

Standing, he made sure to keep his eyes on the man
waiting on him. Without a word, Tate turned and made his
way to the door. Pushing it open, he didn't bother turning
back to see if Logan was following him. He knew that he

was.

Making his way to the narrow alley between the buildings, Tate turned to walk down to the tiny parking lot where he had parked his bike. Halfway there, he felt a firm hand grab his arm and turn him around. Tate knew what was coming, or thought he did, as he was pulled to a stop, facing Logan.

"So, if I say yes, that would make you, what?"

Tate could hear the cars driving by on the main road in front of O'Malley's, and as he searched the face covered by shadows, he tried different words out in his head. *Boyfriend? Am I okay with having a boyfriend? Or what? A lover? A male lover?* It would have been alarming and slightly comical if he didn't want it as much as he now realized he did.

"I thought you didn't like labels," was what Tate finally said.

Logan stepped closer and moved him back farther into the shadows. "I'm warming to one with you."

"I'm serious, Logan. I don't think I'm…" Tate trailed off his jumbled thoughts as rough bricks came up against his back.

Logan's right leg moved between both of his as he pressed in close to Tate and caressed his cheeks, sliding his hands into his hair. Tate winced at the tight hold Logan had taken as he lowered his head until their lips were only an inch apart.

"You don't think, what? I don't like labels, Tate. But I

am being serious about trying this out. If I weren't, I would have paid the bill and told you to fuck off."

Tate blinked several times, dropped his eyes to Logan's mouth, and let his hands drift to Logan's waist where he slid them around to the denim covering his ass.

"You would never tell me to fuck off," Tate murmured, much more confidently as he squeezed the ass in his hands, rocking his erection against the one Logan was now sporting.

"I wouldn't, huh?"

Tate realized that this was the first time he'd initiated things, and as Logan started to really react, he felt a hot sexual thrill skate up his spine. He was anticipating what was yet to come when they got to his place—alone.

"Nope. You want me too bad."

As the last word slipped past his lips, Tate's mouth was crushed in a fierce kiss that had his eyes sliding closed and his breath coming fast. Groaning into the parted mouth above his, Tate dug his fingers into Logan's ass and moved up onto his toes to get closer to the man currently obliterating every thought he had.

Logan wasn't standing idle either. The leg between Tate's thighs moved higher, and as he felt the added pressure to his aching balls, Tate brought his free hand up to Logan's face. When the hair scratched under his palm, Tate's craving for the man tripled as he was reminded of exactly whom he was kissing.

Taking his hand from Logan's ass, Tate quickly

slipped it between them and pressed his palm against the front of Logan's jeans. Curling his fingers around the erection he could feel, Tate began to massage the rigid length.

"Yes," Logan sighed against his lips. "That left hand is such a turn-on, who knew."

Tate chuckled and then took a moment to bite Logan's lip as he dared to ask, "Want to come home with me?"

Logan chased his mouth with his tongue as Tate teased and pulled his head back, all the while continuing to squeeze and stroke him.

"You fucking flirt," Logan accused.

"You love it."

Tate felt and heard the struggle in Logan as his breath caught, and his hips continued to move against Tate's hand.

"So, we're really going to try this, huh?" he asked.

Tate focused and confirmed, "I think so. That means you don't give this"—for emphasis, he stroked the bulge in Logan's jeans—"to anyone else."

Abruptly, Tate found his hand brought up and trapped by his head against the bricks with Logan pressed flush against him. Tate always forgot how strong the guy was until he pulled shit like this.

"So, that means I get to give it to you?"

Tate's heart thundered as he thought of the implications behind that one question and what it meant to

him.

"For the most part," he agreed, hoping that was enough for the moment.

As Logan watched him closely, Tate felt his nerves trickling back in. "I want you in my bed, the same bed I lie in at night, thinking about you, but I don't think I'm ready for *that* just yet."

"Then, what are you ready for?"

"I'm ready to admit that I'm extremely attracted to you and that I can't stop thinking about the way you looked lying in your bed, naked and hard—so damn hard."

"Fuck me, Tate," Logan cursed.

Tate picked up the words and answered on a raspy promise, "That, too. I want to do that, too."

Tate carefully observed Logan as his brow furrowed and he released him. Thinking he'd said something wrong, Tate remained silent and waited.

"What's your address?"

"Huh?" was Tate's brilliant response.

"Your address? I need it to find your place."

"No, you don't," Tate told him. "You're gonna come with me."

"And how am I going to do that?"

"I'll drive us home."

"On your bike?"

Tate rolled his eyes. "No, on my magic carpet."

"I'm not getting on the back of your bike, like some chick."

Tate shrugged and pushed Logan away as he turned and started to walk down the alley toward the parking lot.

"So, you'd give up the chance to be pressed up against my ass the whole way home?" he called out and started to laugh when he heard footsteps behind him.

Logan muttered, "Ah, hell."

* * *

LOGAN STOOD IN front of the shiny, black motorcycle Tate stopped beside.

He shook his head. "No way."

He watched cautiously as Tate moved to the back of the bike and removed his red helmet and then—*yeah, just fucking perfect*—a black one.

"What?" he asked Logan as if he didn't see the problem.

"The seat on that thing is tiny. I'll just take a taxi."

Tate walked back to him and thrust the black helmet against his stomach.

"Suck it up, Logan, and put the damn helmet on."

Logan glared at Tate as he put his jacket on and then pulled the red helmet down over his head. As he flipped the visor up, Logan arched a brow and looked at the black one in his hand.

"How far is your place?"

"About ten minutes."

"Ten minutes is long enough for me to fall off and

lose an arm or leg."

"Don't you trust me?"

Grumbling to himself, his eyes followed Tate as he moved back to the bike, swung his jean-clad leg over the seat, and straddled the wicked-looking piece of machinery.

Finally relenting, knowing that nothing would keep him from getting up close and personal with the man currently sitting with his hands resting on his thighs, Logan shoved the stupid helmet on his head and moved over to the bike.

"If I die, I just want you to know that you have never looked hotter than you do right now, and that is the only reason I'm about to risk my life."

Tate raised a hand, and before he shut the visor, he promised, "I'll look even hotter in fifteen minutes when I'm naked. So, quit bitching, and get on the bike, Logan."

"Fuck you," he responded, climbing onto the back of the bike and clutching the leather waist in front of him.

Tate turned over the ignition, and the bike rumbled to life. His thighs brushed up against Tate's, and as he slid farther down on the seat, his cock nestled up against the man bending over in front of him.

Huh, this might not be so bad after all.

That was, until Tate put his foot on the gas, and the bike actually moved.

* * *

TEN MINUTES LATER, and they were at their destination. Tate pulled into the parking garage, shut off the engine, and felt Logan's hands move to his thighs and then in between.

"You can get off now," Tate informed as he lifted his hands to remove his helmet.

He heard a muffled sound and turned toward his handsy passenger. Reaching out, he pushed the visor up on Logan's headgear.

"What was that?" he asked.

Logan's right hand found his groin, and he repeated his words from a moment before. "That's what I'm trying to do—get off."

Choosing to ignore him the best he could, Tate asked, "It wasn't so bad, was it?"

Logan hummed a little in his throat. "This is the best part."

"Get off the bike, Logan, so we can go upstairs."

Apparently, Tate didn't need to tell him twice. Logan released him and moved back to swing his long leg up and over the seat. Once he was off, he removed his helmet, and Tate's mouth twitched at the usually perfect hair that was now a mess on top of his head. Tate followed Logan's move, removing his headgear, and once the bike was secured, he ran a hand through his own hair and noticed Logan doing the same as they made their way over to the elevator.

When it opened and they stepped inside, Logan looked at him from where he was standing. "So…"

"So…" Tate returned.

"I started *seeing* someone tonight. Did you know that?" Logan quipped.

"I didn't think you were into that kind of thing."

Logan winked. Tate's cock throbbed. "Oh, I can't *wait* to be into this...I think this guy's different."

* * *

LOGAN KNEW HE didn't need to say those words to get what he wanted, but it was imperative to him that Tate knew.

"And why is he different?"

Good fucking question. It was one Logan didn't know the answer to yet.

"I don't know, but I'm looking forward to finding out."

He was about to move forward and kiss Tate just as the elevator stopped and opened.

"This is my floor," Tate told him as he moved out ahead.

Logan followed, quiet and patient, as the man in front of him opened the door to his apartment. Logan turned, shutting them in from the outside world, and when he rounded back to face Tate, he was on him before Logan could blink.

Caught completely off guard, he was easily pushed back against the door as Tate put his entire weight behind the palms planted firmly on Logan's chest. Immediately, their mouths connected in a molten kiss, and Logan groaned as Tate's hand moved straight down between them to his more than interested cock.

Logan's head hit the door, and Tate released his mouth as he began undoing the buttons on Logan's shirt.

"Jesus, what's gotten into you?"

"Nothing," Tate breathed against his neck.

Logan brought his hands up and clasped both of Tate's, pushing him back slightly.

"Yes. Something's different. What is it?" Logan waited and when nothing came, continued. "Tell me, what's changed?"

Tate's breathing came fast as he pulled a hand free. Touching Logan's skin that he'd revealed through the top two buttons, he replied, "I just decided, that's all."

"You decided?" Logan questioned. "You decided, what?"

"That I want to be here. No more pretending. No more fooling myself," Tate continued, sliding his finger down to the button. "So, are you going to shut the hell up and let go of my hand?"

"Depends." Logan moved his head forward to capture Tate's mouth in a fast kiss. "What are you going to do with it? Tell me."

Tate's breath floated across his mouth as Logan released Tate's other hand, and he went back to unbuttoning Logan's shirt.

"You like dirty talk, Logan?"

"I like your dirty talk. That night on the phone was amazing."

Logan rested his head back against the door and—*oh, hell yeah*—Tate placed his teeth along his jaw and sank them into his flesh. Methodically, he worked his way up to his ear with several bites and then sucked on Logan's earlobe.

"I want to give you what I owe you, but you might have to show me how."

Logan turned his head against the door and looked at Tate's face. "You better not be teasing me."

"I wouldn't tease about this."

"Okay then. But not here. Where's your bedroom?"

"You don't want me on my knees?" Tate half-joked.

Logan's arousal intensified as he stared back at Tate. "More than you know, but not your first time."

As Tate stepped away, Logan shrugged out of his unbuttoned shirt and tossed it on the floor as he moved away from the door toward the man who was now walking backward down the hall.

Tate was boldly adjusting the obvious erection he had, and Logan was quickly coming to like this new confidence in him. It was as if Tate could finally do whatever he wanted because he'd given up on denying how he felt.

Logan's eyes didn't leave him as they continued through the tiny apartment. With each step back that Tate took, Logan was advancing toward him. Tate reached down and removed his shirt, tossing it aside, much like he had.

Logan had to physically hold himself back. He let his

gaze wander over what had just been exposed, and when
Tate's back hit what he presumed was his bedroom door,
Logan suggested, "Let me in."

Tate didn't speak or move, but watched as Logan
began to unbutton his jeans.

"You did more than this last night," Logan reminded
him quietly, just in case he was having second thoughts.

That wasn't the case though as Tate turned the
handle and pushed the door open.

"I know. I'm looking. Don't fucking rush me."

Logan stepped forward until they were chest-to-
chest and face-to-face.

"You can look all you like—in there. Now, invite me
into your bed, Tate."

"You need an invitation?" Tate slid his palm over
Logan's tense abdomen and lower still to slide into his open
jeans.

"I want one. I want *you* to invite *me* into your bed."

As Tate's hand found him, Logan's mouth opened
and a hoarse sound left his throat.

"Logan? Please get in my bed—*now.*"

Logan wrapped an arm around Tate, grabbed his ass
hard, and walked the man backward into his room. He saw
the bed, but he would be damned if he was going to get into
it still wearing his jeans.

Releasing his hold on Tate, he stepped away, kicked
off his shoes, and made quick work of removing the denim
and boxers that were left covering him. When he was

completely naked, he brought his eyes back to Tate, expecting the same from him. But no, Tate was standing exactly where he'd left him, except now, he was kneading his erection through his jeans as he took in the sight before him.

Not wanting to take anything away from Tate's intimate inspection, Logan reached down and began his own exercise in self-pleasure.

Last night had been quick and overwhelming. It had been a big whirlwind of Logan pushing Tate along, and in the end, getting spectacular results. Tonight though was all Tate and whatever he decided, and as Logan stood in front of him, he could tell the difference in the look Tate was aiming his way.

The desire etched into the tense expression was that of a man who was looking at and lusting after someone he craved. Not someone who was confused about his feelings. Logan went to move, but Tate raised a hand and stilled him.

"No. Don't. Let me look."

That quietly determined request almost brought Logan to his knees. Tate stepped to him, and reached out a tentative hand and Logan felt Tate's fingertips connect with his nipple. Balling his left hand into a fist by his side, he continued to stroke his other hand over his aching shaft.

"Are they sensitive?" Tate queried.

"Yes."

"Do you like me touching them?"

"Mhmm," Logan hummed.

Tate glanced at what his fingers were touching before he aimed those hot eyes back at Logan. "Licking?"

"Are you asking me if you can?"

Tate nodded. "Yeah."

Logan hoped he had the patience he would need to get through this night of what he figured would be discovery for Tate, and torture on him.

"Tate?"

"Hmm?"

"You can touch whatever you want, *do* whatever you want."

"What if you don't like it?"

Logan held himself back from telling Tate he was insane. "Trust me, I will."

Gently, as though he were testing the waters, Tate skimmed his fingers down over Logan's nipple, across his pec, and then traced his ribs farther south to the V of his groin where he flirted lightly.

"This really turns me on," Tate admitted.

"You *touching* me there is really turning me on. You have it as well, see," Logan pointed out as he indicated the spot where Tate's jeans sat low.

"Yeah, but yours are so defined." Tate lifted his free hand to trace the other side until his fingers were touching Logan's pubic hair. "I never thought I'd be so turned-on by another man's body."

Logan released the hold he had on himself and clasped the back of Tate's neck, hauling him forward and pressing their mouths together. Logan grunted when he felt two hands wrap around his erection. As his tongue touched Tate's, Logan propelled his hips into the hands holding him, and his body shuddered when one of those hands moved to fondle his balls. Tearing his mouth away, Logan panted as he dropped his head back to concentrate on the hands finally learning his body.

* * *

I CAN'T STOP touching him, Tate thought as he stroked the turgid flesh in his hand and played with the soft, tight sacs scrunched up against Logan's body. Lightly, he pressed his lips to a spot Logan had exposed at the base of his neck when he let his head fall back.

Logan's body was unreal. He had muscles on top of muscles, and the evidence of his desire excited Tate to the point where he could feel his own body begging for release.

When Logan had stripped down and Tate had finally allowed himself that moment to really take in and desire everything he was seeing, he'd thought he would come right there in his jeans.

He couldn't explain why, but now that he'd decided exactly what he wanted—and that was definitely Logan—Tate wanted him, bad. He wanted to touch him with his hands, taste him with his mouth, and —*yes*—fuck him with his cock.

As that final thought entered his mind, Tate took his

hands from Logan's body and heard Logan offer a soft
protest against his lips. Removing his mouth as well, Tate
took a small step back and walked around Logan until he
was standing behind him.

Tate watched the hands by Logan's thick thighs
clench. He had the power to really drive this man, who
everyone wanted, out of his mind. Tate placed his hands on
Logan's hips and pulled him back, so his naked ass was
against the erection constricted in Tate's jeans.

"Oh shit," Logan rasped as Tate rolled his hips
against him.

"Can I change my mind?'

"What?"

Logan's entire body went taut against him. Tate
knew what Logan was thinking, but he was so very wrong.

"Can I change my mind?"

"About what? Because if you're about to stop and tell
me to leave, take your goddamn hands off me, and let me
go, so I can calm down."

Tate didn't do any of that. Instead, he put his lips
against Logan's naked shoulder and smoothed his hands
around to trace that sexy V down to Logan's ready and
willing cock. Stroking a fist up Logan's enlarged length, Tate
bit the shoulder under his mouth, hard, as he bucked his
hips forward.

"*Ah*, what the hell?"

Raising his head, Tate put his lips to Logan's ear and
confessed in a voice full of guttural desire, "I don't want to

suck you tonight. I want to fuck you instead."

Chapter Sixteen

LOGAN PHYSICALLY STOPPED breathing as Tate's words seeped into his brain. It didn't matter that warm hands were still tormenting him. With the distinct impression of Tate's arousal outlined to perfection against his naked ass, all Logan could think about were the words, I want to fuck you, coming out of Tate's mouth.

"Nothing?"

Logan heard the question in Tate's voice, and it was the truth. He had nothing. Nothing he could say. Never in a million years had Logan thought that this would happen tonight. He'd never expected Tate to want it so quickly. Logan had thought it was going to take a lot of convincing on his side.

"If you don't want…"

Logan finally made himself turn to face the man who seemed to be second-guessing himself.

"I thought you—"

With one hand, Logan touched his fingers to Tate's cheek and leaned in to take his mouth. As soon as their lips met, Tate's parted, and Logan dipped his tongue inside. Stepping closer, he rested his other hand on Tate's side as the kiss intensified, and desire mounted.

Logan could feel the rough denim abrading his skin as his cock wedged between them, and Tate's remained confined inside his jeans. Logan pushed his hand down and grappled with the button and then lowered the zipper, all the while still sucking on Tate's tongue.

Logan parted the jeans, and slid his palm around Tate's waist, where he dipped his fingers inside his boxers. When Tate's hands grasped his ass cheeks, Logan smiled against his mouth and made sure to stroke a finger down the warm crease of Tate's crack.

"Ah," Tate moaned, pulling his lips away.

"You see," Logan told him knowingly as he did it again, and Tate's ass cheeks flexed. "It feels good, doesn't it? Relax, it'll feel even better." He felt Tate's body physically loosen.

Tracing his finger farther down, he moved back in, so he could gnaw on Tate's jaw. Logan placed his lips under his chin, and then he did as Tate had done earlier. He started to bite him.

The hands on his own ass were shaping the muscle there as Logan made his way up to Tate's ear, telling him, "Nothing in the world could make me walk out of your bedroom right now. So, if you really mean it, then you can have it, Tate."

"Yes. I mean it."

Logan's eyes slid closed for a second as he tried to calm himself, but Tate was hell bent on that not happening.

The strong fingers behind Logan crept between his cheeks and began to spread him slightly. Feeling his own patience running thin, Logan asked, "Condoms? Lube?"

But Tate wasn't listening. He was too busy moving his hips against Logan, who was quickly going out of his mind as the erotic massaging continued. Tate began making a sexy grunt-like noise every time their cocks met.

"Tate?"

Glazed eyes found his, and when swollen lips and wild curls faced Logan, he felt his mouth turned up into a smug smile. "You're one sexy motherfucker when you're turned-on, you know that?"

"So are you," Tate voiced in a tone that had dropped several spine-tingling octaves.

"Mmm. Do you have condoms? Lube?"

Tate released his hold on him and shook his head. "I didn't even think about it. I have lube."

"And I've got condoms."

The look that crossed Tate's face was amusing as hell, and Logan turned to locate his jeans.

"That sure, huh?" Logan heard from behind and rounded back just in time to see Tate push his jeans and boxers off his hips and kick them aside. Logan focused on the thick, veiny erection pointing out in front of Tate's body, and he felt his ass clench in anticipation of having it inside him.

One of the things Logan had missed over the years was a good, hard, fucking. He'd only ever received it from one other before, but as he looked at Tate, he was reminded of the times Tate had wrestled with him and pinned him against a wall. Yes—if anyone could take him on and make him feel it a day later, it would be Tate Morrison.

* * *

TATE WALKED OVER to where Logan was holding out the condom packet, took it between his fingers, and issued his invite from earlier, much more confidently this time, "Get in my bed, Logan."

"Feeling bossy, are we?"

Tate brought the silver square to his mouth where he placed the corner between his teeth and ripped it open. "Horny," he answered as he pulled out the condom, threw the pack aside, and reached down to roll it on. "I feel horny."

He noted Logan's heavy-lidded gaze following the movements of his hand, and then Logan stepped forward and brushed past Tate. As their shoulders touched, Tate looked to the side where Logan had stopped, his mouth pulling into a wicked, sensual smirk.

"You work out at all?"

"Sometimes," Tate told him, slightly confused, as he watched Logan's eyes trail down his body and land on the protected stiff cock he was holding in his hand.

"Good, because fucking me is gonna be one hell of a strenuous workout."

Tate almost came from those words alone as Logan casually walked by him. Turning on his heel, he watched Logan climb up onto his bed, the same bed he had lain in over the last several nights, fantasizing about the guy.

Logan lay down on his back in the middle of the mattress and bent his knees up until his feet were flat, and Tate could see everything, just as he had the previous night. As Tate got up onto the bed and maneuvered himself in between Logan's knees, he was struck again by just how masculine Logan was. He even had big feet.

Seems there is some truth in that saying—big feet, big cock.

Logan's erection was thick and long, and as Tate watched the man masturbate in front of him, he couldn't help but reach down and reciprocate the gesture.

"Let's skip all the bullshit this time around, huh?" Logan's words sliced through the silent room.

"Bullshit?"

"Yeah, all the foreplay. You're hard, I'm hard, and I've been thinking about you naked since we first met."

Tate's balls tingled as Logan slowly spread his legs for him. He could see Logan's hand working his shaft, and occasionally, his fingers would move to the sensitive underside to his balls where he'd cup and push them up his body. From this angle, Tate could also see the dark pucker displayed to him every time Logan moved his hips.

"So, how do I do this?"

Logan gave him a look that screamed, Really?

So, he clarified. "I mean, is there something I need to do, so I don't...you know, hurt you? This will hurt, right? Diana always said—"

"Stop, stop! You're making me lose my hard-on. No one else is in here, Tate." Logan sat up in the bed, bringing his knees under him, and leaning forward, he captured Tate's mouth in a hot kiss. "Just you and me. I'll show you what to do, so you don't hurt me."

Tate rubbed the back of his neck. "Okay."

"Get the lube."

As Logan lay back down, Tate moved to the side of the bed and reached down to a small drawer. Coming back up on his knees, Tate let his eyes rove up the six-pack rippling with each movement of the strong arm pumping back and forward.

"Remember last night?" Logan asked.

Tate's eyelids lowered as his own cock lurched, and he grasped it, pressing it against his body.

"Not something I'm likely to forget."

Logan widened his legs a little more. "I need to get ready before you come at me with that," he pointed out, glancing at what Tate was holding.

Tate nodded and lowered his eyes to Logan's sac and the light sprinkle of hair on the skin leading down to the dark hole. Damn, I really want inside there, Tate thought, and before he knew it, he was asking, "Can I do it?"

* * *

LOGAN HAD HOPED, maybe even silently prayed, that Tate would say exactly those words.

"Definitely."

From where he was lying on the bed, he watched Tate scoot in closer and pour the cool, clear liquid into his palm. He was so aroused by the thought of Tate's fingers in him that he was in danger of once again shooting his load before the real fun started.

When Tate threw the bottle aside and leaned over him, Logan's hand stopped as Tate's fingers lightly grazed up the underside of his engorged length.

"Let me," Tate requested.

Logan released his hold immediately. Sliding his fingers through Tate's hair, he pulled him down until their mouths met. As soon as those slippery fingers encircled him, Logan's hips lifted up off the bed as though he had been shocked. The mouth against his curved into a smile, and that sexy confidence Tate was throwing his way turned him on even more, if that were possible.

Pushing his tongue between Tate's lips, Logan's body heated as the hand between their bodies pumped faster. He could feel Tate's own arousal pressing straight and upright against him, and as Logan moved to return the caress, the body plastered against him shook, and Tate raised his head to stare down at him.

"More, I want more than this," Tate rasped.

Logan lifted his head from the pillow and chewed on

Tate's swollen lip.

"You need to stretch me with your fingers, just like last night."

Logan tried to contain his excitement as Tate's eyes darkened in erotic concentration as he slowly released him. With dexterous fingers, Tate coasted them down the sensitive crevasse until they were pressed firmly against Logan's hot and eager hole.

Logan's breathing was coming in short, quick bursts as Tate's tongue came out to touch his top lip, and Tate continued looking down at him, focused and intense, as he slowly slid his left index finger inside him.

"Tate," Logan hissed out between his teeth, closing his eyes against the intrusion.

Then, Tate's deep voice ordered, "Open your eyes."

Immediately, Logan focused on Tate, who was giving him such a fiery look that he wasn't sure how the hell the tables had turned on him.

"This feels good? Having my finger in you?"

"Hell yes, a second would feel even better," Logan assured him through labored breaths.

Tate pulled his finger back and then pushed forward. This time, he allowed his finger to go as far as he could possibly get it, making Logan's hips snap up and off the bed on a curse, "Fuck."

"That's the plan."

A small huff escaped Logan's throat, and when Tate pulled his hand back and his finger left Logan's body completely, the man lowered down over him and took his mouth in a quick kiss.

Logan's hands came up to cradle Tate's face, as he aggressively took the lips pressing against his while Tate rubbed his sheathed rod over him. With lust riding them both, Logan panted against those lips, "Move back a minute."

As soon as the words were spoken, Tate was back on his knees, and Logan maneuvered himself until he was on his stomach and then pushed up onto his hands and knees. Looking over his shoulder, he found Tate's eyes on his ass while he desperately milked his cock. Logan hung his head for a minute, trying to get himself under control. Once he figured he was good to go, he looked back again, and this time, his stare was met, so he asked, "You okay?"

Tate moved in behind him and ran his finger down the crack of Logan's ass until he reached the hole.

Oh shit.

"Yes. Just looking,"

Ah, pretty fucking sure you're touching, too. Logan grabbed himself with his right hand and tried to keep a handle on his instinct to turn around and attack.

Giving Tate a wink, he issued a strained invite, "Two fingers would be amazing right about now."

Tate pressed the tips of his fingers to Logan's vulnerable skin. As he eased them inside him, a whistle of air left Logan, and he couldn't help from pushing back against them.

"Oh yeah," he barely voiced.

Tate's fingers tunneled in and out of his body.

It had been a long time since Logan had really been taken, but that didn't stop him from using other means to get himself off, and at that moment, he was glad he hadn't been lax in reminding himself how much he loved receiving.

Occasionally, and by sheer accident, Tate's fingers grazed over that magical fucking spot, and a hoarse snarl would leave Logan as he pushed back even harder on the two fingers that were knuckle deep, and driving him fucking crazy. That, however, was no longer enough. Logan wanted the thick shaft he could see every time he looked back over his shoulder to Tate.

Fucking gorgeous Tate, had a look of arousal mixed with first-time curiosity stamped all over him. It was obvious though by the strength and size of his own erection that the arousal was winning out, and as Logan felt those fingers pull from his body, getting ready to plow back in, he finally snapped.

"Now, Tate," he demanded on a growl. "Now."

* * *

TATE HEARD THE demand from Logan and realized, *this is it*. This was the moment he crossed every line. The man in front of him on his hands and knees was spectacular to look at. There was not one thing about him that would allow Tate to confuse the fact that he was in bed with—and about to fuck—a man, not a woman.

The arm holding Logan up was bulging with muscle, as was the one flexing with each stroke he made to his own cock. The legs, dusted with dark hair, were bent, allowing him to kneel before Tate. Strong muscles rippled across his shoulders with every move back towards him, reiterating that there was nothing soft or delicate about this man. As Tate picked up the bottle of lube again, he poured some onto his eager erection, and then spread apart the solid cheeks of Logan's ass and made sure his dark hole was nice and slick as he waited for him.

Damn, this is different. Who knew that staring at Logan while he was stroking his cock would make me so fucking excited that I could come in seconds? But no, he thought as he tightened a hard fist around his own balls, I really want to know how it feels inside him.

Tate noticed that when Logan spread his knees a little wider apart, he angled the top half of his body down toward the mattress, curving his hips and ass back to him.

Touching a hand to Logan's hip, Tate asked, "You okay?"

But Tate had no clue what the hell he was checking for. Logan had been here and done this.

I'm pretty sure he's A-OK. It's me who's the new guy.

Logan looked back at him and licked his mouth. "Yeah, Tate, I'm real good. Just go slow. Okay?"

Slow. I can do slow. Tate smoothed his hand over the

firm ass in front of him and spread the cheeks apart. Once he saw what he wanted, he reached down with his left hand and lined himself up.

As the tip of him touched Logan's rim, the heat from his body penetrated the latex, and Tate closed his eyes from the intensity of that small moment. Then, very carefully, he began to move. The head of his cock met with the resistance of Logan's body, and just when he was about to pull back, he felt the powerful man in front of him drive his entire body backward. Tate's cock slid past the ring of muscle, and he almost swallowed his fucking tongue at the toe-curling pleasure he got from it.

Letting out a loud curse, Tate froze, trying to rein in the desire to surge forward as Logan started to work his way back on him. He kept one hand around himself while Logan's ass slowly engulfed more of his shaft, and as Tate watched himself disappearing inside Logan's body, he felt as if he'd never been as turned-on as he was right then.

"Holy hell," he whispered like a prayer.

Logan changed directions to slide back off him, and then he started to take him inside once again. With each movement, Logan's body swallowed him deeper until Tate was finally fully seated, and his balls were pressed firmly against Logan's heated skin.

Tate remained still as a fucking statue until Logan looked back at him. "Now is the part you should know how to do all on your own."

That smart-ass comment from the mouth that had

teased, taunted, and convinced him into this bed, finally had Tate moving into action. He flattened his palm over Logan's tailbone and ran it up the man's spine until he reached his shoulder where he squeezed as he drew his hips back. Sliding his cock out, he then reversed his movement and thrust back inside the tightest, hottest hole he'd ever been in.

"Oh fuck," was all Tate heard.

He felt the satisfaction and power that came from that response, like a gunshot at the beginning of a race. With his hand on Logan's shoulder, Tate moved down over the man until his other palm was resting on the bedding, and then he really started to move.

"Logan…damn," he groaned as his head came down beside Logan's, and he started to kiss the guy's ear.

Tate could feel Logan's thighs tensing against his own as he pushed back against him in steady a rhythm, and as Logan turned his head, and their mouths met in a tongue-thrusting kiss, Tate's entire body vibrated from, pleasure fucking overload.

He hadn't even felt this way for Diana, but as his hips moved in quick, shallow thrusts against Logan's, and his cock tunneled inside his powerful body, Tate knew he'd never felt this before.

"Jesus, Tate. Harder. I'm not gonna fucking break," Logan barked against his mouth.

Tate's mouth morphed into a feral grin as he moved back up to his knees behind Logan, and placed both hands on his hips. Spreading his knees so he had steady ground,

Tate reached up with one hand and tangled his fingers through Logan's hair, gripping it and pulling his head back.

"Typical. Even now, you can't keep that smart-ass mouth of yours shut."

Logan's head dropped forward, and Tate let him go as he heard, "Come on, Tate, let me have it."

Tate withdrew, and this time, since he had permission, he promised softly, "Wish fucking granted."

That was his only warning to Logan as he slammed his cock hard inside him.

As he picked up speed, he curled down over him, and placed both of his palms on the mattress beside Logan's. Over and over, Tate pounded into him, and every time he did, Logan's body chased his in a way that expressed how much it craved the cock plowing into it.

"Fucking hell, Tate. That's it," were the words Tate could hear coming from the man underneath him.

As his balls slapped against hot skin, he took in that new feeling, too, and added it to the list of things he loved about fucking Logan Mitchell.

* * *

LOGAN WAS LOSING his mind. As he lowered his upper body to the mattress below, he could feel Tate's sweaty chest against his back as he reached down to his lower body and rapidly pumped his cock.

"Tate!" he shouted.

Tate continued jamming his hips into his, driving farther into his ass on every hard downward slide.

There was nothing pretty about this coupling and certainly nothing familiar or practiced. This was a first-time moment for Tate. He was going at him fast and hard, and Logan loved every rough minute of it.

Pushing himself up on his arms, Tate clutched his hips, and Logan looked back and caught eyes with the man who was sliding into him with each sure thrust.

"Jesus, your ass is tighter than anything I've ever been inside."

"And?" Logan challenged, urging Tate to admit what he was feeling.

Tate moved down over him and bit his shoulder as his hips started those fast, shallow digs that—fuck him—hit exactly the right spot.

"And I never want to stop."

Logan turned his head to take Tate's mouth, but before he did, he said, "Then, don't."

"I don't plan to," Tate assured him.

Then, their mouths met as they went at each other like they had been waiting for years instead of days.

It only took minutes this time around, just as Logan had known it would, but within several of them, his own climax raced down his spine to start the familiar ache in his balls that would lead to one amazing orgasm.

Behind him, Tate's hips moved with much more urgency, and the fingers on his hips threatened to bruise as

Tate shouted out an obscenity, and his climax hit him hard. It didn't take anything more than knowing that Tate had come inside him for Logan to come in a hot spray of creamy fluid all over his hand and Tate's sheets.

Unbelievable. Have I ever been so goddamn satisfied?

As Tate pulled out of him, Logan winced slightly at the loss of pressure and shifted, so he was lying on his stomach. When he felt the warm chest and Tate's groin pressed all along the back of him, Logan smiled into the pillow.

"Holy shit," he heard followed by Tate's chuckle.

"No kidding," Logan concurred from under the man stretched out on top of him. He wasn't about to tell him to move.

"That was unfuckingreal. Did it feel good?"

Logan started to laugh at the absurdity that anyone would have to ask that after the way he had just come, and as his whole body began to shake, Tate rolled off of him and landed in—

Yep, the wet spot.

Tate's expression of shock and the quick way he moved made Logan's hilarity increase until he landed on his back and was holding his stomach.

"Yes, you just landed in the proof."

"I'm glad you find this so funny."

Tate's response just made Logan laugh harder. As he turned his head on the pillow to face Tate, Logan couldn't help the grin he gave him.

"I was just thinking how hard it was going to be to convince you to suck my dick if my cum is so horrifying to you."

Tate moved then, quicker than Logan expected, and he found himself pinned under him.

"You'd be surprised at what I might do when asked to try." Tate lowered his head to take Logan's mouth with his own.

Before their lips connected, Logan ran his hands through all those messy curls and told him, "Truer words have never been spoken. Look at everything you did tonight. So, when do you think I should expect that—"

Tate shook his head, brushing their noses together. "Shut up for a change, would you? And just kiss me."

Now that Logan could do.

Part Two

Reaction: An emotional or intellectual response to or aroused by a stimulus.

Chapter Seventeen

THE NEXT MORNING, Logan stood in line at The Daily Grind, waiting to get his much-needed caffeine while thinking about the night before. As far as he was aware, he and Tate had gone from first date to their first time to—

Seeing each other?

That thought alone made Logan almost break out in hives. The idea of tying himself to anyone apparently bothered him more than he'd realized, but he was also willing to try and push past it if that's what it took to keep Tate around.

With that goal in mind, Logan stepped forward and reached out to take the hand resting by Tate's leg. As soon as their fingers touched, Tate moved his aside and shook his head once, before stepping away from Logan and up to the counter.

Ah, so I can touch him—but only in private. Logan couldn't pinpoint why that utterly galled him, since it never had before, but it did. Usually, he was the last person who needed assurance or commitment of any kind, but the fact that Tate was now acting like this, after almost demanding it from him—really got Logan hot under the collar.

As Tate finished his order, he turned and indicated to the corner where he was going to sit. "I'll meet you back there," Tate told him.

Logan found himself biting back what he really wanted to say, which would have sounded something like, *Oh, I'm allowed to sit with you?* But he didn't say it. Instead, he nodded briskly and inhaled the scent of soap clinging to Tate's skin. *The man smelled extraordinary.*

Walking up to the counter, Logan greeted the familiar young woman behind it. "Hey, Libby."

"Logan, hey. How are you?"

Libby had been working at The Daily Grind for the last two years, always on the morning shift when he came in. She was cute and sweet with auburn hair and freckles everywhere. She also enjoyed hassling him at every opportunity she got.

"Oh, pretty good. Running a little late today."

When she looked around his shoulder and over in the direction where Tate had gone, Logan made sure not to turn and follow her gaze.

"For a good reason, I hope?"

Logan chuckled and grinned. "Am I ever running late for a bad one?"

"Good point. Then again, you've never come in here *with* anyone either."

Logan shook his head and then lowered his voice, "Tell me Robbie isn't working today, and I'll love you forever."

"If only it were that easy to win your love, Logan."

Feeling hopeful, he pressed, "So, he's not?"

"I didn't say that."

"Libby, come on, help me out."

"He's here, but I'll keep him away. Sound good?"

"Yeah, thanks," Logan supposed. *What the hell was I thinking, bringing Tate here?* "I'll have an espresso, please."

"Anything else?" she asked with a smile.

Logan gave an absent shake of his head. "Nope, that's all."

"Okay, I'll call it out when it's ready." She paused and picked up the other cup before giving him a mischievous look. "With Tate's?"

Amazing, even his name excites me. Logan turned and made his way over to the booth where the man who belonged to that name waited.

* * *

TATE SAT TOWARD the far back corner of the coffee shop and let his eyes take in his surroundings. Several couches were on the opposite side near the large windows that showed all of the businessmen and women—just like Logan, he supposed—making their way to work. Several of the tables in the middle of the shop were full, and as his gaze finally came back to Logan, who was still talking to the redheaded barista, Tate knew he needed to wake up and get his brain in gear.

Last night was still running on a continuous loop through his head, and when Tate had woken up to find Logan sitting fully dressed on the chair in his room, he'd known it was time to think fast. Real life was about to come calling, and there was no way to hide from what he'd done.

* * *

"I NEED TO go and get clean clothes for work. Meet me for coffee? Nine thirty at The Daily Grind on LaSalle?"

Tate nodded his head against the pillow and could smell Logan's aftershave all over his sheets. He had an insane urge to bury his face in it and then maybe masturbate all over them, but instead, he rolled onto his back. "Yeah, okay. What time is it now?"

"Six."

"Oh shit. Of course you're a morning person," he mumbled.

Logan stood and crossed the space to the bedroom door. "So, nine thirty?"

Tate agreed halfheartedly, resting an arm across his eyes. "Tate?"

As his name was called, he lowered his arm and watched Logan's tongue moisten his lips.

"Yeah?"

"If I didn't have a mandatory meeting today, I'd take the day off, crawl back into your bed, and somehow convince you to lie back and let me have you."

Tate felt his body react to Logan's words, and he knew that he was definitely going to get himself off the minute Logan left.

Last night, after that first time, Logan had told him to sleep. Tate had figured the guy realized how overwhelmed he had been. But this morning, he'd surprised himself because Tate wanted nothing more than to start all over again.

"I'll see you at nine thirty," Logan confirmed, giving him one last look-over, before he walked out the door.

* * *

NOW, HERE THEY were, after Tate had spent the morning lying in bed where he'd jerked off and come all over his sheets. He'd then showered and pulled on jeans with a gray V-neck.

Logan, on the other hand, looked as though he'd had twelve hours of uninterrupted sleep and was immaculately dressed as usual. Tate observed Logan as he made his way through the smaller tables toward him and tried to connect this man with the one he'd had naked and under him just last night.

Dressed in a three-piece suit today, Logan appeared like he usually did when he came into the bar. But this time, as Tate took in the cut and tailored fit of the navy blue material, his palms itched to touch. The perfectly styled hair and the glasses framing serious eyes added up to one seriously hot and sophisticated package—a package Tate wanted to unwrap. He wanted Logan back in his bed. He wanted him naked, and waiting for him on his hands and knees. Just like last night.

"So, am I allowed to sit here? Or should I find a different table?"

Tate blinked at the annoyed tone from the man he was currently fantasizing about, and he tried to work out why the hell he was on the receiving end of the sarcastic remarks.

"Huh?"

As Logan slid into the seat opposite him, Tate continued his bold appraisal until Logan's voice snapped him out of it.

"If you think the way you're looking at me is any less of an indication that you had your cock inside me last night as opposed to simply touching my hand today, then you'd be wrong."

Tate shifted in his seat. "And how am I looking at you?"

"Like you want to undress me."

"I do want to."

Logan placed his arms on the table and clasped his hands together. "But you have an aversion to holding hands?"

Tate leaned across and spoke softly, "Well, I won't be undressing you in public, will I?"

Logan tilted his head to the side and sat back in his chair. "Ah, I think I understand."

"Good," Tate replied, thinking that would be the end

of it.

"So we're...*secret friends*?"

Tate shook his head, rubbing his palm over his face.

What did I think would happen? That Logan would be happy with a quick fuck at the end of each night and that he wouldn't tell anyone? Did the guy ever keep his mouth shut?

No.

"Don't be an asshole."

Logan's expression reflected his incredulity as he responded. "I'm being the asshole? I'm just trying to work out what exactly is going on here, so I know what I can and can't do."

"You can show a little patience while I get used to everything. You've been doing this for..." Tate paused, and then asked, "How long have you, you know?"

"Nope, I don't. If you want to know something, then spit it out."

"Liked both? Swung both ways? Whatever, you know what I mean. Stop being difficult," Tate stated, impatiently.

Logan's laugh was derisive, and Tate knew it had nothing to do with what he'd asked but more to do with *his* discomfort at the question.

"Well?" Tate demanded.

"Since I was nineteen."

"Nineteen?" Tate questioned in a much louder voice than he'd anticipated.

Just as Logan was about to say something else, Tate

heard, "Tate! One, extra-nutty hazelnut latte, and an espresso!"

Tate scooted out of the booth and stood. As he brushed past Logan, he felt a hand grab his wrist. Stopping, he looked down at eyes that were laughing up at him.

"That's the drink you ordered? A nutty hazelnut?"

"Yeah, so?"

Logan shrugged. "Awful lot of nuts for one drink, don't you think?"

Tate scowled as Logan continued to laugh.

"You know, nutty hazelnut fits you quite well this morning, I'd say."

Tate shook his head. "I like the nut flavor, that's all."

"Oh Tate, you make it so easy every time. Go, or I can't be held responsible for what comes out of my mouth."

"Are you ever?"

"More than you'd think, trust me."

Tate pondered that for a moment. "You got the espresso?"

Logan inclined his head without saying another word, and Tate decided that was his cue to go and get their drinks.

* * *

LOGAN REMAINED WHERE he was, staring at the back wall, waiting for Tate to return. He was having an internal conflict, something that didn't happen often with him. He'd been hurt when Tate had pulled away from him earlier.

Hurt.

The concept was almost humorous, considering his stance on relationships in the past, but the thought of Tate being embarrassed by him—

Yeah, that fucking hurt. The guy has managed to turn me into an emotional head case in less than two weeks.

Logan was resolved to telling him that he was not down for the hiding bullshit just as soon as he got back. Before he even finished thinking it though, the seat opposite him filled, and it was not by Tate.

Oh, just fucking great.

"I knew it was you," the new arrival announced.

Logan stared across the table at Robbie.

Blond-haired, blue-eyed Robbie was a one-night several months ago, lapse in judgment.

"Did you?" Logan asked, trying to speed things along.

Robbie wasn't shy at all as he looked over Logan's suit and licked his lips suggestively.

"I did. I told Libby it definitely looked like you even though she swore it wasn't. But I was right, and here you are."

Looking over his shoulder quickly, Logan was happy to see that Tate was still at the counter, waiting behind a group of people. Turning back to face the guy, Logan tried to remember exactly why he'd gone home with him as he replied, "Yep, here I am."

"You're a hard man to get a hold of. Always gone before I see you."

Until today. How could I have been so stupid? Logan aimed a forced smile at Robbie and hoped that Tate took his sweet-ass time getting their coffees.

Robbie leaned in across the table, similar to the move Tate had done a little earlier, and licked his top lip again. Unexpectedly, that night came back to Logan in a hot flash of mouths, cocks, and cum. Specifically, his cock in that mouth.

"I tried calling you," Robbie told him quietly.

Logan remained where he was, but admitted. "I know."

"But you haven't answered."

The guy isn't stupid at least. Logan hated stupid.

"That's true. I haven't."

Some men might have taken offense to that, but Logan was fairly certain that when they'd decided to go home for a quick fuck, he'd very clearly explained the rules up front. So, he was surprised when Robbie continued talking instead of getting up to leave.

"I thought we had a good night together."

Trying his hardest not to lose patience, Logan raised a brow. "We did. And then it was over."

As the word *over* left his lips and seemed to hover in the air, Logan felt, rather than saw, Tate stop beside his side of the booth. He watched as Robbie lifted his eyes to Tate, and then the young man's mouth split into a smile that was pure sexual invitation. It was the same invitation Logan had once taken him up on, and an invitation that was not going to work here. It was a pity Logan didn't have a chance to warn him of that before he opened his mouth and engaged Tate in conversation.

"Well, hello. Who are you?"

* * *

WHO AM I? Tate thought, glaring down at the little dipshit currently seated opposite Logan. *Who the fuck are you?*

Since he seemed to have lost the ability of speech, Tate turned to Logan, who answered for him, "This is Tate. He's..."

Logan seemed to stumble over what he wanted to say, which was completely unlike him, and Tate wanted to get in the blond man's face and say, *I'm his, so fuck off.*

Instead, he remained mute as Logan ended with, "A friend of mine."

Although that completely infuriated him, Tate knew that it was his own fault. He'd sensed the way Logan had backed off when he'd moved his hand away from him earlier. It had been a natural reaction to any guy who'd try and hold his hand. One that was going to be hard to break, but it had really rubbed Logan the wrong way, and now, he was obviously paying him back.

"I'm Robbie. Also a *good* friend of Logan's."

Tate felt the hair on the back of his neck rise at the

implications being thrown at him. It was obvious this guy knew Logan in the we've-fucked kind of way, and Tate wasn't exactly sure what his part in this discussion should be, which also didn't help in his annoyance.

"So sorry, I'm in your way."

"Trust me, you're not. But you are in my seat," Tate pointed out.

"Am I?"

As Tate glared down at the intruder, he noticed that, for once in his life, Logan had shut the hell up. "Yes. You are."

The blond finally removed his eyes from him and looked across to Logan—the man, Tate thought, *he* had met for coffee. Robbie licked his lips like he wanted a taste of Logan's mouth, and Tate almost dumped the coffees on the table, wanting to grab the guy.

Logan must have finally clued in to Tate's mood because that was when he spoke up.

"Well, it was nice catching up, Robbie."

Tate turned his head and pinned Logan with a you've-got-to-be-kidding-me glare.

"It's always nice to see you, Logan, under any circumstances. Or just under you in general," Robbie replied.

That comment was almost enough to make Tate's temper explode, as the little shit slid out of the booth.

As he stood, Tate noticed he was around the same height as him, but Robbie was rail thin. He was wearing black skinny jeans and a black Daily Grind polo shirt. He gave Tate a wide grin, obviously aware of the shitstorm he'd just stirred, and then he turned, and walked away.

Sliding into the vacated booth, Tate glowered at Logan who had an arm across the back of the black seat and one on the table. Tate pushed the espresso over to him and finally spoke. "Him? Really?"

Logan picked up the coffee and brought it to his lips to take a sip. Tate did the same but kept an eye on the man across from him.

"Why so surprised? He's cute, and his mouth rivals the suction of a Hoover."

Tate almost choked on his coffee at that analogy. He coughed, cleared his throat, and stared at Logan, whose eyes seemed to be laughing at him.

"Nice. So, that's how you remember the people you've been with—by their...sucking skills?"

"Not at all. Take you for example. All I can remember is how hard you fucked me last night. Plus, you haven't sucked my cock yet. Want to remedy that?"

Tate shook his head. "Not right now."

"Thought so," Logan responded, lifting the drink to his lips.

Tate watched Logan's lower lip part from the top to take a sip, and that was when he found himself promising, "Later."

"Later, huh?"

"Tonight."

Fingering the cup Logan pointed out, "You work tonight."

"You don't."

"No, I don't, do I? What should I do instead?"

Tate crowded in, wanting this now more than ever. "Come to the bar."

"Now, why would I do that? It's not like you're going to talk to me more than you usually do. I don't feel like sitting in a bar and staring at a man who is too much of a pussy to admit what he's doing behind closed doors."

Oh yeah, Logan is pissed. Just like Logan had once told him, it was an absolute turn-on. Arguing with him was like foreplay. Tate couldn't believe how hot it made him.

Lowering his voice, he suggested, "Call in sick and come home with me. I'll prove you wrong."

"I could," Logan considered. "But I'm not in the mood."

Tate let out a sound of disbelief. "Really? *You* aren't in the mood?"

"Not with someone who acts like I'm no one in public, but expects something exclusive so he can get me on my hands and knees in private."

Logan was right. What he was asking *was* unfair. Tate thought he just needed time, time to get used to it all. But he wasn't kidding himself. He wanted Logan, and he'd probably do whatever the guy asked to have him.

"You're really pissed because I wouldn't hold your hand, aren't you?"

Logan dropped the relaxed posture to lean in.

"Don't you laugh at me."

Tate let his fingers reach out to touch Logan's.

"Why? If this was the other way around, you'd be rolling on the floor, laughing at me."

"Fuck off, Tate," Logan snarled.

Quick as a whip, Tate caught Logan's tie and one of the guys' hands, pulling him across the table. Tate watched Logan's vision shift to his mouth in anticipation.

"You really want me to leave?"

Logan raised his gaze as he warned, "People are watching."

Tate's desire to get his point across was outweighing any kind of fear he might have been having. "So?"

"So? Aren't you the one that—"

Tate cut him off by tugging on the tie. "I told you I needed some time."

"And fifteen minutes is your version of time?" Logan questioned skeptically.

"No, not really. But I want that little shit to see exactly who's going to be sucking you later, and I don't want you going to work thinking about him instead of me."

Logan scoffed. "Tate?"

"What?" He didn't really care where they were anymore. Instead, all he could visualize was this man's mouth on his own.

"Lately, you're all that I think about."

"Perfect." Tate responded before he pushed off his

seat and took Logan's mouth in a blistering kiss.

Logan opened to his lips immediately, and Tate forgot all about his surroundings as he tangled his tongue with Logan's, sinking into the connection. The moan that slipped from Logan's throat made Tate want to drag him over the table and rip off his clothes. It wasn't until the sound of an order being called out, that Tate was brought back to reality, back to the coffee shop, back to where he had just openly kissed Logan in front of anyone who walked on by.

Before he had time to analyze that, Logan flicked his tongue over Tate's bottom lip. "You were jealous, weren't you?"

"What?" Tate reluctantly let go of Logan and sat back in his seat.

Logan followed suit and calmly stated, "Of Robbie. You were jealous."

"And if I was?"

"There's no reason to be. But I like it," Logan informed with a self-satisfied grin.

"Why?"

"Because you looked like you wanted to kick his ass for even talking to me, and that makes me want you even more."

Tate lowered his voice, questioning softly, "You really like that idea, don't you?"

"Hell yes."

Tate felt his erection pressing against his jeans at the

look Logan was giving him. The kiss had gotten him interested, but the look aimed his way had him ready to go.

Then, Logan opened his mouth to add to the torture. "All of that honey-colored skin, naked under me, your curls all over my pillow as I drive my cock inside you—oh yeah, Tate, that's going to happen. Mark my words."

Tate's ass clenched, and he actually pushed his hips up as though he were trying to ease the ache. He was more aroused by the image Logan had just depicted than he'd ever thought he would be.

"What if I don't ever want that?"

"Tate?"

"Yeah?"

"Are you turned-on right now, wishing we were somewhere private?"

Tate closed his eyes, sighed, and then reopened them. "Yes."

"Then, trust me, you want it. Think about it, get comfortable with the idea, and when you're ready, I'm going to make you feel so unfuckingbelievable that you'll wonder why you ever questioned it."

Tate's thoughts were all over the place, and all he wanted was to ease his ache by doing…well, anything with Logan.

"Sure you have to go to work?"

"Yeah, but I'll come by the bar after."

Logan slid out of the booth, and Tate had to wonder how the guy didn't have a raging hard-on like himself. But when he buttoned his jacket and placed his briefcase in front of him, Tate had his answer.

He does, but he has props. Lucky fuck.

Casually, Logan walked over to his side of the booth, leaned down slightly, and relayed in a tone that made Tate look twice, "I don't expect you to announce this to everyone. Hell, I don't even want that. But if you ever pull away from my hand again, like I have the fucking plague, don't be surprised by my reaction."

Catching his breath, Tate dared to ask, "Which will be?"

"Depending on my mood? Either a quick lesson on how much you like my hands or my back as I walk the fuck away."

With that parting shot, Logan turned and walked out, giving Tate a taste of exactly what he did not want.

Chapter Eighteen

SIX THIRTY ROLLED around, and so did the wind and rain. *Damn, that wind is really humming.* Tate had been lucky enough to get to work just before it had really started, but even he had raced against the fat drops of water that had started to fall.

One hour later though, and people were dashing into the bar from the sidewalk, drenched. It made for one messy entryway, but it was a busy Tuesday night with people trying to avoid the downpour.

Tate's mind was preoccupied tonight—consumed by one person in particular. Ever since Logan had shown up, Tate's life had gone from boring to one full of chaos and unanswered questions, but it was time to start working things out. He knew that the further he went with Logan, the more difficult the questions would become.

Dropping his insecurities though was a lot easier to think about than to actually do. Tate didn't want his reactions to Logan to be based out of fear in any way—whether it be the fear of being seen together or the fear of losing what had just started. He wanted his actions to be made because of want and desire and the fact that what he was doing felt good for a change.

So, as he'd gotten dressed for work, Tate had made up his mind. He wanted Logan. He wanted to be able to touch him, kiss him, and do whatever the hell he felt like without having to worry about what anyone else thought.

And that—well, that meant accepting it himself.

As Tate wiped down the top of the bar, he let the thoughts he'd been contemplating start to really sink in. He knew he wasn't quite ready to tackle people head-on, but he wasn't going to hide how he felt either. He was going to act just as they did in private, and if someone wanted to question it, then they could fucking question it.

The bar door opened just as Tate glanced up, in stepped the man who had walked away from him hours earlier—except this time, Logan did not look polished and put-together. No, he looked like the complete opposite. Still dressed in his navy blue suit—well, half of it—Logan had the jacket over his head as he walked through the doors. When he lowered it, Tate saw just how ineffective it had been at keeping the rain from him. Logan was soaked.

As he moved the wet jacket in his hand, he looked to the hostess. She took it from him with a small smile, and Tate saw Logan mouth something, probably a thanks—or a, *Damn, sorry about that*—and then he turned.

Tonight, he was not wearing his glasses, and as their eyes collided and held, Logan raised a hand, pushing his fingers through his glistening black hair, and Tate felt his cock stir and his mouth dry.

The material of Logan's shirt was glued to every muscle of his body from his solid arms to his flat abdomen. Those tailored dress pants were molded to his thighs and cradled the bulge in between, like a lover would, like *he* would.

Fuck, the man is hot.

Logan began walking toward him, and all Tate could think was, *He should always be dressed in wet clothes.* As he passed several other waterlogged customers, Tate noticed them looking him over as well, probably wondering how he still looked so appealing when he was just as wet as the rest of them.

Tate took in the water droplets sliding down Logan's cheek, and his breathing faltered. When those same droplets then continued down to disappear into his shirt—*holy shit*—Tate knew he wanted to follow them with his tongue, and he wanted it now.

After what seemed like hours instead of minutes, Logan stopped in front of him.

Tate knew that the sexual longing he was feeling had to be written all over his face because the first thing out of Logan's mouth was, "Do you have somewhere *we* can maybe dry *me* off?"

Tate didn't hesitate, not even for a moment. If Logan wanted to go somewhere private, Tate was going to be the one to show him there. He was also going to be the one to stand and watch—or participate—as he *dried off.*

"Yeah, break room." Tate stayed exactly where he

was, fearing that Logan would disappear if he moved.

"Tate?"

Tate passed the towel between his hands. "Yeah?"

"Take me there."

Stepping away from the bar, Tate turned, threw the towel on the back counter, and made his way down to the bar pass. He opened it up, and as Logan walked through past him, Tate could smell the aftershave lingering on his body.

Amelia walked up to the bar at that exact moment and looked between the two of them before focusing on Tate.

"Will you be okay for a few minutes? I'm just going to give him a towel from the back."

Amelia's mouth kicked up at the edges. "Yeah, Stacy just came back from her break, so we'll be okay for a while. No rush."

Tate had a feeling she was sizing him up, and more than likely, she was coming up with the correct assumption—especially considering Logan chose to move up and push against Tate's side with his whole body, including the hardening cock he'd admired only moments ago. Before Tate had a chance to step away, he heard Logan whisper, "Hurry up, I want to taste you," and that was all Tate needed.

Turning on his heel, Tate made his way to the back of the bar and into the break room that—*thank God*—was empty. As he entered silently, he was happy to hear the door click and lock. When he turned and saw Logan against the door, all Tate could think was, *Now. I want him right now.*

* * *

LOGAN MIGHT NOT have known the specifics of what was running through Tate's mind, but he knew whatever it was, it was one hundred percent sexual.

The man had tracked him across the bar like a hunter stalking its prey, and for once, Logan had felt his own step falter. The fierce craving in Tate's expression had made it difficult to walk from point A to point B and stay somewhat decent. *But now?* Now, as Logan stood there, with his back to the locked door and Tate looking at him like he wanted to consume him—well, Logan did nothing to conceal the way his cock was upright and erect.

"You're so wet," Tate uttered.

Logan felt an ironic laugh leave his throat. "Now, that's something I bet you never expected to say to me."

Before Logan could even blink, Tate was crushed up against his front with one of his legs maneuvered between his own. A stifled grunt escaped Logan as Tate opened his mouth and teased his tongue along his jaw to his ear where he told him in a voice that was gravelly and full of longing, "You look so hot right now. I wish I had the time to fuck you right here, right against the wall like you once dared me to."

"*Jesus*, Tate."

"Everyone in that bar watched you, all of them. You

might as well take off your shirt with the way it's sticking to you. Christ." Tate nuzzled his lips under Logan's ear where he gnawed gently with his teeth. "And this," he explained, copping a quick feel between Logan's legs, "I want this."

"Then, fucking take it," Logan goaded.

Nimble fingers found his belt buckle, and he heard the metallic snick and clink of it as it came undone. Then, the hot mouth by his ear was back, promising him exactly what he'd been fantasizing about.

"I want you in my mouth."

Logan turned his head against the door and met the eyes blazing back at him. "Yeah?"

"Yeah. Goddamn it, Logan. What have you done to me?"

Logan lifted his hand and pushed it into Tate's hair. Holding it tight, he brought the man's mouth to his own where he breathed against his lips, "Nothing yet, but I have plans. Get on your knees, Tate."

Logan held his breath and congratulated himself for standing still as Tate lowered himself to his knees and looked up at him.

* * *

TATE'S HEART WAS thumping in his chest. He was down on his knees, and Logan's hand was still tangled in his hair. Raising his face, he stared up at the man, leaning back against the door.

With his shirt still stuck to his skin, Logan's tie looked beyond saving. Tate continued to watch his eyes darken. As the fingers in his hair loosened, the same hand smoothing over the back of his head, Tate was able to push aside the slight nerves he felt at what he was about to do.

Getting up onto his knees, Tate quickly undid the button and zipper of Logan's pants. With them hanging open and the belt and water weighing them down, he looked back up to Logan, lifted his hand, and slid his fingers into the elastic of the black boxers.

He paused for a moment and asked, "Yes?"

"Hell yes," Logan replied, thrusting his hips forward.

Tate followed a drop of water as it fell from the end of Logan's tie and hit the back of his hand. Tate leaned forward and licked his own hand, and heard an expletive from above. He slipped his fingers further inside the material and pulled them down. Knowing they didn't have long helped Tate to shove aside any doubt he might have had, and as he freed Logan's erection, he found himself licking his lips.

"Oh *God*, Tate."

Tate looked up to where Logan was watching him like a hawk. "What? I didn't do anything."

"You're looking at me like you're about to eat your favorite fucking meal."

That boosted Tate's confidence to a whole other level, and he smiled up at Logan as he encircled the base of the shaft in front of him. As Logan's mouth fell open, Tate told him, "Who knows? Maybe I am."

"God, please let that be the fucking truth," Logan gritted out between a clenched jaw.

Tate lowered his eyes to his hand and glided his fist up the swollen, aching flesh he held. "What do you like?"

"Think about what you like and just—"

Tate flicked his tongue across the glistening tip, and Logan's entire body vibrated against him.

He finished his thought by saying, "*Ah* shit, yes. Do *that.*"

Feeling encouraged, Tate did it again—lingering, he ran his tongue all around the head and down under to the sensitive glans. Checking to see if he was doing okay, he figured he must have been because Logan had shut his eyes, and his head was back against the door.

Constricting his fist, Tate drew his hand up the long length, and this time, when he lowered his lips, he sucked the head inside his mouth. The salty taste of pre-cum was the first thing Tate acknowledged, just before the rain-soaked, earthy scent that was all Logan hit him. This was definitely different, but as he relaxed into it, Tate became aware of how much he was enjoying it.

"Oh fuck. *Fuck*, Tate."

Hearing his name being cursed out above him was a major turn-on, but when Logan's fingers curled in his hair, Tate knew he could become addicted to this. Down on his knees in front of Logan, he held all the power because, right now, Logan was his.

Releasing Logan's shaft, Tate raised both hands and framed it with his thumbs and fingers. As it pointed out toward him, he sucked the tip back into his mouth, and then he took a deep breath and lowered his lips. He made it as far as he could before drawing up, feeling light-headed from the lack of oxygen.

"Breathe through your nose."

Tate glanced up, slightly embarrassed, to see Logan staring down at him.

"When you do that again—and please, you have to do it again—breathe through your nose."

Taking in the instruction, Tate once again lowered his head, but before he sucked him between his lips, he stopped and blew a breath across Logan's wet skin. It was something he himself always liked, and judging by the hand that pulled his face closer to the cock waiting for him, it was also something Logan liked, too.

* * *

HELL, EVEN WHEN *he's not trying, Tate is a tease.*

Every single move he made was designed to turn Logan on even more than he already was—or maybe it was just who was doing it.

As it was, with Tate on his knees and between his thighs, Logan was finding it difficult not to ram his hips forward and slide to the back of Tate's throat.

Oh yeah, I can't wait until I can do that, and fucking shoot

my load all over his tongue. But Logan didn't want to freak
Tate out, and the slow, tentative way Tate was lowering his
lips down him was sweet torture all on its own.

Closing his eyes, Logan concentrated on the small
noises he could hear, and the fact that it was Tate making
the sucking sounds was almost enough to make him lose it
right there. Tate had his lips wrapped around *his* cock, and it
was driving Logan insane to even think about it.

As the man in front of him seemed to grow more
confident in his actions, Logan felt one of the hands on his
groin move down between his legs, and he couldn't help the
curse that left him when that hand cupped his balls.

"Motherfucker."

"Hmm," Tate hummed as if he was—*please let him
be*—enjoying every single thing he was doing.

Clasping Tate's head, Logan gradually began to
move his hips, sliding past the lips tormenting him. The
hand between his thighs slowly pushed his balls up as Tate
drew his mouth off him and leaned in to press his lips
against Logan's lower abdomen.

Logan hadn't expect Tate to do anything other than
what was the necessary, but as he stood there, Tate shoved
his damp shirt aside and ran his tongue over the muscles
beneath his navel. He rooted his nose in against Logan's skin
as though he loved the smell of him, and then with a hand
on Logan's balls and his chin bumping against his erection,
Tate raised his eyes to meet with his.

The look of absolute lust and acceptance at what he

was doing made Logan want to strip him of his clothes and take Tate on the floor—fuck the fact that he was at work. Instead, he took Tate's head with both hands and urged him up his body. Logan wanted his mouth.

When Tate got to his feet, Logan attacked his lips, lowering one hand to the man's ass and keeping one on his head. Tate's body slammed against his, and he could feel the erection inside of Tate's pants as he thrust hard against him.

Logan tasted the mouth that had just been wrapped around him, and as Tate sucked on his tongue, his hands found Logan's tie, trying to loosen it. As he worked it free of the knot, so it hung loosely, Tate removed his mouth and lowered his lips to Logan's neck.

Logan's head thunked back on the door, and his cock continued to rub over Tate's clothing as he heard the labored breathing by his ear.

"Congratulations," Logan heard whispered as Tate's hand snaked down between them, and his fingers wrapped around him.

"On?" he pushed past the lump in his throat.

Tate raised his head and looked him right in the eye. "Corrupting me."

"I corrupted you? You're the one stroking my dick."

Tate stepped away from him and lowered back down onto his knees. "Yes, and you're the one who convinced me to try, and now, I can't seem to fucking stop."

Logan's mouth curved as he ran his finger down Tate's stubble to his chin where he traced the masculine lips.

"Then, by all means, don't."

* * *

TATE HAD BEEN telling the truth. He couldn't get enough of Logan as he opened his mouth and felt him slide back in along his tongue. Concentrating on his breathing, Tate closed his eyes and enjoyed the feeling of Logan, using his mouth in a way he'd never done before. It was a unique experience—to be giving something and knowing exactly how good it felt to be the one receiving it. Tate knew how it felt to fuck a hot, willing mouth. *Shit, he knew how good it was to slide into Logan's.*

Placing his hands on Logan's legs, Tate felt the power of the muscles flex beneath his palms. Everything about what he was doing was arousing him—the cock between his lips, the soft grunts he could hear coming from Logan, and the hands holding him still, so his mouth could be used. *Oh yeah.* He hadn't been lying. This was exactly what he wanted, and there was no way he was stopping.

Trailing his left hand down between Logan's thighs, Tate moved his fingers in under his balls and pushed a single digit between those hot ass cheeks, and the reaction was immediate. The hands on his head jerked him closer as Tate's finger burrowed higher until he found the warm hole he was searching for. When the tip of his finger touched against Logan, Tate lifted his vision to find Logan staring at him as he huffed through parted lips and continued to jam his hips forward, making sure he filled Tate's mouth.

Tate, curious to see how Logan would react, slid his fingertip inside the other man and watched as Logan bared his teeth at him. His eyes narrowed as his ass clenched around Tate's finger, and then Logan shoved as deep as he could go, making Tate cough and falter. As Logan seemed to realize what had happened, he began to pull out, but Tate chased him and took him back inside, craving that kind of intense reaction.

Gone now was the tease. Gone was the lesson on the hows and whys. Now came the *need*—the need to finish, the need to come, and the need to be part of the other person.

As Tate felt his cheeks become damp, he realized his eyes must have been watering, but he was determined, and he wanted this. When Logan looked down at him, Tate made sure to swirl his tongue around the cock pulled from his mouth.

"I'm really close, Tate. If you don't want this—"

Tate didn't answer verbally. Instead, he slid his lips forward over Logan until the other man got the message and started up a fast rhythm of pumping in and out of his mouth.

Nothing had prepared Tate to feel as he did while he knelt before Logan with his mouth full and his fingers moving. As he watched the man above, who'd somehow crawled under his skin, he realized he was feeling things way beyond sex. He realized that the sex would never have happened if there wasn't more there for him, and just as that realization hit him, Logan's fingers twisted in his hair.

The cock in Tate's mouth pulsated, and then a hot jet of salty fluid hit his tongue, shocking his taste buds. He pulled his lips off the man in front of him, and even though he hadn't expected the heat or the flavor, Tate found his curiosity made him swallow.

"Jesus, you swallowed, too? You *are* perfect."

Tate's eyes crawled up the relaxed-looking Logan, and when they met, Tate touched his tongue to his bottom lip.

"Was it...you know, okay?"

Logan slid down the door until his ass was on the floor. "You literally made my knees give out."

Tate leaned forward, but before he kissed Logan, he stopped.

"What?" Logan asked with a raised brow.

"Do you care if I kiss you...you know, after you just—"

"Are you fucking kidding me?" Logan grabbed him and took his mouth in a tongue-thrusting kiss.

Tate moaned with pent-up frustration and followed Logan until his back hit the door with a loud thump.

"I have to go back to work."

"Be sick," Logan suggested.

"All of a sudden?"

"Yes, *yes*. Be sick and come home, so I can do something about this," Logan proposed, reaching down to milk Tate's cock.

"I can't. It's too busy. Oh *God*," he sighed as Logan's hand continued working him. "God...stop. It's gonna be hard enough to work with you sitting out there."

"Yeah?" Logan teased as he released him.

Tate pushed away and stood up. "Yeah. Don't fuck with me out there."

"Hmm, okay. Maybe I can wait until I get you home. Come on, aren't you curious yet?"

Tate didn't know how to answer that. He *was* curious, especially after last night. He could admit that much, but he wasn't quite ready to say it out loud. Plus, he knew the minute Logan was aware that he'd even entertained the possibility, he would be screwed—both literally and figuratively. So, he decided to ignore the question.

"Logan?"

"Yeah?" Logan responded from where he was busy tucking his damp shirt into his pants and zipping them.

"That was kind of insane."

Logan looked over to him as he stilled. "In a good way?"

Tate nodded as he straightened his own shirt and watched Logan buckle his belt. "Yes, in an I-want-to-do-it-again way."

Once Logan was as put-together as he could get, he strolled forward, and with no hesitation at all, he kissed Tate hard. "Feel free to get on your knees for me whenever you want. I'll never complain."

"Never?"

"Never," he confirmed.

Tate laughed. "You're too easy, you know that, right? You should play hard to get every now and then."

Logan shrugged, and Tate caught himself wishing that he were that sure of himself.

"Why, when I know what I want?"

"And that is?" Tate asked, not really knowing why he needed the verbal confirmation, but he did.

"Are you fishing, Tate?"

"Maybe," he answered.

When Logan moved around behind him, he felt a shiver skate down his spine.

Prickly stubble brushed by his ear and warm lips sucked on his lobe as Logan worked to reassure him. "I want you, and I want to be inside you." He pulled Tate back, so he could roll his hips against him. "Admit it, you've thought about it by now. You can tell me."

"How did this happen, Logan?" Tate questioned almost breathless as Logan's mouth both aroused and did its best to coerce.

"This?"

Tate nodded as he pushed his hips back, so he could feel the ridge of Logan's shaft against him. There was no way he would get rid of his hard-on until the man released him and left the room.

"Yeah, me giving a guy head."

"And loving it?"

"Yes, and loving it. How did that happen?" he asked again, truly mystified.

Logan let him go, chuckling as he made his way to the door where he unlocked it and looked back at him. That was when Logan told him the one thing that Tate knew was the absolute truth. "You met me."

Chapter Nineteen

AFTER HE AND Tate washed up in the break room, Logan was the first to step out into the narrow hall, and as the door shut behind him, Amelia was the first person he saw.

"Well, well, well. I see *you* ended up having better luck in convincing our man in there."

Logan couldn't explain why her comment grated him as *much* as it did. But he was pretty fucking positive it was the way she had said *our man.*

Logan rearranged his knotted tie and walked across the space between them, stopping a few inches from her. "When I set my mind to something, I don't stop until I succeed. What can I say?"

Amelia pushed away from the wall, and raising her hands, she placed them on his chest where she ran them up to his shoulders. "So, now that you've had him, he's free game, right? Have to say, he's definitely someone I'd like to play with. Those eyes and all that sexy hair—he's gorgeous. Since he isn't open to the three of—"

"Amelia?" Logan interrupted as one of her hands slid into his hair where she curled her fingers.

"Yeah?"

Logan bent down by her ear and warned, "Keep your hands off him. He's mine, and I'm not sharing him."

Just as those words left his mouth, Logan heard the door behind them open. He was about to back up when the word, "Typical," reached his ears, and it *didn't* come from Amelia.

Stepping away from the woman in front of him, he turned to see Tate. Now fully put-together in his work uniform, he shot daggers at them both, and as Logan moved toward the man, Tate shook his head and spit at him, "Don't fucking bother."

As usual, the annoyance radiating off of him just made him look hotter and Logan hornier. He knew what Tate was thinking as he stood there, looking from Amelia to himself, and there was no way Logan was going to let him continue along that line. So, instead of heeding the warning to back off, he walked closer and watched in silent fascination as Tate made a move to dodge him.

Completely forgetting Amelia was even in the hall with them, Logan followed Tate's side step and shifted to the left until they were toe-to-toe. Tate glowered at him, and the lips that had just been wrapped around him only minutes ago twisted into an angry snarl.

"Move," he snapped.

Logan felt his adrenaline spike at Tate's demand. "No." He walked closer until Tate's back hit the wall.

"You're incapable of keeping your mouth and your

zipper shut, aren't you? What was it? Two seconds after being with me, and you're out here, trying to score? Fuck you."

Logan's own temper was starting to ride him now as he told the jealous man in front of him, "You've done that, remember? Just last night, and you told me you didn't have time right now."

Tate seemed to have forgotten their audience as well. Logan knew he would have never talked the way he was now if he remembered that Amelia was there. For Logan, that was his cue to remind Tate of exactly *who* he wanted.

"Get away from me until you can keep your dick in your pants."

That was when Logan lost his patience. He raised his hands and pushed Tate's shoulders into the wall behind him.

"My cock *is* in my fucking pants, exactly where I put it after you finished sucking me off a minute ago. Wow, Tate, when did you turn into such a little bitch?"

Logan figured that comment would get him a fist in the face with Tate's fulminating expression, but it didn't. Instead, Tate's focus shifted past his shoulders and obviously latched on to Amelia, who Logan was sure was watching avidly. Then, Tate's returned his gaze back to his.

"Back off," Tate barked, his hard and fast breaths pushing his chest against Logan's.

Logan connected their hips and noticed Tate was either still excited from earlier or newly turned-on since starting their argument.

"No."

"Logan," Tate warned.

Logan didn't care. If Tate wanted proof of exactly whom he was interested in, he had no problem showing him.

"Tate."

"Get the *fuck* off me!"

Logan raised a hand from Tate's shoulder and pushed it up into the hair that Amelia had been talking about only seconds earlier. He yanked Tate's head close and bit his bottom lip. "I will—after."

"After?"

"After I remind you."

With that, Logan brought his mouth onto the angry one in front of him.

* * *

AMELIA IS RIGHT there, Tate thought, as Logan's mouth took his in a brutal kiss. The hand in his hair was punishing in its hold, and Tate could feel Logan's erection as he continued to tangle his tongue with his own.

Yes, this mouth is mine, Tate thought as he parted his lips farther. *Logan's arms? They're mine, too,* he thought, raising his hands from his sides to grip Logan's biceps. As Logan aligned their bodies, Tate groaned and placed a palm on the chest grazing his. *And this body, this powerful body pressing against me, that's mine also.*

Screw Amelia, and as he thought that, Tate's eyes opened and connected with the woman standing across from them. She licked her lips, walked closer, and ran her heated gaze down over the two of them, and Tate made sure to put a hand on Logan's ass, a sign saying, *Yeah, I'm fucking this, too.*

She reached out and trailed her fingertips over the back of his hand gripping Logan, and then nodded as though she got the message, before turning to walk out of the narrow hall. When she was out of sight, Tate put all of his weight behind him, raised his hands, and pushed Logan to the opposite wall where he followed and started to grind on the man with his unsatisfied hard-on.

Lifting his mouth, Tate looked into the face of the man who was making him crazy. "Keep your mouth away from her."

Logan scraped his teeth along Tate's jaw as he rasped, "I thought it was my cock you were worried about."

"Logan," Tate growled.

As he felt strong fingers in his hair, he found it interesting that he didn't give a shit that Amelia had just seen what she had. Tate wanted everyone here to know that Logan was his—for *more* than one night.

"I told you already, I'm not interested in anyone else."

"Didn't look that way," Tate pointed out.

"Well, maybe you should have looked closer. She's

not interested in *me*."

That got Tate's attention. He took a step back and looked at Logan in his crumpled suit as he remained against the wall, eyelids lowered and lips swollen. Tate thought he'd never looked sexier.

"I already told her no," Tate explained.

"Yes, well, she thinks you meant no to the three of us."

Tate shook his head at the casual way shit fell out of Logan's mouth.

"I did mean no to the three of us and to the two of us, meaning Amelia and me. There's no way I'm sleeping with a coworker. It's too messy."

Logan pushed off the wall and stepped to him. "Good, because right now, you're sleeping with me, and that's going to take up all your time."

Tate's erection throbbed even harder at the thought. "God, go, would you? I'll see you at the bar. I need a minute without you in it."

"And why's that?"

"Because you're too fucking much. You make me insane."

Logan leaned into him, and Tate tried to rationalize his *irrational* behavior, but he had nothing—except this man who was bringing out feelings in him that he hadn't felt for a long time, if ever.

Turning his head, Tate couldn't help himself from kissing Logan again, quick and hard, and then he stepped away and watched him walk down the hall.

As Logan came to the door leading out to the bar, he looked back to him once more. "Don't be too long. I like looking at you."

Tate's heart sped up as if Logan had touched him. Instead of saying anything, he nodded, and when Logan winked at him, he felt a whole new kind of ache, but this one was located in his chest, not down between his legs. It was a hell of a lot more terrifying to think about.

* * *

"I WAS RIGHT, wasn't I?"

Tate looked at Amelia with her hip against the back counter.

The initial rush of the evening had finally died down. Luckily for him, they'd been slammed when he stepped back out into the bar area. He'd located Logan at the far end, and he'd felt somewhat relieved to see that he already had a drink. Which meant that Tate could distract himself with other things until he got himself fully back under control.

"About what?" he hedged, but he knew what was coming.

"Don't even. His reputation—it fits him, doesn't it?"

Tate hadn't liked hearing about the gossip before, and now was no different. "I don't know what you're talking about."

"Okay Tate, you can pretend you aren't secretly

enjoying every minute in his bed, but newsflash, I've been there. I know how good he is."

Tate didn't want to cause a scene, but he was really getting sick of people getting in his face today about having slept with Logan. Then again, it wasn't like he hadn't known the man had been with—

Well, in this bar, nearly everyone.

On the other hand, Tate supposed, it wasn't any of his business what Logan had done in the past, just *who* he was doing presently.

"Listen. I don't care about anything he did before. I'm not interested."

Amelia shifted and placed her palm on the counter by his where she touched her fingers to his hand. "I didn't know you swung that way."

"I don't," was Tate's immediate answer, which he then realized was ludicrous, considering what she'd just seen and probably heard in the back.

"Oh, I think you do. It's okay. I think it's hot, and hey, if anyone is going to make you try anything, it would be Logan. He's very persuasive."

Tate swallowed, remembering similar words coming from Logan's mouth about trying things. Tate knew he was way beyond having *tried* something though, and he was now in the *doing* portion.

"I need a cigarette."

Amelia laughed at him. "I didn't know you smoked."

"I don't unless I'm drinking."

"Or having an anxiety attack?" she quipped.

Tate squeezed his eyes shut and then opened them to look down at the petite blonde in front of him. *Why am I not attracted to her? Life would be so much easier.*

"Don't feel bad. He's hard to resist," she comforted.

Yeah, isn't that the truth. Logan was impossible to resist, and as Tate looked over his shoulder at the guy and found him looking right back, he knew that his brain had moved beyond the physical. He had feelings for Logan—emotions that were going to make things messy, tangled, and beyond complicated.

Amelia then broke into his thoughts by confusing him. "You are, too, you know."

Huh? What was she saying?

"Hard to resist. All the girls here wanted you. And who got you? Fucking Logan. Someone we never even considered."

Tate shifted where he was standing, slightly uncomfortable from knowing that everyone had been watching him and probably still was.

Amelia lifted an arm to pat his shoulder. "You better go get him another drink. He hasn't taken his eyes off you, and I'm starting to feel like he's going to jump over the bar and rip off my hand."

"Don't you think you're being a little dramatic?"

Tate pivoted around to face Logan, who *was* aiming daggers at Amelia, and then she caressed his fucking arm, making Logan's eyes narrow.

Amelia laughed. "Um, no. Considering he warned me off you earlier in the hall, I'm pretty sure I'm reading him right, which is interesting. He's *never* given a shit before."

Tate's head snapped around to her and he glanced at the hand massaging his arm and then up to the mischievous grin on her face. "He did what?"

"He didn't tell you?" she asked, finally removing her hand. "When you came out and saw us, he was telling me to back off."

For some reason, that piece of information made Tate hot as hell even though he figured it probably should have annoyed him. Distracted by his own thoughts, he told Amelia he'd be back, and made his way toward the man at the other end of the bar.

* * *

LOGAN'S EYES WERE fixed on Tate as his long legs ate up the space behind the bar. When he stopped in front of him and placed his hands on the counter, Logan lifted his face and waited.

"Want something?" Tate asked without any kind of greeting.

"I don't remember service being so sloppy in here."

"Sloppy?"

"No greeting, no smile, no how's-your-day-going."

Tate crossed his arms and aimed a fake smile his

way. "Hi, how's your day going?"

Logan pushed his tongue into his cheek and glanced over Tate's buttoned black shirt and vest. *Yes,* he thought, *Tate looked fucking spectacular on his knees in front of me. I was right—that pompous vest looked even better from above.*

"Fantastic as of thirty minutes ago when—"

"Don't."

"No? Why not?" Logan quipped. "I thought you might need a reminder."

"I don't. I remember it all perfectly, but you left out a few details."

Sitting back on the stool, Logan frowned. "Did I?"

"Yes, you did."

Logan tracked Tate's hand as he pulled the white towel from the back of his pants and started to wipe down the bar top. *Ah, that nervous gesture. I love his tells.* "What did I leave out?"

Tate bent in closer than even Logan would have expected. "You get just as jealous as I do. *You* just hide it better."

Logan's jaw ticked as he thought about Amelia touching Tate, not knowing what she had been saying. He had to admit, he was one hundred percent jealous. That was something he'd never been in his life—until Tate. Logan didn't want her anywhere near him, not while he was his.

"So?"

"Oh, so it's okay if it's you but not me? Not so funny now, is it?"

"It was never funny. I've worked hard to get what I want. She can take a fucking hike if she thinks she's going to get a piece of it."

Tate placed a steadying palm on the bar, as his mouth parted slightly. He sucked in a quick breath and then he let it out, confessing, "I don't know why that's so hot, but it is."

"Don't you see, Tate? She's just like me. The ones who resist us are the ones we want the most."

"So, this is just a game to you?"

Logan thought about that for a second, and then he reached out to the hand on the bar. "Maybe at first, but not now. It stopped being a game the night you showed up at my front door."

Logan removed his hand and sat back, while Tate reached up to rub his cheek.

"So, let's talk. Tell me something I don't know about you," Logan said, deciding to move to a topic that was more comfortable.

Tate lifted a shoulder but played along. "I hate mushrooms."

Not expecting that, Logan started laughing. "Okay, I'll keep that in mind for pizza night."

"And anchovies," Tate added.

"Who likes anchovies?"

"I don't know, but I hate those salty, fishy things."

"Noted. Anything else?" Logan asked.

Tate took the empty glass in front of him and put

them with the other dirty ones. When he turned back, he asked, "What night is pizza night?"

Logan thought about that and decided he really liked the idea of a regular date night with Tate. "I'm thinking Sundays."

"Sundays, huh? I'm free on Sunday nights."

"Yeah?"

Logan noted the way Tate's eyes darkened, and he felt all kinds of excited at the thought of spending the night with this man again.

"Yeah."

"Then, you should definitely come." Unable to look away, Logan was enjoying this relaxed side of Tate.

"Well, that could certainly be part of the evening, I'm sure."

Logan hadn't even caught himself on that, but as Tate threw the pun back at him, he felt his anticipation heighten at the flirtatious grin crossing the lips he was now imagining against his own.

"Careful, Tate."

"Why's that?"

"You think you're safe because I've already tasted you. You think I'm just sitting here, but you're wrong, I'm constantly imagining it. All it did was make me want you more. I'm about two seconds away from hauling you across the bar. So, back the fuck up unless you're ready for that."

* * *

TATE BACKED AWAY, eyeing Logan's mouth. "Well, everyone I work with will know by the end of this shift anyway."

"Does that bother you?"

Tate thought that over and realized that it *didn't* bother him. It was actually a relief that he wouldn't have to be the one to tell people. They would just know, and if they were brave enough to ask him about it, then he'd deal with it then. Most people though never actually said what they were thinking to your face. It was usually gossip behind your back, and he didn't give a shit about that.

"No. It doesn't."

"Really?"

"Yes, really. I don't care what they think. I hardly know them."

"That's true," Logan agreed. "What about people you *do* know?"

Tate crossed his arms. "Like?"

"Like your family."

Tate didn't understand. Logan had balked at the very mention of family just the night before. *Why is he bringing it up now?* "Family is different."

"Is it?"

Tate got the impression that Logan was annoyed with that answer.

"Yes, it is. Anyway, you're the one who made it very clear that families aren't an issue right now."

Logan's mouth twisted into a smile that Tate suspected was fake. "You're right."

"Am I?" He was slightly confused by the turn in the conversation.

"Yep. Can I have another drink?"

"Why? Do you *need* one?" Tate asked, reaching under the bar for a glass.

"Maybe."

The usually calm and put-together man now looked…bothered.

"Logan?"

"Yeah?"

"Do you *want* me to tell my family?"

Logan's eyes rose to his own, and Tate felt his heart thudding in his chest.

"Not really my decision, is it?"

Tate put his hands back on the bar and pushed his face in close to Logan's, not giving a fuck who was looking. "No, it isn't, but I think you *want* me to tell them."

When Logan didn't say a word, Tate knew he was right on the money.

"I know why that thought scares me, but what scares *you* about it? The fact that you'd have to admit to the commitment or the thought of someone giving a shit about you?"

Logan frowned, and just like that, the reality of where this was all going was laid out in front of them.

"I don't know what you're talking about."

"Yes you do," Tate whispered and straightened. "Still want that drink?"

"Yeah, let's make it tequila."

Laughing at Logan's mumbled request, Tate questioned, "Liquid courage?"

"Enjoying yourself at my expense?"

"Immensely." Tate turned his back, poured the drink, and then moved to slide it over to Logan. That was when he heard a question he'd never expected to hear.

"Why are you attracted to me?"

This was something that Tate had asked himself over and over. At first, it had seemed essential for him to know the reasons for his reactions to a man. But the more time Tate spent with Logan, the more he realized it wasn't the feelings he had for a *man* that he needed to work out, but the feelings he had for Logan in particular—and there were many.

"Your confidence."

Logan scoffed. "Really? Because I was under the impression you hated that about me."

"I did," Tate responded automatically.

"*Ah*...I don't understand then."

"I hated it—at first."

"But now?" Logan pushed.

"Now, I think it's...exciting."

Lifting the shot to his mouth, Logan downed the liquid and didn't even flinch as he placed the empty glass on the bar. "Well, that was a different answer than what I'd expected. Thank you."

"I'm not finished. There's more," Tate taunted with a chuckle, wondering what exactly Logan *had* expected. "Want another drink to hear the rest?"

"Oh, nice. Laugh away. The only reason I'm behaving is because you're at work. Otherwise, you'd be just as uncomfortable right now."

"Since when has the fact that I'm at work stopped you?" Tate asked. "I can stop if you'd like."

"Don't you dare."

"So, you like hearing about yourself? Why doesn't that surprise me?" Tate raised his hand to stroke his chin, pretending to be deep in thought.

Logan clarified, "I like hearing what *you* think."

"I think you're sexy, but everyone must tell you that, so that's nothing new. It must get boring."

"Are you kidding? Do you know how long I've waited to hear you tell me something like that?"

"Not that long. I've only known you for a little over two weeks," Tate reminded him, tongue-in-cheek.

"Has it really only been that long? I swear it feels like I've wanted you forever. God, you have no clue what I want to do to you."

Tate's mouth went dry at the way Logan's voice deepened, and his eyes moved to linger on his throat. Reaching for the white towel tucked into his pants, Tate brought it between his hands and twisted it. "Stop it. I can't think when you look at me like that."

"I know. You start playing with that towel, or you push your hands through your hair. But damn, Tate, I can't help it. The minute I saw you, I wanted you."

Tate's erection pressed against its confines as he studied Logan's mouth. "I also like that."

"What?" Logan exhaled.

"How much you want me. It's a fucking rush. The way you watch me, and look at me is so shameless."

"Tate?"

"Yeah?"

"Walk the fuck away from me—right now."

Tate twisted the towel and raised a hand to push it through his hair as he nodded, understanding Logan's lack of self-control. "But later?"

"Later, you're coming home with me."

Tate managed a one-word promise. "Yes."

Chapter Twenty

BARELY TWO FEET inside Logan's condo, Tate was spun around, and his mouth was taken. *Taken* was the only way to describe it. Logan wasn't gentle, and neither were the hands at Tate's waist.

The door was kicked shut, and a light switched on as Tate was walked backward while his work shirt was pulled from his pants. The mouth on his was ravenous, and the tongue that dipped between his lips tasted him like a starving man.

Bringing his hands up to Logan's face, Tate caressed his cheeks and chased the agile tongue back into Logan's mouth. *Hell, as if the man isn't potent enough, his mouth tastes like tequila,* Tate thought as nimble fingers began playing with the bottom of his vest.

Sliding a hand around to the back of Logan's head, Tate flirted with the black hair that had finally dried out from the rain. He gathered Logan in as close as he could until their hips met, and the proof of Logan's arousal was pressed up against his own. Tate pulled his head back and pushed his body against the hard one in front of him.

"Naked. I want you naked," Logan rasped as he

started to undo the buttons of Tate's vest.

Tate took Logan's full bottom lip between his teeth and pulled at it gently before swiping his tongue over it. A hoarse sound came from Logan's throat as he reached the top button of Tate's shirt.

"This damn uniform. It's like unwrapping a fucking Christmas present. Layers and layers," he breathed out, exasperated, while continuing to unbutton, "before I get to what I want."

Tate lifted his hand to Logan's tie and stroked the crumpled material down his chest. "I could say the same."

"So, undress me."

Tate loosened the tie, removed it, and threw it to the floor. Two hands finally parted his vest and shirt, sliding inside, while he unfastened the top two buttons of Logan's shirt.

Before he got any further, Logan lowered his head and pressed warm lips to Tate's nipple. Tate dropped his hands, and let out a shaky sigh.

Oh yeah, bite me, come on, Logan.

Sharp teeth nipped over his chest, and then Logan's tongue flicked out across the pointy nub. When Tate clutched the back of Logan's head, Logan bit down.

"Oh...*shit*, Logan."

Logan's mouth curved against his heated flesh before he moved across to the crease of Tate's arm where he nuzzled in and continued to gently bite the skin and muscle of his bicep. Tate grunted in pleasure at each sharp bite until

Logan lifted his head, and that teasing mouth was back on his.

Tate braced himself, as Logan's hands moved to his waist and then slid around to pull him into full-body contact.

"God, Tate, your skin"—Logan kissed his way across Tate's jaw to his ear—"is so smooth...and tanned...all over. It's so lickable."

Tate's head tipped back, exposing his neck for Logan, and when firm lips started to suck the skin covering his Adam's apple, a rumble left Tate's throat.

Logan lifted his head. "Do that again."

Tate felt the lips back against his throat, and he groaned for Logan, causing a vibration to hum out of him. Then, a wet tongue licked up the side of Tate's neck, and strong teeth sank into his jaw. He lifted his head and stared back at Logan.

"I want you so fucking bad," Logan cursed.

Tate raised his hands to Logan's shirt, and this time, instead of bothering to unbutton it, he tore it apart. As the buttons popped free from the material, he yanked Logan in by the edges of his shirt, so their bodies were back to touching.

"Hope you didn't want your shirt."

"Fuck my shirt."

Tate chuckled, and then he asked seriously, "Logan?"

Logan's body tensed. "Yes?"

Pushing the white material off Logan's shoulder, Tate relayed his thoughts clearly. "I want to be inside you, just like last night." He kissed Logan's neck, and when he got to his ear, he sucked the lobe into his mouth. He made sure to add, "And I want to hear *my* name when I make you come."

* * *

YES, LOGAN THOUGHT as Tate's mouth hovered over his ear, whispering the hottest promise he'd ever heard.

Logan hadn't been lying about how much he wanted Tate. It was insane. Basically, Tate just had to look at him, breathe near him, or be in the same vicinity, and he was ready to go. Usually, Logan could control his body better, but one flirtatious comment or smile from the man currently kissing his way up his neck, and he was useless.

"Feeling possessive?" he goaded, knowing exactly what was riding Tate.

Not one, but *two* of Logan's past acquaintances had gotten in Tate's face today, and Logan knew that tonight was about two things—*want and possession*. Tate was out to prove something, and who the hell was he to stop him.

As his shirt landed on the floor and Tate's mouth came back to his, Logan ran his hands through the curls he obsessed over and pushed against the determined man in front of him. When Tate shoved back as though he wasn't giving up the upper hand, Logan bucked his hips forward, loving the resistance. As two hands moved between them to his belt buckle, Logan lifted his head, and Tate's tongue licked into his open mouth.

"So sexy, Tate. You're so fucking sexy."

Tate's lips curved. "Where to? Bedroom?"

Logan glanced over to the couch. "No, not close enough. There."

"Here?" Tate confirmed as he released him and turned to walk over to the black leather couch. When he stopped in front of it, he unfastened the button of his pants, his zipper, and then sat down with his legs spread wide in sexual invitation.

Logan could hardly take his eyes away from him as he kicked off his shoes. He knew what was coming and what he wanted, and it was sitting on his couch, waiting for him to come and take it.

Bending down, Logan removed his socks, and when he straightened, he came eye-to-eye with Tate, who was watching him and stroking himself. With his lowered eyelids and swollen lips, Tate looked like he'd been fucked hard already, and Logan couldn't wait for that day. He knew that once he got inside Tate, he was going to spend a good portion of his days, weeks, and months getting back in there as often as possible. Until then, he would happily take him the only way he could.

"You want something, Tate?"

Tate looked him over, starting at his bare feet. Unhurriedly, they grazed over his boxers to the trail of hair that pointed down to Logan's upright shaft, and when Tate's eyes finally connected with his, they were so dark they were almost black.

"So? You want something?"

"You already know what I want. I told you."

Logan moved across the room to open a drawer in the bottom of the entertainment center. When he came back in front of Tate, he dropped a condom on the glass coffee table and a bottle of lube on the couch beside Tate's leg.

"Tell me *exactly* what you want," Logan urged as Tate looked at the items he'd deposited.

When he brought his eyes back to Logan's, Tate reiterated, clear as a fucking bell, "I want to hear *my* name, on your tongue."

Now, it was Logan's turn to reach down into his boxers and take a hold of his straining erection. "And then?"

Tate watched Logan's hand and proceeded to shock the hell out of him. "And then, I want to come all over you."

Faltering on Tate's words, Logan stepped between his legs as Tate pushed up to sit on the edge of the couch. Tate grasped his hips between those wide palms and pressed moist lips to Logan's lower abdomen.

"I watched that today before work," Tate admitted against his stomach, causing Logan to almost fall over as his fingers weaved into Tate's brown waves.

"You watched, what?"

"Two guys having sex, and then they came all over each other. It was so damn hot."

Tate watched gay porn? Oh shit, I am so screwed, Logan thought because he knew he needed all of those details right fucking now.

* * *

TATE NIBBLED THE warm skin under his lips as the fingers in his hair knotted, and he knew Logan was undoubtedly reacting to what he'd just said. He wasn't lying. This morning, after the coffee shop, Tate had spent a lot of time going over his emotions, and by the end of it, when he had decided what he wanted—well, he'd done some research.

It hadn't taken him long to find a good free site, and for the next hour or so, he'd educated himself in a very pleasurable way. *Who knew gay porn would be so sexy?* Or more to the point, he hadn't known that watching it and imagining doing all of that with Logan would be such a turn-on.

Obviously, it also excited Logan because he was practically fucking his face through his boxers. As Logan's fingers continued to play in his hair, Tate's head was pulled back, so he was staring up at the man looking down at him.

"What else did you *learn* today?"

Tate hesitated for only a second before he told Logan the one thing that had really gotten him off. It was something he hadn't thought about previously, but now that he'd seen it, he couldn't get it out of his head.

"That I can take you face-to-face—with you on your

back under me."

When Logan remained silent, Tate continued, "I want you like that. I want to watch you."

The seconds following that comment were palpable. All Tate could hear was his own harsh breathing, and then before he knew it, his hair was released, and Logan was straddling his thighs.

It was an odd feeling to have a man slightly bigger than himself kneeling over his lap. But as soon as Logan's cock, which was straining against his boxers, brushed against his own, Tate leaned back on the couch and clutched Logan's ass, pulling him forward.

As their mouths met, Logan agreed, "All right, do it."

Tate thought about it for around three seconds, and then he moved. With a hand on Logan's head and one on his ass, Tate maneuvered them, so Logan was lying flat on his back, and he was hovering over the top of him. Logan's mouth parted as he stared up at him, and Tate couldn't help himself from tracing his finger across his thin top lip and then the bottom.

Tate shifted on the couch until he was situated between Logan's thighs, and he felt his own erection line up with the one beneath. Stretching above Logan's head, Tate clutched the arm of the couch, just as Logan once had, and started to rock his hips. With eyes full of heated lust, Logan bent his legs on either side of him and arched up to meet him halfway.

Tate heard an uninhibited roar rip from his own

chest. *This is what it's going to be like,* he thought as he continued to writhe against Logan. *When I'm inside him, I'll get to watch every thought and feeling on his face.*

Then, Logan's arms wrapped around him, and his hands slid inside Tate's pants to fondle his ass, making Tate desperate for the mouth inches from his. Gliding his tongue between Logan's lips, Tate went crazy as the thighs on either side of his waist tensed, and Logan lifted his body up to drag against his own.

With a grunt, Tate lifted his head, "Oh *hell,*" as Logan's fingers crept between his ass cheeks and spread him while bringing him in even closer.

"*Damn*, Tate. Feels good," Logan praised.

When Tate couldn't stand it anymore, he pushed back and knelt between the spread legs in front of him. As he looked down at the man lying back on the couch, his mouth practically watered. Logan was irresistible, and Tate couldn't wait to get inside him.

* * *

AS TATE LOOKED him over, Logan raised one of his arms behind him. He slid his other hand down into his boxers to stroke his erection, showing off his entire body to Tate's hungry stare.

"God, I stood no chance," Tate told him in disbelief. "Look at you."

"Look at *you*," Logan retorted, his voice pitched-low,

so he had to consciously project it for Tate to hear.

Logan's eyes drew heavy as Tate extended his arm and curled his fingers into the elastic of the black cotton, preparing to free his cock. With a husky groan of sheer relief, Logan quickly raised his legs to allow room for Tate to pull the fabric off and throw it aside. Resuming the same position, Logan gave Tate a thorough once-over as he began to work his length under Tate's keen gaze.

"Get naked, Tate."

Quickly, Tate stood and removed his remaining clothes. As his erection came into view and he bent to pick up the condom, Logan couldn't help the raw noise escaping his mouth.

Tate kept his eyes on him the entire time he sheathed his cock. When he picked up the bottle of lube and unsnapped the lid, Logan took a moment to wonder where the curious and nervous Tate had disappeared to. In his place seemed to be an entirely confident man, who was getting ready to fuck the hell out of him. Either way, he wanted Tate inside him.

Logan widened his legs as Tate got on the couch and braced one of his arms over him, so he could lean back down. As their bodies finally brushed up against each other, Logan brought his hands around to grip Tate's ass, bringing his thick shaft, against his own.

"Ah, you like that?" Tate continued thrusting down on him.

"Yes, I fucking like it."

Tate took his lips in a quick kiss. "So testy. I like this position."

"Jesus, you're talkative all of a sudden."

When Tate stopped the slow roll of his hips, Logan almost shouted in frustration.

"I'm sorry," Tate taunted. "I'm not supposed to talk?" He lowered his head until his mouth was beside Logan's ear. "I thought you liked it when I told you what I wanted to do to you."

"Holy shit, Tate, I do."

Never in the past had he liked talkers. In fact, Logan had hated them. He'd preferred to get the deed over and done with. *As long as it felt good, why would I care what was being said?* But with each new discovery Tate made, Logan would get more turned-on, and he couldn't wait to hear the next thing that would tumble out of this guy's mouth.

Case in point…

"Good, because I really want to watch your face when I slide my fingers back inside you."

"Fucking hell. *Do it,*" Logan implored. He took Tate's lips with his own, trying to shut him up, before he came from his words alone.

Tate's free hand burrowed down between them, and his slick palm gave Logan's shaft a firm stroke, making Logan's back come up from the couch. He didn't linger there though. Tate merely lubed him up enough to create an easy glide for Logan's own hand. Then, Tate trailed his fingers down until he was probing at his hole.

Logan closed his eyes as Tate hesitantly massaged his fingertip over the puckered skin. It wasn't until Tate lowered his other arm and hooked it around his left leg that Logan lost his fucking rhythm. Tate steadily pressed his thigh back, stretching him wide open. *Holy shit.* Tate *had* been watching and learning.

With his leg trapped at that angle, Logan was about as vulnerable as he could get. Not a position he particularly enjoyed, but as he lay underneath Tate, he had never been more aroused. Logan was *more* than happy to be this particular man's experimental body.

As Tate shifted slightly, Logan knew he was open for Tate to do with as he pleased, and for now, Tate took pleasure in looking him right in the eye as he slowly slid his index finger inside his body.

* * *

HOW FUCKING SEXY is that? Tate thought as he looked down at Logan who was wide open and holding his hard length as his body sucked Tate's finger into his depths.

"Incredible, fucking incredible," Tate marveled, pulling his finger from Logan, only to slip it inside again.

Looking down to where his finger was disappearing into the deliciously masculine body below, Tate slowly removed his long digit and added the second. Watching the quiet, intense man, Tate slowly pushed forward until they were all the way inside Logan, and then he stopped and left his hand there. "What would make this better for you?"

Logan's eyes widened slightly. "It's pretty perfect as is, but if you like, pull them out and push them back in *real* slow. Then, come down here and kiss me."

Tate watched in fascination from his view as he *slowly* did what Logan had instructed.

"*Ah*," Logan moaned.

"Again?" Tate asked. His own cock now aching with the need to bury itself where his fingers were.

"Again," Logan approved even as Tate's fingers were already moving.

Tate angled down over him, bringing up Logan's left leg until it was pushed back against his chest, and then he took his mouth in an unyielding kiss.

"I want you so bad," he rasped against Logan's mouth.

Logan's lips slid into a provocative smile as his hips shoved up toward Tate's fingers. "Then, take me."

Removing his fingers from the snug heat of Logan's body, Tate kissed him again quickly before moving back to kneel and grab the bottle.

Looking down at the naked man waiting for him, Tate watched as Logan bent his legs and spread them wide while he pleasured himself. Tate tried to calm his breathing, but when Logan's lips parted and he told him, "I can't wait to feel you inside me," it was no use.

Gripping both of Logan's calves, Tate hauled him down the couch until he was directly between Logan's legs where he needed to be. Taking his cock in his hand, Tate lined himself up with Logan's hole, and then hooked his arm under Logan's leg, bending it back slightly to give him a better view of what he was about to do.

Tate pressed against the rim of Logan's body, and grit his teeth. He glanced up to see Logan's eyes were closed, and his black lashes were lying on his cheeks. He seemed to be waiting patiently for Tate to push forward. Meeting with the initial resistance of Logan's body, Tate's heartbeat quickened as he flexed his hips, and the muscle gave way, allowing him to sink inside.

Feeling it the night before had been unreal. *But seeing it and feeling it? Total fucking ecstasy.* Tate heard a rumble come from Logan as he sank in deeper. *What a fucking sight,* Tate thought. *It looks and feels perfect.*

Fully seated inside Logan's body, Tate once again checked on the man under him to make sure he was okay.

And this time, Logan told him, "Move."

Tate's mouth twitched. He wanted to smile, but he was too tense. "I'm sorry. I didn't hear you. What was that?"

A growl definitely left the man as Logan repeated, "*Fucking* move."

A third invite was not required.

* * *

LOGAN LOOKED UP to Tate and tried to remind himself that he was new to this. Drawing his knees back to his chest,

Logan's shaft lay rigid against his stomach as Tate's withdrew and then surged back into his body.

Tate's eyes were glued to what was going on between Logan's legs, and he couldn't blame him. It felt mind-blowing. He *also* wanted to see, and this time, when Tate slid into him, Logan reached down to his cock, and he greedily watched all the muscles in Tate's body flex.

"Fuck, *fuck*," Tate was chanting over and over, like a prayer.

Logan had to agree. This was definitely prayer-worthy. It was that good.

Logan was dying to taste Tate's lips, so when Tate's hair flopped forward into his face, Logan took the opportunity to pull on that hair as he leaned up and grabbed Tate's neck, bringing the man down with him.

As Tate came to him, he placed an arm on the couch and groaned as Logan wrapped a leg up around his waist. Taking Tate's mouth with his own, Logan engaged him in a tongue-thrusting, kiss that drove him wild.

Their tongues met while Tate's thick length moved in and out of him. Logan's left leg was still hooked over Tate's arm, and Tate pushed it back against his body, spreading him apart. As he did, Logan couldn't help the throaty curse that fell from his lips.

Tate stopped moving completely and asked through labored breaths, "Sorry. Did I hurt you?"

"No. Hell no. You're just so...so," Logan panted. "It's intense this way."

When Tate brushed a hand over Logan's hair, he felt the intensity triple from the emotion flickering over Tate's face.

"Yeah, it really is."

"Do it again," Logan urged.

Tate drew his hips back and then punched them forward into him, and this time, Tate watched his face for a reaction, and Logan gave it to him.

He bared his teeth and arched his back, demanding, "Again. Do it again. *Harder*."

Logan yanked Tate's hair, and as Tate obeyed, Logan lost his grip on reality.

* * *

TATE STARED DOWN at the man he was working his cock in and out of. Logan had shut his eyes and was fiercely stroking his own erection as Tate pounded into him. Over and over, he slid inside Logan, and each time he bottomed out and his balls hit Logan's body, Tate thought he'd come right then.

He leaned down over Logan and slid so far inside that he felt like he would split the man in two. Instead of complaining, Logan just urged him to do it harder and faster. So, he did, and as Tate connected their mouths, he knew he'd never experienced anything more stimulating before.

He felt as though he were truly inside this man in

every conceivable way, including his mind, and what an experience it was. Watching every expression of lust, want, and pure need cross Logan's face was like a wet dream come to life.

He is gorgeous.

Gone was the time where Tate thought that word didn't apply to a man. As Logan lay under him with his body open, there was no other word that fit. He was as gorgeous as he was strong and sexy.

Logan's cock was long and stout and dripping all over his stomach. It amazed Tate that Logan was getting off, considering how hard he was thrusting into him, but Logan was, and Tate loved every hard hip-fucking moment of it.

It wasn't until Logan craned his neck to watch Tate slide inside, that Tate felt his climax race down his spine. He needed and wanted release, but he wanted Logan to first.

"I need to come," he told the man beneath him. "But I want to watch you."

As if Logan had been waiting for him, he instructed, "Hard and fast. Give it to me as hard and fast as you can, and you'll get one hell of a show."

Tate hooked Logan's other leg with his free arm and braced himself on the cushions by Logan's sides, and he started to fuck the guy as if he never would again.

Hard and fast, as requested, he slid into Logan, and Logan's ass clung to him on every withdraw. Tate's breathing came faster with every flex of his hips, and as his eyes locked with Logan's, he felt the hand in his hair twist as

Logan jerked his cock with the other.

"Ah, Tate. *Fuck!*" he shouted.

Tate watched avidly as Logan came in a sticky mess all over his own hand and stomach as Tate continued to tunnel into him. Logan continued to curse as Tate's hips repeatedly made quick shallow digs inside him.

As Logan's breathing calmed, he grunted softly when Tate pulled out of his body and quickly rolled the condom off. Throwing it aside, Tate picked up the bottle of lube and squeezed some into his palm. He then looked down at Logan, who'd raised his arms back over the couch, with his cock lying against his body now covered in cum.

That was all the visual Tate needed. Grasping his throbbing erection in his hand, Tate watched the satisfied man under him. Logan lazily ran his gaze over him as he lowered his fingers and started to rub his cum into his body.

Without a word, Logan lowered his hand to cup Tate's balls. As soon as his warm, wet fingers touched his flesh, Tate's lips parted, and he shouted a loud, satisfied sound as he, too, came all over Logan's stomach and chest.

As his breathing slowed and his eyes found Logan's, Tate licked his lips and continued to milk his cock until every last drop was on the man under him.

"Fuck," Tate managed on a shaky breath.

Logan sighed, fully satisfied, and placed both hands behind his head. "We've definitely done that."

"You're phenomenal."

Logan crooked a finger up at him and invited,

"Come here."

Tate leaned down over Logan, who brought his legs up to entwine them with his, and their bodies joined together with the sticky evidence of their arousal sliding between them. Logan took his mouth in a sensual kiss.

When he pulled back, he whispered against Tate's lips, "*That* was phenomenal."

"Hmm," Tate hummed in agreement against Logan's mouth. Then, he finally voiced something else he'd been thinking about, "Maybe next time, you can do that to me."

Logan pulled Tate's head up by his curls. "What did you just say?"

Tate grinned down at him. "Maybe next time, you can do that to me. Well, maybe not that hard, you know, being that it will be my first time, and it will probably—"

"Tate?" Logan interrupted. "Shut up for a minute. Do you mean it?"

"Would I be this fucking nervous if I didn't?" Tate asked.

Logan smiled and raised his eyebrows. "I don't know what porn site you watched this morning, but if this is the result, we need to buy a subscription."

Tate chuckled, moving against Logan's body. "I learned a lot of things."

"You did, huh?"

As Tate nipped Logan's mouth, he nodded. "Yep, let me tell you about it, and then we can see if there's anything you want to try."

"I can guarantee that anything coming out of your mouth is going to be something I want to try. I'm easy, remember?"

"I do seem to remember something like that."

Tate lowered his head and rested it against the large chest under him. He thought about how weird it should have felt, but as Logan's arms wrapped around him, it didn't. It felt...*right*.

"Is this okay?" Tate questioned against the short hair on Logan's chest.

"It is until you say otherwise."

Tate couldn't have said why, but that small whispered reply hurt his heart.

Chapter Twenty-One

THE FOLLOWING MORNING, Tate woke with a raging hard-on and a warm tongue on the inside of his thigh. With his eyes closed, he slowly spread his legs farther apart and felt his mouth tug into a smile as a low laugh reached his ears.

"Sure glad you're straight, Tate. Gay guys never let me do this."

Tate opened his eyes and looked down to where Logan's chin was resting on his thigh.

"I highly doubt that. You really *do* only shut up when your mouth is busy, don't you?"

"You like my mouth." Logan licked across one of Tate's balls. "Admit it."

Tate's hips arched toward the teasing tongue as he answered with a soft groan, "It has its good points."

Logan opened the mouth in question and drew his tongue across the base of Tate's cock.

"*Very* good points," Tate stressed.

Logan raised his head and winked up at him. He shifted to place his hands on the bedding next to Tate's hips, rising up over him.

"Give it to me," he suggested.

Tate reached down and pointed his erection up at Logan, who then lowered his head and sucked the tip into his mouth. Letting out a heavy sigh, Tate raised his other arm back behind his head, plumping the pillow up, so he could watch what was going on between his legs.

Logan was on his knees, and Tate watched as a hand brushed his aside, and when a firm palm took its place, Logan's hot mouth drew him all the way inside until his nose was touching Tate's short curls.

Holy fuck! Tate thought as he raised his hips and moved his free hand to the back of Logan's head.

As Logan removed his lips and started to suck the swollen head, Tate wondered why he'd ever questioned getting head from this guy. Logan's eyes flicked to his as he swirled his tongue over the slit, and then he licked his way down the underside of his shaft until he reached his balls. With a quick swipe over them, he came back up and swallowed Tate to the root.

"Oh *Jesus*, Logan," he called out as he palmed the silky black hair in his hand.

Logan drew back up and off him. With a demonic grin, he darted his tongue out and tickled the underside of Tate's cock. "Love sucking on you."

Tate closed his eyes, deciding that was the only way he would last longer than the thirty seconds he figured he had left in him with Logan's teasing. Bending his left leg back felt natural to Tate as he widened his straddle and pushed himself closer to the mouth feasting on him. When a groan came from between his thighs, he figured Logan approved of this new position as well. That was confirmed when a large hand clamped onto his shin and pushed his leg farther up onto his chest, keeping him open and in place.

* * *

LOGAN DREW HIS mouth off of Tate's luscious cock and watched as Tate opened up for him to play, and he planned to take full advantage.

With one hand on Tate's leg and the other on the mattress, Logan lowered his head and took one of Tate's balls into his mouth. As he gently sucked on the sac of skin, he heard a grunt from above, and when he pulled his mouth away and released the tender flesh, a sigh reached his ears. Several times, he repeated the move, stopping only to lick across the base of Tate's solid erection.

He could see the pucker of Tate's ass, and it was calling to him to come and take it, but he knew he'd have to move slowly or Tate would put an end to it before it even began.

Looking up to Tate, Logan watched him stroke himself and then leaned back in, touching the tip of his tongue to Tate's rim. Tate's eyes flew open, and his body tensed as he tried to move, but the hand Logan had on his leg and the look he aimed up at Tate held him in place.

"What the..." Tate questioned, as he stared down at

him.

"Trust me."

Logan blew a breath of air over the wet skin he'd just licked. Tate's ass clenched, and he cursed, causing Logan to close his own eyes to keep his desire in check. As Tate flopped back down on the pillow in defeat, Logan took that as a sign, and he repeated the move, flicking his tongue out to tease.

"What the hell are you doing to me?" Tate groaned.

"I'm gonna make you lose your fucking mind," he promised.

Logan lowered himself to the mattress, so he could bring his free hand up to Tate's body. With a finger against Tate's ass, Logan eyed him as he licked the pucker. Tate's hand was desperately jerking himself now as he watched what was going on.

Pushing his leg up a little higher, Logan got a great angle and tongued his way up to his balls where he sucked one into his mouth as he pushed his finger inside Tate. He heard Tate shout out his name, but Logan didn't stop what he was doing. Instead, he sucked and kissed his way back to where his finger was penetrating Tate, and sucked around it, making sure to keep Tate's hole nice and wet.

"*Ah*, your mouth is going to kill me."

As the words hit Logan's ears, he shoved his finger back inside, and—*oh yeah, there you go, Tate*—he grazed it over Tate's prostate causing his ass to clench Logan's finger, as his hips snapped up hard.

Logan continued fingering him while his tongue devoured him, and it took less than a minute for Tate to come on a loud bark, his cum shooting out all over his stomach and chest in creamy spurts, which made Logan want to come up there and—

Oh, fuck it.

Removing his mouth and fingers from Tate's body, Logan crawled up between his thighs and licked up the cum leading from Tate's navel to his nipple. When he was finally hovering over the shocked and satiated man, he greeted him, "Morning."

As Tate's mouth fell open as if to answer, Logan couldn't help but kiss him. He wasn't sure what kind of response he'd get, considering he'd just cleaned up the guy's stomach with his tongue, but Tate grabbed the back of his head and aggressively returned the gesture.

When he was finally freed, Logan announced, "I've got to go to work," and then he rolled off the bed.

As he made his way over to the bathroom, he heard Tate call out his name. He stopped and turned to see Tate lying exactly the way he'd left him—naked with his legs spread and a glistening stomach from his mouth.

"Yeah?" he finally responded.

"What about you? Don't you want to—"

"Oh, I want to, but I don't have time. I do, however, plan to use my hand and a five minute shower *very* well."

Tate's gaze lingered over him. "Want some company?"

Logan gritted his teeth. "Of course, the day you get experimental is a day I have to go in early."

Tate climbed out of the bed and started walking over toward him. "Okay, how about I just stand and watch?"

Logan shook his head. "No."

"No?" Tate asked as he got closer.

Taking a step back, Logan made it into the bathroom. "If you stand and watch, it will take me a lot longer than five minutes, and I need to go."

Tate started laughing as Logan began closing the bathroom door.

"Seriously, I *can* just watch and not touch, you know."

"Oh, I'm sure *you* can," Logan agreed, "but I can't." He shut the bathroom door and locked it for good measure.

* * *

"YOU'RE LATE," WERE the first words Logan heard as he stepped off the elevator.

With his briefcase in one hand and a coffee in the other, he glared at Cole. "You don't say."

"You know you were supposed to be here early. Mark likes you. He works well with you—"

"What? Did you poll the guy? Should I expect a proposal? Jesus, Cole, I'm only ten minutes late."

Cole took his briefcase from him and gave it to Jane with a restrained smile. "Can you please get this to Mr.

Mitchell's office? He needs to get to the conference room *immediately*."

"Yes, Mr. Madison."

"Cole, Jane," Cole reminded his personal assistant as he did every day.

"Yes, Mr. Madison," she repeated back with a smile. She moved around them to make her way toward Cole's office.

Logan frowned and unbuttoned his jacket. "Why do you even bother? You know Jane will never call you by your name."

Cole nodded. "That's not the point."

"No? Then, what is?" Logan asked as they started walking toward the conference room.

"The point is, for her to always know that she can."

Logan stopped and turned to face his brother.

Cole shrugged. "It's our thing."

Laughing, Logan took a sip of his coffee. "Your thing? I wasn't aware that you two were dating."

"Shut up. Rachel says it's sweet."

"Rachel doesn't count. She sleeps with you. Of course, she thinks it's sweet."

Cole narrowed his eyes and took the coffee cup from him. "Go in there, and run your mouth where it will actually *do* us some good."

"And where are you going?"

"To call my wife. I now feel the need to hear about how *sweet* she's going to be to me later."

Logan lifted his arm and looked at his watch. "You're calling the wife this early?"

Cole raised a brow. "Yes. Unlike you, *I* was here on time."

Logan reached out and twisted the handle, but before he opened the door, he smirked at Cole. "Well, I always said you were the boring one. I'm only ten minutes late, and I already had something sweet today. I left him naked in my bed. Have a nice phone call."

* * *

TATE HAD SHOWERED and dressed after Logan left, and he was now standing in the man's kitchen, drinking a cup of coffee. His damp hair was cooling against his neck, and as he looked around the condo, he found himself trying to learn about the man who lived there.

The first thing he noticed was the lack of photos. There wasn't even one. *Not so unusual*, Tate thought. He didn't have any photos up either, but then again, he'd only been living in his crappy apartment for a short period of time, ever since directly after his—divorce.

Putting the cup down on the counter, he ran a hand through his hair. *Am I really considering taking this all the way?* As he looked at the couch and remembered last night, not to mention this morning, he knew that if they continued, then yes, he would eventually need to find a way to tell his friends and family. *I mean, what's the alternative?* There wasn't one, and Tate knew when it came to Logan, the feelings he was starting to have were already starting to escalate.

Moving over to the couch where Logan had put his jacket, Tate heard his phone start to buzz. Pulling it out of the pocket, he noticed he'd missed—*oh fuck*—six calls. While taking his cigarettes out of the other pocket, he answered the call and brought the phone to his ear.

"Tate?" his mother greeted him.

Tate sighed. "Hi, Mom."

"Where on earth have you been? I've been calling you since last night. I thought maybe you forgot to pay your bill, and they turned your phone off."

Tate wandered over to the door leading to Logan's balcony. He unlocked it and stepped outside. Leaning back against the wall, he crossed his legs and looked out at the building next door, wondering if he could see inside if he looked hard enough.

"When has that ever happened?"

"Well, okay, never," his mother answered.

He could hear a drawer being opened and what he thought were utensils being moved around.

"Then, why would it happen now?" Tate pulled a cigarette out between his lips and grabbed the lighter. Holding the phone between his ear and his shoulder, he waited.

"I don't know. Why else wouldn't you answer your phone?"

There was a pause as Tate tried to think of a likely reason, other than the real one. Unfortunately, he wasn't quick enough.

"Were you on a date?"

"No."

"Did you have a woman over, and that's why you couldn't answer?"

"*Mom*. No," Tate stressed.

But it was beyond containment.

"What's her name? What does she look like?"

Tate took a long drag of the cigarette and closed his, picturing his *date* from the night before. Yeah, somehow, he didn't think his mother would appreciate that his date was around six-feet-two and had dark stubble to match his short black hair.

Oh, not to mention, Mom, his dick is slightly longer than my own.

Yeah, maybe not.

"Mom, there was no date."

Tate could hear some water running and knew that his mother must be in the kitchen, cooking. She loved to bake, and that was his opportunity to get the hell out of this sticky conversation.

"What are you cooking?"

"Don't you try and change the subject, William Tate Morrison," his mother warned jokingly, pulling out the full-name card.

"There *is* no subject."

Then, as if she could see through the phone, she asked, "Are you smoking?"

Tate gritted his teeth. "I'm going to hang up the phone, just so you know in advance, and don't get mad."

"Don't hang up, don't hang up," she grumbled.

"Are you going to quit hassling me?"

"I suppose. But don't worry, I promise not to tell everyone that you're seeing someone."

Tate's jaw started to tick. The woman was as stubborn and pigheaded as...well, himself.

"I'm. Not. Seeing. Anyone."

"Okay, son. You'll bring her around when you're ready." His mother paused and then asked, "So, what time will you be here Sunday?"

Tate rolled his eyes and told her a time. Hanging up the phone, he chose to ignore the nervous thumping of his heart at the mere thought of bringing Logan anywhere near his family.

In fact, to settle his nerves and any lingering doubt he had, Tate selected Logan's name on his contacts list, opened up a message box, and began typing.

I'm convinced my shower would have been so much better with you in it this morning.

* * *

LOGAN HAD JUST sat down at his desk when Cole wandered in and shut the door.

"What now?" he asked.

Cole walked over and sat in the chair opposite him. "Tell me how it went."

Breathing out a sigh of annoyance, Logan leaned back and brought his ankle up to rest on his knee, tapping his fingers on the wood. "Well, I walked into the conference room, offered him a blow job, he accepted, and then we signed the papers."

Cole remained silent, obviously not believing him.

"Oh, fuck off, Cole. Why do you suddenly need a play-by-play? We signed the client, so get off my ass."

"Maybe if you'd said that this morning to Mr. Morrison, you would have been here on time."

Logan's mouth fell open, and the words he was about to say got stuck. When his phone vibrated on the desk, he glanced at the message quickly and saw that it was Tate. Knowing Cole would not be leaving anytime soon, Logan looked back to his brother as he absently hit a button to Ignore the message. He'd call Tate back as soon as his over-attentive business partner left. "That was last night's activity, if you must know. And aren't you the comedian today?"

"I try."

"No, you don't—*ever*. So, what gives?"

Cole tilted his head to the side. "You *were* with the bartender, huh?"

Logan sat forward and clasped his hands together, glaring across at Cole. "Yes, Counselor. I know you're not stupid, so you already know all of this. Get to the point."

Cole raised a hand and stroked his chin with a shrug. "Bit messy, don't you think?"

Logan knew exactly what he meant, but he'd had just about enough of Cole's veiled comments. "Sure it is, but he's so much fun to lick up, and he's so…vocal. *Oh yeah, Logan.*"

* * *

TATE STARED AT the phone in his hand and felt something between panic and burning rage. Surely, what he was hearing at the other end was *not* what he thought it was, but as he watched the seconds on the display change, it was confirmed. The call from Logan was *definitely* connected.

When his message had first gone through, his phone almost immediately began to ring. Sitting down on the couch, Tate had relaxed back into the leather, thinking he was about to talk with the man who'd left him in bed this morning.

Instead, he was sitting on the couch, listening to—

What? A conversation between Logan and—Tate could only assume—*Cole?* One in which Tate was not only the central character, but also the comedic relief.

* * *

COLE DIDN'T EVEN flinch at Logan's reenactment. After years of knowing one another and working together every day, Logan figured it would take a whole hell of a lot to shock his brother.

Instead, Cole asked, "What are you doing with this guy?"

Logan couldn't help himself. "Well, last night, he was actually the one who did…"

"Logan?"

"Yeah?"

"Stop fucking around and answer me. I walked in on you doing and *being* done all through college. I hardly think I'm going to be horrified now. So, cut the crap. What are you doing with this guy?"

Logan glared at Cole. *The asshole is right. He knows me better than anyone.* "I'm just having fun, okay? It's nothing serious. Just the usual."

Cole's eyes pinned him in place as he sat forward in his chair. "Really?"

"Yes, really. Do you even remember what fun is?"

"Kind of. Yes," Cole answered stoically, not a smile in sight. "Does he know he's just a piece of ass?"

Logan frowned, discovering he hated that fucking description, but he offered no defense. He didn't need Cole all over him about this.

"How is this your business? And yeah, I'm pretty sure he knows we aren't running out to buy wedding rings."

"You know, it's okay to admit that you like the guy."

Logan shook his head. He had no idea why Cole was being such a pain this morning, but it was getting really damn aggravating.

"What the fuck, Cole? Get off my case, would you? I *have* dated before."

"When? College?"

"Maybe," Logan replied vaguely, knowing of only one other person he had ever *dated*.

Cole stood and placed his hands on the desk and looked down at him.

"If you mean Chris, *that* is not dating. That was fucking, hiding, lying, and then him bailing like a pussy when everyone found out. And *he* was gay."

Logan sat back at the anger on Cole's face. He *had* been referring to Chris, but he hadn't really wanted to rehash it, especially not *that* way.

"It wasn't that bad."

"Yes, it was. So, I will ask you again," Cole began. "What are you doing with this *straight* guy? You know how things like this end, and I don't know why, but you always end up giving a shit about the wrong people."

"That's not true, and it doesn't matter. I told you, this isn't that serious."

As soon as the words had left his mouth, Logan recognized them for the lies they were. But he wasn't about to confide in Cole, not when he was royally pissing him off.

* * *

TATE WONDERED HOW he hadn't hurled his phone

across Logan's living room as he glared into the brightly lit surface shining back at him. He was livid. With every word that passed between these two, Tate's temper rose, and the trust he'd been so reluctant to give crumbled.

Not sure how much more he could listen to, Tate was about to end the call when Cole's voice came through the phone, breaking the silence.

"After Chris, you have not had one serious relationship. You fuck and run. And the first person you decide to focus on is straight?"

Tate sucked in a breath. He didn't want to hear Logan's response, but he also found it impossible to ignore.

"You know, when you got married a week after knowing Hot Cheetah Pants, I wasn't this much of an asshole."

"No, but you were quick to point out how I tied myself to one person. Just make sure the person you decide to put all your effort into is the right person."

"You're really starting to piss me off."

For once, Tate had to agree with Logan. Cole was really pissing him off, too.

"Am I? Truth hurts, huh?"

"Whatever. What's your point? If you even have one."

"My point is, Logan, don't delude yourself into thinking he's going to magically switch teams."

"Well, thank you, Cole, for being so damn supportive. Good thing I'm not delusional."

Still furious, Tate pushed aside his own anger and disappointment for a moment. He thought he'd caught something in Logan's tone, but before he could pinpoint it, it was gone.

* * *

LOGAN WANTED TO hit something, and he was afraid if Cole didn't leave, it would be him. So, he advised, "You know where the door is. Why don't you go and fucking use it?"

Cole stood and walked over to where Logan was now standing behind his desk. Logan hated that he had to look up, even slightly. When he did, he saw a flash of sympathy cross Cole's face, and he almost gave in to the urge for violence, something he hadn't done in years.

"I said, get out," he repeated.

Cole shook his head. "Don't become someone's mistake."

"Why? It's what I'm good at. I was your father's *biggest* mistake."

Logan knew it was low, and he knew the blow was uncalled for, but Cole was hitting too close to all of his fears and insecurities. When Logan was cornered, he always fought dirty.

"That was low, even for you."

"Are you really surprised? Now, get out."

Cole turned on his heel and left the office, leaving

Logan just the way he wanted to be—alone. As he moved over to the window, he wondered when exactly he had decided that being *alone* was all he deserved.

* * *

TATE HIT END on the call and threw his phone on the couch, cursing Logan and admonishing himself. *How could I have been so damn stupid? This whole thing had disaster written all over it from the beginning.*

But after last night, he'd thought—

What? That Logan was serious about all of this? That he cared? Well, there you go. There's your fucking wake-up call. Loud enough for you?

Tate tried to block out everything he'd heard, and he jumped slightly when the phone beside him started to ring. Looking down at the screen, he saw it was Logan. He picked it up and hit Answer, but he remained silent.

"Tate? You there?"

Tate closed his eyes and turned to lie down on the couch.

"Hello? If you don't answer me, I'm going to call the cops and tell them to go check my condo just in case you were attacked or—"

"Shut up, Logan," Tate finally cut him off. He wasn't going to lay there and act like everything was fine just because Logan was putting on one hell of a show.

"What's wrong with you?" Logan had the audacity

to ask.

Tate couldn't help the snide tone that crept into his voice. "Oh, nothing *serious*."

There was a lengthy pause and then, "Well, obviously, something's wrong."

"And obviously, I don't want to talk to you."

"Um, what the fuck, Tate?"

Infuriated at himself and Logan, Tate sneered through the phone, "Exactly. What the fuck? Maybe we should go and get Cole for this? Make it a conference call. He seems to know all about our relationship. But hang on, we don't have one of those, do we? It's just some *fun*?"

From the silence that stretched through the phone, Tate knew that Logan had no clue that he'd heard his recent conversation with Cole. He was about to inform him when Logan's bad temper seemed to finally catch up and he lashed out at him.

"Don't fuck around with me, Tate. I'm not in the mood."

That was the exact moment that Tate felt his own rage boil. "Well good, Logan, because I'm not in the mood for you either. You might want to check your recent calls, *asshole*. Have a nice fucking day."

With that, Tate ended the call and threw his phone onto the floor. *Don't fuck around with you? Fine by me, Mr. Mitchell, fine by me.*

Chapter Twenty-Two

IF LOGAN HAD to make a list of things he hated, it would include being hung up on and being ignored. Tate had done both of those in the last three hours. He'd tried calling him back several times after their not-so-pleasant conversation, and the stubborn ass had let all of his calls go to voice mail where, of course, he'd left *seven* different messages.

Christ, how was I supposed to know I hit Call instead of Ignore earlier? Plus, Tate had it all wrong. Logan hadn't meant things the way they'd sounded. Tate just needed to hear him out.

Opening the door to the bar, Logan stepped inside and noticed it was quiet for a Wednesday night. *Good,* he thought, *it will make it easier for us to talk.*

Making his way over to his usual spot, the first person he saw was Amelia.

She gave him a small wave as she walked over and then stopped in front of him. "Evening, Logan."

Logan was not in the mood for small talk. "Hey. Is he here?"

Amelia sucked her top lip into her mouth and grabbed a glass. "Gin and tonic?"

Annoyed at her change of topic, Logan nodded and tried again. "Amelia?"

She mixed the drink, and slid it over to him. "He told me to take your orders tonight."

Logan's jaw actually hurt from how hard he clenched it shut. He looked down the length of the bar, but he saw no sign of Tate. He turned on his stool and looked around the dimly lit area, and still, no Tate. *Where is he?*

As Logan faced Amelia once again, his eye caught Tate walking out from the back hall. He threw a towel over his shoulder and made his way up to the counter with a smile for—Logan turned to check—a redhead with huge—

"Logan?"

"What?" he snapped, aiming his glare at the woman in front of him.

"You want anything else?"

Logan picked up the glass, brought it to his lips, and before taking a drink, he mumbled, "No."

Amelia leaned across to him, as Logan continued to sit, irate.

Once upon a time, he would have been looking at a way to get her out the back, but now, all he could do was think about how she could help get Tate to talk to him again.

"He's been looking at the door all evening, if that helps."

It did, but Logan wasn't going to admit it. Instead, he brought his eyes to hers and hated the fact that they no longer did anything for him.

"Tell him I'm here?"

Amelia stepped back with a laugh. "Oh, he knows. That's why he went out the back." She started to walk away, and then at the last moment, she looked back at him. "It's nice to finally see *you* having to work for the attention."

Logan raised his glass to take a sip, and eyed Tate as he continued laughing with the redhead. Yes, he'd worked damn hard for Tate's attention, and he would be fucked if someone else stole it—*even* for five minutes.

* * *

TATE COULD SENSE Logan's eyes on him. There was no way he was going to serve him tonight. He was too mad to even talk to the guy, let alone have a verbal sparring match with him. So, he'd sent Amelia instead.

She, of course, had been curious about what was going on, but surprisingly, she had not asked any questions. She'd merely smiled and agreed to do it. It was, however, killing Tate not to look over at the other end of the bar. He hadn't realized how strongly he was drawn to Logan until he was ordering himself not to be.

With a wide smile and a view directly down her pink blouse, the woman in front of Tate was trying her very best to convince him to take her number, or perhaps give his own.

"So, what's your name?"

Tate gave her a quick grin knowing exactly what his

role was in this little game. "Well, if I tell you that, you'll know all the important facts and leave me."

"Oh, I'd never leave you," she purred. "You're too nice to look at."

Somewhat flattered, Tate eyed the drink in front of her. "I think your drink has impaired your vision."

"No, it hasn't. This is only my second one, and you are just...*mmm*...delicious."

Tate knew it was her third. He'd been counting.

He wondered, not for the first time, *How do I always end up in conversations like this?* It was part of the job, he supposed.

Knowing that if he played it up, the tip would likely be a good one, he leaned his side against the bar and continued chatting. "Hard day at the office?"

Red took a sip of her Manhattan and raised a brow. "Are you changing the subject?"

"Not at all. What would you like to talk about?"

"How about you? Are you single?" she daringly inquired, letting her eyes roam all over him.

Tate wasn't shocked that her look provoked zero response from him, but he was surprised that the mere thought of the man in the gray suit at the other end of the bar had his cock twitching and his skin heating. *Fucking Logan.*

"Not much to tell," he replied, choosing to ignore the relationship question.

"Oh, come on," Red coaxed. "Gorgeous guy,

bartender. I bet you have the best stories."

Tate almost groaned at the irony and wondered how she would feel if he told her, *Well, that man down there with the sexy glasses? Yeah, he started flirting with me, just like you are now, and we had sex. It was absolutely mind-blowing sex that I can't stop thinking about it even though he was a total asshole today about something that could totally change my life. How's that for a story?*

But Tate didn't tell her that. Instead, he shrugged. "A bartender is just like a priest. We listen to all kinds of confessions, but we never speak of them after they have left the customers' lips."

Red moved her drink aside, and reaching across the bar, she traced a finger over the back of his hand. "So, I could tell you anything, and you wouldn't tell a soul?"

Looking into her eyes, Tate tried to see if he could feel the way he did when Logan stared at him, but as she dropped her gaze to his mouth, Tate felt, *nothing.*

"That's right." He glanced down, finally allowing himself a chance to appreciate that she had an amazing set of breasts. The problem was, he was much more interested in the dick at the other end of the—

"Is this seat taken?"

The redhead turned first to see who'd spoken. Of course, the second her attention landed on Logan, she pulled her hand back from Tate, the less-than-accommodating bartender, and instead, she focused on the seductive and interesting—

Asshole.

"It is now. Please, feel free…" she invited.

Tate fired a drop-dead glare in Logan's direction.

"To do?" Logan drawled as he looked to Tate with aggravation swirling behind those glasses.

"Whatever you like," she told him. Reaching out, she ran her fingers, the same ones that had just stroked *his* hand, over the suit covering Logan's arm.

"You know what I'd really love to do?"

The clueless woman leaned in, and for some reason, Tate braced himself with his palms on the edge of the bar. He wasn't sure why, but he felt that whatever Logan was gearing up to say, was not going to be even remotely appropriate.

"No, what?"

Logan also moved forward until his lips almost brushed against the woman's, but at the last second, he turned his attention on him. "Your bartender."

Okay, Tate thought, *there's no doubt here. My cock definitely knows who it wants.*

"Huh?" Red asked, clearly not understanding.

But Tate wasn't confused by the words or the look Logan was aiming at him. It screamed, *You're mine, not hers.*

"Your bartender," Logan repeated and turned back to face her while Tate held the wood under his hands. "I want to *do* him, as in take off his clothes and fuck him, and you're in my way."

Tate witnessed the woman, whose mouth had parted

in shock, turn and face him as if waiting for—

Sorry, lady. I'm used to his mouth.

As the three of them remained locked in an awkward silence, Tate decided he needed to do something since it was apparent Logan was just going to stir shit up if left to his own devices.

Looking across to him, Tate managed, "Can I get you something?"

Logan licked his lips. "You. Alone in a room."

"No," Tate countered.

"Why? Scared of me? You should be. I don't like being ignored."

Tate stared at him in disbelief. "I'm not scared of you, and we had this conversation a week or so ago."

"Yes, and this morning in bed, it certainly seemed you'd come around, but not so much now, with the avoiding routine."

That was when Red slid down off her seat. "Uh, I'm sorry, I didn't realize that you two—"

"Are together?" Logan announced before Tate could even utter a word. "Well, we are, so go hit on someone else. He's mine. I found him first."

* * *

LOGAN WASN'T KIDDING. That was how he really felt, and Tate needed to know that *right* now.

"I don't like to be ignored or hung up on," he told

Tate again as the redhead finally took a hike. He detected a small twitch in Tate's cheek, and he was satisfied at the thought that he, too, was suppressing his outrage.

"Yeah? Well, I don't like hearing that I'm just a piece of ass. So, why don't you get lost? I'm not in the *mood* for you."

Logan pushed off the stool quickly and grabbed Tate's vest, hauling him in close until he was up against the counter. "Well, that's too bad because I'm in the mood for you, and I wasn't lying to her. I want you, and I'm going to have you."

Tate scoffed at him, and Logan had to control the urge to take that mocking mouth with his own.

"Yeah? Well, excuse me if I don't believe you. You say one thing to me and then something else when I'm not there."

Logan looked around and saw several people focused on their display. He then faced the furious man in front of him. "You think so, huh? I don't know, right now, everyone in this bar knows exactly who I want. So, I'd say I'm expressing it very well. Want me to put my tongue in your mouth and really make it obvious?"

Tate's eyes darkened, and Logan knew the idea appealed to him even as he continued to seethe.

"I'm not talking about now, and you know it. But why should you care anyway? It's not like this is serious. Now, let me go."

"Meet me in the back," he ordered softly.

Tate's glare didn't falter. "Not in a million years."

"Why not?" Logan rasped, getting more turned-on by the second. He wanted Tate's lips under his, so he could turn that sneer into a groan.

"Because I know you."

"And?"

"*And*...you'll get your hands on me, and I'll be fucked."

Logan revealed his teeth in a savage grin. "It's not my hands that I use for *that* particular activity, and even I wouldn't let your first time be in the back of a bar. Your first time is going to be in my bed under me."

"Let. Me. Go," Tate sneered, this time enunciating each word. "Everyone is watching us."

"Yeah, they are. They're all wondering, *Are they going to punch each other or kiss each other?* They're so confused. What about you? Are you confused?"

"Me? Are *you*?" Tate demanded.

Logan finally released him, sat back, and watched as Tate ran his hands down his vest. "I'm not confused at all. I just didn't feel like giving in to Cole's twenty questions, so sue me. If you answered your phone or listened to your messages, then maybe this would already be sorted out."

Tate looked down the bar quickly and then back at him. "I have customers, and I *did* listen to your messages. And you know what? I heard everything you had to say, but one thing was missing."

Logan lifted his hands. "What, Tate? What didn't I

say?"

Tate glared at him and said simply, "Sorry."

* * *

TATE'S HANDS WERE shaking as he walked away from
Logan, and the semi he was sporting in his pants was
maddening. He'd wanted nothing more than to kiss and bite
those lips that continually spouted suggestive comments at
him, but with all eyes on them, Tate hadn't dared.

He knew from experience that once he and Logan got
started, they would forget *who* and *what* was going on
around them. Plus, Tate had been serious. He wanted a
fucking apology. He understood that Logan hadn't wanted
to explain their relationship to Cole just yet, but the way
Logan had casually dismissed him was not cool at all.

He reached two women at the end of the bar and got
them their cocktails. Then, he moved on to several others
who had taken their seats and needed drinks. When he was
done, he turned back to see Amelia had started to talk with
Logan. She was resting up against the bar, and her arms
were crossed as they continued to talk and look over at him.
Amelia gave him a smile, and Logan just stared him down
from behind those thick black frames.

Tate knew that stare. It either led to fighting or
fucking.

Aggravated that they were no doubt discussing him,
Tate grabbed a tray and moved down past them both to go

and collect some empty glassware. He needed to get away
from that look, or he'd end up doing something stupid.

Lifting the bar pass, he made his way through and
over to the tables. He collected a full tray, brought them
back, and handed them off to Amelia, who was now
standing there on her own. Logan was nowhere in sight.

"Where'd he go?" he asked.

When she shrugged and turned away, Tate glanced
back around the bar area.

He didn't see Logan anywhere. *Well, isn't that great,
you idiot? You sure solved that.*

Picking up the tray, Tate headed toward the booths
on the sidewall. Just as he made his way past the entry to the
second room that was closed off for the night, his arm was
grabbed, and he was pulled into the dark empty space
where he was propelled, face-first, up against the back wall.

Logan's mouth was instantly by his ear, and his free
hand was unbuttoning Tate's pants.

"Stop it," Tate growled as he bucked back against
Logan.

Logan didn't budge. He merely held him immobile
while he unzipped his work pants. "You're one stubborn
piece of ass, Tate Morrison," he accused against Tate's hair.

"And you're *just* an ass," Tate fired back, disgruntled
with the position Logan had him in. He'd been like this once
before, and although it was turning him on, it made him feel
weak.

"You're so pissed, yet if anyone should be angry, I

think it should be me."

Tate tried to think, tried to formulate words, but the nose nuzzling into his hair with the tongue flicking his ear was driving him crazy.

"Letting some woman hit on you, flirt with you," Logan breathed right against Tate's ear as his hand found its way into his boxers. "She even *touched* you."

Tate's mouth parted, and when he heard his own moan, he knew Logan did, too, and he would take full advantage.

"Oh look, I think you like this position, don't you? Me behind you, ready to…fuck."

Tate shook his head the best he could. "Logan, get off me."

Logan chuckled, and the depraved sound raced down Tate's spine to his balls.

"No I don't think so."

Those words whispered against Tate's ear made him catch his breath as Logan's hand wrapped around his cock.

Logan placed a foot between his legs. "Spread your legs, Tate."

Turning his head, Tate's eyes found Logan's, and the heat in them lit a fire in Tate's veins. "No."

As the side of Logan's lip quirked up, Tate felt his cock weep as the hand around him squeezed.

"Spread your *fucking* legs, Tate," Logan ordered.

Tate was aware that doing this here was stupid and risky, but it only added to the high Logan was building in him. There was no door separating this room from the other, and anyone could walk in at any moment—but as Logan thrust his hips forward and the ridge of his hard-on nudged against Tate's ass, Tate didn't give a shit.

"Do it," Logan cajoled. "And you'll get your apology."

Licking his dry lips, Tate's focus zeroed in on Logan's mouth that was only an inch away.

"Most normal people apologize first," Tate explained on an edgy breath as he slowly widened his legs.

When the hand around him began to stroke, a strong thigh worked its way between his, and it moved upward to add pressure against his balls. Tate cursed under his breath as he pushed back against Logan's unyielding frame.

"Haven't you noticed by now that I'm not like most *normal* people?"

Tate looked over the face beside his own, and then he gave in. He lunged forward to take Logan's lips just as he'd been thinking about doing since the man had left him this morning. As soon as Logan's mouth opened, Tate dropped the empty tray by his feet and shoved his tongue inside, tangling it against Logan's. Tate's trapped arm between them was pulled out from behind his back and pressed up against the wall. Logan ripped his mouth away and tugged on Tate's erection. Logan rolled his hips forward in a way that suggested he was imagining being inside him.

"*Fuck*, Tate," he hissed as though he was in agony.

If the steel-like rod massaging Tate's ass was any

indication, Logan *was* suffering.

"Don't blame me. You started this," Tate accused.

Logan released Tate's straining flesh and gave a caustic laugh. Tate eyed the hand that slammed down by his head, mirroring the position Logan had his trapped one in. He could barely breathe as the tense body behind him caged him in.

"No. You started it this afternoon, and you've been seething ever since. But now you're just irked because you want me. So, I suggest you put your hand down your fucking pants and finish it."

"Fuck off. I'm not gonna do—*ah, fuck, Logan.*"

Tate's indignation left him as Logan's teeth found his neck, and his thigh pressed higher between his legs.

"You better hurry. Pretty sure someone will notice you're missing soon," Logan taunted, moving his entire body against Tate's back as if they had all night.

Tate finally gave in and reached down inside his pants to start jacking himself off. His boxers were damp with the pre-cum leaking from his cock. He flattened his cheek to the wall and began to quickly pump his demanding erection.

He could feel Logan's broad chest against his back, pinning him to the wall, as he continued to grind his hips over and over into him. Tate closed his eyes, and he wasn't sure what to think about the fact that with every rough stroke of Logan's erection, his ass seemed to crave what it didn't yet know.

The loud huffs of breath that were warm against

Tate's ear accelerated as he fisted his length and shoved back against Logan harder. Wanting a smoother and quicker friction over his cock, Tate raised his hand and spit into his sticky palm.

Logan groaned loudly behind him. "*Jesus*. You're a dirty fucker," he growled.

Tate started stroking himself again and saw Logan's hand leave the wall before weaving through his hair to pull it aside.

"I fucking love it." Logan's strong teeth bit down into his neck while his hips rammed against Tate.

Tate cupped the head of his cock and turned to clamp his own teeth into the arm that Logan still had propped against the wall. As he grunted against the fabric of the suit, Tate felt Logan's body slam him into the wood as he exploded into his own palm in a toe-curling climax.

He pulled his mouth from Logan's sleeve, and as he let his breathing slow down, Tate heard against his skin, "I'm sorry."

Making sure to keep his hand closed, Tate shut his eyes as he rested back against the man still pinning him to the wall.

"I'm sorry for not saying everything that I should have to Cole. Things like, *this is serious*, and *he's so much more than just some fun I'm having*. It's just been a while since I've had to think about someone else."

Tate pressed his forehead to the wood as Logan's mouth moved up his neck. He tried to remember what they'd been discussing. *Apologies, wasn't it? And having to think about others?* That was something he was having great difficulty with at the moment, considering what had just happened.

But Tate managed to ask, "And now that you are?"

"Now that I am, you're *all* that I think about," Logan stressed.

Tate felt the hold on his arm finally release him from the wall as the body behind him relaxed for the first time since he'd been pulled into the room.

"You caught me mouthing off to Cole. We'd argued earlier, and obviously, it's no excuse, but it carried over. I'm sorry I said those things, and I'm sorry you heard it."

Regaining his composure, Tate turned his head to look over his shoulder. When their eyes met, he told Logan, "I don't have any expectations of how you should act, you know. I don't even know what I'm doing half the time. Just don't play around with me, okay? If you want this, fine. But if you don't, tell me, so I'm not wasting my fucking time. I just want the truth."

Logan focused on him, and he looked slightly shocked. Then, in a tone that Tate had never heard, he explained, "You're not the only one who has changed in the last two weeks." He paused and brought a hand up to touch Tate's mouth before taking a step back. "You make me want things that I'd forgotten I wanted."

As Tate was freed to turn around, he felt his heart beating rapidly until it overshadowed the throb that had, for now, subsided between his thighs. "That's probably the most sincere thing that I've ever heard come out of your mouth."

Logan lowered his eyes to Tate's hand. "Now, that's not true. I was very sincere this morning when I told you that I loved sucking your—"

"Don't ruin it," Tate interrupted.

Logan stepped in close and took his closed hand with his own. Tate shook his head at the sensual look crossing Logan's features as he raised it up to his mouth.

"But it's true. I love sucking you almost as much as I love the taste of your cum."

Logan's tongue came out and licked Tate's palm and fingers clean before raising his head and tracing it over Tate's swollen lips.

"And you think I'm dirty."

Logan let his hand go and reached down to adjust the obvious erection Tate could see in his pants.

"You are. But I'm much dirtier."

"You really like the taste of it?" Tate asked, wanting to know.

"Well, I'm not lying just to get in your pants. Plus, didn't you just say you wanted the truth?"

Logan stepped away quickly zipping his pants back up, before looking over to where Tate was standing. Tate watched him run a hand through his hair as a frown formed on his face, and the atmosphere in the small, dark room changed from sex to serious.

And with them both staring at one another, Tate asked, "So...what's your truth, Logan?"

Logan stared at him so intently that Tate wondered what was going on inside his head before he replied, "I think you are," leaving Tate speechless.

Chapter Twenty-Three

LOGAN HAD LEFT the bar not long after he and Tate had each agreed that they needed a night off—a night to breathe and reflect. Or in Logan's case, as he sat on the balcony with his feet propped up on the table and half a bottle of whiskey, he needed a night to get fully loaded. Resting his head back on the chair, he stared out at the scattered lights in the buildings surrounding him.

Tate Morrison. Logan hadn't been lying. There was nothing easy about what he was feeling when it came to that man. *Scary and surprising—yes.*

He wasn't one to give much credence to the whole love notion. Very little of it had been passed around in his life so far, and he just figured it was something people made up to make themselves feel better. That was, until Tate.

He'd managed to make Logan feel something only one other before him had, and Logan wasn't sure if that made him happy or terrified. All he knew was that whatever it was, he needed to keep a close handle on it.

Raising the bottle, he took another sip, well on his way to the relaxed state he was craving.

Cole was also running through his head tonight. It

had been a long time since he'd fought with that guy, and he hated it. They'd decided many years ago that it was neither of their faults that life had dealt them an asshole for a father, but every now and then, the old resentment came through, and Logan couldn't help feeling pissed that he was the one their father had thrown away.

Placing the bottle down beside him, his cell phone started vibrating on the table. Reaching forward, he picked it up and saw Tate's name flashing across the display. Sitting back in the chair, he snagged the bottle again and answered.

* * *

TATE SETTLED INTO his couch and waited for Logan to pick up. He'd been thinking about their conversation ever since Logan had left the bar earlier. A lot had been said in the few words Logan had actually spoken, and when he'd told Tate they should just meet up sometime tomorrow, Tate had known he, too, felt their relationship had shifted directions.

Glancing at the digital display on the DVR, he saw that it had just turned one fifteen. *Maybe he's sleeping?* It was late. Just as he was about to hang up, the phone connected, and Logan's voice washed over him.

"I was just thinking about you."

Tate lay back on his couch and placed his head on the end pillow. "Should I even ask?"

There was a longer pause than he would have

expected before Logan spoke.

"I don't know. Do you want to?"

Tate knew this conversation could go one of two ways, and as much as he wanted to take the easy way out, he also wanted some answers if Logan were in the mood to give them.

"You asked me that like you expect me to say no," Tate stated, and when there was no response, he asked, "Do you? Expect me to say no?"

"I don't know. I think maybe I do."

Wow, well, that's honest, Tate thought as he closed his eyes. "Want to tell me why?" He heard something—*liquid, maybe*—through the phone.

"I don't know. Maybe because a couple of weeks ago, the thought of kissing a guy disgusted you."

Logan sounded so different compared to the way he usually did that Tate couldn't help himself from asking, "Are you okay?"

"Not really," he admitted.

Tate wasn't surprised that Logan was just as blunt when it came to the hard truths as he was with the easier ones.

"Want to talk about it?"

"Does it still disgust you?"

"The thought of kissing a guy? Or the thought of kissing you?"

Silence met his question as though Logan was thinking about it. "Isn't it one and the same?"

Tate tried to imagine himself kissing another man, other than Logan, but since he'd never even entertained the thought before, he really didn't have an answer. "It might be, but before you, I'd never thought about it."

There was another louder swish in his ear, and Tate knew what the sound was. Logan was drinking.

"What are you drinking?"

"Jack."

"You're drinking cheap whiskey? Why not the usual?"

"Because Jack was here, and he's real nice to swallow."

"Do you just come up with this shit? Or do you have it all written down somewhere?"

"Hmm, I should write it down, shouldn't I?"

Again, the sound of Logan taking a drink came through the phone, and then he asked, "*So…*why did you think about kissing me?"

Tate couldn't help the laugh that escaped him. "How much have you had to drink?"

"What?" Logan questioned. "Why?"

"I'm asking because it must have impaired your brain. I thought about it with you because you wouldn't give me a minute *not* to think about it. Every time I turned around, you were there."

Awkward and tense silence greeted Tate after the final words left his mouth.

"So, you only did it because I was always *there*?"

Tate wasn't quite sure, but he was almost positive that Logan sounded unsure, on the verge of vulnerable. That was something he'd never heard in him—*ever*. Logan didn't strike him as the type of guy who usually poured his heart out.

"I did it because you got in my face and made me see how irresistible you are, regardless of your gender. And Logan?"

"Yeah?"

"I still think that, but now, there's so much more to it. I really like you."

The laugh that met Tate's ears was devoid of humor and full of mockery. "Really? Ninety percent of the time you're furious with me."

"Yeah, I know. You drive me crazy *because* I like you," Tate stressed. "A lot."

"A lot, huh?"

Closing his eyes, Tate imagined—*finally*—the smirk he could hear in Logan's voice.

"A whole lot."

"Like how much?"

Tate started laughing. "What are you? Twelve?"

"No. I'm drunk or really close."

"So, now is when I should ask you all the hard questions?" Tate queried only half-serious.

"Do you have hard questions?"

"Yeah, I guess I do."

"Sure then. Fire away," Logan replied flippantly.

Tate heard the underlying tone, and he recognized it for what it was—caution. "Okay. What really happened with Cole today?" Tate hadn't realized he wanted to share that burden until it came out of his mouth.

Logan sighed. "You heard everything that happened."

"Yeah," Tate agreed, "but I only understand half of it."

Tate wondered if this was the moment when he would see that this all meant more to him than—

"Well, you know he's my brother, right?"

Tate let out a sigh of relief. Logan wasn't going to shut him out. "Yeah."

"We didn't know that until I turned eighteen, and our father's trust was made known to me."

Logan stopped talking, and Tate waited.

"And I already told you that his father had an affair…well, obviously, he didn't choose my mother and I…"

Tate couldn't even begin to imagine how that would affect a teenager. *Not only growing up without a father, but then also learning that he had a whole other family? A family that included a brother he had never known about.*

"The asshole died when Cole was five, so at least I never had to meet him…" Logan revealed, and his voice trailed off, leaving Tate to wonder if he really meant it.

"Anyway, you didn't ask all of this."

"No. Don't do that," Tate finally spoke.

"Don't do, what?"

"Don't change the subject or assume that I don't want to know about you. Talk to me. Tell me." Tate held his breath and waited, hoping that Logan would open up and trust him.

"Okay. You want the details? Let's see…my mother never married. She told me that she had fallen in love once and that the pain she'd felt from loving someone she shouldn't far outweighed any joy, so there was no point."

When Logan paused, Tate had to ask, "Someone she shouldn't?"

"Yes. Sounds familiar, huh?"

"As in me? I'm hardly married, you know that."

"But you're straight."

Tate swallowed and remained quiet, not really knowing what to say.

"I promised myself, I'd never have regrets, like the one she had."

"What does that mean?"

"It means that I didn't care one way or another what you said. I was willing to try anything just to taste you once."

Tate knew that to be the truth, but decided to ask anyway. "And how did that work out?"

"I haven't regretted it yet," Logan answered right away. "But that's a different conversation. You want to know why Cole was upset. Hmm, well, I tracked Cole down the minute I got to college. He was just starting his second year, and he hated me as soon as I told him my name."

"Well, that's bullshit."

"Is it? All he knew was that his father, a man he'd idolized, had left a college trust fund to another kid—his *other* kid. I would have hated me, too."

Tate sat up on the couch and shook his head. "But it wasn't your fault."

"That didn't matter. I represented everything bad that his father had done."

"But you work together, so obviously, you get along now," Tate queried.

"Oh yeah, I was a total pain in his ass the first month of college. Everywhere he went, I showed up."

"Imagine that."

Logan's voice took on that same serious edge he'd had earlier. "When something is important, I don't give up."

Tate was about to pursue that, but then Logan started again. "Then, I found out where he was living off-campus, and I made myself at home on his doorstep until he talked to me."

Tate couldn't help the loud laugh that escaped him. He could only imagine how annoyed Cole had been to find Logan on his steps every day.

Then, Logan confirmed it. "He was furious. We got into a fight that first day. He punched me right in the mouth." Logan chuckled. "I thought he was going to do it again today."

And there they were, back where they'd begun. "Why? What made him so mad?"

"You did."

And with those two words, Tate felt his breath leave him at the blunt confession.

* * *

LOGAN PUT THE bottle down next to him and sat up. *God. The alcohol was making him run his mouth even more than usual.*

"What do you mean, I did?" Tate's voice finally filled the silence.

"He's worried about me."

"Well...yeah."

Logan ran a hand over his face and up through his hair. *What the fuck? Might as well put it all out there. Tate heard everything anyway.*

"You asked me the other night, if I'd ever dated anyone else..." He trailed off, finding that for the first time, he was uncomfortable with discussing his sexual encounters—well, *this* particular encounter. When Tate stayed quiet, he rushed out, "If I'd let anyone else *be* with me like you are. And obviously, you heard I was with a guy named Chris."

"Yeah, I remember."

Logan nodded and waited. When he heard nothing at the other end, not even breathing, he probed, "Tate? You there?"

"Yeah," Tate sighed.

It sounded to Logan like he had been holding his breath.

"Sorry. I was just thinking."

"About?"

"You and Chris."

"And?"

"It pisses me off."

Logan felt the nice buzz in his head finally relax him a little. "I told you, you're always pissed-off at me."

"And I told you why."

"Because you like me," Logan repeated Tate's words from earlier. "*A lot.*"

"I like you too fucking much, Logan."

Logan swallowed and let that admission warm the rest of his body. "Chris and I met at college. We had the same algebra class. I was good at it. He wasn't. So, I tutored him."

"In algebra and…"

Logan could hear the veiled question hiding in Tate's comment.

"And nothing. *I* only taught him algebra."

"But he taught *you* things?"

"He taught me everything," Logan confided and sat back in his chair.

He tried to picture Chris in his mind, but he came up blank. All he could see were Tate's brown eyes and unruly curls and the lips that snarled or smiled at him, and he had to stop and really focus to even remember *who* Chris was.

"I don't like him," Tate's voice interrupted matter-of-factly.

"You don't know him."

"I still don't like him."

"Because..." Logan drawled.

"Because he had you," Tate told him much more boldly than Logan would have expected. "He fucked you, didn't he?"

Enjoying Tate's jealousy a little too much, Logan answered, "Yes. Quite a bit."

"How much is quite a bit?"

"Want all the juicy details, Tate?"

Logan heard a long-suffering sigh, and then Tate cursed, "Fuck."

"Tate?"

"What?" he barked at him.

Logan couldn't help the way his dick reacted to it. "I can't even remember what he looks like because all I can picture is you." Logan's heart ached as he waited for what felt like hours until Tate finally spoke.

"You really mean that, don't you?"

"I do, and it scares me."

"Why?" Tate whispered into the phone.

His voice had Logan wishing he hadn't gone home alone and that he was instead lying in bed beside him.

"Come on, Tate. Don't you think I wonder what will finally change your mind? What will make you think, *what the hell am I doing*?"

There—he'd finally voiced his biggest fear.

He could hear movement through the phone, and then Tate asked, "Is that what he did? Is that why Cole's worried? He thinks I'm playing you?"

Logan sat back in the chair, and answered the question. "Yeah, that's what Chris did. It wasn't so much he changed his mind as denied everything when people found out."

"Why? Was he straight?"

Logan almost choked on the bitter laugh that left his mouth. "In public, yes, but in my dorm room? Not even a little bit."

"But you said *he* taught *you*. As in he'd been with others before, right?"

"As in, yes, he was gay, and it was my first time with a guy. And when someone found out and told all of his friends, he denied it and stopped talking to me."

"Fucker," Tate cursed through the phone.

"Yeah, well, Cole saw us arguing one day. Chris pushed me into the wall and threatened me. Before I even had a chance to respond, Cole beat his ass, right in the middle of everyone."

"Good. Stupid dick deserved it," Tate mumbled vehemently. "So, what happened after that?"

"He started dating every girl he could. I'm pretty sure he wasn't fucking them though."

"How do you know?"

Logan felt his own satisfaction come racing back to

him as he said, "Because I made sure that *I* was fucking them *while* he was dating them."

Tate started laughing so loudly that Logan had to pull the phone away from his ear. *Good.* He hadn't been sure how that piece of information would go over.

"Only you, Logan, I swear." Tate chuckled and then finally calmed. "So, that's it? After that, you were with girls only?"

"No. After that, I was with whoever the hell I wanted to be with. He'd already told everyone I tried to come on to him, so I figured, why not. But never like that again."

"In other words—"

Logan interrupted, "In other words, I haven't bottomed since—until you."

"Really?" Tate asked.

And it sounded to Logan like he was holding his breath.

"Really."

Silence stretched between them, and then Tate promised, "I'd never hurt you like that."

"That's easy to say," Logan agreed. "But no one knows your secret yet."

"Because it's been two weeks. Actually, less since it got physical. Cut me some slack. I just got used to the idea. I want to enjoy it before I have to defend it."

Logan closed his eyes and asked the one question he dreaded, "And will you?"

"Will I..."

"Defend it?"

Logan heard Tate sigh in a way that didn't bode well for his question at all. But he remained quiet, determined to let Tate say what he must, and then he would move on from there.

* * *

"YES. I'LL DEFEND it. But I won't lie to you, my family is not going to understand this *at all*," Tate told him candidly.

"This?"

"You, me. Us."

A low *hum* of approval came through the phone, and Tate found himself stretching along with that contented sound.

"Us. I like the sound of that," Logan confided.

Tate lowered a hand down between his thighs to rub it slowly against the erection swelling in his sweatpants. "So do I. So, tell Cole to stop trying to think for me."

"I can't *tell* Cole anything. But I will advise that he back off."

"Good. Because I know what I want."

"Oh?"

"Yeah. Logan, my family is traditional as hell. We all go to church on Sundays. Trust me, there's not one part of this that's going to be easy, but..." Tate felt his heart racing in his chest with his hard-on throbbing beneath his hands.

"But?"

"I want you. Am I supposed to walk away because you're a man? Maybe. They'll say yes for sure. But I'm sick of all the questions running around in my head." Tate stopped and licked his lips. "I want the man who sat down across from me and changed the way I look at the world. And if that's wrong, then I'm confused because when I'm near you, it feels so damn right."

"Tate?"

"Hmm?"

"I wish I was in your apartment right now instead of out on my balcony."

Tate took a moment and pictured Logan sitting outside among the glittering city lights.

"Are you still drinking?"

"No."

Tate slid his hand into his pants and stroked his palm over his naked flesh, remembering this evening in the bar up against the wall.

"Do you feel better?"

"Yeah, I do. Tate?"

"Yeah?"

"Are you falling asleep?"

Tate looked down his body and pushed his sweats over his hips. "Not yet."

"What are you doing?"

"Listening to your voice and getting hard."

A groan was Logan's answer. When Tate heard a chair scrape, he knew that Logan had stood and was

398 Ella Frank

moving.

"What are you doing?"

"I'm going into my bedroom to get naked. Want to come over?"

Tate played with his balls and let out a soft grunt at the invite. "It's too late now."

"What does that mean?"

"It means, I'm already hard, and I want to come."

"Selfish," Logan admonished gently. "If I remember correctly, you already came twice today. The least you could do is get on that death trap you call transportation, and come and return the favor."

"*Ah...*" Tate sighed into the phone as he thrust up into his hand. "But then I'd have to stop what I'm doing."

"Yeah," Logan agreed.

There was a whole lot of shuffling going on, and then he was back, promising, "But I'm dying for it, and if you come here, instead of your hand, you can fuck me."

Tate gritted his teeth. "You play dirty."

"Come over, and I'll show you how dirty. You know you want to."

Tate glanced at the DVR clock, and it now read 1:40.

Am I really going to—

Oh, what the hell?

Tucking himself back into his sweatpants, he winced as he sat up, and then he stood, looking around his apartment for his helmet and jacket.

"Logan?" He located them both and picked them up.

"Yeah?"

Tate snagged his keys off the counter and said into his cell, "Fifteen minutes. Be ready."

With that, he ended the call and walked out his front door before slamming it behind him.

Chapter Twenty-Four

TATE WAS BUZZED into Logan's condo lobby the second he arrived, and now found himself stepping out of the elevator and onto Logan's floor.

What a difference a week could make, Tate thought as he rapped his knuckles on the door. *Has it really only been a few days since I was standing here the first time around?* There was no question in his mind this time. He wanted to be there.

As he stood in the empty hall in his gray sweatpants, white T-shirt, and leather jacket, he reached down to adjust the erection that hadn't completely subsided since he'd left his apartment.

Seconds later, Logan's front door opened, and Tate decided that the ride over had been worth leaving his place at two in the morning. His fingers tightened around his helmet as he quickly took in the wet hair swept back from Logan's face, the dark growth shadowing his jaw, and every single inch of skin on display—and there was a whole hell of a lot.

Logan must have just stepped out of the shower because the light covering of hair on his chest glistened as he stood with his hand up on the open door. Tate's gaze trailed

down the hair of Logan's chest and across his rippling abs
until it narrowed and then disappeared behind the bright
white towel secured around his hips.

Bringing his eyes back up to the ones watching him,
Tate stepped forward, causing Logan to back up and drop
his hand from the door. Once he was inside the condo, Tate
kicked the door shut with his foot, dropped his helmet onto
the floor, and advanced as Logan started walking backward.
Shrugging out of his jacket, Tate kept his eyes on the man in
front of him, who had a grin on his face that made Tate want
to kiss it right off. As they made it out of the foyer and into
the living room, Tate dumped his jacket on the floor and
kept advancing on Logan.

"What's on your mind, Tate?"

Tate reached over his shoulder, gathered the material
of his shirt in his fist, and drew it up his back and over his
head before tossing it on the ground.

"Just wondering if it's a habit of yours to answer the
door dressed like that?"

Logan looked down at himself and then brought
devious eyes back up to his. "Why? What's wrong with
what I'm wearing?"

Tate felt his own mouth morph into a suggestive
smirk. Reaching down to the top of his sweatpants, he
loosened the drawstring as he kept moving forward. "It
doesn't hide much, does it?"

Finally, Logan came to a standstill when he backed
into the kitchen island. He placed his hands on the solid

surface behind him, which caused his body to thrust forward, showing Tate exactly how exciting this particular game of cat and mouse was for him.

"Well, my aim wasn't really to hide so much as to provoke."

Tate reached out to finger the spot where Logan had secured the towel. As Logan stood rooted to the spot, Tate pulled the material out of its hold, and when the towel loosened, Logan sucked in a breath.

Bringing the material up between them, Tate looked at it and then focused back on Logan as he dropped it onto the kitchen floor. Taking the final step he needed for his body to be pressed flush against Logan's naked one, he placed his palms on the counter and penned Logan in.

With chests and hips locked together, Tate replied, "Well, mission accomplished. I'm provoked. Now, turn around."

* * *

LOGAN'S EYES WIDENED slightly at the demand as Tate took a step back. Instead of moving right away, Logan stayed where he was, fully erect and completely naked. He couldn't stop himself from looking at and drooling over the picture Tate made, dressed only in loose sweats hanging from his hips, as he stood, waiting on him.

"Turn around?" he questioned, knowing full well that had been the order, but enjoying the game just the same.

"Yes," Tate confirmed in a voice that made Logan's shaft pound just a little harder. "Turn around. I want to see you. *All* of you."

Logan turned but couldn't help himself from saying, "Yes, *sir*."

As the final word left his mouth, Tate crowded in behind him and shoved him up against the counter, so it was digging into his waist. Logan glanced back over his shoulder as Tate's hand came up and gripped his chin. Slowly, he moved his face in until their lips met.

"Such a smart mouth," Tate acknowledged as Logan's lips parted, "and tongue," he made sure to add, licking them as he ground his hips in against Logan's backside, making him very aware of the erection he was packing.

"Everything I want, and everything I crave, is *you*. Now, face forward," Tate instructed as he let go of Logan's chin and ran his fingers down his spine to his tailbone.

"Spread your legs," Tate whispered against the back of his head.

Moving only slightly, Logan hardly widened his stance at all, and he heard Tate laugh at the smart-ass move. He started to feel the thrill of victory at his small win until Tate put his foot between his and kicked them apart.

"Spread 'em, Logan, nice and wide. Stop acting like you don't want it when we both know that you do."

This time, he couldn't help the huff of air that came from him as Tate urged him down onto the cool, unforgiving surface of black marble with a firm palm between his shoulder blades.

Against his back, Logan could feel Tate's warmth as he bent down with him, curling his front against him. Then, Tate smoothed his free hand over his bare ass and ghosted his fingers across the dark shadowed crease of his body.

Logan clenched his teeth against the pleasure that made his body quiver from the sure touch, as a shiver of pleasure made his entire body tremble. All the while he was thinking, *I'm screwed. With this guy, I'm fucking screwed.*

* * *

"DAMN. WHAT IS it about you?" Tate wondered out loud as he straightened to run his palms up and down Logan's sides, enjoying the feel of his skin under his hands.

Logan remained bent at the waist with his face against the counter and his legs spread wide.

"My sparkling personality?"

Tate brushed his fingers down Logan's crack and smiled as the man's entire body tensed.

"Nope, it's not that."

When Logan's eyes met his, the best they could from his prone position, Tate's fingers pushed between his cheeks to the heated pucker waiting for him.

"Although, it may be part of it," Tate joked as he felt slick moisture on his fingertips and realized exactly *how* ready Logan was for him. "You're already lubed up? You fucking deviant. Just begging for it," Tate whispered as he grazed his fingertip against Logan's hole, "aren't you?"

"*Yes*, I fucking am," Logan admitted readily around a curse.

"Just how badly do you want it, Logan?"

"Jesus, Tate, how bad do you think? Look at me. You think I do this for everyone?"

Tate had to agree, the man had a point. With a quick pinch to his ass, Tate grinned when Logan flinched.

"Oh, I'm looking, trust me. Spread out, bent over your kitchen counter," Tate relayed all that he could see. Then, he brought his lips down to Logan's ear as his finger probed for entry and found it. "I think I like it—*a lot*. And so do you," he confirmed as his finger thrust forward, causing Logan to move up onto his toes.

"*Ah…*" was the unintelligible sound that ripped out of Logan as Tate watched his toes curl against the tile while his body got used to the invasion.

Gradually pulling his finger free, Tate brought two fingertips back to Logan's rim to play. "Did you have fun putting this on without me?"

Logan looked back at him once again. He tried to regain some control of the situation, but it was useless. Tate held it all, and Logan fucking knew it. So, instead Logan gave him a seductive once-over. "No need to feel bad, Tate. I thought about you the whole time."

Pulling the edge of his sweats down, Tate freed his hard-on from its confines as he continued fingering Logan.

"Who said I felt bad? I want to know if you had *fun*?" Tate asked again, emphasizing his point by pushing the tips of his fingers back into Logan's body.

There was a loud groan and then Logan replied, "Yes. *Yes!* Fuck yeah."

"And what were you thinking about?"

As Tate slid his fingers in and out, methodically stretching him as he'd been taught, Logan's breath became labored.

"Was thinking about this."

"This, huh?" Tate queried, knowing exactly what he meant. "My fingers inside you? Or maybe you were thinking about more than that."

"*Yes.*"

"Yes, what? These one-word answers are not working for me." Tate came down over Logan again and placed his mouth on his shoulder. "Yes, you were thinking about more?"

Logan's hips bucked back as his ass clenched around Tate's invading fingers.

"Come on, Logan, tell me your dirty secrets. Just how many fingers *do* you want?"

Logan clenched his teeth, and whispered, "Another."

Tate stood back up and looked down to where his fingers were disappearing and reappearing. Smoothing his free hand over Logan's ass cheeks, he spread him apart and slowly pushed three thick fingers inside the hot body bent before him. *Holy fuck, what a sight.*

"This is unreal...*Logan*, so sexy," were the words that left him as he twisted and flexed his fingers.

When he pulled them out, he apparently hit Logan's prostate because he shouted out Tate's name and jammed his hips backwards, demanding roughly, "*Again.*"

As Tate eased them inside, Logan let out a loud groan. Tate was mesmerized by how wide he was stretching him and how much Logan was loving it.

Unable to help himself, Tate lowered down over the spread-out man and put his mouth to Logan's upturned cheek, licking the stubble there. After kissing the corner of Logan's mouth, Tate's eyes held his as he vowed, "I don't care what anyone says. *Love* being with you like this. I fucking love it."

* * *

LOGAN HEARD TATE speaking as his fingers were grazing against that perfect spot, but he'd lost the ability to comprehend. He was spread apart and bent over, and he was quickly falling harder and faster for the man giving him exactly what he wanted.

For years, he'd denied this side of himself, but he'd always loved bottoming for Chris. The bite of pain, the roughness, it had all added to the pleasure. Although thinking back now, that was probably more due to Chris's selfishness than a want to fulfill Logan's own desires.

But not here, not this time with Tate. Tate was

watching and reading every single move he made, and he
was relishing in the power he held while *he* was busy getting
off on being at Tate's mercy.

"*Hell*, Logan. You weren't lying on the phone, were
you? You were dying for me to come take you. *That's* what
makes you so goddamn sexy—the fact that you don't wait
around when you see something you want, and you don't
stop until you're...*absolutely*...fucking...satisfied."

Logan sucked in a breath as Tate shoved his hips
hard against his ass with each enunciated word, and his
fingers spread inside him. With every rub of the guy's cock
over his flesh, he could feel the sticky proof of Tate's
excitement against the skin on his backside.

He squeezed his eyes shut and shouted as Tate
removed his fingers from his body. Logan knew what was
coming next, and when he felt the bare head of Tate's shaft
brush up against his ass, he clenched his jaw and barely
remembered to ask, "Protection. God, please say you have a
condom."

Tate's fingers dug into his hips, and he cursed out,
"Hell, wait here. Do *not* move."

Logan couldn't have moved even if he tried. His cock
was pulsating, his ass was needy, and his body was just
about to go into a meltdown. The only cool parts of him
were his stomach and the right side of his face, which were
pressed up against the marble. He stretched his arms out to
the sides, and a moan of pleasure escaped his lips when he
felt Tate's body come back and line up behind him, wedging

his thick shaft between his cheeks.

Closing his eyes, Logan tried to calm himself as warm fingers spread him apart. When the head of Tate's erection pressed against his stretched rim, Logan let out a breath of air as he was penetrated one slow inch at a time. He could feel a palm resting flat on his back at the base of his spine, and as the pressure increased, he relished the delicious fullness of having Tate inside him.

"Nothing feels like you do," Tate admitted hotly behind him.

Logan had thought that this coupling would be hard and fast, but as Tate lodged himself inside and stopped. Tate came down over him and spread his arms out to the sides where Logan's lay, and he entwined their fingers. The mouth by his ear kissed the shell of it, and the hips pressed up against him moved in a slow rotation.

"Every time we do this, it convinces me that I'm exactly where I need to be."

Logan shuddered and pushed himself back, trying to get Tate closer somehow. He couldn't find the words for the emotions he was feeling, so he remained silent and instead allowed himself to sink into the feelings. For the first time, he let them wash over him and wrap around him, much like Tate was.

"I don't care how hard it might be. I need to know why it's you who makes me feel this way. If it's just sex or if it's more, I need to know if you feel this way, too." Tate professed.

Logan remained uncharacteristically quiet for a change as Tate's words came to a halt. Then, he felt a tongue touch his lobe, and Tate's hips rocked forward.

"You feel the same, don't you? You told me this scares you. Tell me why, Logan."

Logan felt Tate lift slightly, and when he pressed a kiss to his cheek, Logan nervously licked his lips. "Playing dirty, Tate?"

"If I have to. Tell me," he replied, refusing to give Logan an easy way out.

Shutting his eyes, Logan admitted, "It scares me because of how much I want it."

Tate nuzzled into his neck and shoulder, and Logan's body trembled under the man behind him.

Suddenly, he couldn't shut his mouth. "I've never wanted something more. But with you, I can't seem to stop myself. I want to look at you and know that you're mine, and *that* terrifies me."

Tate's fingers wrapped around his own as he brought their arms in close to his sides, and then Tate asked again, "Why?"

Logan found Tate's eyes and finally acknowledged, "Because I think I could love someone like you."

Tate's breath left him in a quick rush of air, and then he was gone. He released Logan's arms and straightened up behind him. Logan felt strong fingers holding him in place as Tate slowly pulled from his body before surging back inside. He heard a low moan behind him, and as he pushed back onto the body moving inside his own, Logan enjoyed the wicked slide into oblivion.

* * *

TATE LOOKED AT the smooth skin of the muscled back laid out for him and wondered when this had gone from a quick fuck to making love. As he slowly pulled his hips away from Logan, he knew that was exactly what he was doing. He was making love to this man.

Logan's eyes were shut, from what he could see, and his hands were braced under him, so with each of Tate's thrusts, he could move back on him. But all Tate could think about were the words, *because I think I could love someone like you*, and all of a sudden, Tate wanted more.

Pulling out of Logan, Tate heard him groan from the loss as he managed in a gruff tone, "Turn around."

Slowly, Logan stood and turned to face him. As soon as they were face-to-face, Tate took the back of his neck in his palm and pulled him forward. Capturing his mouth in an urgent kiss, Tate heard a moan slip free from Logan as one of his hands cupped Tate's cheek.

Their tongues tangled, and their cocks bumped against one another.

Tate ripped his mouth away, breathless. "Need you, but not like that."

"How then? Tell me what you need."

"Bed. You in your bed."

Logan nodded once and didn't waste any time. He
turned and made his way into the bedroom with Tate
following close behind, keeping his eyes on the ass he
planned to take as soon as they were on a soft mattress.

When Logan stopped by the side table and opened it
to remove a bottle of lube, Tate bumped into him and
ordered softly, "Get in the bed."

"I like this bossy side of you almost as much as the
aggravated side. Am I demented?"

Tate felt a grin hit his lips for the man who
continually threw him off guard, but he wanted more from
Logan than smart-ass comments. He wanted to see inside
this man. He wanted to know all of him.

"Earlier tonight, you told me that I was your biggest
truth, but that's not right. You know what the biggest truth
is, here in this room?"

Logan looked down at their bodies and then back at
him. "Other than the glaringly obvious?"

"Yes. Other than that."

"No, I don't."

"The biggest truth is that we're *both* trying something
new, and you know what?"

Logan's face changed and became serious at that
comment. "What?"

"We *both* love it." Tate's eyelids lowered, and he
gestured with a tilt of his chin. "Get in bed, Logan. I want
you."

Tate watched as Logan climbed into the bed and lay

down on his back. He turned his head on the pillow, his black hair stark against the white, as he reached out his free arm and crooked his finger at him.

"Come here."

Placing his knee onto the mattress, Tate took the bottle of lube in his hand, poured some into his palm, and gripped his erection, stroking it several times.

God, he liked this man. In fact, Tate thought he was pretty damn amazing, and that was when it hit him. *Somehow, this man is perfect for me.* Tate brought his eyes back to Logan's face. *How can that be? And more importantly, how am I okay with the fact that my perfect person is a,* him?

But as Logan stared back at him and Tate crawled between his legs, he knew without a doubt that he was. Kneeling between Logan's thighs, Tate's heart started to pound.

Logan's lips tipped up, and a smile split his mouth. "What are you thinking about?"

Tate laid down over him, and as Logan's mouth parted and that sexy bottom lip pouted out, Tate couldn't help but take a gentle bite of it, watching as his eyes slid closed.

"You don't want to know. It would terrify you."

Logan's eyes opened immediately. "Really? That bad?"

Tate rocked his hips on top of the body under him. "Really. That good. Now, *shh*, would you?"

Raising himself up and over Logan, Tate gripped his

cock in his hand and directed himself toward Logan's waiting body. Logan bent his legs, and Tate easily slipped inside the man and groaned, lowering his head into the crook of Logan's neck.

Resting his forearms by Logan's head, Tate began to move slowly in and out of him.

"*Tate*," Logan sighed, turning his head until his face was nestled in against his hair.

Tate closed his eyes from the pleasure of having him there. Bumping his hips back and forth, he threaded his fingers into Logan's hair, and he raised his head to look down into a face, full of emotion and desire.

As Logan raised his knees and wrapped his legs around Tate's waist, he whispered, "Terrify me."

Tate's breath caught in his throat at the sincerity in those two words. The look on Logan's face was one of absolute ecstasy, and every time Tate pulled out of him and then pushed back inside, a breath of air left from Logan's lips.

"So perfect," Tate praised as he stared down, captivated by the face that had become essential to him.

He fingered the black hair in his hands as Logan's palms trailed down his spine to his ass where he caressed him before pulling him closer.

"*Tate. Tate...Tate*," Logan chanted.

Tate picked up his pace, and he knew he had him.

Kissing his ear, Tate snaked an arm down between them, taking Logan's dripping cock and stroking it.

"Gonna make you come, Logan. Come on, I want to *feel* it. Hot and sticky all over me. All over us."

"*Oh God!*" Logan rammed up, slamming their hips together.

Tate started to pump into him, and he felt his balls tingle, threatening to explode on every downward glide, while Logan's fingers grabbed his hips, pulling him closer against his needy body.

"So good, Tate. So, *very* fucking good." Logan praised as his body tensed under him, and his hips pushed up. A throaty growl left Logan, and the veins in his neck pulsated as he arched back in an explosive release, and the sight was enough to make Tate want to come. As Logan came down from his high, his eyes opened, languid and full of desire, and his mouth curled as Tate quickly pulled out of him and rolled the condom off his body. Tate grabbed the lube and poured some into his hand as he kneeled between Logan's legs, running his gaze over the other man.

Logan licked his lips and started to run his fingers through the sticky mess on his stomach as he murmured, "Perfect, sexy Tate. First time I saw you, I wanted you under me. Are you ever going to let me have you?"

Tate felt his breath coming fast at the thought of what Logan was proposing, but he was beyond talking now. As he continued pumping his cock furiously, Logan quickly sat up and kneeled in front of him. Reaching down between them, Logan took him in his strong hand now covered in his own cum.

Pressing his lips against Tate's, Logan promised, "I want to lay you on your back and kiss and lick every inch of your body, and then, Tate…" He paused, biting Tate's lip. "*I'm* going to take *you*, and you're going to love it."

Just like that, Tate came all over the both of them with a shout and a sharp punch of his hips with no other thoughts except how amazing his orgasm was and how much he wanted Logan to take him that way. He could feel Logan's hand soothing his sensitive skin as his lips kissed and sucked their way down his neck.

Tate almost whimpered when Logan let go, and he raised his hand to Logan's cheek where he leaned in and kissed him.

When Tate finally pulled his mouth back, Logan whispered, "Stay?"

"Yes," Tate replied easily.

"Good. I want you to stay."

Tate leaned in again and gently pressed his mouth to Logan's. "Then, I'll stay."

Chapter Twenty-Five

THE FOLLOWING MORNING, as they stood outside of The Daily Grind, Logan looked over to where Tate was leaning back with one of his feet propped up against the brick wall and a cigarette in his hand.

Usually, this kind of thing did nothing for him, but as Logan moved in beside Tate, he had to admit the look Tate had going reminded him a little of *James Dean,* and it was flat-out sex.

The white shirt, jacket, and jeans—not to mention, the black steel-toed boots—with the wind-ruffled curls all meshed together in just the right way to make Logan's palms itch to touch. Logan squinted against the rising sun as Tate glanced over to him and lifted his hand to take a drag of the nearly finished cigarette.

"Quit it, would you?" Logan ordered at the thorough once-over Tate gave him.

"Quit, what?"

Logan aimed his eyes at the lips surrounding the tobacco stick. "Staring at me like you just spent the night, naked, in my bed."

"But I did. I hardly think it's making you

uncomfortable," Tate stated, lowering his arm, as he straightened off the wall.

"Trust me, uncomfortable is not what it's making me feel."

"Mhmm, and since when has *that* bothered you?"

"Since I'm out on a public street and can't rectify the issue," Logan pointed out.

"So, I shouldn't tell you that you in that suit makes me really fucking excited? I've never dated anyone who wears a suit. Well, I've never dated a guy, so—"

"Tate?" Logan interrupted shifting his briefcase in front of him to hide the erection he could feel swelling even further between his legs.

"Yeah?"

"Stop it."

Tate laughed, clearly enjoying his discomfort, as he turned to press the butt of his cigarette into the tall, cylindrical black ashtray by the door.

"No, I don't think I will. I had to deal with this shit from you for a week before you finally told me what the hell you were looking at."

Logan stepped around him and pushed his face in close to Tate's. "I thought I was more than obvious. I was looking at you. And by the way, why are you smoking again? Stressed? Nervous?"

Tate arched a brow and offered a roguish grin. "How about satisfied?"

Rolling his eyes, Logan reached out and pulled the

door open to the coffee shop. As the smell of ground beans reached him, he watched Tate maneuver his way through the people waiting to take a spot at the back of the shortest line. Following his lead, Logan moved in beside him and then reached down between them and slid his palm into the one by Tate's side.

Tate turned toward him, and Logan made sure he was staring right back with a neutral expression. When Tate's fingers parted slightly and entwined with his own, as they had last night, Logan couldn't help the way his heartbeat nearly flew out of his chest. Tate winked at him and went back to facing the front, and Logan found it almost laughable that he was the one standing there with a shocked look on his face.

Pulling his shit together, he leaned in, so their shoulders bumped, and he whispered, "You look good in my jeans. I especially like that you aren't wearing anything under them."

Without even turning, Tate chuckled as he continued to scan the chalk-written menu. "Can't help yourself, can you?"

"What?" Logan protested with his eyes on the strong side profile Tate's jaw presented.

Tate turned to him as they shuffled forward in the line. "That right there."

"What? I was just making a comment."

Shaking his head, Tate moistened his lip with his tongue. "You never just make a comment."

"I don't?"

"No. You make suggestions, or you turn things into an invitation."

Logan shifted where he stood, very aware of the heat of Tate's body and the hand in his own, as he turned back to look at the menu even though what he wanted was standing right beside him.

"Maybe that's just what you hear," he added quietly.

He was shocked to feel a set of warm lips by his ear as Tate told him, "That's what you want me to hear."

Logan faced him with only a slither of space between them and admitted, "Damn right, that's what I want you to hear. And it's *still* what I want, every minute I'm with you."

Silence slipped between them, but it wasn't uncomfortable in any way. Logan wanted to call Cole and tell him he was taking the rest of the week off, and then he'd convince Tate to do the same, but really, there was no need. It wasn't as if they only had two weeks to work this out. They had as long as they wanted, they had forever if need be.

Wait—damn, that's exactly what we have, Logan thought as he turned back to face the front, and once again, they moved farther up the line.

"So, I'm meeting with Diana and your brother today. Finally, all of this shit will be over," Tate told him.

As Tate's words interrupted his current train of thought, Logan blinked several times and tried to refocus. "Oh, that's bound to be fun," he answered absentmindedly.

"Yeah, I'm sure. A root canal would be more
exciting."

Logan didn't mean to ignore Tate, but he found
himself standing there, trying to imagine how to ask Tate if
he were interested in—

What exactly?

Yeah, Tate had expressed that he was feeling things
that were more than just sex—feelings that were strong, that
would terrify him—

But did he mean this? Forever?

Because this, *this* was terrifying him.

* * *

TATE CONTINUED WATCHING Logan, as he seemed to
zone out on him. He knew that he was teasing him with
every move and word that had come out of his mouth, and
Tate loved it. Logan's reactions to him solidified that what
they were doing was right. Logan was feeling the exact same
way he was, and that was the kind of reassurance Tate
craved to move forward with their relationship.

This morning, Logan looked exactly as a high-paid
lawyer should, all suited up. It wasn't as though Tate hadn't
seen him dressed this way several times before, but this time
was different. This time, he'd sat and watched as Logan had
dressed.

Oh yeah, I like my choice of lover, Tate thought as he
continued studying the man who had gone from seductively

playful to pensive. *Lover? Yes, that is exactly who Logan is to me now.*

"What's on your mind? You seem very serious all of a sudden."

Logan turned and acted affronted. "I *can* be serious on occasion, you know."

"Really? Have to say, it must be a rare event. Actually, I'd love to see you in court. I think that would be a total turn-on."

Logan laughed and told him flat out, "No way in hell are you going anywhere near a courtroom that I'm supposed to be in."

"Why?"

"Because you step into a room, and everyone else disappears."

Tate caught the expression of shock that had crossed Logan's face at his own admission, and he jumped right on it. "So, right now, here in the coffee shop, it's just me, huh?"

When the person in front of them moved aside, they both turned back to the front, and Tate smiled as he looked at the back of the barista. That was, until he turned. Tate almost groaned at his luck, because right there, standing in front of them, was Robbie—the same guy that he and Logan had run into the last time they were in here, the *same* guy that Logan had admitted to being with. As Tate glared at the man, he felt Logan's hand squeeze his own.

Tate turned to Logan, and he realized he was still wearing his scowl as Logan's eyes widened as if to say, *Is this a problem?*

And is it?

Not really.

He was the one holding Logan's hand. He was the one who'd been in his bed last night. As he turned back to face Robbie, Tate took a second to check him out, only to see if Robbie had something that *he* didn't—

Right?

"Hey Logan, and, Tate, isn't it?"

Tate was surprised that the guy remembered his name. He was about to say something caustic when Robbie continued, "I see you're both back in here again *together*."

"Robbie, come on, can we just order?" Logan replied just as Tate stated dryly,

"Good to see there's nothing wrong with your eyes."

When the guy started laughing, Tate wasn't sure what the hell to think.

"Oh, he's touchy, isn't he?"

That question was *definitely* directed at Logan, and before he could answer, Tate snapped, "No. *He* just wants to order a coffee."

Robbie rested his hip up against the counter and leaned over, so he was slightly closer to them both. "That's fine. I can help you with that. But while you're both here, let's chat."

"Let's not," Tate fired back as Logan groaned out, "*Robbie.*"

"Oh, come on. That's no way to talk to a friend."

Jesus, this guy just doesn't know when to quit, Tate thought as he looked from Logan, who shrugged and rolled his eyes, and then back to Robbie, who was beaming at him as he chatted casually almost as though they had all been doing this for years instead of...*never.*

"You're not his usual type, you know."

"Robbie, just take our fucking orders, would you?" Logan suggested as he released Tate's hand to press his thumb and index finger to his forehead.

"What? It's true."

Knowing *who* he meant but not quite *what,* Tate managed, as politely as he could, to ask the question pounding in his brain, "What do you mean?"

"Well, you're nothing like me, are you?"

He was definitely nothing like him. Robbie was shorter to start with, probably around five-ten, and had blond highlights throughout his hair, which was slightly longer in the front and swept to the side. Down the side of his neck was a tattoo of some kind that snaked into his black polo shirt, and in each ear, he had black gauges. He was also wearing—

Is that eyeliner?

He looked like a runaway from a punk band.

And he is criticizing me?

Without taking his eyes off Robbie, Tate asked, "So? What's that supposed to mean?"

"It means nothing. He's talking out of his ass," Logan interjected.

But it was too late. Tate wasn't paying attention to Logan, and Robbie was having too much fun messing with the both of them.

Robbie straightened and shrugged. "Nothing, I guess. Just that, usually, he goes female or, you know, my kind. You...you're...well—"

"Well, what?" Tate demanded, and felt Logan grab his hand.

Not realizing quite how loud he had spoken, it wasn't until the woman in the line beside them turned their way with a frown, that Tate mumbled, "Sorry."

"Well, you're like him. Big, tall..." Robbie joked, lowering his voice to a false baritone as he turned to Logan, and then Tate before trailing off. He seemed to be concentrating on something very important, then whispered, "And really sexy. I bet you two look so damn hot when you get together. Who tops?"

Tate almost choked as he heard Logan mumble, "Oh fuck," beside him.

"Jesus," Tate cursed. "No wonder you two get along. You have no filter either."

Robbie frowned at him and looked toward Logan, who was still muttering something under his breath. "What do you mean? Who has no filter?"

"Nothing, forget it," Tate grumbled, irritated that he was slightly amused by the entire conversation.

"Okay," Robbie answered with a quick grin and then asked again conspiratorially, "So, who tops? I can't imagine

Logan as anything else, but *then*—"

He was cut off by Logan's phone that started ringing at that exact moment. Tate turned just as Logan looked down at the screen and then back at him. He indicated the waiting area behind them.

"I've got to take this. Will you be okay *here*?" He emphasized the word *here* as he glared at Robbie.

"I guess," Tate answered with much more surliness than he knew he possessed.

"Okay, just black for me."

Nodding, Tate watched him walk away and then turned back to face Robbie on his own.

"Can we just have our coffees?" Tate requested through clenched teeth, his jaw starting to ache.

"Well, you could, *but*…" Robbie drawled in a way that was more than a little obnoxious.

"But what?"

With a quick, flirty wink, Robbie shrugged. "You haven't ordered yours yet."

Tate lost all of his annoyance that quickly, and he found instead that he was laughing and shaking his head. *Great, just what I need — to actually find him humorous instead of annoying.*

"Okay, Robbie, you win. God, I need a coffee now more than ever. Can I have a hazelnut latte? And his espresso. To go."

"Sure. Want me to bring it over?"

Tate looked at him in a way that screamed, *Not if you*

value your life.

Robbie's smile was full of mischief as he finally put Tate out of his misery. "Got it. It'll be ready here in just a minute."

* * *

TATE MADE HIS way over to where Logan was standing with the phone pressed to his ear. Just as he got to the table, he heard, "Sorry, hon. It just isn't going to happen again."

Frowning, Tate came to a standstill, and Logan glanced at him across the table that was between them.

"No, it was nothing you did."

Logan's tone and his words made it abundantly clear that he was not talking to a work colleague or a client. Tate was trying his hardest not to pay attention to his insecurities as they knocked on the door in his brain when Logan reached over and took his hand.

"Jess," Logan said and paused.

Jess? Jess? That name is familiar, Tate thought as he stared at Logan.

"Look, since we last spoke, I started seeing someone."

The bar. That was where he'd heard the name, back when they had first met. He remembered Logan on the phone with a Jess, promising to see her *or* him, without their clothes on.

"Yes. It was fun, but this is serious," he told the

person on the other end of the phone as he moved around
the table toward Tate.

When Logan was beside him and their hips and arms
were brushing, he looked right at him as he said clearly,
"This is exactly what I want."

Tate felt his body heat at the words as his heart
skipped in his chest, and everything finally fell into place.
He was so ready to be with Logan in *every* way, and if he
hadn't been sure before, this confirmed it.

"Good-bye, Jess," Logan said, ending the call and
then placing the phone down on the table where he twirled
it slowly. "What have you done to me, Mr. Morrison?
Turned me into some relationship guy?"

Tate focused on the man studying him from behind
the thick black-rimmed glasses. "You didn't really think this
through, did you?" he asked Logan.

Logan looked at him with an expression that relayed
the words he then spoke, "I don't understand. What do you
mean?"

Tate leaned closer, so their faces were only inches
apart, and he lowered his eyes to Logan's mouth. "You
never actually thought about what would happen if you
finally got me to try what you wanted, did you? Did you
actually believe that this wouldn't turn into more? With this
kind of heat?"

"Why should I have thought that? It never had
before."

Tate shifted his eyes back to Logan's. "Yeah, but it

wasn't with me, was it? Have you ever stood in a coffee shop and wished that every single person in here would get out, so you could do exactly what's on your mind?"

"Not until right this second. What's on your mind?"

Tate looked around at everyone milling about, waiting on their drinks. "What you've always wanted—me under you. I'm ready to give it to you."

Logan visibly swallowed. "You're fucking trouble."

"Yeah? Well, it's your own fault. Once I make up my mind, that's it. You should probably remember that."

"So," Logan started and then cleared his throat, attempting to change the subject, "Robbie didn't give you any more problems?"

"No, nothing other than that comment regarding your type and how I'm not it."

Logan looked over his shoulder and glanced at the counter where Robbie was working, and when he turned back, he stepped in much closer than they had been before and placed a hand on Tate's chest. Brushing his lips over his cheek, Logan told him, "He's so very wrong."

"Hmm, is he?" Tate questioned, openly enjoying Logan as he felt firm lips move up to his ear where Logan murmured, "Yes."

Turning his head to Logan as though hypnotized, Tate heard his name called out to come and collect their coffees. He was sure his feet could take him to the counter, but they didn't move him anywhere as he continued to stare at a grinning Logan.

"Better go get our drinks," he teased as Tate finally stepped around him. "Oh, and by the way, Tate, so much better this time. You didn't even flinch when I touched you."

That smart-ass comment was all it took for his brain to kick in, just as Logan had known it would. Tate glared at him, flipped him off, and moved toward the counter.

Just as he got there, Logan called out to him, "I've got to take Cole's call. This is the second one I've ignored this morning."

Tate looked over his shoulder. "When was the first?"

Logan winked and laughed, leaving him to only imagine, as he walked toward the door. Tate turned back to the counter where Robbie stood, holding out their coffees, with a huge smile on his face that told Tate he'd been watching the entire interaction between Logan and himself.

"So, come on, tell me. Who tops?"

Tate held his hands out with a bored look on his face. He took the coffees and turned without saying one damn thing, but as he left to go and find where Logan was waiting on him, he realized he was happier than he had been in a long time.

Chapter Twenty-Six

COLE HAD BEEN terse on the phone with him when Logan had finally called back. He was obviously still worked up about their argument. Logan knew that they needed to patch their shit up and soon. The problem was, neither of them was particularly good at saying sorry, and instead, they enjoyed avoiding one another more. Although, that was no longer an option since Tate's soon-to-be-ex had shown up already for their nine o'clock meeting—at eight.

After he'd told Tate, Logan had heard him mutter something along the lines of, *Fucking early as usual,* and then they'd made their way over to the office. Logan figured the sooner this was over with, the better.

Having made good time, they moved into the elevator that would take them up to the offices, and he pressed the button for his floor. Logan stepped back to stand beside the man who had him hyperaware of every single move he made. Ever since Tate had dropped the bombshell that he was finally ready to let Logan be the one to do the taking—*well, fuck*—his brain hadn't fully recovered.

One thing was for certain—he was more than ready to take. His manners were wearing out, and the restraint he'd being hanging on to was stretched to its limit each time they got naked together. So, yes, he was more than ready.

Logan glanced at Tate from the corner of his eye and saw that in his usual relaxed way, Tate was propped against the back of the elevator with his legs crossed and one of his hands resting on the brass bar that ran across the panels.

Who would've ever known it would be this guy that I want above anyone else? The not-so-straight bartender, Logan thought.

The elevator stopped at a floor, and several people got on. Tate shuffled beside him, and they moved closer until their shoulders bumped up against one another. As they faced forward in the confined space, Logan felt the hand Tate had on the bar shift until it was against his back. Figuring it was just by accident, Logan didn't say anything until he felt that same hand move, and a sinful pressure was applied to the base of his spine.

Clearing his throat, Logan once again looked to Tate, who was still facing forward, staring at the doors, as he raised his coffee cup to his lips and took a sip. That was also the moment the hand on his back glided down over his ass and then up under his jacket.

Careful not to attract any attention, Logan moved the briefcase in front of himself, knowing that the fingers now tracing a line up the back middle seam of his dress pants were going to make him hard as a rock.

Once again, they came to a stop in their ascent, and the hand teasing him paused as several more people got on.

One of them, a work colleague, smiled in his direction and greeted him. Logan replied with a brisk nod of his head and was about to say more until a long index finger worked down the crease of his ass, making him cough instead.

Christ. Tate touching him, even above his clothes, was driving him out of his mind. Turning his head, Logan was ready to pin Tate with a look designed to stop him from his sensual torment. He wasn't, however, expecting to come face-to-face with the fervor in Tate's eyes.

Holy fuck. That look alone was as effective as Tate sucking his dick. It was molten, it was incendiary, and it was all for him. So, instead of doing anything to stop him, Logan stepped back into those fingers, wishing they were somewhere where he could unbuckle his belt and really let Tate have at it. But no, he was stuck in an elevator going to work where, ironically, Tate's ex was already waiting for him.

Finally, the elevator stopped on the firm's floor, and when the other people parted, Tate removed his hand and sauntered out as if fondling him had never happened. That wasn't going to last long though—that casual ease Tate was carrying around. *Oh no.* Logan planned to set Tate straight about how today was going to go.

Moving out of the elevator, Logan struggled to make sure that no one saw exactly how exciting his morning ride up to the office had been—*up* being the operative word. He made his way through the doors and into the lobby, empty except for the receptionist, and walked over to stop directly behind Tate.

Tate didn't turn, and he didn't look back at him, but his body stiffened as Logan placed his fingers in the same position on the lower part of his back.

Making sure his mouth was close enough for Tate to hear, Logan relayed exactly what was on his mind. "You've tested me and my patience for the final time today. You better be ready tonight. I'm going to enjoy making you pay for *that* particular cocktease."

* * *

TATE FELT A shiver race down his spine as Logan's dark promise penetrated the lust inside his brain. He was starting to rethink his actions as Logan's fingers moved across his back before he stepped around him, making his way across the marble-floored lobby of the firm.

Logan seemed different here, larger than life, and Tate could feel the sexual waves rolling off of him. This was a man who had finally been given permission, a man who now knew he could do what he wanted without being told no. This man was dangerous to his very being.

Tate took a steadying breath, determined to at least act as though he were calm. Making his way over to the doors, Logan opened one for him, looking ever the professional. It wasn't until Tate passed him that the word *professional* took a flying leap out the window because Logan brushed a palm over the back of Tate's jeans and warned him, "Tonight, it's *my* turn, and *this* is finally going to be mine."

Stopping beside him, Tate locked eyes with the silver-tongued lawyer as Logan continued, "But for now, you have a meeting in the conference room. Good morning, Mr. Morrison."

Logan stepped around him, and Tate watched in silent awe as he made his way down the hall and through the desks of people, who were all busily working. Tate noticed as Logan passed each of them, that nearly every person lifted his or her head and greeted him. *Made sense really. Logan is the boss*, Tate thought and then lifted a hand to run it through his hair. *And in case I ever doubted it, he just made that abundantly clear.*

Making himself move, Tate walked through the many desks of workers to the conference room. *How strange is this going to be? Sitting in a room with my soon-to-be-ex and her lawyer, who just happens to be my lover's brother. My new* male *lover.*

Tate shook his hands by his thighs and tried to push aside thoughts of Logan and what was going to happen tonight. Then, he made his way over to the open door of the conference room.

Tate walked inside, looked at the back of Diana's head, and frowned, *Time to get this over with.* He must have made some kind of noise because she turned and looked over her shoulder, pinning him with her eyes and a grimace, which spread across her face as she looked down over him.

What-the-fuck-ever. She could think what she liked. He wasn't here to impress her anymore. Making his way around to the other side of the table, Tate pulled out a chair and sat down, placing his coffee cup in front of him.

"At least you're on time today," were the first words out of her mouth.

"Jesus, do you ever say anything nice anymore?"

She looked at her tailored dress and pretended to brush a piece of lint off of it, and then she glanced back at him. "I can. I just don't want to. Besides, don't crawl all over me for stating the damn truth. "

"Why? What did I ever do to you that was so bad, Diana?"

Aiming a look at him that should have made his balls shrivel up and die, she leaned over the table and placed her hands on top of it. "Gee, let me think. Letting our marriage fall apart."

"That was not my fault alone, and you know it."

Sitting back in her chair, she shrugged and crossed her arms. "You were always pigheaded, Tate. You never take responsibility for anything."

"Bullshit. I take responsibility for every goddamn action I make."

"Oh, I know you take credit for leaving. That's the easy part. But what about the reason why? You never admit to any fault when it comes to the *why*," she sneered.

"Excuse me?"

"The *fault*, Tate. You never took any blame for what

was *your* fault. It was only due to your laziness that we ended up where we are, and you know it."

"Lazy? How can you sit there and say I was lazy? I worked two jobs the entire time we were together."

"Lazy when it came to us. You just didn't give a shit. Then, you quit. Just walked right out the damn door. You didn't even care that your family loved me, that *I* loved them."

Tate ran a frustrated hand over his face. *Where was Logan's brother?* Sighing, he dropped his arm down onto the table. "Funny, in that entire sentence you never once said that you loved me or that I loved you."

Unexpectedly, Diana reached across the table and clasped Tate's hand. "But you did, didn't you?"

Tate looked into the eyes of the woman he thought he'd once loved, and all he could think of were blue eyes, glasses, and a stubbled jaw.

"Whatever I did or didn't feel burned itself out long ago."

"And now you feel nothing?"

Tate considered her question carefully, trying to gauge her angle. "Am I supposed to?"

So quietly he almost didn't hear her, Diana whispered, "Maybe, if you tried."

Just as he was about to pull his hand away and ask her if she'd forgotten she was engaged, the conference room door opened and in walked Cole followed closely by—

Logan. What the hell?

Both of them looked as formal and businesslike as they possibly could.

Immediately, Tate saw Logan size up the situation. Those eyes he had just been imagining zoomed in on the hand that was covering his own, and as Tate removed his, Logan's eyes lifted and locked with his.

"We're sorry we got held up," Cole stated. "Mr. Morrison, it seems your lawyer is running late."

Diana let out a snort of laughter that had everyone turning to face her, and Logan then tilted his head to the side studying her for the first time as one would a petulant child.

"Is something amusing, Ms. Cline?"

Under Logan's direct stare, Tate watched Diana straighten her spine and lift her chin. "No. Is there a reason you're even here? I was under the impression you were only needed if Mr. Madison wasn't available, and clearly," she stated as she turned to Cole, who Tate only now realized was staring at him with a pensive look on his face, "he is."

"Oh yes, I'm here for a reason," Logan announced as he unbuttoned his suit jacket and brushed it aside to slide his hands into his pants pocket.

And yeah, Tate thought, *he knows exactly what he's doing to me.*

Tate felt his palms sweat as he stared at the man squaring off with Diana, and he wondered for a split second just how far Logan's outrageous behavior extended. *Would he really say something to her just to gain the upper hand?*

"I'm here for Mr. Morrison. I need him," Logan stated and moved toward the conference room door. When he reached it, he looked back over his shoulder to Diana, who was completely ignoring him, and promised in a voice that seemed to have a direct link to Tate's cock, "His lawyer wants to speak to him. Don't worry, I'll send him back to you as soon as he's done," and then he left.

Tate's erection noticeably throbbed between his legs, and he was curious about how exactly Logan expected him to get up and walk out after the sensual threat he'd just heard in his voice. Several seconds passed, and it wasn't until Cole moved to stand beside Diana that Tate looked up at the blond guy and saw him raise his brows.

"Your lawyer's waiting for you."

Tate nodded silently, understanding that both Cole and Logan were *not* referring to Mr. Branson. He looked to Diana, who aimed daggers back at him, and finally having gained some control of his body, Tate pushed back from the table. "I'll be back in just a minute then."

Cole inclined his head but said nothing as Tate hurried around the table and made it out the door, walking toward the office where *his* lawyer was waiting for him.

* * *

AS SOON AS the knock sounded on his office door, Logan yanked it open and stared at Tate. Without a word, he stepped aside as the man walked inside. Turning to watch him, Logan lightly pushed the door closed as to not disturb the thick silence that had engulfed them. As he made his way over to the man with his back to him, Logan's palms itched to slide into Tate's jeans pockets covering that perfect ass. *That ass which is soon going to be mine.*

"You came to me," Logan murmured from where he stood behind Tate, not yet touching but close enough that his suit jacket was brushing the material of Tate's clothes.

"You said you needed me. How could I refuse that?"

Isn't that the fucking truth? Logan thought, looking at the back of Tate's head, wanting to remind himself that this man was his.

When he'd walked into the conference room and seen Tate's ex wife with her hand over Tate's, Logan had felt a moment of—

What? Jealousy?

But as quickly as it had surfaced, it disappeared because Tate had looked up at him, and the eyes that had met his own had been full of want, full of need, and full of everything he himself felt, and it had all been directed at him.

So, Ms. Cline can go fuck herself.

Raising his hand, Logan brushed his fingers on Tate's shoulder where he trailed them down his arm until their fingers met and interlaced.

"I do need you," he confessed so close to Tate's hair, that his breath made the curls shift. "I've never been so distracted in my life, thinking about you in there with her."

Tate turned, and as Logan stared into the dark eyes hooded with desire, he lifted their hands.

"Look how far you've come? Holding my hand and everything?"

Tate's mouth curled up on the sides as he took Logan's other hand in his. "I want to do a lot more than holding hands. And look at you, finally admitting you're jealous."

"I did not."

"Yeah, you did."

"Hmm, so tell me more about what you want to do," Logan said.

He stepped in close until Tate's legs hit the desk, and he settled, allowing Logan to maneuver between his legs. Bringing their hands around his waist, Logan placed Tate's palms over his ass and sighed when he felt him squeeze and bring him closer. Removing his hands, Logan placed them on Tate's chest.

"I can't stop thinking about coming to your place tonight after work."

Logan rubbed himself between Tate's legs and fingered his hair. "And?"

"And"—Tate chuckled—"you know why."

Logan pressed his lips to Tate's. "Yeah, but I want you to say it."

"Do you?"

"Yes. Tell me you'll be mine, that I can finally have you."

Tate blinked, and this close, Logan thought it was astonishing that he'd never noticed how thick his eyelashes were before.

"Yes, you can fucking have me. I *want* to be yours."

Logan threaded his fingers through Tate's hair and tilted his head back, so he could take his mouth. As Tate's lips parted, Logan eased his tongue inside, and he could taste the hazelnut and the lingering hint of tobacco as they seeped into his senses and rolled into the deliciousness that was Tate.

The hands on his ass increased in pressure as Tate stood up from the desk and his body brushed directly against Logan's, ripping a raw groan from them both as their lips parted. Tate then lifted one of his hands to cradle Logan's cheek as he pressed a gentle kiss to his lips, and in that simple moment, Logan knew that he'd never experienced such perfection in his life.

As his mind spun and his brain kicked into overdrive, Logan didn't hear the door to his office push open. He didn't hear Cole's wife, Rachel, as she knocked on the door, but as she stepped inside, he did hear a soft laugh, which had him pulling his mouth away from the one that was still clinging to his and turning to see Mrs. Madison with a woman he didn't know.

Just as he was about to greet Rachel, Tate moved out from behind him, obviously realizing it was no one that they—

"*Tate?*" the woman beside Rachel questioned

incredulously.

Logan turned to the man beside him who looked as though he'd seen a ghost and thought, *Okay, scratch that. Apparently, it is someone Tate knows.*

Chapter Twenty-Seven

TATE STARED AT the two women standing in front of both him and Logan. He knew that he had to say something, but he found himself ironically incapable of speech. One minute, he'd been in the middle of the best kiss he had ever received, and the next, he was standing in front of—

My sister.

"Tate?" the all-too-familiar voice questioned again.

This time, Jill stepped around the other woman, who Tate didn't know, and moved closer. "Oh my God! It *is* you."

Tate swallowed several times and ordered himself to, *Speak, speak. Open your mouth and fucking speak!*

But nothing happened, and Jill continued, "But you were just…just…were you *kissing* him?"

Yes, I was definitely kissing him, Tate thought, but still nothing left his brain via his mouth.

Finally, Logan spoke up, "Excuse me? *Who* exactly are you? Rachel, what's going on?"

But before Rachel—whoever she was—could answer, his sister took another step toward them, and Tate saw her mouth open and shut several times as though she, too, had lost the ability to speak. Jill, however, found it again, much quicker than him.

"I thought you were meeting with Diana, and instead, you're in here, kissing a...a..."

"A man," Logan added dryly. "I'm a man."

"Is this who you're dating? Does Diana...does she *know*?"

Jill's voice had risen to a high-pitched shout, and the questions she was demanding answers to were hitting Tate with the force of a sledgehammer. Still standing mute and apparently immobile, Tate watched Logan take a step toward the two women.

"Look, I don't know what is going—"

"Wait," Tate finally spoke up.

Logan looked over his shoulder, and the expression on his face was one of concern. But he also appeared as if he figured this was the moment Tate would take to lie and deny everything. That was the problem. Tate didn't want to deny one damn thing, and as he stood there, he'd been trying to work out exactly what it was that he *did* want to say.

Taking a fortifying breath, he stepped forward until he was shoulder to shoulder with Logan, and he looked down at Jill. "This is my sister, Jill. Jill, this is Logan, and yes, he *is* who I've been dating, but he is not the reason I left Diana. That was over a long time ago, months before I even met Logan."

Tate watched his sister's eyes widen, as she seemed

to take in the information he'd just supplied her with, and then she shook her head. "What?"

"This is Logan—"

"I heard that part, Tate! What are you thinking?" she demanded and spun on her heel ready to leave. "Where's Diana? Does she know?"

Tate lunged forward and gripped her arm, spinning her back. "You don't need to—"

"Don't *fucking* touch me," she hissed at him with so much acidity that Tate literally dropped her arm as though it had burned his hand. She glared at him and then shifted her glare to Logan, who was standing deathly silent beside him. "This is disgusting. Mom and Dad will *never* forgive you for this."

"Jill," Tate warned, his breathing stuck somewhere inside his chest, knowing exactly how well this would *not* go over with his family. As he watched her march out of the office, he called after her, "Jill!" but it was too late.

She was now standing out in the middle of the law firm in front of Diana and Cole, who had apparently come out of the conference room to see what all the noise was about. Diana looked at her best friend, his sister, before raising her eyes to meet his.

That was when Tate felt someone move up beside him, and without turning, he knew it was Logan because Diana's eyes moved to him, and a scowl crossed her features. Slinging the strap of her purse over her arm, she walked forward and clasped his sister's arm. When they both reached him, she laughed in a way that was both as ugly as it was spiteful.

"Good luck explaining *him* to your family, Tate. They already hate you for what you did to me. They're going to hate this even more."

Tate knew she was right. Introducing Logan to them was going to be a nightmare, one they were going to have to deal with sooner rather than later.

"This is for *me* to tell them," Tate told them both, "not you."

Jill looked away as though she couldn't even stand the sight of him.

Diana cackled like the witch she was turning out to be. "Well, we'll just have to see who gets there first."

"Diana," Tate cautioned, becoming more and more pissed.

She completely ignored him, turned to Logan, and said in a voice dripping with malice, "So, do you fuck the exes of all your clients? Or just the men?"

"Diana!" Tate shouted and got in her face. "Stop it."

Narrowing her eyes, she didn't back down one bit. "Fuck you, Tate. Oh, hang on," she said, making sure to spread her venom as she moved past them with his sister in tow, "maybe he can do that."

* * *

LOGAN STOOD IN the middle of Mitchell & Madison with

all of his coworkers, including Cole, staring at him and the man standing beside him. It didn't bother him in the slightest that they knew he was seeing Tate, but never had he blatantly displayed his personal relationships before. Then again, this was his first.

"Okay everyone, show's over, go back to work. Tate, can I see you in my office, please?"

Logan moved to his door, and glanced inside to see Rachel sitting on his couch with her lip caught between her teeth as she stared at him with an I'm-so-sorry look plastered all over her face. Logan winked at her and tried for a smile, letting her know it wasn't her fault, as he stepped aside to let a traumatized Tate walk back into his office.

Standing, she glanced in their direction and indicated she was going to go and almost ran out of the room, pulling the door closed behind her. As it clicked shut, Logan turned to face Tate, who was still silent and looked as though he was in shock, which he probably was considering everything that had just happened.

Logan was just about to suggest they sit down when Tate turned and grabbed his hands.

"We need to go and see my parents."

Wait…what? Logan thought as he looked at the desperate expression on Tate's face.

Tate nodded manically as he clutched Logan's hands, and then he started talking rapidly.

"Yeah. We'll go there now, my mom is home, and she can call my dad. We can sit down, tell them how we met, and that this is all good, that we…you know…that this is…"

He trailed off, and Logan felt his own anxiety starting to swirl and race through him. *Meeting parents? Meeting family? Family that won't like me because of who I am? No, thanks.* He'd already had one of those in his life with his own father.

Plus, are we really that serious that we have to jump into this right now? Tate is just nervous, he is rushing things, he is—

"I *want* to tell them, Logan. They need to hear it from me—the right way, not the distorted, warped version that she'll tell."

Okay, so apparently, Tate is very coherent.

Logan took a step back and rested up against his desk. Removing his glasses, he pinched the bridge of his nose and sighed. "Tate, I don't know. I'm not good with families. I don't think you need me there."

Tate stepped toward him and reached out to touch his shoulder. "Of course you need to be there."

"I don't think it's a good idea." Logan stared up into the brown eyes now staring at him with confusion.

"I don't understand."

Glancing away from that all-too-knowing stare, Logan said once again, "I don't think it's a good idea."

"*What's* not a good idea?" Tate demanded, his voice so loud that Logan knew it could be heard outside of his office.

Standing, so they were on equal footing, Logan put his glasses back on and slid his hands back into his pockets for something to do. Suddenly, the whole day looked totally fucked-up. "I just don't think we're at that stage yet. I mean, I get you need to tell them. But they don't need to meet me."

Tate blinked several times and almost staggered back from him. "Are you fucking kidding me?"

Letting out a sigh, knowing this was not what Tate wanted to hear right now, Logan raised a hand and stroked his chin. "No."

Tate launched himself at him before Logan even had a moment to counter it. He shoved him so hard in the chest that Logan stumbled back and landed on the desk.

"You fucking asshole!" Tate boomed as he crowded in against him.

Taking a hold of his jacket lapels in his fists, Tate yanked him up, and Logan had never, *ever* seen him look so volatile. He also had never realized how fucking strong Tate was when he was angry.

"You ask *everything* of me, everything, and risk absolutely nothing in return."

Releasing him with a rough, hard push, Tate glared at him in a way that made Logan feel like the piece of shit he knew he was being.

"I don't know why I'm so surprised. Did things get a little too real for you, Logan? Well, fuck you! My whole goddamn life just changed, and here you are, backing away like a pussy."

Logan straightened and stood up as Tate moved to the door. He was about to call out to him, stop him from leaving, when Tate placed his palm on the handle and turned back, pinning him with a look that shouldn't have, but did, cut him to the core.

"Why don't you understand that everything I've done and *just* did, I did because of how you make me *feel*, Logan? Even when I knew my family wouldn't understand, I did it anyway, just to get closer to you. How stupid was I?"

Logan couldn't find the words to even begin to explain what he was thinking, and as Tate walked out of his office, Logan knew that Tate hadn't wanted to hear them anyway.

* * *

LOGAN STOOD IN the deafening silence that Tate had left behind. He felt the ache that had been growing, since Rachel and Jill stepped into his office, fester into a wide gaping hole that was now threatening to swallow him.

One minute, he'd been kissing Tate and planning exactly what he was going to do to the man that night, and the next, World War–fucking-female broke lose. Tate had pushed him for more, Logan had shut down, and now, Tate was gone. *Fucking gone.*

Jesus, he thought, storming around his desk to take a seat.

Just as his ass hit the leather, there was a knock on the door, and Rachel, Cole's wife, poked her head into his office. "Hey."

Looking up at her, Logan rested his head back against the chair and tried for a smile. "Hey."

He watched the woman he loved as a sister walk in and stop on the other side of his desk. She placed her pink-tipped fingers on the surface and leaned in. "Oh God, how badly did I screw this up for you?"

Logan's mouth quirked as he thought about how angry Tate had been, but the fault wasn't anyone's but his own. "You didn't."

Rachel made her way around the desk and when she was beside his chair, she turned, rested her hip up against the wood desk, and looked down at him.

Logan had known Rachel for a little over three years, and as usual, today, she looked gorgeous in her black leather pants and pink polka-dotted blouse. She was beautiful in a wild in-your-face kind of way, the complete opposite to her—

Knock, knock.

"Hello?" Cole called out as he pushed open the door.

Husband.

"Hey," Logan replied.

Cole stepped through the door before shutting it behind him. Rachel was still staring down at him as though she was waiting for him to speak, but he really had nothing to say.

Huh, that has to be a first.

"Did Mr. Morrison leave?"

Logan raised a brow at his brother. "His name's Tate,

and he's not here, and neither is the bitch you're working with, so you can cut the polite shit."

"Look, I was just—"

"Just what?" Logan snapped.

Rachel cut in by moving forward and placing a palm on his shoulder. "Hey, relax. He's just trying to—"

"Tell me what I did wrong? That he was right? No, thanks, heard it all before."

Rachel laughed softly. "You're just like him."

"*Him* is right here, Mrs. Madison," Cole reminded her in a tone Logan figured worked for Rachel since she looked back over her shoulder to where her husband was standing.

Smoothly, she told him, "Oh, I know exactly where you are, smartass," before turning back to face Logan, "Like he's easy to ignore. But what I was going to say is, Cole's just trying to see if you're okay. He knows how much Tate means to you."

Logan took off his glasses and tossed them onto the desk. "Yeah, well, it doesn't matter. I'm pretty sure he just dumped my ass."

Rachel frowned. "What? But I don't understand. He said—"

"What'd you do?" Cole questioned, stepping forward to the desk.

"Excuse me?"

"What. Did. You. Do?"

Logan glared across at Cole with a look that

screamed, *Fuck off.*

"That *straight* guy just told his ex-wife and sister that he was dating you, then you came in here, and now, you say he left and dumped you. So, what did you do?"

"Nothing."

"Bullshit."

Logan stood, hoping that would make him feel better about the situation, but it didn't. Cole, meanwhile, stared him down until he had Logan rolling his eyes.

Screw Cole and his ability to wait me out. Two can play at that game.

"Go away. I have a busy morning and a boring night to look forward to, so please, leave."

"He said something about family, didn't he? His sister, his ex? What happened, Logan? He wants you to meet the parents?"

Rachel stood beside him and touched Logan's hand. "Was that it? Because that's great. He must really like you."

Logan looked down into the wide blue eyes staring up at him. They were hopeful, sweet, and not-so-innocent since he knew his brother.

"Look, not everyone's like you two. It's too soon for all of that."

From across the desk, he heard a mocking laugh, and his head snapped around, so he was once again facing Cole.

"You dumb shit. He just got outed to everyone he knows and stood up for you, and you told him no to meeting his parents?" Cole laughed again. "I would have fucking punched you before I left, if I were him."

He very nearly did, Logan thought, remembering the rage on Tate's face. But then he also recalled the disappointment and pain in the expression he'd seen right before Tate had walked out.

As Logan stood there silently, Rachel ran a hand up his arm to his shoulder. "Go to him, and apologize. Swallow your pride."

Logan looked down at her and tried to diffuse the much-too-emotional moment with inappropriateness. "It's not pride I'd have to swallow."

A small smile tipped her lips as her eyes sparkled. "I'm not rising to your dirty bait, Logan Mitchell. If it's not pride, then swallow your fear." She looked over to Cole and whispered, "I did. It was the best thing I ever could have done."

Logan glanced at the other man in the room, and the look on Cole's face as he stared back at his wife made Logan—

Envious?

"You're right. You're both right. I have a few meetings, and then I'll go and track him down."

Rachel practically squealed as she bounced up on her toes and kissed his cheek. "See? Family can be a good thing! We just did a good thing, right? And we're family. Now, make up you two, so Cole can ask you something."

Logan frowned over at his brother.

"Go on," Rachel urged.

Shaking their heads, they both grumbled out a pathetic excuse of, "I'm sorry," and then Rachel patted his arm and moved around the desk to go and stand by Cole.

Taking her husband's hand in hers, they both looked over at him, Rachel grinning and Cole looking as serious as ever.

"Okay, ask him."

"Rachel," Cole warned as though he wasn't sure he wanted to right now.

"You told me you wanted to ask him as soon as we knew, but you both had a fight, and—"

"Rachel?" Cole interrupted.

"Yes, dear?"

"Why don't *you* ask him?"

Logan stood there, looking back and forth between the pair, and when Rachel turned and placed her hands on her belly, Logan felt a genuine smile spread across his face.

"Will you please be one of our baby's guardians? You know, in case—"

"Don't say it," Logan grumbled quickly, raising a hand. Then, he laughed out loud. "Congratulations, you two! But are you crazy? Me? Are you sure?"

"No, not really," Cole replied dryly.

Rachel whacked him in the chest. "Yes. We wanted both of our brothers."

Logan looked over at Cole, extremely moved by the gesture he never would have expected, and when his brother finally smiled, he felt their relationship shift back to where it belonged. The only thing that was missing was the one thing that he'd driven away.

"Then, I'd be honored."

As Cole hugged his radiant wife to his side, he glanced over at Logan and mouthed, *We good?*

Logan tipped his chin in agreement as his mind began spinning—spinning, planning, and plotting his next move. It all revolved around one thing—getting Tate back into his life.

Chapter Twenty-Eight

THREE AND A—fuck, something hours later, and I still can't stop thinking about him, Tate thought as he stared at the fan rotating slowly above him. Nothing would have been odd about that, except that his fan was turned off. Yep, the alcohol was doing its job, and he was nice and buzzed.

Lying on his back, he picked up his cell phone from his bare chest and stared at the screen. *Still nothing. No calls of outrage from the family and not one call or text from that asshole telling me how sorry he is.*

Well, fuck him, Tate thought, dropping the phone back to where it had been, as he lifted the bottle of Cuervo to his lips. *Actually, don't fuck him. He'd like it too much,* Tate told himself just as his phone vibrated.

Picking it up, he made out the name and text he'd been waiting for. Swiping open the message, he stared at the two words on his screen and felt his mouth fall open. Twisting around and sitting up way too fast for his head, Tate continued to stare at the screen.

That arrogant fuck. Instead of the two words he'd expected—I'm sorry—there, staring back at him, was, **I'm coming.**

Tate glared at the phone as if the man who had typed it would be able to see. Placing the bottle down on the floor beside him, he typed back.

You're not coming here.

Logan was in for a rude surprise if he thought Tate was going to let him in, and an even ruder one if he thought he was going to come in any way, shape, or form near him until he apologized.

Logan: Be ready.

"Unbelievable," Tate sputtered, reaching down for the tequila.

Fuck you.

Not ten seconds later, there was a loud pounding on the door that startled him as his phone lit up. Looking down at it, Tate read a reply that made his buzzed brain take notice and his traitorous cock stiffen.

Logan: No, Tate. I'm gonna fuck you.

"Open the door!" Logan called out.

Tate stood, making his way—*one foot in front of the other*—to the door. "Go away, Logan. I don't wanna talk to you," Tate called out, leaning against the wood as he raised the bottle back to his lips.

"That's too damn bad because I have a lot to say to you."

Bringing the bottle down by his leg, Tate closed his eyes. "Then, say it."

There was a long pause, and then Logan's voice, softer this time, vibrated through the door. "This morning at my office—"

"Yes, *Lo-gan*—" Tate half-sang through the door.

"Are you drinking?"

Again, Tate repeated, "Yes, *Lo-gan*."

"Open the door, and say that to me," Logan demanded, calmer this time around.

Tate rolled his shoulders along the door until he was resting his left side up against it. "And why would I do that?"

He heard a thump and wondered if Logan had used his fist or his head to hit the door. "Open the fucking door, Tate."

"Apologize," Tate countered, determined to hear the words.

"Open the door, and I will," Logan argued back.

Sighing, Tate knew they were at an impasse. He unlatched the dead bolt, turned the lock, and opened the door. Logan was standing there, with his arms stretched out, bracing him against the door frame, with his jacket parted and his tie falling forward.

Guy's all fucking sex, Tate thought as he stared at the eyes behind the glasses.

Being this close to Logan with only his jeans—*oh shit, they're Logan's jeans*—between them, was not going to help him resist the man in front of him. So, as soon as Logan dropped his hands off the frame, Tate raised the bottle to his lips and downed more of the smooth, warm alcohol, trying to keep some distance between them.

"You going to let me in?" Logan asked.

Tate had a feeling that statement meant a lot more than permission into his apartment.

"You going to apologize?"

Logan ran a hand along his jaw. "You want me to do this here?"

Taking another drink as he thought about it, Tate scratched a hand over his naked chest, and then he moved it down to the button on his jeans. "Yeah, I think I do," he agreed, and then blamed the alcohol when he added, "Down on your knees. That's where most people grovel."

* * *

LOGAN MANAGED TO keep his mouth from falling open—*barely*—as the words Tate had just spoken made it to his brain.

Glancing at the bottle of tequila in Tate's hand, Logan questioned much more calmly than he felt, "How full was that?"

Tate lifted the quarter-empty bottle and shrugged. "Unopened. Why?"

"I'm just thinking about how *brave* you're being," Logan drawled out suggestively.

"Maybe I should always be drinking around you then."

Logan reached up to loosen his tie. "No doubt. Now, what exactly is the criteria for me to get into your place? Me on my knees, apologizing, right?"

Tate dipped his head forward and gave Logan a confident leer. "That's right."

Looking up and down the narrow hall he was standing in, Logan lowered down to his knees in the doorway and had to admit that the game, which was most definitely *on*, was making him horny as hell.

Tate took a step back from the door and then another before he stopped, widened his legs, and unbuttoned the top of his jeans. Logan's mouth practically watered as he remembered exactly what Tate did *not* have on under the denim he'd borrowed this morning.

"Tate…"

Tate focused his eyes on him and unzipped his jeans. *The cocky shit is going to tease me to death. When I finally get my hands on him, he is in so much trouble.*

"Yes, Logan?"

"I'm sorry."

"For?" Tate urged as he slowly pushed his hand into his jeans.

Logan was finding it difficult to concentrate, as he remained kneeling in place. "For being an ass."

Tate moved his hand around behind the material, and then he pulled his erection up straight with a relieved groan. It was visible through the open zipper, and Logan wanted it. He wanted it so bad that he was close to crawling across the floor and begging for it, but why crawl when—

"And…"

And? There's supposed to be more? Logan thought and then decided, *Enough is enough.* Moving to his feet, he took a step inside, and he was satisfied when Tate did nothing to stop him.

Shutting the door with a loud slam, Logan loosened his tie further and pulled it over his head before throwing it to the floor. *Game on.* It was his turn to hunt.

This time, it was *he* who was stalking Tate, *and if Tate knows what is good for him, he'll run and hide.* Or at least, he would run if he didn't want to be caught and attacked because that was exactly what was about to happen.

Something must have triggered Tate's flight response because he started to slowly back up, and *that* only made this all the more fun in Logan's opinion.

"Where are you going? I thought you wanted me to elaborate." Logan shrugged out of his jacket and tossed it on the ground.

"Not going anywhere," Tate told him stubbornly, the alcohol making him slightly less aware of the calculation in Logan's eyes.

"You sure look like you're going somewhere," he pointed out as he pulled his shirt from his pants and started to undo the buttons one by one.

Tate stopped by his kitchen table and placed the bottle on it. "I'm still angry at you. It's going to take more than that half-assed apology before you're forgiven."

Logan yanked his shirt open after becoming impatient with the small buttons, and removed it as he stopped in front of Tate and threw it on the table, next to the bottle of tequila. Swiftly, he took Tate's chin between his thumb and forefinger.

"Yeah, I figured as much since you're pretty much buzzing and *still* drinking."

"Yeah, well, you're enough to make anyone drink," Tate fired back, surly as hell.

"Is that right?" Logan asked with a curl to his lip.

He didn't know what this said about him, but this was the attitude he loved on Tate, and he hadn't seen it for a while. It was pissed-off, it was confident, and as his eyes remained locked with Logan's, it was arrogant as fuck.

"Yeah, it is. I'm not going to give in until *you* really mean it."

Logan couldn't help the taunting laugh that escaped him as he took Tate's bottom lip between his teeth. Pulling it out and then letting it go, he ran his tongue over it and tasted the tequila as he promised, "Well, we'll just have to see who gives in first, won't we?"

He covered Tate's mouth in a furious mating of lips as he pushed his free hand down into Tate's open jeans. As Logan's fingers curled around Tate's hard cock, Logan felt him shudder, and he smirked against his mouth.

"I'm going to make you tremble so fucking bad, your knees are gonna give way."

Tate breathed heavily against his mouth and challenged, "Bet you can't."

Letting go of Tate's chin, Logan cupped the back of

his head and twisted strong fingers into his hair. Pulling
Tate's head back, Logan sucked on his neck and throat and
then licked over Tate's Adam's apple where he promised, "I
will, or I'll die trying."

A harsh moan left Tate as Logan worked the
responsive flesh in his hand and then kissed Tate's jaw. He
bit it gently, and then with a tinge of desperation, he
pleaded with the man, "Say you forgive me, say we're fine."

"No," Tate refused.

Logan could see how this was going to play out. He
just wondered who would win.

"Okay, if you won't forgive me, then at least let me
taste you."

Logan released both hands from Tate's body as he
dropped down onto his knees and quickly pulled the jeans
to Tate's thighs. As soon as the denim revealed what he
wanted, Logan went for it.

Wrapping his arms around Tate's legs, Logan
kneaded his ass cheeks and nuzzled into Tate's groin,
reveling in the scent that hit his nose. Exhaling slowly,
Logan looked up to see Tate staring down at him.

"Well? I'm waiting."

Oh, are you? Logan thought as he circled the base of
Tate's erection and dragged his tongue from the root of the
shaft to the tip.

When he got to the head of the thick erection, Logan
licked the slit, and Tate's fingers found his hair and grabbed
on as he tongued the sensitive glans.

"Come *on*, Logan. Suck it. You know you're dying to," Tate ordered.

Logan would be damned if that demand didn't ramp up his urge to take Tate, that much more. But first—first, he was going to drive Tate fucking crazy.

Running his hand down Tate's ass cheek, he brought it around the front of his thigh and up between to cup his full and heavy balls. As soon as he was cradling them, he squeezed and glanced up to see Tate fixated on him. Feeling a smirk cross his lips, Logan rose up on his knees and bent his head over him.

"*Holy shit*, Logan," he heard reverberate through the silent apartment as he brought his lips back up Tate's steely length.

"Your mouth was fucking made for this."

Logan could feel his own cock pressing painfully against his zipper.

"Hmm…mouthy lawyer equals one sexy cocksucker."

He's going to kill me, Logan thought as he pulled his lips from Tate. He was about to tell him he was going to get it, and hard, if he didn't stop running his mouth, but before Logan even had the chance, Tate's hand was on the back of his head, increasing the pressure.

So, instead of talking, Logan locked eyes with the sexed-up ones looking down at him, and he silently parted his lips as Tate pushed his hips forward, and slid back into his mouth.

Logan could hear the soft huffs of air leaving Tate with every flex of his hips, and when Logan closed his palm around the firm sac he was fondling, Tate cursed loud enough that Logan was sure that everyone on Tate's floor had heard. But this wasn't where Logan wanted this to end. *Oh no.* He had so much more in mind for Tate.

Rising to his feet, Logan took Tate's lips in a hard kiss, before lifting his lips.

"Not yet, Tate. Your mouth is *very* dirty tonight. I think you need to cool down and wash it out. Time for a shower."

Tate pulled back from him. "I'm not fucking you in the shower."

Logan reached down between them and took Tate's erection in his palm. "Good. Because in case you've forgotten, that's not on the agenda today."

Tate lowered his hands and stilled Logan's. "You're *not* fucking me either."

Logan stared at Tate as he removed his hand and stroked the back of his fingers along his cheek. "Even if that was an option, I'm of the opinion that I want you to have a clear head. So, let's get rid of this buzz you have going because, Tate?"

Tate's dilated eyes blinked at him as Logan assured him, "You *will* sober up, you *will* forgive me, and then I'm going to take what you promised me."

* * *

TATE CONCENTRATED ON Logan as he thought back on the morning. "You hurt me today. I knew she would, but I didn't expect you to."

Tate knew it was the alcohol that had him relaxed enough to say things he never normally would, but when Logan was being gentle, when he was touching him like he cared, it was so easy to slip into the stronger emotions.

"I know," Logan admitted. "I know I did."

Tate let out a shaky breath, and for the first time in four excruciatingly long hours, he relaxed under Logan's admission. "Okay, as long as you know."

That was when Logan stepped back, removed his glasses, and tossed them on the table. Tate tugged his open jeans back up his body, and as Logan ran a hand through his own hair, he let out a breath and muttered, "I know, believe me. Watching you leave, with no plan to return, isn't something I want to witness again any time soon. Now, let's shower."

* * *

LOGAN FOLLOWED TATE down the hall toward the bathroom and for once, he really wanted this to be special. For the first time in his entire adult life, he cared about what happened to the man in front of him.

Just as Tate turned to his left and was about to disappear through the door, Logan reached out and took his arm. Pulling him back, so he was in the dimly lit hall, Logan stepped in to him until Tate's back was against the wall, and he was against his chest.

Cupping Tate's face, Logan pressed his lips to the parted ones in front of him. He was relentless in his quest to hear the answer he craved. "Do you forgive me?"

Tate reached down between them and began unbuckling Logan's belt as he denied him once again, "No."

Logan rested his forehead against Tate's, as fast fingers unfastened his button and zipper.

"Tell me why I should. Give me a reason," Tate suggested.

"Because," was all Logan could come up with as Tate's hand pushed down into his pants, taking him in his palm.

"Because?" Tate repeated back to him.

"Yeah, because."

"But you told me that *because* is never a good reason," Tate reminded him as he let go of Logan's aching skin. He slipped away, making his way into the bathroom.

Frustrated with himself for this entire situation, Logan squeezed his eyes shut and counted to thirty. He was close to finally being in control of himself when he heard the water turn on in the next room.

Oh hell. He had no chance of winning this game, and he knew it. He would do anything to hear Tate say he was forgiven, even if that meant sitting outside the bathroom *while* he showered, but hopefully that wouldn't be the case.

Making his way into the tiled room, the first thing Logan saw over in the corner was the pair of jeans Tate had been wearing. He then focused on the man who was standing under the spray of water, and he felt his cock weep as he watched him run a soapy sponge all over his tanned body. When Tate then turned toward him, he dropped the sponge and lifted his hands to smooth them back through his hair, and Logan was rendered useless.

How did I ever think that I'd be the one to win this battle of wills? The man is gorgeous and stubborn, and he has the ability to bring me to my knees.

Kicking off his shoes and pushing his pants and boxers down, Logan was happy to see that even though Tate was still mad, his body was responding to him, regardless. Tate's erection, both veiny and thick, pointed right at Logan before Tate reached down with a wet hand and stroked it while his eyes stayed on him.

Logan made his way to the glass shower door, pulled it open, and stepped inside, facing the soaked man in front of him. As the water sluiced down over Tate's body, making his hair stick to his head, Logan couldn't stop himself from wrapping his own hand around the blushing thick erection Tate was fisting.

Stepping forward, Logan met Tate halfway, and the second their mouths collided, every thought Logan may of had about slow and sweet went straight out the door. *God, this is pure heaven.* Tate's mouth was hot and wet as it moved under his, and the noise that rolled out of him was like music to Logan's ears.

Raising a hand to Tate's shoulder, Logan pulled his mouth away as he ran his palm down along the smooth, wet skin and ordered, "Turn around, and face the wall."

Tate blinked at him, and the water that was caught on his eyelashes sparkled under the bathroom lights as he sucked his bottom lip and slowly moved forward. Then, without question, he turned around.

Before Tate was even in place, Logan encroached on that perfectly bronzed back and wedged himself between Tate's rounded ass cheeks. Loving the feeling of finally having his cock where he'd been dying to put it, he sank his teeth into Tate's shoulder, sucking up the beads of water as he felt the spray hit his side.

Tate bucked into him, and Logan asked again, "Do you forgive me?" as he bent his knees and slid his erection up through the most toned ass cheeks he'd ever seen.

Tate's palms flattened against the tile wall as he used it to drive back on him, telling Logan once again, "No."

Cursing out his frustration, Logan licked his way up Tate's neck to his ear and threatened, "Don't you fucking move, you hear me?"

"Or else?" Tate dared to ask.

"Or else, when you *want* to move, I won't let you."

Tate turned his head and looked back at him, "Is this how you ask for forgiveness by being a bossy, mean—*ohhh…*"

Tate's words stopped on a groan as Logan dipped his

Ella Frank

knees again, sliding his rod against him.

"No. This is me showing you with my body that you're the most spectacular thing I have ever had against me. I'll beg for forgiveness later. For now, don't move." He instructed.

Speechless, Tate nodded as Logan lowered down onto his knees and looked at the perfect ass in front of him. He reached out and cupped Tate's cheeks, pushing them up and together, kneading the firm, wet flesh under his palms as the water hit his side and swirled down around his knees.

Tate pushed back into him, and when Logan ran his thumbs down his shadowed cleft, he looked back over his shoulder and Logan gave him his most devious smile.

"You're not surprised, are you?"

As Logan kneeled up, sipping the water from one of Tate's rounded cheeks, he dropped a hand down to squeeze his solid erection, and Logan bared his teeth, biting the same spot before he murmured, "I'll take that as a no. In fact, I think you're dying for this."

With strong thumbs, Logan spread Tate's flesh apart.

"Aren't you, Tate? You want it, and you *know* I'll give it to you. Let me guess. You want my mouth here"— Logan nibbled along the dark crevice of fresh wet skin— "and you want my tongue here," he told him, and swiped his tongue across the top of his crack. "Or maybe...maybe, you want it all, just a little bit lower."

As he teased the tip of his tongue farther between Tate's cheeks, Tate automatically widened his legs, a gruff sound pulling from his throat. Logan chuckled against him before he sat back on his heels, releasing Tate, as he looked at the picture spread out before him, almost forgetting they were in the shower.

"God, from the minute we met, you've been nothing but pure fucking temptation for me."

Tate glared back at him over his shoulder, and his eyes were as dark as Logan had ever seen them. *Oh yeah.* Tate was on edge, and he was frustrated that Logan had stopped.

As he knelt back up behind Tate, Logan appealed to him once more. "Do you forgive me?"

The question now became something of a quest.

This time, instead of an immediate denial, Tate's eyebrow rose, and his lips twitched. "No."

Logan smoothed a palm over Tate's ass, and promised, "You will."

* * *

TATE KNEW WHAT was coming. Logan had very briefly—

Holy shit.

Okay, so Logan had never quite done *this* to him before. He could feel Logan's fingers holding him apart, and unbelievably, the scratch of Logan's stubble against his ass was incredibly stimulating. Tate reveled in all of those feelings until the warm, wet tip of Logan's tongue grazed his rim.

Tate shut his eyes and ordered himself to relax and enjoy the—*ah, fucking hell*—experience. But every sure flick of that tongue made his cock painfully aware that it wanted to come.

Arching his back, Tate shoved away from the cool tiles and onto the hot mouth that was savoring him from behind as he heard and felt a groan vibrate out of Logan. This was probably the most depraved thing he'd ever done in his life, and as Logan's tongue returned time and time again to his sensitive hole, Tate realized he loved every second of it.

Moving his legs even farther apart, he grunted when a fingertip poked against him, and as the tip slipped inside, Tate started to pump his shaft. Letting his imagination fly, he pictured the way they would look right now if anyone were to walk in on them.

Him standing, facing his shower wall, legs parted, and Logan—raw and uninhibited Logan—down on his knees, holding my ass wide apart while his wicked tongue dips inside of me.

Christ, the mental snapshot Tate had given to himself was unbelievably erotic. The intense stimulation Logan was providing was turning him on so much that when the fingertip turned into a full thick digit, Tate shouted and jammed his hips back onto it.

He could feel Logan's tongue swirling around the spot where the finger was wedged, and as it dragged out of his body, it hit his prostate, and Tate saw fucking stars. His hips snapped forward as he started to masturbate as if this were the last time he would ever hope to come in his life.

Tate could feel Logan's mouth against his ass cheek, and his finger working back inside him as he started to glide it in and out, hitting all the right spots. It didn't take longer than probably three more thrusts of that finger, and Tate was shouting out Logan's name, as he came with such force that he thought he might rip his cock clear from his body.

With his erratic breathing subsiding, he become aware of the lips on his ass cheek, and the tongue that was drawing circles against his flesh. Releasing his hold of his overly sensitive skin, Tate looked down to Logan, who gave him a wicked grin and bit his ass gently.

"Dirty, *dirty*, Tate. Good thing we're in a shower."

Tate turned as Logan got to his feet, and he leaned back against the shower wall, noticing that Logan's own erection had subsided. Logan winked at him and then stepped under the spray, turning back to face him where he remained against the tiles.

"Come and get clean, would you?" Logan suggested and frowned as if just remembering. "Am I forgiven?"

Tate stared over at the man looking back at him, and he realized that even though this had turned into some kind of game, he still wanted something...*more*. So, with the effects of the alcohol having somewhat dissipated, Tate stepped forward with his eyes locked on Logan, and he replied, "No."

Chapter Twenty-Nine

"SO, TELL ME something," Logan said an hour later as they lay in Tate's bed.

They'd ordered and eaten a pepperoni pizza between them, and then Tate had called in to work after some not too subtle urging.

"Something," Tate replied into the shadows of the room.

"Comedian."

"*Hmm*, not really."

When they'd made their way in here, Tate had closed the blinds, but as they lay naked in the center of the bed, the rays had somehow slipped through and made it seem as though Tate's skin was burnished by the sun.

Logan rolled over onto his side and looked down at Tate's face. His left arm was up behind his pillow, and as Logan stared into his eyes, he knew that this was the moment they'd been building up to. *This* was what he'd been looking for—the one thing that would make him stop *trying*—and he was here, lying beside him.

"Are you still mad at me?" Logan questioned as he reached out and traced a finger down Tate's ribs.

Tate turned his head on the pillow and stared up at him. "No…"

Logan narrowed his eyes at him. "But?"

"*But*…you still aren't forgiven."

Flopping onto his back, Logan started to laugh.

"What?" Tate queried, turning over to lean up on his elbow.

Logan stared at the serious face that he knew he wanted to see every day. "You really are pig-headed. You never let me get away with anything. That's why you're perfect for me."

As Tate's lips twisted into an ironic smile, Logan frowned. "What? Come on, don't tell me, that's it?"

Tate said nothing. He just grinned and lay down onto his back. Quick as a flash, Logan moved over him, placing a palm on either side of Tate's head.

"That's it? *That's* what you've been waiting for?" Lowering his head, Logan pressed his mouth against the corner of Tate's. "What? I haven't told you how much I need you in my life? How much I want you here in it, everyday?" Logan raised his hand to touch the hair by Tate's face. "How can you not already know?"

Tate raised an eyebrow at him, and Logan couldn't help but run his finger over it as he mumbled, "So damn stubborn."

"It's your own fault. You never told me. What am I, a mind reader?"

"I don't know, but I'm a fool," Logan stated.

"Why?"

"This morning, you accused me of risking nothing, and you're right."

Tate went silent as though knowing if he spoke, Logan would never get out what he wanted to say.

"You've changed me, and you don't even realize it. Just being with you, near you? It makes me want to be a better person. *You* make me want to take a risk."

Tate touched one of his fingertips to his lower lip.

"What do you want to risk?"

Logan let go of all the emotions he'd held so carefully at arm's length. Finally, with those feelings surrounding and engulfing him, he answered simply, "Everything."

* * *

TATE COULDN'T BELIEVE all that he was feeling as he stared at Logan hovering over him. In the last couple of weeks, Logan had ignited in him things that he'd never thought possible. He'd challenged him to try things Tate had never *ever* considered, and as he looked up into Logan's face, he wondered if he was in love with him.

He knew that he was close. He could feel himself sliding, falling over that edge into madness—a madness that, for him, had already ended badly once before.

Am I really ready to risk it all again on someone who has never done this before? My family is going to—

"Hey, what are you thinking about?"

Tate pushed thoughts of family out of his head. Right now and right here was all that was important for the moment. They had plenty of time for the rest of the world—*later*.

"Nothing important."

"That usually means the exact opposite."

Tate lifted both of his hands and ran them through Logan's hair. As he pulled his head down, Tate kissed his lips lightly.

"It can wait."

Logan's mouth curved against his own as he lowered his body down on top of his. "Can it?"

"Yeah. But you know what?"

"No. What?"

Moving his mouth to Logan's ear, Tate kissed the lobe as he told him, "I can't wait anymore."

Logan lifted up over him. "What can't you wait for?"

Tate lowered his head back to the pillow and bent his legs, pressing his hips up into Logan, as he sighed, "You."

* * *

LOGAN CLOSED HIS eyes at the pleasure he got from the slow drag of Tate's hips against his own as Tate's voice filtered in past all of his anxiety.

Right now, all Logan could focus on was the man underneath him.

"Will you take me?"

As Tate's voice filled the silent room, every muscle in Logan's body tensed at the enormity of the request. Opening his eyes, Tate's serious expression focused on him, and Logan discovered that once again, with this man, he had no words.

"You don't have to if—"

"Oh, I want to," Logan assured him as he moved back to kneel between Tate's bent legs.

Tate moved up on his forearms. "But?"

"But I want this to be"—he rubbed his chin—"right for you."

Tate smiled at him then, and Logan was reminded of the very first time they had ever met. That moment when he'd turned around to stare across the bar at the most gorgeous man he'd ever seen, and Tate had been wearing that same exact smile.

"Logan?"

Logan shook himself out of his daydream, and then refocused. "Yeah?"

"What you just said?"

"Yeah?"

Tate reached down his body to palm his hardening length. "Just made it right."

Logan looked at the hand Tate was slowly stroking over himself.

"Are you sure? I mean, if we do this, you can't go back. You can't change it. This makes it real."

Logan watched as Tate lay back down, pushing his

hips up to him in invitation, and when he raised his eyes, Tate's expression answered before his words did.

"It's been real since the moment I realized that I couldn't stop thinking about you."

Logan couldn't help himself from reaching down to his own erection. Steadily, he began to glide his fist up its length.

"And when was that?"

Tate's eyes grew heavy, and his lips parted as he admitted, "The first night we met."

Logan trailed his gaze down from Tate's face to his tanned throat and then on to his leanly muscled chest. "I thought you were fucking gorgeous that night. I was determined to have you."

"And now?" Tate asked, drawing his attention back up to his face.

Logan released his shaft and ran a finger down Tate's knee and shin before he looked back at the face staring at him.

"Now, I think you're gorgeous and about to be mine."

* * *

TATE'S BREATH CAUGHT as Logan's finger continued to draw a simple path from his knee to his ankle and then back up again. It was nothing, it was everything, and it was driving him out of his mind.

"Logan," he finally said when the touch alone was no longer enough.

"Yes, Tate?"

Tate swallowed and then just decided to say it. "Lube and condoms are in the side table."

So what? He'd been preparing for tonight. He'd thought about it several times, and he wasn't ashamed of that at all, and as Logan slowly backed off the bed, Tate forgot about everything except for how impressive he looked naked.

The muscles of Logan's thighs bunched as he climbed off the bed and then walked around to the side table where he opened the drawer and grabbed what he needed.

When he turned around to face him full-on, Tate thought he'd never seen someone so attractive in all his life. He'd always known that Logan was sexy, there was no question. Everyone looked at him, both men and women. But as he stood before him—naked, aroused, and looking at him like he wanted him more than his next breath—Tate realized he'd never known physical attraction as strong as this until now.

"God, I love looking at you like this," he admitted out loud for the first time.

Logan's eyelids lowered to half-mast as he sheathed and lubed up his cock. Tate couldn't help but stare at the muscles of Logan's flexing arm as he began to pump his fist. Reaching down between his own legs, Tate matched the rhythm Logan set and watched as he masturbated with him.

"Keep going," Logan instructed as he walked back around to stand at the end of Tate's bed.

Tate tracked him with his eyes, raised his palm, spit in it, and then continued to stroke it over his taut flesh.

"Bend your legs, Tate. Show me everything."

Logan's gruff voice filled the room, and Tate didn't hesitate. He raised his feet until they were flat on the bed, and he widened his legs. He knew that Logan had a full view of his balls and ass, not to mention his cock, and the more Tate thought about it, the more turned-on he became.

"Show me what you did that first time we spoke on the phone. You do remember that night, don't you? That was the first night you admitted that I made you hard, that you wanted me, that you *watched* me."

Logan placed a knee on the mattress and then climbed up onto the bed until he was between Tate's legs. "You told me that night that you were so hard you could go all night."

Almost as though in slow motion, Tate watched as Logan reached forward and wrapped his greased up fingers around his own. Tate groaned and pushed his erection through their fingers as Logan asked, "Let's aim for that."

Tate spread his legs even wider and pushed his ass off the bed as his slippery cock slid through their fists.

"I want you as hot, hard and desperate as you've ever been before, and once you're there, then I'll take you. Okay?"

Tate had to wonder how much more desperate he

could get, and then he felt it—a slippery finger slid down over his balls and the tight skin behind until it made its way to the cleft of his ass.

"Okay, Tate?"

Tate stared at Logan, and when he saw the sinful smirk that the other man's mouth had given way to, he knew that he was about to be taken in ways he had never imagined.

Chapter Thirty

LOGAN KEPT HIS eyes on the silent man under him as he bent down between his legs and drew his tongue across Tate's cock. Tate's legs tensed and drew up, and Logan immediately moved his hands to Tate's thighs to hold them apart.

"Hours," he murmured. "One day soon, I'm going to spend hours down here, touching you, kissing you, sucking on you." He kissed the skin that had drawn up tight to Tate's body. "Do you like that idea? My mouth down here for hours? I think you do."

Logan glanced up Tate's long torso to the scorching eyes above. He should have known the guy would fire back, even when receiving a thorough tongue-lashing.

"I like it better down there, occupied, than giving me hell as it usually does."

Logan chuckled and stroked his fingers up the inside of Tate's tense thighs, running them over the crease of his legs as he continued to taste and suck the heated skin nestled safely between Tate's legs.

"Careful, Tate, I'm already turned-on. You know how hot I get when you're mean to me."

Tate managed to buck up against Logan's mouth as he lowered his own hand down to stroke his neglected shaft.

"You're a seriously demented man, Logan," Tate huffed.

Logan swiped the base of his erection with his tongue. "You love it. Admit it."

Tate craned his head up to look at him, and Logan began drawing circles with his tongue.

"Admit what?"

"You love everything I'm doing to you," he mumbled and then maneuvered himself up to his knees.

Once he was there, Logan reached out and clasped one of Tate's legs under the knee. Lowering down over him and pressing Tate's thigh to his chest, Logan kissed him as he braced his palm by his shoulder.

"You do, don't you?" Logan asked again.

This time, he dipped his free hand over Tate's balls to run his fingers down the hot strip of flesh between his cheeks. Tate's body tensed, and Logan advised gently, "Relax. Breathe out, and let me in. We've already done this, and you loved it."

"*Yes*," Tate sighed against his mouth.

Logan pressed his fingertip to the hot little pucker of skin. "Yes?"

"Yes. I love all of it," Tate answered.

Gently, Logan eased his finger into Tate's body as he pressed his lips against Tate's parted ones. He arrogantly confided, "Oh, I know."

Tate's eyes closed then as Logan pushed his tongue into his mouth. He slid his finger farther inside him, and as he felt Tate's body suck him in, Logan moaned into the mouth moving beneath his own.

"That's it. *Yeah*." He started to push and pull his finger in and out of Tate, over and over. "I can't wait until this is my cock."

Tate shuddered, and Logan knew he was thinking it, too.

"Me inside you," he vowed over Tate's lips as he pressed two fingers against his rim, "stretching you, taking you, fucking you."

"*Yes*, fuck yes," Tate agreed, jacking himself a little faster.

"It's gonna be *so* good that you'll be thinking about my cock even when I'm nowhere in sight."

Logan could feel his erection responding to his words as he oh-so slowly eased two of his fingers forward into Tate's body. Logan could feel him take in a breath and push it out as he worked his index and middle finger inside.

"Oh God, that's…that's…"

Tate seemed stuck for words, but it didn't seem to matter because Logan chose that moment to twist his hand and rub his fingers directly across Tate's prostate. That well-practiced move had Tate's hips jamming up sharply into the air and his hand squeezing his cock, *hard*.

Again, Logan pushed his fingers inside, stretching Tate and trying to get him ready for what was about to

488   Ella Frank

happen to him. Tate looked magnificent, lying beneath him. He had one leg bent back against his chest, where Logan held it in place, and the other angled at the knee, against the mattress. His busy hands were frantically working his rigid flesh, and as he stared up at Logan with absolute trust in his eyes, Logan asked, "You okay?"

When Tate nervously licked his lips and nodded, Logan lowered himself and followed the same path, tracing Tate's mouth with his tongue, before he cursed out at his lack of control. Tunneling his fingers back into the hot, snug home where his cock wanted to take up residence, he admitted, "I want in here so bad, Tate. I have wanted it since we first met."

Logan pulled his fingers free, and Tate's breathing came hard as his lips parted, and he told him, "Then, take me."

* * *

HE WAS READY. *Fuck.* He was beyond ready as Logan's fingers worked inside him. *It wasn't the most comfortable feeling,* Tate thought as Logan pulled his thick fingers out of him. But every time he'd done it, his fingertips had knocked against that spot where the pleasure was off the fucking chart. So, yes, he wanted to feel the pressure and fullness that Logan's cock would give to him when it pressed inside him.

"You ready?" Logan asked as he stared down with

what looked like an angry expression.

But Tate knew better. He knew it was restrained lust, not anger that was making Logan look like he wanted to kill. Logan wanted him so badly that it was physically hurting him to wait.

Tate nodded, and he expected Logan to remove his hand and push into him. What he hadn't expected was for Logan to shift out from between his legs. As he lay down on his back beside him, Tate turned his head and looked at him with a frown.

"I don't understand."

With one hand, Logan palmed his cock. "The best way for you is going to be like this."

Tate's ass pulsed and burned slightly from the fingers that had been moving inside him, and as he looked at how Logan was casually lying on his back, he asked, confused, "What do you—"

"Straddle me, Tate."

"What?" Tate questioned, feeling his brow rise.

"Knee on either side of me. You know what straddle means, right?"

"Fuck you," he heard himself mumble as he moved closer to Logan.

"You can, if you prefer."

Tate glowered at him, not really annoyed at Logan but irritated by his own sudden apprehension. He'd been ready to lie down under Logan or be on hands and knees. But this, this was not what he'd expected. They had never done this before.

"This way, you'll be in control. You can go as slow or as fast as you like, trust me."

Well, that makes sense, Tate thought. But as he came to a stop beside Logan and looked down at the hand fisting the covered, large cock, Tate couldn't believe that this was the first time he'd wondered, how *that* was going to—

"It'll work," Logan assured, seeming to read his mind. "Trust me. Stop thinking. Come down here, and kiss me."

Tate moved down and kissed his mouth, and Logan's hands grabbed his arms and pulled him close. As he fell down with a soft huff, Logan's hands slipped around to his back and slid down his spine to his ass.

Tate moaned as Logan's tongue pushed between his lips, and when strong fingers gripped the backs of his thighs and urged them apart, Tate spread his legs to either side of Logan. As Tate bit at the full lip he loved and placed his hands by Logan's head, he kissed him passionately and began to grind his shaft against the one under him. He could feel Logan's hands slide up the sides of his thighs to his waist and across his ass as he continued kissing and rocking against him from underneath. As a rumble left Logan and moved through him, Tate knew what he wanted. He wanted to give this man everything.

Lifting his head, Tate looked down into the dark blue eyes peering back at him and placed his palms on Logan's chest as he slowly sat up, straddling Logan's stomach.

His cock sprung up in front of him, and Logan's hands came around to rest on his thighs as Tate reached down and began stroking it and sighing from the sheer pleasure.

"Oh Jesus, Tate. You look amazing," Logan told him as his eyes wandered over his body.

As Tate kneeled over the man, he *felt* fucking amazing. He noticed Logan look over to the side of the bed and reach out to grab the bottle he'd left there. Opening it quickly, Logan lifted it to Tate and poured some into his palm before he recapped it and threw it to the side. He then began to massage his hands over Tate's thighs.

"Okay, whenever you're ready, just reach back, oil me up, and take your time." Logan paused as he placed his hands behind his head, trying to convey a sense of calm. "There's no rush, and if you want to stop, you stop."

Tate appreciated that as his nerves made his heart pound erratically in his chest.

Reaching behind himself, he found Logan's erection. Curling his fingers around it, he ran his slippery palm over the sheathed rod and felt his whole body shift as Logan pushed up from underneath him.

Tate looked down at the powerful man under him and released him as he then began preparing his own body. As he started to run his wet fingers over his hole, he licked his lips nervously and grabbed his eager erection dripping with its excitement—excitement from the unknown.

Logan's eyes looked heavy, but the relaxed pose

didn't fool Tate for one second. The arms Logan had placed behind his head looked tense, and the muscles were bulging as Tate slowly rose up on his knees.

"Logan?" Tate whispered hesitantly.

"Yeah?"

Tate focused on the serious face staring back at him. "Can you help me?"

A soft expression loosened Logan's tense features, as he lowered his hands and smoothed them up Tate's thighs. "Of course."

Tate gripped Logan's cock and pushed it toward his body until he felt the tip nudging between his cheeks. That was when Logan's palms smoothed around his hips, and his fingers gently spread him apart.

At first, Tate began to tease himself, moving back and forward over it, feeling the way the wide round head parted his ass as it massaged his hole. He heard a hiss of air and looked down at Logan, who had squeezed his eyes shut as though the pleasure was too much to bear, and *that* made Tate brave.

Remembering what Logan had told him, he took in a breath, and then he slowly released it as he lowered his body down over the waiting hard cock. The first sensation was the immediate pressure of something so thick trying to penetrate him, but from this angle it was much easier to control how much he could take at a time. Gritting his teeth and placing his palms on Logan's chest, Tate stared at the face that was pulled taut as he continued to slide down on

him.

The second Logan pushed past that initial tight ring of muscle, Tate was hit with the sting and burn. *Fuck.* The pressure in his ass was unlike anything he'd ever felt. Just as his cock was beginning to soften, and he was about to remove himself, one of Logan's hands wrapped around him and started to stroke his erection.

"Breathe, Tate. You feel and look so damn good. *Jesus Christ.* Breathe."

Tate focused on Logan's face, which even when twisted and distorted with his own pain and pleasure was still sexy as hell. He kept one hand on Tate's hip and continued to stroke him with his other.

"Your ass feels *unfuckingreal*—so hot and so fucking tight."

Logan's words were both dirty and provocative, and as they made their way to him, Tate found that they distracted him from the burn inside him as he continued to lower himself, feeling Logan stretch him wider and wider as he sank in even deeper.

Logan snarled like a caged animal under him as his hand clasped Tate's thigh. Tate squeezed his eyes shut, trying to get used to the feeling, trying to get used to being filled, but it was so foreign and felt so different that he didn't think it would ever feel right.

"You're so fucking big," he heard himself say out loud.

Logan gave a strained laugh. "Words no man minds

hearing ever."

Tate didn't have any smart-ass comebacks this time as he finally seated himself fully, and Logan's flesh pulsated inside him. Tate remained as still as possible, trying to let his body become used to the invasion.

As Tate stared down at Logan, he gave him one of his slow sensual smiles, and Tate felt his cock become roused. He couldn't help the swift thrust he gave, trying to push himself into... *something*, and just that quickly, Logan curled a fist around him.

The minute Tate had moved, the shaft inside him shifted, and the pleasure he got from it surprised him. It surprised him so much that he did it again, this time causing a curse to rip from Logan.

With his hands on Logan's chest, Tate slowly raised himself up on his knees, allowing Logan's erection to slide a little ways from his body. Then, he re-seated himself, and this time, that wide, rigid shaft hit the right spot, and Tate's eyes rolled to the back of his fucking head. Breathing hard, he did it again, a little faster. He raised himself up and then came back down, his body sucking Logan inside.

"Oh fuck, Tate, *fuck*!" Logan shouted as he arched his head back against the pillow. His neck strained against his pleasure, exposing all its veins. "*So* good."

Loving the sound of that, Tate began to rock his hips over the cock inside him. The burn had now been replaced with a satisfying ache, and Logan was right about how good it felt. As Logan half sat up, causing all of his stomach muscles to ripple, Tate's erection lurched at the sight, and he bent down to take Logan's mouth.

Forcing his tongue between his lips, Tate began to writhe on top of him as Logan lay back down, bringing Tate with him.

"Mmm, again," Logan requested, but it sounded more like a demand.

Tate shifted forward to chase Logan's mouth, and the erection inside him slipped free.

"How does it feel, having me inside you?" Logan asked by his ear.

Tate slid back and once again took Logan *all* the way inside him.

"There are no words," Tate confided.

Then, he felt the hands on his ass clench as Logan shifted and bent his legs up, so his feet were on the mattress.

"Good, because I need to move inside you the way I've been dying to," and that was all the warning Tate got.

* * *

LOGAN'S CONTROL WAS at an end. With his cock inside Tate as he rubbed a wet trail of cum all over Logan's body, he was surprised he hadn't already lost his cool.

As soon as Tate had sunk down on top of him, Logan had started to count backward from one hundred. The agonizing pleasure of seeing Tate's body take him was too much.

When Tate had straddled him and his chest had been heaving with each anxious breath, Logan had worried at first that Tate had changed his mind. But after some gentle coaxing and a few quick thrusts to the right spot, that gorgeous man had begun to move, and Logan's patience ended.

As Tate lay down over him, Logan could feel his body clenching around him. Palming his ass cheeks, Logan spread him open as he raised his feet to plant them on the mattress. When Tate placed his hands on either side of his head, Logan leaned up and bit his bottom lip as he pushed off the bed and drove up into him. He wasn't exactly sure what Tate was feeling at that moment, but when their eyes met and Tate dropped his head, whispering, *"Again,"* Logan just about lost it.

Propelling his hips upward, Logan pulled Tate down, penetrating him deep and hard. Tate's neck arched back, and then he surprised the shit out of Logan by sitting up and taking him as far inside his body as possible.

With a loud curse, Tate leaned back and placed a palm on the mattress between Logan's legs, stretching his entire body out for him to look at. With frenzied eyes, Logan tried to take in everything, and there was no way he could not grab on to that stiff cock.

Reaching out to stroke Tate's erection, the visual Logan had was something from his dirtiest fuck fantasies, and he couldn't help but pound his hips up into Tate, hard. The sounds and words coming from Tate's mouth were low, gravely, and filthier than a fucking sailor as he continued to roll his hips. Apparently, he'd found the exact right angle to continue hitting the spot he needed to drive himself crazy.

"Oh *yeah*. Right *there*, Logan. Fuck. *Oh fuck*!" and that was all it took.

Like a goddamn fountain, Tate's cock erupted, and white ropey jets of his cum spurt out over Logan's hand and stomach. As he gritted his teeth, holding off on his own climax, Tate rode out his, and what a fucking sight it was. Logan had known that once he had Tate, he'd never want to stop, and he'd been dead-on with that prediction.

Knowing Tate's shaft would be sensitive, Logan reluctantly let go of him and lay there, his own breathing coming hard as he waited for Tate's next move.

* * *

TATE SHIFTED AND heard Logan let out a quiet grunt, and he was surprised to feel that he was still hard. Tate's orgasm had been fucking spectacular, and he was shocked to discover that being *taken* by Logan was just as addictive as *taking* Logan.

Staring down at the aroused and agitated man beneath him, Tate asked, unsure, "Now what?"

Logan bit his top lip as though in pain. "Slide off—slowly."

Tate did as instructed, and the minute Logan slipped free from his body, he was almost overwhelmed by the sense of loss he felt. He didn't have long to think it over though because Logan moved quicker than Tate thought possible. He sprung up off the bed and rolled them over until Tate was lying facedown on the mattress, and Logan was situated against him from head to toe.

Tate moaned as Logan bit his shoulder and held him down.

"Goddamn it, Tate, *damn you*."

Tate shoved back, and when he felt Logan's bare cock against his ass cheeks, he knew he'd removed the condom.

"Your ass, clinging to me as I slid out and then *pushed* back in," he replayed seductively as Tate felt a hand push his hair aside and lips began sucking the skin of his neck. "Nothing has ever felt that good. And *no one* has looked as fucking mouthwatering as you riding me like you were made for it."

Tate bit down on the pillow as Logan's hips continued to move over his ass, and he promised, "Next time, I'm going to have you just like this. Facedown, ass up. But for now, I'm going to give your poor little hole a break. Just lay there, and let me look at what's finally mine and no one else's."

Tate felt Logan's body weight move back off him, and he remained where he was told with his legs spread out behind him as he heard the bottle open up once again. Closing his eyes, Tate imagined what he would see if he turned around—Logan kneeling between his legs, the wet slide he could hear of his fist moving frantically. When a large hand came down and began to smooth over his ass, Tate couldn't help but move into it.

Logan cursed behind him, and Tate could feel a fingertip probing his well-used body. It actually felt good, so he widened his legs, and as soon it slipped inside him, he heard a harsh shout followed by his name, and then he felt hot, sticky liquid hit his spine and lower back as Logan came all over him.

Tate closed his eyes as Logan's tongue licked over the skin of his back, and his hands smoothed up over him before he lay down, joining their bodies chest to back.

"Hmm," Logan hummed in his ear. "You don't taste like a cherry anymore."

Tate turned his head on the pillow. "A cherry? I don't—"

"Yep," Logan interrupted, kissing his cheek. "I popped it, sucked on the seed, then licked it all up, and made it mine. "

Tate heard Logan's chuckle in his ear, and he had a feeling he was doing it to get a rise out of him. "So, what does that make you, my little cum-licker?"

Logan's mouth froze where it was, and as a loud booming laugh left him and filled the sex-filled space, he rolled off of Tate. "Oh my God. That was good. I have to give you that one."

Tate stayed where he was but smiled as he closed his eyes. "Good. Now, leave me alone. Since you've had me, you finally owe me some sleep."

"*Aw*, have I been keeping you up at night?"

Tate cracked one eye open. "Logan?" He was about
to tell him to shut up, but that was when the sound of his
cell phone peeled through the room.

Tate knew that ringtone immediately. That was his
mother—or his father, which would be worse. He didn't
move as he lay there, intent on the man lying beside him.

"You need to get that?" Logan asked, his expression
now serious instead of the relaxed humor from seconds
before.

They both knew that whoever was on the other end
of that phone was going to change things.

So, instead of reaching for it, Tate scooted closer to
his lover, laid his head on the same pillow, and told him,
"I'll call them back."

"And then?" Logan asked, his body relaxed, but his
eyes betraying his easy calm.

"And then...everything is going to change."

Logan swallowed visibly and asked the question that
Tate knew must have just about killed him, "Are you really
ready for what's about to happen here, with your parents?"

Tate raised his palm to stroke Logan's jaw. As he
leaned in and pressed their mouths together, he decided that
now was the time. This was the moment where he asked
again and hoped for a different outcome. It would either be
the bravest thing he'd ever done or the most stupid. He
looked directly into Logan's eyes, and told him, "I always

was. What about you—are you ready now to *try*?"

And patiently, Tate waited for the answer.

Special Thanks

As always, Candace, thank you for being available for me to laugh, cry and scream with. This book would *not* have been possible without you.

Xx Ella

P.S. We made it!! What a ride!!

About the Author

Ella Frank is the *USA Today* Bestselling author of the Temptation series, including Try, Take, and Trust and is the co-author of the fan-favorite contemporary romance, Sex Addict. Her Exquisite series has been praised as "scorching hot!" and "enticingly sexy!"

Some of her favorite authors include Tiffany Reisz, Kresley Cole, Riley Hart, J.R. Ward, Erika Wilde, Gena Showalter, and Carly Philips.

CPSIA information can be obtained
at www.ICGtesting.com
Printed in the USA
BVOW09s0102290417

482683BV00001B/1/P